A CONUNDRUM OF WIZARDS

K. R. BADY

CONTENTS

ACKNOWLEDGMENTS

To Lexi and Jax for being my friends and inspiring me with your antics.

To Eric for giving me a title too good to waste.

CHAPTER 1

Magic discovered Ari Jamison when he was nine years old, when he was still young and impressionable, but old enough to know weird bullshit when he saw it. He'd been too young to trust his instincts back then, though, so he kept Magic to himself like a secret, like something that didn't matter so long as he—and everyone around him—ignored it.

Magic did not like being ignored, though. It made puberty a truly horrific experience in retaliation. Years later and well into his thirties, it was still trying to beat the lesson into him.

"I'll be right with you, sir!" Ari said to the old man approaching the sales counter.

Glancing at his customer over his shoulder became an awkward spin as Ari's hand hit the door marked "Employees Only," then he stumbled into the bookstore's kitchen. Mid-motion, he closed his eyes so he could shake the golden-blond hair out of his face without getting it in his eyes, then—

"What the fuck," Ari whined.

The door closed behind him before he could catch it. Just like that, Ari was stuck gaping like an incredulous loon, not at the stainless steel appliances of his shop's backroom, but at the overstuffed couch and sequined cushions decorating his apartment three blocks away.

Ari propped his hands on his hips and fumed at nothing.

"Oh, hello," came a sleepy voice from the direction of his bedroom. "Aren't you supposed to be at work?"

"Aren't I?" Ari scoffed as he turned to grab the handle of the closet door behind him. His knuckles whitened around the knob as he hissed under his breath, "Knock it off and send me back."

He yanked the door open to reveal folded linens organized by color and uniform glass dispensers full of cleaning supplies.

Ari tossed his head back with a miserable laugh. The stack of towels on the top shelf promptly tumbled onto his face as if shoved by an invisible hand.

"You should probably fold those."

Face hot and fist clenched at his side, Ari glared at his roommate. The white Bengal cat strutted from the bedroom unperturbed and hopped onto the couch's armrest. Val gave Ari an innocent grin as she stretched out and flopped onto her tummy.

"By the way," Val purred, "I had a package delivered today. Would you mind grabbing it for me, dear friend?"

Ari huffed as he collected the spilled towels from the floor. "No."

"Pretty please? I'd do it myself, but it's so difficult without opposable thumbs. Also, we don't want the neighbors talking about us again."

Ari shook out the last towel with a loud snap and folded it with sharp movements as he addressed the cat. "The universe did not teleport me away from the job that pays for our housing just so I could fetch your catnip from the doorstep. Why the hell am I here, Val?"

"I have no idea. Oh, wait." She rolled off the armrest and popped to her feet with attentiveness. "Is this because you left the stove on again? Because I already took care of that for you—"

"No."

"You're welcome—"

"No," Ari repeated, louder. "We've been over this. Witch Magic doesn't give a shit about small stuff like that."

"Is that so?" Val said as she made a show of peering around Ari's legs at the towels he was restoring on the shelf.

Ari shut the closet before Magic could mess up his towels again, then he threw up his hands in defeat and headed for the front door.

"Don't forget my package!"

Ari kicked the brown box at Val and slammed the apartment door closed. He stomped two paces away from the welcome mat before he hesitated.

He didn't have his apartment key on him. Like the keys to his shop, it was safely attached to the fluffy pink dice key chain hanging out of his jacket pocket. In the back room. In the shop.

Face turned heavenward, Ari nearly wept with frustration as he asked, "How am I supposed to lock—"

The lock engaged behind him with a click as loud and quick as a sucker punch to the gut. Wincing, Ari walked back to the shop without another word.

It was a short walk, fifteen minutes at most, and one he could transverse blindfolded if need be. Ordinarily, Ari enjoyed strolling through Olde Town Arvada, but autumn in Colorado was a much nicer experience with a jacket. Ari's plaid sweater-vest and button down provided little protection from the chill, and while it wasn't raining, it still dampened his appreciation for the falling leaves and charming historic backdrop. In a huffy attempt to warm his forearms, he tried rolling down his shirt sleeves without slowing his stride. He was graceful enough to pull off such mundane tasks despite his poor attitude, provided Magic was done fucking with him.

Magic was, in fact, not done fucking with him.

Ari wasn't the most observant guy, but he didn't typically trip over random bums taking a rest on the brick sidewalk. Today, he did.

"Shit!" Ari cried as he skipped and flailed. He caught himself before face-planting on the ground, but barely.

"Dude!" The bum gaped up at him without moving an inch. He remained just as he was, slumped against the building with his knees raised as a perch for his folded arms. His foot was braced outward, but not imposing on pedestrians. There was no good reason Ari hadn't noticed him with amble time to avoid the mishap.

"Sorry." Ari's face warmed as he composed himself. "I didn't see—"

"Yeah? Where's your cane?"

Ari blinked. "What?"

"Your cane," the bum repeated, glaring up at Ari through his haphazard beard. "I've been sitting here for an hour, and you weren't distracted by a phone or whatever. If you didn't see me, you must be blind. So, where's your cane?"

He mimed holding out the described tool and tapping it back and forth. Between his drawn hood and rampant beard, Ari couldn't make out much of his expression, but the snap to the man's voice was plenty harsh on its own.

Ari frowned and his hands popped to his hips on reflex. "I am clearly not blind, just . . ." He faltered, and the blush rushed back to his cheeks. "I was simply not paying attention," he admitted, matching the bum's attitude. "There's no reason to be rude about it."

"I'm not the posh bastard strutting around like he owns the sidewalk."

Ari's jaw dropped as he watched the stranger spring to his feet and stride off. Still scoffing with incredulity, Ari unglued his feet and continued his way back to the shop. He took three or four steps that might have been a bit heavier than normal before he slowed down with a stifled groan.

He and the bum were going the same way.

Ari blew out a harsh breath and folded his arms as he made a conscious effort toward his usual pace. "I'm not following you," he snipped seconds later as he neared the hooded figure ahead of him, "I just happen to be going the same direction."

"Oh my god!" the bum hissed. With no further acknowledgment, he shoved his hands into the front pocket of his hoodie and made an abrupt turn onto a convenient side street.

Ari scoffed again, but kept his voice low and private as he told the universe, "Oh, fuck off, already."

He took a bracing breath and kept walking. He gave his usual shortcut, and, not so coincidentally, the rude bum a dejected stare as he crossed the intersection. If he noticed the literal bum of said bum had a nice shape to it for someone resigned to sitting on curbs, well, no one needed to know.

"An ass like that is supposed to be attached to frat boys or gym bros," Ari complained four hours later, "not homeless jerks."

Like the true, if blunt, friend he was, Dazzle leveled him

with a concerned stare and asked, "Be honest, honey: when was the last time you got laid?"

Ari ignored the heat on his cheeks as he glared across the service counter at his friend. "Not helpful."

Dazzle shrugged with a smile that said Ari should have known better than to expect anything else, then he returned his attention to the smartphone in his hand. Without pause, Dazzle resumed typing away at high speed despite his two-inch-long rainbow nails. His short hair was neon pink that day, and even his understated shirt and jeans couldn't stop him from drawing attention.

Dazzle had that effect everywhere he went. Ari doubted he could help it, but even if he could, Ari wouldn't want him any other way.

With a sigh, Ari went to check off the next item on his "List of Closing Duties." As he cleared the few remaining pastries from the glass counter display and chucked them into a bag, he asked, "Hey, did you help Val order something again? She got another surprise package today."

Dazzle lowered his phone with a thoughtful look that was way too innocent.

Ari sighed and sealed off the bag of baked goods. "What was it?"

"I don't remember."

Ari swung the bag over the counter and smacked Dazzle's shoulder with it.

Dazzle flinched with a dramatic squeal and folded before the bag even made contact. "I promise it wasn't another dildo!"

"What was it?" Ari demanded.

"I plead the fifth!"

"Too late! Now fess up!"

The bookstore was empty, and there was less than five

minutes till its official closure. It was just him and Dazzle, who was at best a nonpaying customer by this point in their lives. Ari calculated the risk for potential damage to his professional image and decided it was well worth it to hop the counter with his bag of overstock raised high.

Dazzle scampered from the retail counter.

It was uneventful, as far as chases went.

Grimoires and Goodies was a small shop with only one high ceiling-ed room open for the public. Bookshelves lined each wall from the polished wood floors to the exposed rafter, with a spiral staircase in the corner leading to the balcony level. The main floor included a few mismatched tables and assorted chairs scattered among a few shorter display shelves.

Dazzle scurried around the furnishings and attempted to use them as shields, but Ari was faster.

"Ears!" Dazzle shrieked after Ari herded him into a corner.

Ari was mid-swing with his makeshift weapon, but he pulled back, so the blow landed on Dazzle's pink head like a love tap. Hoisting the bag over his shoulder, Ari arched an expectant brow.

Dazzle kept his arms over his head like a shield as he reluctantly said, "We ordered a pair of cat ears and paws."

Ari frowned and hesitantly asked, "Why?"

Dazzle sank to the floor with his clenched arms still protecting his head. "It came with a tail, Ari! You know I can't say no to free add-ons!"

Ari brandished his bag of treats with narrowing eyes. "I repeat: why?"

Dazzle squeezed his eyes shut like the Drama Queen he was and admitted, "We thought if you had a costume already on hand, we had a better chance of getting you into Furry Con."

"Wow," Ari said dryly, unimpressed.

Dazzle opened one eye to peek at him. "So . . . wanna come get freaky with us at the convention?"

Ari hit him again in reply. He used enough force to make the loose books behind his friend wobble.

"Ow." Dazzle pouted as Ari abandoned him to go lock the door.

"For the last time, I am not closing the shop during a high-traffic weekend to chaperone your nerd orgy."

"We're inviting you to the Con," Dazzle whined, bouncing along behind him. "Though the after-parties might interest you if it's orgies you're—"

"No!"

Ari swatted at him with the baked goods again, but Dazzle danced out of range. Ari couldn't follow him and flip the open sign to closed at the same time. On his way back to the counter to finish clearing the display of the last few crumbs, Ari sent his friend a baffled glower.

"Why does Val want us to go so badly anyway? She's a cat, for fuck's sake. It's not like she would be picking up guys any more than I would."

"There are a lot of answers I could give to that, but I doubt you're ready to hear them," Dazzle said as he hopped up to sit on the counter.

Ari gave him a look that clearly expressed his confoundment, but Dazzle quite literally waved him off and kept talking.

"First of all, cats are as entitled to a bit of consenting voyeurism as anyone else, and we don't kink-shame around here, do we?"

Ari rolled his eyes, but Dazzle pretended not to notice.

"Second, your little experiment with celibacy is out of

control. Haven't you noticed how hard it's been on Val now that she can't live vicariously through you?"

Ari gave an incredulous scoff.

Dazzle straightened and began channeling his inner diva as he admonished, "Do you even care?"

Ari pointed at the door and said, "Get out."

"No, I don't think I will," Dazzle said as he inspected his nails for blemishes. "The truth's hard sometimes, honey bunch, but as your friend, I am duty bound to lay it on you. You and Val got needs to meet, girl."

"Why are you like this," Ari groaned as he retrieved the ceramic spray bottle from under the register.

He began spritzing the counter top and interior of the display case. By the fourth pull of the trigger, the countertop, cash register, and credit card reader were sparkling and pristine. By the fifth spray, the display was crystal clear and ready for the following day.

"God, I love wizardry," Ari moaned, hugging his ceramic bottle to his chest like it was a newborn kitten.

"You're welcome," Dazzle sassed.

Ari sighed. "Fine, I guess I'll keep you around, but only because you give me gifts that cut my maintenance expenses in half."

Dazzle grinned and patted Ari's cheek. "Aw, I love you too."

In truth, Grimoires and Goodies would have never worked without Dazzle, and they both knew it. When Ari turned eighteen, his parents' life insurance bought him the time and means to attend business classes at the community college and kept a modest roof over his head for a time, but it was nowhere near the amount he needed to launch a business as niche as Grimoires and Goodies. His dream of opening the shop should have remained just that, a dream, but he was lucky enough to have powerful friends with deep pockets.

Dazzle and Val were wizards. Not merely geniuses in their chosen fields, they were real, trained magic users.

"A little cleaning potion here and there really isn't that big a deal, Ari," Dazzle said in that tone he used whenever he thought Ari was being difficult. "You know I'll never charge you for more than the cost of ingredients."

"That's beside the point." Ari gave his potion a covetous caress. "I'm not like you; I'll never take your magic for granted."

The lights went out. The electrical whir of the register and card reader went silent at the same time.

In the pitch-dark shop, Dazzle whistled. "Smooth, Ari."

Ari set down the potion with a resigned sigh. He shouted into the void, "I didn't mean it like that!"

The power turned back on, but only for the split second necessary for the card reader to issue an offended beep, then the blackout resumed.

"God, I love witches," Dazzle mocked.

"Oh, shut up."

Dazzle left shortly thereafter, leaving Ari with ample privacy to do his groveling. Ari rolled his eyes and laughed at his friend's continued insinuation that witch Magic acted more like a jilted lover than a major power. Dazzle meant it as a joke; he didn't know any better.

Ari was the only witch Dazzle knew. He was the only witch most wizards tolerated.

Alone in his shop in the dead of night, Ari felt his way back to the retail counter. Once he located his emergency séance kit, Ari made his way to the round table stationed at the exact center of the shop.

All Dazzle's teasing aside, Ari was nervous as he untied

the velvet purse and set out the candles. He couldn't remember the last time he practiced real witchcraft. He usually went out of his way to avoid it.

The last thing he needed was Magic feeling encouraged to fuck with his life.

Witchcraft was a fickle thing, based on intangible factors like emotion and divine investment. While most witches seemed to embrace the chaotic energy and unpredictability, Ari abhorred it. It lacked the reliable results and scientific finesse of wizarding counterparts. Witchcraft was more of a subjective art, and Ari didn't have the time or patience for that kind of mess.

Magic didn't usually interfere in his daily life to such extremes, though, and it was never so obvious about it.

Enough was enough. Ari interlaced his fingers and swung his arms out in a gratifying stretch, rolling his neck as he did so. Then his hands came down on the table, bracketing the velvet bag and the pagan paraphernalia spilling from it's opening. He reached for the tarot deck like he had half a dozen times before.

A little witchery tonight would mean business as usual tomorrow.

That was his plan, at any rate. As usual, Magic had other things in mind.

CHAPTER 2

*I*t is time, Magic said.

The message resonated throughout Ari's head as he opened the shop the following morning. Try as he might, he couldn't stop it from replaying like a broken record.

It is time.

He flicked on the lights, and the Gothic chandelier bloomed to life. Ari stared at it for a moment, even though the occult symbols in the ironwork were only visible from the upper level.

It is time.

Ari shook his head and turned away. Maybe it was time he redecorated. He tossed the thought out in the same moment it occurred to him. From the glowing, bubbling cauldron in the shop's window display, to the demonic bust centerpiece on the largest table, or the taxidermy bat hanging from the balcony's safety railing in front of the Natural Sciences section, Ari's shop was nothing if not dedicated to its theme.

Besides, he wasn't stupid enough to think the shop's atmosphere was the reason Magic wanted his attention.

It is time.

Magic didn't have an actual voice, of course. It didn't speak with words, but its meaning was clear whenever it chose to douse him in emotions and abstract concepts that didn't belong to him.

It is time.

Cryptic impressions were no help to Ari, though. Magic obviously wanted something from him again, but he couldn't do much about it when all his questions were answered with the same vague warning. Ari couldn't afford to let it paralyze him, so he continued willfully shoving the matter aside so he could get another task done. The moment he relaxed into autopilot, the wariness would creep over him again. It was a vicious cycle, but a necessary one.

Ari never closed the shop without advanced notice. He tried a few times, long ago, but then he learned it was easier to come in sick as a dog than to deal with the headaches a closure inevitably brought him.

He had money to make, but Grimoires and Goodies was about more than that.

The mundane world saw Ari and his shop as a strangely successful gimmick, but there was only so much profit to be made off tourists and Denver's local eccentrics.

No. Ari's bustling business had more to do with the supernatural community. Ari might have been a witch himself, but his appreciation for other magical means led to him carving out a very specific place among his peers. He didn't just cater to all kinds of magic users, he welcomed them.

As if his thoughts had summoned them, the day's first customers were a pair of witches.

The elder witch was a regular since the day he first opened the shop, but Ari never bothered to learn her name.

Hag Number Six was drowning in her usual garden-stained poncho, and the stark, manufactured neatness of her tennis shoes made Ari roll his eyes. She only wore them because Ari wouldn't let her in the shop barefoot.

Her usual accomplice, who he privately referred to as Hag Number Two-hundred-and-four, came bounding after her in a cloud of teenage musk. He kept tossing his head to displace the overgrown mop of brown hair from his vision, and Ari denied the urge to lecture the boy on the merits of deodorant and regular haircuts.

Like most witches, Two-hundred-and-four wouldn't listen to him anyway. Ari was an oddity among witches like that: too useful to openly disdain, but too independent to be worth their respect.

"Good morning, Ari!" Six said, a cheery grin turning her roundish face into a perfect heart.

"Morning," he said, nodding in her direction. Most people read this greeting tactic as polite enough to feel welcomed in his space, and just cool enough to discourage direct chitchat.

Most people were not Hag Number Six. Along with being a recognizably skilled witch, she was obnoxiously persistent. Ari knew the former trait was an adequate reason for Two-hundred-and-four to hang off her every word; the boy was the latest in a running comic strip of wannabe apprentices loitering in her shadow. As for the latter trait . . . Ari begrudgingly accepted that proximity to Six seemed to carry a certain fringe benefit among Denver's baby witches.

Six was the penniless witchling's free ticket into Grimoires and Goodies.

It was an unspoken thing, floating in the air like a hex waiting for him to imbue it with the strength of acknowledgment. He wouldn't, of course. Hexes normally required a witch's intent and certain ritual impetus, but he decided long ago that he would never risk giving Magic such an open invitation. Whether he endorsed it or not, the fact remained that Hag Number Six was a Goodies regular and a big spender. He couldn't turn her money away, no matter how much he wanted to at times.

Six rarely came to see him without company. At least this teenage lackey didn't waste his breath trying to pressure Ari into joining their coven, only to get himself banned from the shop entirely.

Six tutted and cooed to the teenage boy about a couple odds and ends, as she always did, but she ended up on the other side of the café counter sooner than usual. Between the previous day's hiccups and Six's disinterest in pretending to shop around, Ari's wariness spiked.

He slipped his smartphone into his apron pocket and gave her his undivided attention. In his experience, bookkeeping could wait more patiently than any witch.

It is time.

Yeah, now was definitely not the time to assume Six was here to make pleasantries.

Ari met her eye with a put-upon sigh. "If you're here to deliver another message from your Morrigan—"

"Not at all!" Six leaned on the counter with a conspiratorial light in her eyes. "A little birdie told me you were looking for help around the shop."

Ari snorted. "That bird's a liar."

The glint in her eye didn't fade as she scrutinized him. "Sure about that, are you?"

The door chimed as another customer came in, and Six's attention was diverted.

"Councillor," Six said with a strained smile.

Ari stood a little taller and offered the newcomer a more

genuine grin. "Welcome back, Councillor Sanchez. I'll be with you in just a moment, yes?"

Councillor Maria Sanchez spared Six a sour glance before beaming at Ari. She gave him a quiet nod before wandering off toward the romance novels. Her yellow sundress made the sparse graying of her dark hair look almost like natural highlights, and Ari wondered yet again if she used magic to supplement the signs of aging. Regardless, she was poised and refined as she perused the shelves in a way Ari couldn't help but envy.

He didn't envy himself for dealing with her, though. Sanchez rarely visited the shop in person, preferring to do business via email or the occasional video call. Her presence during the day could only mean a headache for him.

"Why you let her kind in here, I'll never know," Six huffed.

Ari frowned. "She's not bothering you—oh!"

Six clamped her fingers around his wrist. They struggled for a brief moment, but she pulled his hand toward her, despite his resistance.

"Not this again," he groaned in defeat as she splayed his fingers out with a satisfied smile.

"Oh, hush." She proceeded to trace the creases in his palm with an earth-stained finger.

Ari cringed even as he braced his free arm on the counter and dumped his weight on it. "So help me, if you start spouting shit about inconsiderate blackouts or the state of my linen closet, I will chase you out of here with a broom."

She paused the palm reading to quirk a questioning brow at him.

Ari sighed. "Just get on with it."

She pursed her lips as if fighting back a smile, then refocused on his open palm. Ari let her work in silence.

Six did this every now and then, and Ari had yet to gather the courage to ask her what she was looking for. She rarely said anything, be it during or after, and he didn't know her well enough to read the collage of expressions that always crossed her face as she read him. The only thing he knew for sure was that if Six came in with a mind to look at his life lines, there was no making her leave until she did it.

Resigned to the path of least resistance, Ari relaxed into her earthy hands and entertained himself by scanning the shop.

Over Six's head, Ari watched Two-hundred-and-four settle at the corner-most table with a thick novel pulled from a nearby shelf. Ari made a mental note to remind the boy that Goodies was not a library, and he would have to buy the book if he wanted to keep reading it every time Six visited the shop.

While annoying, the lounging teen was commonplace. Ari's attention slipped away with the ease of routine and sought out the other customers.

He spotted Sanchez flicking through a fashion magazine, with a pair of tourists snickering behind her near the romance section. He found the back of a dark-purple jacket and black beanie wandering along the balcony level. Ari watched the figure browse for a moment before determining he must be another tourist.

Six continued making faces over his hand, so Ari diverted his attention to the windows with a stifled sigh. He didn't know how other witches operated, but he preferred practicing the craft in relative silence; in theory, the less distraction he caused Six, the sooner she would move on. She would shop for a bit while her underling read and Ari made her and the boy their usual coffee order, then she'd pay for the beverages and whatever else caught her eye, and they would each go about their lives without incident.

In the meantime, Ari would entertain himself with people watching. It was the first weekend of fall break for local academics, and the pedestrian traffic was picking up despite the early hour. He watched families trundle by with their bouncing children and packed strollers, and the fit individuals power walking with their dogs or jogging partners. He smiled each time he spotted a little old couple with their arms latched and sporting the occasional cane, and rolled his eyes at every gaggle of teens pretending they couldn't feel the chill as they forwent jackets for the sake of aesthetic.

He perked up whenever the right person passed his shop windows. After so many years, Ari knew the type of person that made up his clientele, even when they were regular people with zero magical affinity. He saw the spark of interest in their eyes the second they caught sight of Goodies; it was a siren call that invariably drew in people of all sorts.

It was a nice and predictable correlation, just the way Ari liked it.

By the time Six released him from her clutches, a dozen or more people roamed the shop. As he reasserted use of his hand, Ari asked, "Your usual?"

"Actually . . ." She gave him another assessing stare. "I'm thinking of mixing things up today. Let's try something new."

Ari's brows shot upward in mild dismay.

"What would you recommend, Ari?"

Ari frowned at her suspiciously. When all she did was continue smiling, he spat out the first drink that came to mind, "The Bella Lugosi. It's a raspberry truffle macchiato."

She beamed. "Perfect."

His eyes narrowed. "Yeah?"

She reached over the counter to give his wrist a squeeze, and her voice dropped to a giddy whisper, "Chaos is part of every witch's nature, you know? Yours too, no matter how hard you try to deny it."

Ari yanked his arm free and stepped back from the counter with his arms crossed over his button down.

She let him go with an impish grin. "Just saying. There are worst things than accepting who and what we are."

"Thanks, but if I needed vaguely foreboding advice, I'd call a priest." With a mean little smile, Ari added, "Or join a coven."

She didn't argue, which was a prime example of why he never had cause to kick her out over the years. Instead, Six clucked at him in gentle rebuke before trotting off.

Ari shook himself to keep the mild irritation from billowing into something problematic. He probably looked like a fool, shuddering behind the counter like he'd been doused in ice water, but it couldn't be helped. It was unacceptable to start throwing rude hand signs at a person's back in public, and he needed some kind of physical release for the tension suffusing his muscles.

It is time.

This was bullshit, Ari decided.

Six seemed to respect his need for space. She stayed clear of him and the counter for the next hour. She even sent her lackey over with her purse to pay for her drink when it was ready. Ari busied himself with other customers and forced himself to stop replaying her words.

It gave him the perfect opportunity to play detective with Councillor Sanchez.

"This should be sufficient, I think," Sanchez said as she set a hefty envelope on the counter between them.

Ari barely had to touch it to know it was a thick wad of cash.

He arched a brow at her. "This is for the scroll?"

"Of course."

Ordinarily, Ari wouldn't accept such a significant fee outside of a private meeting. Sanchez was a rare exception; while he didn't consider her a friend, she was cordial and reliable. She and Ari had a history of working well with each other, and the particular scroll in question was an established deal.

Unfortunately, Ari could see Six and her lackey eyeing them from across the shop.

Ari lowered his voice. "I can't give it to you in public. Certain people get touchy about these things, you understand."

Sanchez's mouth tightened into a thin, hard line, but she folded the envelope back into her purse without complaint. "You do have it in your possession, then?"

Ari blinked at her surprising acquiescence. "I do. Would you like to make an appointment?"

The North American Council of Wizards wasn't known for their flexibility, but Sanchez seemed to be in a good mood. It took a bit of back and forth to find an agreeable date, but the Councillor seemed happy enough to shake on it once they did. She strode out of the shop with the air of a woman who owned the ground beneath her feet, and left nothing behind for Hag Number Six to gripe about.

In fact, the conversation with Sanchez seemed to have put Six off entirely. He expected her to come grumble at him for consorting with wizards so openly, but she contented herself to shooting him pouty looks for another hour or more.

For better or worse, Ari was left to his usual business. He rang up sales, filled drink orders, and otherwise busied himself with customer service. It was a good, easy afternoon.

He was making idle conversation with a middle-aged

couple from Oklahoma when a vaguely familiar voice scoffed behind him.

"No way."

Ari glanced over his shoulder and promptly stopped listening to the couple's continued chatter.

The tourist in the purple jacket and beanie cap stood there with a few books tucked under his arm. He was taller than Ari first realized and nearly drowning in his coat, which accounted for his substantial bulk despite the leanness to his neck and face. His face wasn't one Ari recognized, for that matter; his tan skin was mottled with green and yellow bruising along one side, and the signs of healing were stark enough to show through his close-trimmed beard.

Even without the bruises, his blank expression seemed beyond exasperated as he stared at Ari.

Ari gave him a stiff smile. "How can I help you, sir?"

The guy blinked at him, face stoic beyond the twitch of a jaw muscle. In the awkward silence, Ari couldn't help but notice that while one eye was still a little swollen, the guy's irises were a spectacular array of greens and browns.

A throat cleared, and Ari jumped at the light touch to his arm.

"It was lovely talking to you," the Oklahoma wife said with a forced smile as her husband led her toward the exit.

Ari flushed, but the couple took off before he could apologize for his inattention. He stopped himself from shouting after them like the poor-mannered idiot they must think he was, and turned back to the wounded stranger with a wince.

The guy didn't look impressed. "You work here?"

Ari straightened his posture and put on his best customer service smile. "Yes. In fact, I'm the owner."

The stranger's lips pressed into a hard line. "Of course you are. Fantastic."

The derision in his voice kicked Ari's memory into gear, and he gaped. A hushed exclamation slipped out of his mouth without his permission, "The bum!"

"Wow." The guy closed his eyes to take a deep breath, then shook his head. "Whatever. I'll wait for someone else."

"Actually . . ." Ari began with a haughty laugh, but he had already been dismissed.

Ari watched the guy plop down at the farthest of the shop's two smallest tables and fumed. He told himself not to take it personally, that the table was the obvious choice for privacy from the other shoppers, and it had nothing to do with maximizing distance from where Ari stood near the counter. It took an absurd amount of time for the heat to leach from his face and neck, but Ari refused to question it further.

He would give the not-necessarily-a-bum some time to chill out before he approached him. Or maybe he would let him figure out that Ari was the only employee on his own time.

Two hours later, and Ari knew he miscalculated. The not-bum had more patience than he did.

"Thanks!" a young lady said as she accepted her change and a steaming cup of espresso and sugar.

Ari smiled and nodded, following her out the door with his eyes. She was the last tourist from the morning throng, and her departure marked a good opportunity to take his lunch break before business picked up again. Even if he didn't have Val's enchantments reinforcing the security cameras and sensors to keep the peace, Ari trusted his regulars to behave while he stepped away for ten minutes.

That said nothing about the potential bum keeping to the smallest table and pretending Ari didn't exist. If he was still there when Ari finished eating, he would insist the guy buy something or get out.

He had a business to run, dammit.

"What's for lunch?" Hag Number Two-hundred-and-four chirped, appearing by the door to the back room before Ari could make his escape.

Ari bit back a rude remark about minding one's own business and waved him off. "I'll be back in ten."

"Perhaps you could ring us up first?" Six said from behind him.

Ari paused with his hand on the employees only door and glared from one witch to the other. The door was right there, but in light of his recent poor luck, committing to that trajectory had a good chance of dumping him in his apartment again.

Or worse.

Deciding not to risk it, Ari trudged back to the register with the two happy witches trailing behind him.

Six's latest haul was a series of historical fiction novels and a garden-themed sudoku that took mere seconds to ring up and bag, but she hesitated to hand him her debit card.

"Could I bother you for another drink before we go?"

Ari sighed. "Sure."

"Excellent! How about . . . a Ghost Milk Latte?"

Ari jerked his head in a nod. "If it gets my break started any sooner, sure. On the house."

"Wonderful!" She beamed and threw him off guard with a conspiratorial wink. "And you'll add some cinnamon and caramel to that, hmm?"

Ari shook his head in bemusement and finished the transaction. While Six heaved her bag of books off the counter, Ari marched to the back to work on her second uncharacteristic order for the day. He should have known better than to make her that macchiato; Six usually took her coffee black, but now she was discovering her sweet tooth. It was bound to become another way for her to prolong conversations and irritate him in general. She looked far too smug when he agreed to give her the damn latte for free.

He finished the drink in record time, but Six and her henchman were gone when he returned to the counter.

The two witches weren't the only missing customers, either.

"What did you do?" Ari demanded as he set the drink on the counter between himself and the only other living soul in the shop.

The potential bum raised his unfairly pretty eyes from his stack of books to glare at Ari. "So, you treat paying customers with the same shitty attitude you use with innocent bystanders on the street, huh?"

"No." Ari planted his palms on the counter and smiled through gritted teeth. "I reserve it for rude assholes who like jumping to conclusions and meddling with my livelihood."

When Ari's brow lifted pointedly, the guy set a hand on his chosen books like he expected Ari to confiscate them, then he turned to take in the empty shop. When those obnoxious hazel orbs returned to Ari, they were noticeably wider than before.

"Where did everybody go?"

"You tell me," Ari retorted as he leaned back and crossed his arms expectantly.

Ari braced for an aggressive or reliably derisive response, but it never came. Much to Ari's surprise, the man's forehead crinkled, and his lips shrugged down in a deep frown. His stare went unfocused, as if momentarily lost in deep, unpleasant thoughts.

With a heavy sigh, Ari yanked the books out from under a heavy hand. "Let's see what you got— Oh."

Ari froze, his eyes fixated on the topmost tomb: *The Twenty-First Century Witch's Digest.*

Deliberately not looking at his suspicious customer, Ari moved the book aside to reveal the one beneath it. His confusion and alarm only grew when he read: *From Morgana to the Modern Coven: Centuries of Witch Histories.* The third and final selection was none other than Volume 1 of the *Encyclopedia of Magical Academia and Subsequent Elevation of Wizardry.*

With unfocused eyes on the books, Ari cleared his throat.

"How did you find these?"

The cold steel in his voice made the possible bum pull back and stand up straighter. "They were on your shelves. Why?"

Ari looked up to see the pronounced unease of the guy's voice reinforced by the wariness in those hazel eyes. Ari watched the gold flecks amid the greens and browns grow brighter in real time.

Pretty eyes notwithstanding, there was nothing special about the guy that Ari could see.

Ari held the Digest up between them like a prosecutor brandishing evidence. "How did you manage to pull this from the shelf? It should have escaped your notice entirely. I know for a fact the average person can't just pick up my decidedly non-average goods by chance, Mister . . . ?"

It took a long time to get a name. As the strained silence dragged on, the suspicious stranger kept shifting his attention between Ari, the books, and the exit. A part of Ari expected him to run off instead of replying; it was the same part that had him holding his breath as his gut clenched with inexplicable nerves.

"Osondu," he said in a reluctant whisper. "And you're Ari Jamison. You're the witch."

Ari bristled. "I'm a witch, yes. But you're sure as hell not."

As the Digest thumped down on the counter, the stranger seemed to startle out of his indecision. His gaze darted to Ari and stayed put with a laser focus that stole Ari's breath away for no good reason.

The guy's jaw tightened hard beneath his facial hair. "It's true, then. You can tell what I am just by looking at me."

Ari bit the inside of his cheek to keep from broadcasting his alarm. No one was supposed to know about his special gift, about his little, inexplicable quirk. Plenty of witches could sense the presence of other magic users, but only while magic was being worked, or in its close aftermath. Ari had never met another witch who could reliably identify magical talent at a glance, and as far as he knew, no one ever suggested witches should be able to sense a wizard's magic at all.

Far as he knew, Ari was the only one who could read magical ability on sight. Too much of his formative years were spent pretending witchcraft wasn't real, and he dedicated most of his young adulthood to navigating around it with minimal consequence. Sensing the gifts of others didn't require any silly rituals or dedicated spell casting, so it wasn't something to be learned.

It was something innate to Ari, and Ari alone. It was the super power that made Grimoires and Goodies possible.

No witch, wizard, or supernatural creature got within spitting distance without Ari clocking them. Not ever.

"Look, I need your help," Osondu responded to Ari's prolonged stillness. "I can't tell you who sent me, but they gave me your name once it became clear the wiz database was a dead end."

Ari's lungs deflated in a hurry as he stepped back from the counter, sweating.

The International Wizardry Database was a remarkable bit of magical finagling with all the shiny newness and fame of being the biggest breakthrough in modern magic. It bent time and space to bring every wizard's research together from every corner of the globe. It was accessible at any time, from any place, so long as a person knew how.

Only certified wizards were privy to that secret.

Without thinking, Ari blabbed in confusion, "You're a wizard?"

Osondu moved too fast for Ari to read the emotions that played across his face. The words flew off Ari's tongue with too much astonishment, perhaps even accusation. Either way, the outburst sent Osondu racing from the shop like a wanted criminal reacting to sirens.

In his wake, Ari collapsed against the pastry display. His head swam with dawning realization.

He was blind to this wizard. Try as he might, Ari looked at him and saw only man. Granted, he was an irritatingly attractive man now that his facial hair was groomed and his strong features weren't hidden in a hood's shadow, but still . . . Osondu gave off none of the magical knowing Ari always keyed into on instinct.

"This isn't possible," he muttered.

Naturally, the Magic running the universe chose that moment to mock him. Something nudged his stunned hand, and Ari looked down to find Osondu's books neatly stacked with Six's abandoned latte resting on top. The spines of all three books faced him, but their titles were nowhere to be seen.

Ari wasn't proud of it, but he loosed a piercing shriek that would make a grown-ass banshee proud.

The spine of the first book read: It.

The second read: is.

And the third read: time.

CHAPTER 3

Gladys: The Nosy Neighbor was Ari's favorite bar in all of Denver. It was the sort of place a magical being could hide in not-so-plain sight from their peers. The indulgent and materialistic atmosphere tended to turn off the witches, and the unrestrained energy and lack of refinement had a similar effect on most wizards. The excess of perfumes and sex pheromones served as ample deterrent to other supernatural beasties as well.

As a bonus feature, mundane eyes didn't have a hope of noticing anything truly magical when copious amounts of alcohol and flamboyance demanded their attention.

There was a certain kind of eccentric anonymity to be had in such spaces. Dazzle and her fellow Queens were the natural exception.

"Get that mopey expression off your face," Dazzle demanded in place of greeting.

Dahlia Dazzle slid onto the bench across from him in a blinding cloud of glittering tulle and rhinestones. Her dress for the evening was an extravagance of blue, with a stuffed

31

top that made the illusion of her breasts seem impossibly large when combined with the right makeup technique.

She was an absolute vision, and Ari couldn't help but notice the sparkling blue of her dress matched his corset vest by pure coincidence. A shared taste for fashion was practically the cornerstone of their friendship, and the unintended color coordination was a testament to their closeness.

"Ari deserves to mope after the week he's had," Val defended as her head popped out of his bag on the seat beside him. She sported a bow tie around her neck in place of the collar she usually wore in public. It, too, was sparkly and blue.

"Oh my god! Is that a kitty?"

A young woman wobbled over to them on stiletto heels. She either didn't care or didn't notice her pink mini skirt riding up with every step.

Without missing a beat, Dazzle shooed the drunk woman away. "She's a working girl, and you can't afford her."

The woman's face fell, so Ari gave her a sympathetic smile as he muttered the words, "Emotional support animal." She cheered back up and trotted on her way with an understanding wave.

"I hate you both," Val reminded them in the aftermath.

Ari and Dazzle ignored her, and they weren't the only ones. God, but Ari loved this bar. There were precious few places in public domain where a talking cat wouldn't draw attention.

Whipping her long sapphire wig back over one shoulder, Dazzle snapped her fingers under Ari's nose. "Spill the tea, honey bunch. What's got your panties in a twist now?"

"Apparently, *The Twenty-First Century Witch's Digest* is quite a harrowing read," Val said before Ari could formulate a reply. "It even includes—what was it again? Right! '365 homebrews guaranteed to help you live a healthier and happier life.'"

Sighing, Ari placed a hand on Val's head and shoved her back into the tote.

"I need context," Dazzle admitted with an impatient flutter of her gaudy lashes. "Or maybe another drink."

"Both," Ari and Val chimed as one.

Dazzle stuck her tongue out at them as she snapped her fingers for the waiter's attention. It wasn't the sort of entitlement Dazzle would demonstrate anywhere else or in any other circumstance, and that was precisely why it worked. Before Ari could utter another word, one of the staff was already depositing a drink in front of the Drag Queen.

While Dazzle sipped her signature martini, Ari and Val regaled her with the tale of Ari's recent string of magical mishaps and the inconvenience that was the wizard Osondu.

"At the risk of toeing the line of certain boundaries," Dazzle hedged, "this sort of sounds like a problem a Morrigan could help with."

Ari grimaced and turned away as he downed half his beer.

Val took the opportunity to hop onto the table and sit so she and Dazzle could stare him down as a united front.

"You don't have to reach out to Fuckman," Val said, sharing a meaningful glance with Dazzle, "but there are plenty of other covens around."

"You know I can't do that," Ari huffed.

He didn't often talk about his early encounters with other witches, but Val and Dazzle were the closest he had to confidantes. If anyone understood his reasons for remaining unaffiliated to a coven and consequently beholden to said covens leading Morrigan, it was them.

Ari didn't view Magic's influence on his life as the

blessing witch culture proclaimed it to be. He never wanted to be someone's apprentice to begin with, and the one and only time he gave it a try ended in absolute disaster. It nearly crippled his career long before he got the chance to buy the real estate for Grimoires and Goodies.

Val and Dazzle didn't know all the details, but they knew enough. As a rule, witches and wizards did not mix. The three of them were the exception.

"There's no reason for a wizard to be buying books on witchcraft," Ari complained, and if it happened to redirect the conversation to safer topics, all the better.

"Yeah, it's definitely weird," Dazzle agreed, but without full understanding.

Unknown to his friends, Ari's ability to detect the magic of others was at the heart of the shop's success. Grimoires and Goodies had a reputation as the rare neutral ground between witches and wizards by design. No one was better than Ari at running interference between customers of differing backgrounds, often times without either party noticing the other's presence. There were the occasional incidents, but rarely the sort of thing Ari couldn't diffuse with good ol' fashioned customer service and mundane threats. The magical community's joint commitment to secrecy meant a clash between the factions wouldn't be dangerous in the physical sense of the word, but it could do irreparable damage to Ari's business.

For the love of any and all possible deities, but his wizard patrons barely tolerated him on a good day. Most witches got their broom handles shoved up their asses any time they knowingly shopped within glaring distance of a wizard.

"What if I said the wrong thing to the wrong person while Osondu was there?" Ari grumbled after draining his glass. He couldn't forget how closely his confrontation with the potential bum followed Six's impromptu palm reading. "What if I sold him those books first, and one of my regulars figured out he was a wizard before I did?"

Finally, they seemed to understand. Ari was relieved to see Dazzle's spine straighten with alarm and Val's fur standing on end.

"I'd have no idea the covens were boycotting me till the loss of business put the shop at risk," Ari muttered, dropping his head into his hands.

"Ari," Val whined. "That didn't happen."

"But it could have," he countered. "Fuck. I can't keep the shop open without the covens. They make, like . . . half my income!"

Val rolled her eyes in an uncomfortably human expression. "That's an exaggeration—"

"It's really not."

"It could be worse," Dazzle offered without meeting his eye. "At least he wasn't a witch slipping under your radar. Could you imagine the fallout if a coven member witnessed you closing on that sale with Councillor Sanchez?"

Dazzle laughed, but it died quickly when he realized neither Ari or Val were joining in.

If anything, the new hypothetical made the blood drain from Ari's face even faster.

"The special order from Romania," he murmured in horror. "It took me two years to get that scroll. And Sanchez is not just a wizard. She's on the Council!"

That was all it would take for covens all across the United States to label him a traitor. They already struggled with Ari's decision to remain independent and magically limited, and that was a generous take on the situation. Someone like Hag Number Six wouldn't see the deal with Councillor Sanchez as good business, but a serious betrayal of all his fellow witches.

That was precisely why Ari wouldn't join a coven. Even if he was interested in the power boost—which he wasn't—the shop would never survive if he was bound to a coven. He would have no choice but to turn over any and all magic items of significance over to the coven's Morrigan.

That wasn't the only thing Morrigans throughout the western world wanted Ari for, either. It was just the easiest one to accept.

Ari slumped backward, sinking into the pleather booth as he tried to reconcile with the massive risk of Osondu's earlier visit.

"I don't care how pretty his eyes are, or how cute his butt is," Ari decreed, "if that wizard shows his stupid face again, I'll ban him from the shop."

And with that, Ari sat up and tossed back his beer for emphasis. He forgot he already finished the drink, so he got a face full of melting ice for his trouble. As he sputtered and grabbed for the napkin dispenser, his chosen wizards cackled mercilessly.

They were still laughing at his expense minutes later when the lights dimmed and the pumping music made way for a low, warbling note designed to amp up a crowd's anticipation.

Dazzle choked on her laughter and sprang from the booth with her martini in hand. After one last sip and frantic gesture, she abandoned them with a chipper, "That's my cue!"

Gladys was a typical bar where the dark walls, high tops, pool tables, and scattered seating were concerned, but their stage was special. It was larger and more glamorous than stages of the nearby bars that catered to a more heteronormative crowd. The colorful backdrop and lighting elevated karaoke nights above the usual off-key spectacle, and the staff wasn't quiet about their excitement for a good drag show.

The stage lights fluttered, and a Queen decked in ruby and orange tones marched to center stage with a microphone to introduce the first act. The show began with thunderous applause. Dahlia Dazzle wasn't the first performer to grace the stage that night, but she was the third in a stellar lineup of glitz and glam. By the time Ari saw Dazzle waltz forward to claim the mic with an exaggerated hip sway, Ari's face ached from his persistent grin.

There was nothing legitimately magical about Gladys, but that was the whole point.

Who needed magic when Drag Queens were prancing around?

When Dazzle crooned her last note and took a bow, Ari cheered himself hoarse. He had almost forgotten about mystery bums and any close calls to his professional standing.

"Brava!" Ari cried as Dazzle returned to their table a bit later.

Ari blew her a smacking kiss and carried the gesture into an unceremonious grab for one of the three emerald-green drinks Dazzle held clumped between her fingers.

"And she comes bearing gifts!" Val cheered. A glass touched down in front of her, and she sat on her haunches with her back to the room so she could lap up a taste. "Like a liquid jolly rancher! I love it."

"Thanks," Ari told Dazzle as they clicked their glasses together. "I'll get the next round."

"No need." Dazzle stabbed two long nails into her cleavage and pulled out a few folded bills. "My fans got us covered. Least I can do since this round was covered by yours!"

With a wicked giggle, Dazzle bopped Ari on the nose with one of her talons.

"Aw!" Val cooed, "You have fans, Ari!"

"And this one's got the brains to buy drinks for your entourage too!" Dazzle said, raising her glass with a pointed look.

Ari rolled his eyes, but he was grinning, and his face felt warm. "I hope you said thanks before warning him about wasting his money."

Val lapped up some more booze with a low, "Boo!"

Dazzle pursed her lips as she swallowed like her mouth was full of cheap tequila instead of sweet cocktail. "What's the point of being a flaming twink when you're determined to waste it on celibacy? Witches are supposed to be nymphos who dance naked through the woods, not boring monks."

Ari frowned at her in thought. "I feel like that's racist."

"That's because you're drunk," Dazzle said. "Witches aren't a race. The joke was prejudicial with no genuine belief behind it, which you know, because you know me, and we love each other."

"Speak for yourself," Ari scoffed into his glass.

"Shut up," Val huffed. "You love love."

"I really don't, though," he said, matching her snark. "It's not my fault the two of you have a kink for the idea of me gagging on every dick in my general vicinity." He pointed to them in turn as he said, "You need to get laid, and you need to at least re-evaluate your personal definition of bestiality again. My asexuality is not the problem here."

Both wizards guffawed at this.

"Asexual, my ass," said Dazzle.

Val was quick to follow up by saying, "I've seen your search history, Ari. You're a filthy liar."

"Fine. I'm willfully aromantic then!" Ari adjusted,

throwing up his hands. "I don't need a partner, regardless of my sex drive, and I'm not arguing semantics with either of you. I'm finishing this drink, maybe one or two more, then I'm going home. Alone. Like always. Because that's the way I want it."

He took another long draw from his glass for emphasis. They stared at him with the same hefty exasperation that always warned him they were about to spout some insightful bullshit.

Ari smacked his glass back onto the table and announced, "And that's the end of that discussion."

Val and Dazzle exchanged a look. Even after so many years, Ari wasn't privy to the messages being exchanged. Val and Dazzle shared a history that went farther back than their awareness of his existence.

Val cleared her throat. "Maybe it's time you got over that drama with—"

"I swear," Ari cut in as the nonverbal talk became miraculously clear, "if either of you mentions his name again, I will dump this glass over your heads and leave."

Ari raised his drink like a threat, and let his cold and sober tone make it clear he wasn't joking. Without a word, Val and Dazzle refocused on their own cocktails.

"Good deal," Ari said and stood in a hurry. "Now, I need another drink."

Dazzle didn't look at him as she raised a wad of cash between two pinched nails; Ari snatched it up on his way to the bar. There was a bit of a crowd, but more than one person decided to go elsewhere when they caught sight of his face. He didn't have to slow down more than once before reaching the nearest bar stool. He plopped onto the seat to wait for the bartender and tried to shrug off his irritation.

"Looks like you enjoyed that drink."

Ari froze. He knew that voice. He shouldn't, but he did.

Shoulders slumping, Ari spun on the stool to stare up at Osondu. His oversized jacket and beanie made the wizard stick out like . . . Well, rather like a straight man in a gay bar.

"Why?" Ari sighed.

With a defensive hunch and astounded chortle, Osondu asked, "Why what?"

"Just in general, why?"

Why was Osondu visiting Gladys? Why was he stalking Ari? Why, on God's green earth, was he interested in witchcraft in the first place? And why was he making it Ari's problem? Just why, why, why, why?

Ari had so many questions, and he was getting really fed up with the giant neon arrow the universe kept pointing at Osondu whenever he dared ask.

"I need your help."

Ari craned his neck back in exasperation. "Not this again."

Osondu's brow pinched lower than ever with displeasure. He grumbled something under his breath, then unzipped his jacket as he took an aggressive step forward. He loomed over Ari's seated figure with his jaw clenched tight, and Ari felt an inexplicable shiver stutter up his spine.

"Can you at least tell me what the fuck this is?"

It wasn't the first time a guy flashed his body at him, but it was the first time Ari's heart iced over in reaction.

He was prepared to see abs and a surplus of smooth, caramel skin, not the black-and-purple bruise spanning the side of Osondu's ribs. It wasn't like the wizard's facial injury, which was almost unnoticeable at this point. No, no, no, the mark on Osondu's ribs was dark, with a pattern to the mottled colors that wasn't natural. There was a distinct absence of swelling despite the apparent freshness, and it painted a definite shape.

A thick outline of a black square tilted onto one corner above a matching 'y' shape. Two additional lines jutted down from the letter's symmetrical top lines. Ari recognized the symbol from a few academically interesting curses he would never be tempted to try himself.

"It's a nemiza," Ari whispered as he abandoned the stool without diverting his horrified gaze from the thing. "A witch's mark."

"I figured that much," Osondu huffed as he yanked down his shirt. "But you know what it means."

It wasn't a question, but Ari nodded as if it were. He swallowed the spontaneous rock in his throat so he could talk, and it hurt like gulping back a clump of raw and jagged diamond.

He made a decision then, and after shooting a quick text to Dazzle, Ari grabbed hold of a purple coat sleeve and dragged its owner to the exit.

CHAPTER 4

Osondu didn't look happy about it, but he didn't resist his apparent abduction either. He let Ari shove him into the back of a ride share, and he said nothing in response to Ari's sullen silence the entire ride from central Denver to Arvada. It was not a short trip, nor was it comfortable.

Ari was stone-cold sober by the time he let them into Grimoires and Goodies. The antique grandfather clock between the bathroom and the backroom said it was one in the morning.

Osondu hesitated by the locked door as Ari marched up the spiral stairs like a man on a mission. "Does this mean you're willing to help me now?"

"No," Ari said with a cold laugh. "This means I'm keeping my conscience clear and covering my ass."

A glance over his shoulder told Ari he wasn't the only one thinking about his ass. Not for the first time, Ari applauded his outfit choice; he appreciated the illusion of security he got from the snug fit, almost as much as he enjoyed the way it snatched his waist and accentuated the perfect fit of his jeans.

It was so nice of Osondu to notice.

"I can give you info," Ari said pointedly as he leveled a smug smirk at the wizard from the higher ground, "but that's it."

Osondu's complexion was too dark to display a vivid blush, but his perpetual grumpiness pinched in a telling way. It inspired a snide laugh from Ari, and he knew the wizard heard it by the way he hunched his shoulders and averted his gaze.

That was for the best, Ari decided. He didn't need the wizard watching while he retrieved what they needed.

Ari hid all his magical products and decor from mundane notice with a few clever runes carved into the walls behind the bookshelves and biannual rituals to keep them working. Val added a few spells over the years to keep some higher-end stuff secure but visible to magic users, and that was usually more than sufficient to keep curious hands off the trickier merchandise. He didn't usually need to waste a year's salary on faerie charms.

The Fae were expensive like that. They were a rare breed of magic to begin with, and their affinity for deception was unmatched by even the strongest coven casting or elite wizardry. They could afford to set their prices sky high, even if it bordered on extortion. Faeries were that good.

As a result, Ari's one and only foray into Fae magic was the upstairs safe. The small cabinet appeared as a shadowy corner stacked with boring boxes of overstock, too crammed and unassuming to draw anyone's attention. Ari was the only soul alive who could see through the glamour to the sealed glass lock box and its precious contents.

The glamour never faltered as Ari reached through the facade, and the lock undid itself the moment his fingers made contact. He ignored the small chest of enchanted jewelry he had yet to identify, and took the split second necessary to ensure the black velvet cloth properly obscured the cursed skull on the bottom shelf. He bypassed the scroll wrapped in aged muslin and tagged with Sanchez's name, then he snagged the book he needed from the elite selection of ancient texts on the cabinet's top shelf.

His skin crawled as he carried the book downstairs with both arms weighed down. The words "Book of Shadows" were painstakingly etched into the leather cover, and despite the years it spent in Ari's safe, Ari still wasn't sure what to make of it. The kind of witch who would name their spell book after a stereotype didn't seem like the kind of witch who'd fill their grimoire with spells for torture and mayhem.

Peculiar title aside, *Book of Shadows* was precisely the dark reference Ari needed in that moment.

"I'm not telling you what that mark means without irrefutable corroboration," Ari explained.

He set the genuine grimoire on the nearest table with a substantial thump. Ari's religious cleaning habits were put to shame as a small cloud of dust billowed up from the crackled pages and peeling leather face.

Osondu inched closer while Ari flipped open the cover. Ari could hear the sneer in his voice when the wizard commented, "I didn't know you sell used and abused copies too."

"Believe it or not, there isn't any other kind for this title." Ari glowered as he flipped through the frail pages. He found what he needed and shot Osondu a sarcastic smile before opening to the necessary page and saying, "At least this one doesn't have bloodstains."

"I can't tell if you're joke—"

Sweet, victorious silence fell as the wizard joined him at the table and got a look at the graphic illustrations. The nemiza was there, front and center, but so were a few of its victims.

"You weren't joking."

"Nope."

Ari yanked out a chair and dropped into it like this was precisely how he expected to spend his Friday night— or Saturday morning, as it turned out. If he rubbed his hands on his thighs like the book left something tangible and nasty on his skin, at least Osondu didn't call him on it.

Although, it didn't look like Osondu was in the right headspace to notice Ari's jitters anyway. He stood over the open book with a dumb, pallid stare.

Giving him a moment to collect his brain cells, Ari crossed his legs and tapped a slow beat on the table with his fingertips. He counted to ten in his head without so much as a twitch from the troublesome wizard.

Ari sighed. "I don't know what you did or who you pissed off, Mr. Osondu—"

"It's Taye."

"Sure. Taye. Right." Ari uncrossed his legs and leaned forward to interrupt the man's line of sight with his face. "So, here's the deal, Taye: you've been marked for death."

With Osondu's full attention locked on him instead of the gruesome book, Ari reclined again with his fingers laced together over his stomach. The posture was a soothing reminder of all the times he sat just so and lectured a rich patron on the history of a certain writing or the influence of whatever on a given arcane subject. Confidence settled over him like a cozy blanket ready to fend off his nerves with dependable warmth.

"Judging by the clarity and size of the symbol across so many of your vital organs, I'm guessing you either angered a scary powerful witch, or you have multiple covens coming together in ways they haven't dared since the Satanic Panic of the '80s."

He waited for a reaction, but Osondu only blinked at him.

Nodding to himself, Ari cleared his throat and tugged at the bottom hem of his corset like the sense of propriety would do him any good.

"I won't lie," Ari hedged, eyeing the open book, "it's a nasty way to go. The nemiza's the sort of curse designed to affect every aspect of a person: mind, body, soul, you name it. If it's a part of a person, the nemiza shreds it to pieces. By all accounts, you should be dead already."

Osondu opened his trembling lips, but he barely had time to suck back a lungful of air before Ari cut him off.

"I don't want to know how you're still alive. I don't want to know what you did, and I definitely don't want any further involvement in whatever shit you got yourself into."

Popping to his feet, Ari braced a hand on his hip and gave Osondu a pointed look that directed him toward the door.

"I'll thank you to stop coming around my shop and inconveniencing business moving forward."

With that clear dismissal, Ari heaved the ugly grimoire into his arms and turned to leave. He promptly stubbed his toe on the leg of a chair that shouldn't have been in his way.

"Seriously?" Ari huffed down at the displaced chair.

Behind him, Osondu gave a dismayed grumble, "I didn't do anything."

"Not you!" Ari rolled his eyes as he balanced the heavy book on one hip so he could have a hand free. He shoved the chair back toward the table it belong with and stomped toward the staircase a second later.

The twice-damned latte from Six's latest visit sat on the third step, like a tiny, terrible trick meant to fuck up his entire evening.

Jaw tight and stomach lurching, Ari sighed, "Okay. I got the hint."

"Who are you talking to?"

"You, apparently," Ari spat as he gingerly lifted the latte from the step. It was still steaming and emitting the sweat and spicy notes of freshness. "Here. Drink this while I secure the grimoire and make myself a coffee."

Osondu stared at him like he was starting to suspect Ari was dangerously crazy. "I don't drink coffee."

Ari's eye twitched. "It's tea."

Without pausing to see if Osondu would taste it, Ari raced up the spiral staircase and returned the grimoire to safety. While his late-night treat brewed, Ari scrubbed his hands in the kitchen sink till his knuckles were raw and his palms burned. When he carried his coffee back into the shop between red and smarting hands, they still didn't feel clean enough.

Ari made a mental note to wear gloves next time he handled that particular book.

He found Taye Osondu sitting at the same table Ari first allocated for them. To his surprise, the wizard not only brought himself to taste the Ghost Milk Latte, he seemed to really enjoy it from the way he tossed back his head to tip the final drops into his open mouth.

Ari sat down across from him with his eyes narrowed on the wizard. Somehow, when Osondu lowered the empty cup to reveal zero signs of recent injury to his perfectly sculpted face, Ari wasn't surprised.

"Feeling better?"

Osondu held the cup in his lap, studying it with an impressed frown as he nodded. "Not bad. It tasted like chai tea—"

"Tea-tea? Imagine that."

Osondu scowled and flicked the cup so a few specks of latte splattered in Ari's direction. Ari's chair shrieked across the floor as he avoided the droplets, and when he next refocused on Osondu, the wizard's scowl was replaced by something intrigued and thoughtful.

"What did you put in that tea?"

Ari snorted and sipped his coffee, complete with a self-important shimmy that straightened his posture.

Osondu's suspicious scowl came back full force as he sat forward. Then he went still as a statue. He blinked a few times, then jumped to his feet and began pacing as he crushed the latte cup in his fist. His other hand went to his torso, patting and prodding at the area where the nemiza should be. His long strides were graceful and unhurried, and Ari realized he never saw the guy move without prominent pain before that moment.

With three fingers enclosing the crumpled cup, Osondu pointed at Ari. "You healed me. Why?"

Ari considered lying for a moment. It wasn't the first time Magic hijacked something Ari made, leading to misconceptions about his magical prowess. He enjoyed another leisurely mouthful before setting down his mug. He trained his gaze on the creamy brown liquid and decided he really didn't need Osondu thinking him capable of miracles.

"I did nothing."

"Liar."

Choosing to ignore the insult, Ari circled the rim of his mug with a diligent finger and watched the coffee swirl in a predictable and fully controlled pattern.

He didn't react when Osondu's hand came down beside his mug and the wizard loomed over him.

"Witches don't go around doing favors for random

wizards. They don't do favors for anyone or anything outside their coven."

"Hmm. Know many witches, do you?"

"I've heard my fair share of stories."

Ari raised his head, ill-prepared to find those vibrant eyes inches away from his own. He kept his surprise to himself and didn't back down. It was beyond gratifying to see Osondu's gaze flicker down toward his mouth when Ari resumed talking.

"You don't know me," Ari murmured.

Things went wrong then. The air grew warmer as the last word left his lips, and that was the moment Ari lost control of his tongue. It was like a waking dream; he was aware, and it was his voice, his mouth doing the talking, but he didn't know which words would come out of him until the moment he and Osondu heard them with their very ears. He had no control over the tone, no involvement in the message's creation.

Even as he spoke with the authority of limitless power, Ari felt powerless.

"You are merely a wizard," Magic said from Ari's throat. "Everything you know and everything you can do is a direct result of the abilities and resources of those who came before. You think because you do magic, it makes you special, but I was born a witch. I am a creature of magic."

Ari wasn't sure what happened, but Osondu's eyes widened before he yanked away and backed himself into a bookshelf. Ari didn't move to follow—he didn't think he was capable of it just then—but the seeds of confusion blossomed into full alarm as Osondu stopped eyeing him like an irritating puzzle and more like a genuine threat.

Magic either didn't notice, or didn't care.

"You came to me for a reason, Tayvon Conall Osondu. I

suggest you remember it and make your case before I tire of your petty intimidation tactics."

A sharp squeak accompanied the movement as Osondu's abandoned chair scooted an inch from the table all on its own.

"Sit," Ari heard himself say. "It is time."

Between one blink and the next, Ari was back in the driver's seat of his own body.

"The fuck was that?" Osondu asked. "You were fucking glowing."

He sounded disturbed, but he covered it well enough as he made his way back to his seat with slow, deliberate steps.

Instead of answering, Ari raised his mug in both hands and hid his face in its aromatic steam. He needed a minute to slow his pounding heart and covertly calm his breathing before the encroaching panic got a solid hold on him.

After a careful sip of coffee, Ari cradled the mug in his lap and spoke with totally feigned calm. "I don't have a satisfactory answer to your question, but I . . ." He hesitated, licking his lip. "I think it's time you tell me exactly why you sought me out."

Osondu squirmed a little in his seat as he rubbed a fist into the adjacent palm. His expression was contemplative and distant as he stared down at the table and gnawed on his wide lower lip.

Ari turned his mug in a circle between shaky hands. "I doubt you know much about witch magic or how it differs from wizardry, but I need you to understand; I don't belong to a coven. I never have, and I never will."

With that, Ari clamped his mouth shut. He wasn't about to tell Osondu about the years he spent fending off power-hungry covens led by Morrigans who saw him and his unique connection to Magic as a tool rather than a person. He'd seen all manner of tactics, from brute force to congenial manipulators. In the end, their priorities were always the same; they never cared about Ari, only the power he was capable of.

It wasn't a story Ari was inclined to share with his closest friends, let alone a stranger.

Osondu must have read something of that truth in Ari's expression, because he didn't push the subject. With a curt nod, he surmised, "I get why she sent me to you, now. You won't turn me over to a Morrigan's mercy."

Ari sighed, and he knew he would regret asking before he voiced the question. "What did you do and to what witch?"

The mangled latte cup was discarded on the table between them, but Osondu stretched out of his seat to pick it up. He fiddled with it, keeping his eyes and fingers busy as he thought. Batting the trash between his hands, he eventually looked up through his lashes and offered a tight smile.

"Would you believe you're the only witch I've met?"

Ari frowned and settled on repeating himself. "What did you do, Taye?"

"It's easier to just show you," he grumbled as he began plucking at the garbage.

Frown deepening, Ari watched Osondu unfold the paper cup like he intended to salvage it. Ari stood to retrieve the small trash bin from the corner so they could get rid of the distraction, but then he noticed the intent in Osondu's movements. There was a wealth of focus in his expression as he unfurled the trash and balanced it on its wrinkled bottom.

"Watch," Osondu said as he shoved his hands in his jacket pockets, his eyes never straying from the cup.

It shouldn't have been possible, but Ari watched it happen. Without a conduit item, without any kind of invocation or ritual, Osondu stared at the used cup.

The cup reacted.

At first, it barely wiggled. It started so subtly, Ari first thought he imagined the movement. Then a deep fold smoothed out of existence, then the bottom evened out and the cup stabilized. Then, like a plastic bottle rather than a mangled paper cup, the damaged container popped back into its perfect and useful design.

Ari stepped forward in time to see the telltale foam of a fresh latte rise from the bottom. Ari snatched the open cup from the table and held it with the base flush to his palm as the drink finished refilling itself.

Stunned, Ari turned his gaping face toward Osondu.

The wizard shrugged with a strained smile that mirrored Ari's own dismay.

Still starring at Osondu, Ari raised the cup to his mouth. Osondu didn't stop him, so Ari dipped the tip of his tongue into the steaming liquid. It was delicious, and just as frothy and substantial as the drink Ari made days ago with his own two hands.

Ari set the cup down with a soft and possibly hysterical laugh. "You meant to do that?"

Osondu shrugged. "Mostly? I mean . . . I meant to fix the cup, but the rest . . ."

"Not intentional."

"Yeah."

Ari stared at the cup, his mind racing. He thought back to all the times something similar happened to him, when one little spot of witchcraft went off the rails and gave him something more than he bargained for.

For one heart-stopping moment, Ari wondered if Osondu was like him: cursed with an inexplicable connection to Magic.

Except . . . Osondu was supposed to be a wizard. His

magical ability was supposed to be dependent on study and use of a specific medium.

Ari eyed Osondu critically. "You have your certification from the North American Council of Wizards?"

He nodded.

Ari's gaze darted from man to latte and back again. Before he could ask what Osondu's chosen medium was, the guy scooted forward on his chair and started talking.

"I can't control it. Not entirely. Even when I try my usual wizardry, things have been"—he weighed his options before choosing a word—"intense. It's like my magic's on steroids or something."

Slow and deliberate, Ari reclaimed his seat at the table. Osondu needed no more encouragement than that.

"I tried to help someone," he said, gaze distant with memory. "A client. He was sick and suffering. I can usually help him with some subtle wizardry, but this time . . . Well, let's just say the miraculous healing I ended up performing would have exposed the supernatural in a pretty big way if the Council hadn't stepped in."

Ari shook his head, hands on his hips as he continued staring at the cup. "I don't know what to say. That's . . . I mean, it's definitely not witchcraft, and it's not like any wizardry I've ever heard of."

Osondu made an absent gesture. "I trained and earned my certification with a guitar as my conduit."

Ari nearly fell out of his seat in surprise.

"A wizard musician," Ari mused aloud. "That's . . . unorthodox."

Wizards typically required a medium that was less subjective. As Dazzle once put it, wizardry needed less art and more science. It wasn't unheard of for a wizard to master something like music as their chosen conduit, but the people who chose it rarely handled the kind of power that garnered widespread attention.

Ari couldn't imagine how a wizard and his guitar deserved the nemiza branded on his torso. Then again . . . there wasn't an instrument in sight, was there? Osondu hadn't needed it to perform impressive magic.

Osondu didn't react to Ari's stunned stupor. He merely accepted it and carried on the conversation.

"Two weeks ago, I couldn't work any magic without strumming a few notes, but now . . . As soon as I realized it wasn't a fluke, and the universe really was spontaneously bending to my whims for no apparent reason, I went to my mentor." Osondu hunched his shoulders, and Ari realized the wizard was trying hard not to look at him. "He told the Council."

Ari winced.

"Instead of helping me, he blamed me."

Osondu's careful stoicism began to crack with rising temper. Ari didn't blame him. For all their differences, witches and wizards shared a healthy respect for the unique relationship between a skilled magic user and their apprentice. It was nothing as formal as adoption, but the connection was often as strong and insoluble as any chosen family could hope to be.

The betrayal Osondu described was uncommon. Worse yet, in Ari's opinion, it was familiar.

"I showed him something similar"—Osondu gestured to the latte—"and instead of asking questions, he jumped straight to the most damning conclusion he could think of. He started yelling at me for fucking with unsanctioned magical experiments."

The angry sneer warping Osondu's features was a thinly veiled mask for his devastation. It made Ari want to reach out to grip the guy's arm in solidarity, but he aborted the motion before Osondu noticed.

"I knew I had to run when he said my abilities threatened the secrecy and stability of the magical world as we know it. And he was right."

While Osondu wiped the growing wetness from his eyes, Ari tried to collect himself. He took a few measured breaths and willed his gut to unclench. He cleared his throat and hoped his professional affect was back in place so they could continue with less emotion slowing things down. He meant to distance himself.

He didn't. He wasn't delusional enough to blame Magic for his actions this time.

Ari set a hand on Osondu's knee and asked, "Was he the one who gave the black eye?"

It took a long, tense moment before Osondu nodded. He looked away from Ari as he did it, but he didn't yank his leg out from under his touch either.

That one moment of shared hurt was brief but irrefutable. It killed any chance of further conversation, and they said nothing else that night. By unspoken accord, the first involuntary yawn saw them rising from their chairs and exiting the shop. Ari said nothing as he let them out onto the sidewalk, and the wizard ran off in the time it took Ari to lock up behind them. It was just as well.

There was nothing more to say.

"You know all those times I suggested you bring a man home?" Val asked the following day as she lounged beside the register. "That wasn't what I meant."

"I'm aware."

They were the only two souls in the shop, because for the first time ever, Grimoires and Goodies was closed on a Saturday with no notice. Ari never took a sick day because he never got sick, and he never had emergencies to attend to because he never engaged in that sort of drama. Now though, with the fresh image in his mind of Taye Osondu involuntarily dozing off in his shop and clutching a magically induced tea like an emotional support stuffy, Ari reckoned his luck had run out.

Ari was both sick to his stomach and certain this constituted as an emergency.

Val shifted uneasily. "You're positive he was subjected to a death curse?"

"Yep."

"And why isn't he dead again?"

"I don't know."

A contemplative silence stole over them as Val continued pondering and Ari resumed distracting himself by deep cleaning the cash till. He knew there were easier and quicker ways to get the job done, since he had plenty of Dazzle's cleaning potion in stock, but he needed to keep his hands busy. He needed simple and consuming tasks that were well within his ability to handle.

Customers were too much for him that day, so cleaning with mundane products and elbow grease would have to suffice. The physicality was rather cathartic, not that he would admit it aloud.

Val left him to it for a long while. He almost forgot she was there when she piped up again. "Do you really think he can work witchcraft?"

Ari hesitated.

He really didn't want to waste another hour trying to get Val to understand the astoundingly huge difference between witchcraft and whatever Osondu did the previous night with nothing but his brain. On the other hand, the whole situation was so far beyond his scope that Ari physically itched to pass the ordeal onto Val.

Val's dainty little paws were clearly not up to the task, though.

Sighing, Ari set down the scrub brush and leaned his hip on the counter, arms crossed. "Let's say yes, this wizard woke up one day able to commune with Magic more effectively than any witch since Morgana herself. If he came to you for guidance, what would you do?"

Val craned her neck to meet his eye. "As a wizard?"

Ari frowned. "As opposed to . . . what?"

Val sighed. "As a wizard with a social obligation to the

community, I would tell the closest Council member at the earliest convenience."

Ari made a disgusted face, but she didn't let him get a word in.

"His mentor wasn't entirely wrong, Ari. From the sounds of it, no one knows what he might be capable of, or why, himself included. No one's comfortable with unknowns when magic's involved."

Ari considered that in light of what he experienced the previous night, not twenty feet from where they stood now. The unprecedented power that manifested through Ari's own body last night wasn't any more normal than Osondu's spontaneous paper cup restoration. Ari wondered if he ought to tell Val about it.

Shit. If he did, he'd probably have to confess about the rest of Magic's unsolicited assistance since he and Osondu crossed paths.

"Now, as a thinking and feeling person," Val continued in blissful ignorance of Ari's troubled thoughts, "I would have advised Taye to remain calm and sit put till he knew the extent of his new powers. I would have offered a safe place to stay while he tested his limits and I contacted the Council on his behalf, and I sure as shit would have advocated for asking questions and conducting a fair investigation before jumping to conclusions and passing judgment."

Val had a few more choice words about Osondu's former mentor and the Council of Wizards as a whole. Her general affront about the situation's poor handling washed over Ari like a balm, dousing him with reassurance that his sympathy for Osondu was both reasonable and deserved. The cat knew the effect she was having, too, because she continued ranting beyond the rant's natural end just for his sake. Eventually, she ranted to the point Ari was chuckling aloud as he resumed cleaning the till at a more sustainable pace.

He disappeared to the back room for a few minutes to grab his third coffee to make up for his lack of sleep. On a whim, he made an extra cup for Val.

He returned to find Val utterly uninterested in refreshments. The white Bengal was on her feet, fur bristling as she stared toward the shop's entrance.

Ari nearly spilled the drinks when he saw who stood on the street glaring back at Val through the clear glass of the door.

"Either he leaves, or I do," Val hissed.

"Hush," Ari scolded, setting the mugs on a convenient table as he passed.

Councillor Robert Gaines stood on the cobblestone like the embodiment of Ari's childhood hopes and dreams. He was striking in his three piece suit and dark, slicked back hair. The symmetry of his clean shaven face and the overt strength of his chin was a work of art that made up for the fact his lips were so thin and his eyes so unfeeling. He exuded a chilling competence that could be felt even through the glass and across the length of the store. Physically beautiful and refined, hardworking, predictable, and disciplined, Gaines was almost the perfect man in Ari's opinion. It was a shame he was such an asshole.

Ari flipped the lock without touching the closed sign, and the overhead bell chimed as he yanked the door open a few polite inches.

"Hello, Councillor. Perhaps you could stop glaring at my friend like she owes you money? Then you'd be welcome to stop by another time when the shop's open."

"Send Lady Valkyrie on her way," Gaines said with a dismissive glance at the cat now pretending to sunbathe in the window display and coincidentally flashing her booty hole. "There's no need for her involvement."

Ari slipped onto the sidewalk and pulled the door shut behind him. He planted himself two feet from the wizard with arms crossed and his own proverbial witch's broom good and tight up his backside.

"Val has an open invitation," Ari explained. "If you'd like to schedule a private—"

"I'm not paying your exorbitant consultation fee," Gaines interrupted with a mean smile. "I wouldn't be here at all if I had any other recourse. As it is, there are no wizards who can assist me."

Ari sighed as his heart plummeted. "What do you need that's so pressing, Councillor?"

Gaines raised a brow as he gestured at Val again. "I must insist on privacy."

In the end, Val wanted to be in the same room with Gaines about as much as he wanted to be near her. After a brief and nearly wordless discussion, Ari let the cat out the back door so she could walk home via the alleys and rooftops. She was wearing her pink collar with his phone number inscribed on the tag, so he wasn't worried someone would mistake her for a stray.

He came back to find Gaines seated at the random table Ari deposited the mugs on, and sipping from the one meant for Val. Sucking back a breath that begged for patience, Ari pulled out the opposite chair and palmed his own drink.

"I don't know the extent of your wizardry knowledge, but I assume the likes of Valkyrie and Davenport have explained the Council's authority to you."

"I never needed them to. I have to be familiar with the Council and their responsibilities, since I count several members among my patrons." Ari smiled his favorite customer service smile, the blatantly fake one he rarely used when the store was open to the public. "Despite your disapproval."

"The Council of Wizards controls and serves the wizards of a given area the same as a Morrigan serves their coven," Gaines explained as if Ari never spoke. "You owe me the same respect you would show a Morrigan."

Ari's fake smile widened. "That would be the same basic decency I show all my customers, then."

Gaines glared at him in a most unimpressed manner. "I'm sure a man of your apparent intelligence can appreciate the comparison anyhow."

Ari said nothing to that, so he drank deep while arching a sardonic brow over the mug's rim.

If Gaines wanted to draw useless comparisons between witch and wizard governance, than Ari would leave him to it. Despite his personal dislike for the man, Ari tended to agree with Gaines's outspoken opinion that wizards had the superior system of checks and balances.

The Morrigan concept was a little too archaic and monarchical for his comfort. It didn't seem right for one person to hold so much power over all others, but any time he complained within another witch's ear shot, all he got was pitying looks and the occasional guilt trip one might expect from a cult follower addressing an outsider.

Wizards on the other hand, organized themselves by region instead of charisma. Miraculously enough, Gaines was an elected official.

"While I maintain there's no practical reason for your seeming success," Gaines droned, "I am, unfortunately, forced to admit you hold a unique position in the wider magical community."

Elbow on the table so he could prop his chin on his palm,

Ari gave a malicious grin. "My, my, Councillor. Are you propositioning me?"

Gaines wrinkled his nose like he smelled something foul. "This isn't a business transaction, Mr. Jamison. It's an interrogation."

Ari blinked and sat up straight.

"I'm searching for someone."

"Oh?" Ari drawled back as if bored, but his guts were twisting and wriggling into knots.

"A rogue wizard by the name Osondu."

A chill ran up Ari's spine. Rogue was not a word often used within the magical community. The term implied much worse than a lack of affiliation with a council or coven; it labeled the individual as uncontrolled and dangerous, criminally so.

"I'm told you can help me locate him."

Ari took another gulp of coffee to buy himself a second to figure out what to do next.

"Do you have a picture?" he asked, the words tasting like charcoal. "I'm not familiar with the name, but I've always been better with faces anyway."

As Gaines reached for his jacket's inner breast pocket, a gust of wind invaded the closed shop for the express purpose of stealing Ari's air supply. His throat didn't lock up, but his breath was stolen just the same. The sensation passed before Gaines noticed anything was wrong, only to be replaced by the squeezing of an invisible band around his rib cage. The experience included no words, only feeling.

It is time.

The message reverberated through Ari's being. His body and soul translated it into some sort of alarm. It felt like panic and exhilaration, like he was hyper-alert to the point of numbness. Nothing and everything made sense.

Ari froze in place as Gaines unlocked a sleek black cell phone before setting it on the table between them.

The man staring back at him from the screen was clean shaven and decked out in a nice shirt and tie. There were no lines of age or stress, no unkempt stubble or curious bruising, but Ari recognized those pretty hazel eyes in a heartbeat. It was undeniably Taye Osondu.

Ari wanted to believe he was staring at the troublesome wizard's younger brother. Unfortunately, the harder he tried making up a different narrative than the inevitable truth, the tighter Magic hugged him around the middle. Chest tight, Ari resorted to rubbing his sternum uselessly.

"You've seen him," Gaines murmured, his tone somewhere between accusation and victory.

Ari couldn't draw enough breath to speak. He winced as Magic clamped down harder, till his bones crackled with pain.

"When was he here?"

On instinct more than thought, Ari set a single fingertip on the corner of the smartphone and slid it back to Gaines. Breathless, Ari shook his head in the negative.

The pressure disappeared, and Ari sucked back a beautifully long, deep inhale. The confused emotions and impressions swarming his mind and heart fell to the wayside to make room for an all-encompassing relief. Rightness. Yes, this was right. It was so profound that Ari began panting, his eyes leaking as he collapsed in the chair.

Gaines didn't seem to care. He stood and loomed over Ari with a tight jaw and expectant grimace. "You must tell me everything. When and where you last saw him, what he was doing. All of it. I must know every word he spoke within your hearing."

Blond hair fell into his face as Ari shook his head again.

He tried to compose himself and regain his breath, but his speech came out as a wheezing laugh.

"All due respect, Councillor, but no."

The table clanked and rocked with the impact of the wizard's fists as he leaned in, his teeth bared. "You have no idea the risks this man poses to the community, but if you have half a brain in that pretty little head of yours, then you will trust me when I say he is the greatest threat to our security since The Inquisition."

Since Ari's lungs were no longer screaming at him, he clutched his hands over his heart and gaped up at the Councillor. "Aw, you think I'm pretty?"

Gaines jerked upright, gaping and blinking as if he'd been splashed with a face full of scalding coffee. "You really think this is the best time to mock your betters?"

Ari scoffed up at him. "Wow. You come into my territory and waste my time with insults and—forgive my phrasing— but an actual fucking witch hunt, and now you want to pull some prejudiced bullshit on top of that?"

Ari got to his feet with another cynical laugh, and it was strangely gratifying to see Gaines turn red and curl his hands into fists at his sides.

"I'm not one of your wizards, Councillor." Ari was impressed by how cool and calm his voice sounded, considering how much his legs were shaking. "For the sake of the peace and neutrality Grimoires and Goodies represents, I'm asking you to leave."

"Gladly." Gaines brandished the picture on his phone like a weapon. "But only after you tell me what you know. I may not have formal authority over you, Jamison, but I do have a working relationship with the local Morrigans. One word from me, and they won't remain so accepting of the egotistical loner making a fortune off their covens."

Magic didn't like the threat any more than Ari did. He felt it tickle his fingertips and creep up each digit like tangible vines twisting around his limbs. All traces of humor gone, Ari asserted, "We're done here. You're welcome to return to the shop once you've remembered your manners, but—"

The pain came out of nowhere. Ari gasped, stumbling as his head whipped to the side courtesy of the backhand to his face. His cheek throbbed, hot and already swelling as he blinked away the shock.

"You don't have the protection or might of a coven," Gaines sneered as he watched Ari press a hand to his stinging cheek.

Ari didn't expect it, but Magic's presence danced around his fingers like a balm. No, wait. It was a balm.

"While I'm sure you believe Valkyrie and Davenport are misguided enough to stick up for you," Gaines continued in the background, "I'm equally sure they wouldn't dare."

The power collecting at Ari's fingertips seeped into his wounded flesh and banished the hurt before the bruise could become visible. The amazement of it stole the air from Ari's lungs. Magic had never healed him before, not even when it was the cause of his aches and pains, as was so often the case.

Staring down at his fingers like they owed him answers, Ari tuned back in to Gaines and his sanctimonious tirade.

"All true wizards understand the consequences of defying the Council of Wizards. Now, you will answer my questions without further attitude."

"My apologies for the misunderstanding," Ari said in a daze as he retook his seat. "I'm not much for confrontation."

"I don't care—"

"But I am practical," Ari finished as he made a point of leaning back and crossing his legs. He retrieved his coffee with one hand and snapped his fingers with the other.

Silence reigned.

When Ari next lowered his mug, he was blissfully alone. There was a faint odor of something like burning rubber, for lack of a better descriptor, and the half empty mug commandeered from Val sat abandoned on the other side of the table. There was no other sign Councillor Gaines was ever there.

"Good to know the most extensive witchcraft of my career still works," Ari mused aloud before taking another leisurely sip of coffee.

He chose to overlook the startling reality that he finally activated the defensive wards. He would have to close the shop an extra day so he could reset the runes carved into the baseboards, but that was a worry for another time. For now, Ari was going to ignore the fact he just banished one of the most powerful wizards in the Northern Hemisphere to who knows where. At least for as long as it took for him to finish enjoying his beverage, he wouldn't be considering all the life-altering implications or potential ramifications of such actions.

Holy fucking shit balls, but he needed more than a single cup of coffee.

CHAPTER 6

*A*ri adopted the phrase "one step at a time" as his own personal mantra for the remainder of the weekend. It was more like managing one crisis at a time, but he didn't have the mental or emotional bandwidth to argue semantics with himself.

He had a rogue wizard potentially stalking him, an entire shop to reinforce against a slew of unwanted visitors, and a shit ton of magical shenanigans to get to the bottom of. None of it was business as usual, and if Ari wasn't shocked into hyper-compartmentalization just then, he would be a sobbing mess over it.

"Now I get why you got home so late last night," Val commented as Ari carried her into the shop Sunday morning. "You were busy with a demolition."

"The mess is a necessary evil," Ari grumbled.

He deposited Val on the nearest chair that wasn't serving as a temporary shelf for various merchandise. He grabbed hold of a displaced bookcase in the next second to resume dragging it a sufficient distance from the wall.

After the Councillor's departure, Saturday was spent

hanging drapes over the shop's front wall, closely followed by unseemly amounts of manual labor as he removed decor and hauled furniture toward the center of the main floor. While the former action ensured the vital privacy he needed to reset the wards without rousing mundane notice, the latter was the bigger priority. He needed access to the full perimeter of the space, specifically the carved baseboards.

If there was any fairness to the universe, it would have the decency to do some of the heavy lifting for him.

"I'm begging you, Ari," Val mewled as if on cue. "Please tell me the hunk of milk chocolate on the doorstep isn't Osondu."

Ari stopped ineffectively yanking on the antique troll leg masquerading as a floor lamp. Peering around the artifact, he found Val peeking through an opportune divide in the curtains.

A jolt of agitation shot up his spine, and Ari found himself throwing open the door before he knew what he was doing.

Taye-fucking-Osondu leaped back like an unsuspecting pedestrian crossing a viper's nest.

Temper abruptly fizzling out, Ari leveled a deadpan stare at the wizard.

Those big hazel eyes blinked once, twice, then a third time before Osondu concluded Ari wouldn't be starting any conversation. Hefting a raggedy backpack higher on his shoulder and shoving his hands in the pockets of his ill-fitted jacket, Osondu cleared his throat.

"Why's the shop closed?"

"None of your business. Why are you here?"

Osondu bristled. "None of your—"

The wizard cut himself off when Ari arched a brow.

"Yeah, okay. It is your business." Osondu indicated the

shop's interior with a poignant look. "Look, you have resources I need. Your website said you'd be open, so . . . yeah."

Ari sighed and stepped back, wordlessly holding the door open like an idiot who didn't know when to quit getting pulled into other people's drama.

Osondu's face split into a grin. With no signs of recent injury and his facial hair more closely trimmed than ever, he seemed young and so very, very handsome. Ari was still frozen in the doorway like a deer caught in headlights when the damn wizard flounced into the shop in full advantage of the open invitation.

Dazed and wondering why his stomach was turning somersaults, Ari refocused on the task at hand. Rearranging furniture. Right. That was it.

Ari spent the next twenty minutes avoiding the heavy troll in the corner and pretending he couldn't hear Osondu and Val making cautious small talk in the background. It was unseasonably warm in the shop, and the return to heaving and hauling didn't help. Sweat was starting to pool at the small of his back, and with the store closed, Ari was almost tempted to remove his casual button down.

It wasn't quite warm enough to make him forget Osondu was loitering in his periphery, though.

"Stop before you hurt yourself," the wizard huffed.

Ari's spine went ultra rigid as broad hands gripped his biceps and redirected him away from the latest mammoth of a bookshelf. Ari didn't need much persuasion to stop straining against the furnishing, but he didn't inform Osondu. Rather, Ari found himself resisting a bit just for the thrill of the contact lasting a moment longer.

"Could you levitate it?" Ari asked, curious gaze darting between wizard and bookshelf.

Osondu hesitated. "Normally? Sure, so long as I had an instrument in hand and enough time to formulate the right melody."

"And now?"

Osondu eyed the sturdy furnishing warily. "You're okay with the possibility of this rocketing across the room, maybe going through a window? Or we might risk everything in here going airborne."

"I see. Let's not, then."

Despite the lack of magical assistance, Osondu had a much smoother time rearranging things. As he watched the wizard move the bookcases with comparative ease, Ari lamented the drab clothing that hid what must have been an impressive physique.

Val wove herself between his ankles and purred, "You're drooling, dearest."

Ari kicked her. He made a halfhearted attempt, anyway, but the cat was faster.

Shaking himself back to mindfulness, Ari shifted gears and made a beeline for the kitchen.

"Don't forget to move the last three shelves near the stairs, while you're at it," Ari ordered his newfound helper as he ran away. "I need at least two feet of clearance from the wall."

Osondu puffed out a resigned laugh. "Are you planning to pay me for all this work?"

Ari poked his head back out of the kitchen with an expectant smile. "Are you planning to pay me for access to my private collection or research materials? What about my nighttime stint as a therapist?"

Osondu scowled, his hands going to his hips in a most distracting way that emphasized his narrow waist. "You're the one who let me in."

"And you're the one who took over my self-appointed task without discussing terms. What's your point?"

Without waiting for a response, Ari flounced off to make another strong pot of coffee.

Ari almost slipped into autopilot as he prepped his and Val's usual morning sustenance. Somehow, he ended up putting together a chai latte as well. He never had a conscious thought to make one; it wasn't part of his usual routine, and he did it without Magic blatantly commandeering his body, but there it was, in his hand.

Sighing, Ari snagged a cheap serving tray from the appropriate cabinet. He couldn't carry three sloshing mugs in two hands any more than he could justify wasting a perfectly good drink.

He emerged from the back room just as Osondu finished moving the requested shelves.

The wizard grinned. "Another chai tea?"

Ari glared at him as Val cackled, "Ah! Another tea-tea aficionado!"

Ari pinched her snout shut. "Don't encourage him."

Osondu grinned as he lifted his mug from the tray, and Ari just knew the asshole was trying to irritate him on purpose.

Raising the drink, Osondu paused to give Ari a suspicious glance. "Should I expect any unintended side effects, or are you intending to poison me this time?"

Ari stiffened as the heat leeched from his face. He braced himself for the uncomfortable explanation Val would no doubt demand, but the cat surprised him.

Val's claws pinched into his side as she wheezed a stunned laugh. "Ari! It's like he knows you!"

Osondu met Val's eye and lifted his mug an inch in a toast of solidarity that Ari did not appreciate in the slightest.

Unfortunately for him, the man looked too pleased with himself as he drank his latte, and the cat was giggling back at him like a school girl with a burgeoning crush.

Ari stared at them, speechless as he tried to compute what just happened. He felt like he'd just dodged a bullet. He was shaking, but it was such a fine, full-body tremor that went unnoticed by anyone else.

"What a nice change of pace!" Val chirped in blissful ignorance. "It usually takes years for Ari to get comfortable enough to drop the snobby librarian persona. You must be special, indeed."

An unreadable expression flittered across Osondu's face before settling on a confused smile. "You don't say?"

Ari hugged his own coffee to his chest and stepped away, muttering, "I don't know what this is, but I don't like it."

Behind him, he heard Val's delighted whisper clear as day. "Bratty antagonism is Ari's love language. You'll get used to it."

Osondu sputtered, quickly followed by Val's distinct shriek from getting caught in the spray.

Ari didn't turn around to make a sassy comment about Val deserving it. He had the disconcerting idea that he would regret engaging with the two of them further.

ARI AVOIDED DIRECT CONVERSATION WITH OSONDU FOR THE rest of the day. It was annoyingly easy once the wizard began browsing through Grimoire's inventory. By the time Ari finished tracing his runes with the carving knife and was ready to add some arcane finesse to the project, Osondu had chosen a spot on the floor near the entrance to park his perfect ass.

He was reading intently. Val read with him, draped over his shoulders like the traitor she was.

Neither wizard gave Ari any notice as he pricked the tip of a finger with the knife and began whispering in pig Latin.

According to his independent studies, the banishment wards required him to make his request in ancient Greek, Latin, or Egyptian, but Ari had neither the time nor inclination to learn an entire foreign language. After a decade or more of using the pretend language in spoken rituals, Ari was confident that Magic didn't give a shit. Ari couldn't speak for other witches, but it always seemed like Magic cared less about the particular language than it did the gesture. It just wanted to feel special by forcing witches to speak outside of their comfort zone and with all the grandiose ceremony of a marriage proposal.

Shit. Maybe Dazzle was right, and Magic really was more his lover than his power source.

Setting such thoughts aside and focusing on his intent, Ari made his way from rune to rune, tapping each with a drop of his blood.

Back when he first collected the keys to the shop from his commercial realtor, Ari doubted he would ever need to banish anyone from his place of business. It was a precaution, nothing more. He'd been conservative with his application, placing the runes every six feet or so along the perimeter of the ground level.

Ari liked to think he was wiser now.

It took hours to creep around the full shop, stopping every two feet along the way to instill his essence and extension of his will. He was far more thorough than he'd been for the original wards.

Dusk was in full swing when Ari finished the spell casting. He'd almost forgotten he wasn't alone.

The two misfit wizards remained still and silent as Ari approached them. Val was no longer on the man's shoulders, but seated on the floor beside him as they stared at the book with matching intensity to their grave expressions.

Ari crouched in front of the wizards and twisted to read the title printed at the top of the open page.

"*A Divergence of Magic*," Ari read with a frown. "You got this from my stock?"

Osondu nodded without lifting his gaze from the page.

Sitting back on his heels, Ari gave a nervous hum. "Interesting."

Val glanced at him, but Ari just shrugged. He wasn't familiar with this book, and he made it a point not to sell magical texts without vetting them for himself first. There was no telling how Val or Osondu would respond to the idea that Magic itself had manifested this book for them to read. Something told him now wasn't the time to worry anyone with that particular nugget of information.

"It's getting late," Ari announced.

Both wizards jerked their heads toward the curtained windows like they doubted him.

"How about this," Ari said as he slid *A Divergence of Magic* from Osondu's hand and eased it shut. "You help me put the heavy stuff back tonight, and I give you this one free of charge?"

Ari held his breath, anticipating an unpleasant sensation in return for his blatant interference in whatever message Magic was trying to give Osondu. To his surprise, nothing happened.

"Deal," Osondu agreed, holding out his hand.

Breathing freely again, Ari accepted.

Oh, but Osondu's hands weren't just big. They were warm and rough, the long, agile fingers of a musician with calluses that prickled Ari's palm in new and fascinating ways. It was . . . distracting.

Sparks didn't literally fly, but it was a near thing.

"You guys good?" Val asked. "If you'd like me to leave you two alone—"

"That's enough out of you," Ari announced as he scooped Val up under one arm and the mystery book in the other.

Maybe he imagined it, but he thought he heard Osondu chuckling under his breath as Ari made his escape.

CHAPTER 7

Thanks to Osondu and his deceptively lean but capable muscle, Ari was in a good position to reopen the shop as usual on Monday morning. By all rights, he expected to wake up with a lazy stretch a good five minutes before his alarm, as usual.

So why on earth was he waking up hours before dawn to a pissy Dazzle?

"I've had nightmares that started like this," Ari admitted as he stared up at his best friend from a sea of downy pillows and luxuriant sheets. "Granted, there's usually less pink, but still. I think it's the suit and the mean mugging."

Dazzle braced his hands on his hips. "If you're done being a smart-ass, we have real problems to address."

"Easy for you to say," Ari grumbled as he lifted himself more or less upright in bed. "I can count on my fingers how many times I've seen you in corporate attire."

In a bizarre mesh of personality and professionalism, Dazzle's pink hair was combed back in keeping with his collared shirt, navy jacket, and matching slacks. His star-studded tie was the same color as his hair, and his lengthy nails were glittering gold. Combined with the patent leather loafers on his feet, it was the closest Darren Davenport would ever get to blending in at his day job.

Being a literal wizard in a field as lucrative as pharmaceuticals had its perks.

"Why yelling?" Val yawned as she swayed into the bedroom. "What for?"

"I need you alert, kitten!" Dazzle shouted with an unnecessary clap of his hands. In the next moment, he yanked the bedding off Ari's drowsy form and poked a lengthy nail at the witch's chest. "Tell me you did not banish Robert-fucking-Gaines to the Sahara Desert."

Ari woke up in record timing.

"Come again?" Val said with nary a yawn or sleepy squint in sight.

"Ari," Dazzle gritted through his teeth. "Open your stupid mouth and say the words I need to hear. Now."

Belatedly, Ari sat up and ran a hand through his hair. "The Sahara Desert, huh? The farthest those wards can go is a dank alley in downtown Denver."

"This isn't real," Val decided form the sidelines. "I'm still asleep. Or really fucking high."

Ari and Dazzle broke their staring contest so they could scowl at the cat.

"I thought we agreed no more catnip in the apartment," Ari commented.

"I wish you were high, too, but no." Dazzle sighed and pinched the bridge of his nose with two sparkling talons. "This is real. Ari fucked up."

"Woah now!" Ari raised an affronted hand. "Gaines hit me!"

"He did not!" Val yowled, back arching and claws

popping out like some sort of berserker kitty jonesing for a fight.

"You should have sent him to an abandoned warehouse one town over!" Dazzle shrieked over Val's hissing. "You don't strand an elite member of the North American Council of Wizards to a wasteland on the opposite side of the globe!"

"I didn't!"

"You did! And now I have three of his peers commandeering my office and demanding I reel you in! I don't even know what that means!"

"For fuck's sake, Dazzle, I couldn't banish Gaines that far even if I wanted to!"

Ari tried to jump out of bed in his rush to explain, but his feet slipped and tangled in the pricey sheets. He narrowly avoided crashing into Dazzle's chest, and wound up kneeling on the mattress. Nose-to-nose with his fuming best friend, Ari was too frazzled to make further attempts to recover his dignity.

He had bigger problems to address, apparently.

"Those wards were designed as an afterthought," he stressed, shaky hands waving in all sorts of earnest gestures. "You can ask Val. Every time I tested them on her, she ended up in random parking structures or alcoves well within the city limits."

Dazzle crossed his arms with a huff and angled his face toward Val.

"It's true," she admitted with a furious nod that was uncomfortably human on a feline. "Besides being his guinea pig, I helped with the research and watched him carve the symbols myself. Those wards don't have the structure for great distances."

"Even if they did," Ari added, "what you're suggesting isn't possible for a single witch."

It took a significant amount of emotional energy from a witch and an uncommon agreeableness on Magic's end to cross large distances to begin with, and loads more to cross a body of water. A swift stream was a notable hindrance to most spells and supernatural creatures. An ocean was an immeasurable blockade by comparison.

The right wizard with the right tools and enough time could do it, but not any witch Ari knew of.

"The Council is exaggerating," Ari assured them as his heartbeat finally calmed.

Dazzle had yet to relax his crossed arms, his expression still distressed, but Ari could see the belief in his eyes. Dazzle believed him. As Val rubbed her head against his hip, Ari knew she did, too.

"I'll admit, I was unusually angry when I used the wards," Ari explained, "but if you heard the way he was talking—"

A sudden, shrill buzz made everyone jump, and more than one voice rang out with an unflattering yelp. On the nightstand, Ari's cell phone lit up like a beacon.

"What the hell kind of morning alarm is that?" Val hissed.

But it wasn't a wakeup call. It was the triggering of the shop's security system.

It took time to get dressed, and even more time than he liked to convince Dazzle and Val to let him deal with the intruders on his own. In the end, his friends only relented once he explained he recognized the witches on his app's security feed.

Ari didn't bother telling them he only recognized one of the seven witches setting up camp in his store. He had an idea what these witches wanted, and he was done dancing around everyone else's insanity.

Besides, it wasn't like an entire coven was trespassing on his property. The smallest coven he knew of had at least twenty witches operating under a single Morrigan's umbrella.

Hag Number Six was the only one he could identify with any confidence, and she wouldn't meet his eye when he finally joined them under the cover of predawn.

"What's this about?" Ari demanded as he manually locked the door behind him. It was unlocked when he got there, and the handle was still warm and static from magical finagling.

An old man in a grass-stained sweater stepped forward, his lined face drawn taut with blatant dislike. "Don't play dumb, boy. We're here because of the wizard."

Ari nodded, having assumed as much. He wasn't Osondu's friend by any means, but he was getting tired of people acting like the poor guy was a criminal. Enough was enough.

He went to the counter to set down his wallet and keys like this was business as usual. "What wizard?"

The old man scoffed. "The one that threatened you."

Ari concealed his surprise, but the ball of dread in his stomach began to loosen.

"You should have told the coven the moment he approached you, Ari," Six added, her voice uncharacteristically intense. "This wouldn't be necessary if you just called me. I gave you my number for a reason."

Ari nodded as he leaned back against the counter and crossed his arms and ankles with every semblance of ease. "Yes, I still have it on my fridge for a rainy day." He leaned sideways, exaggerating his movements as he gazed out the window. "That sky looks pretty clear to me."

"Ari," she said with a wealth of maternal disappointment.

"Enough games," said a dangerously thin woman with poorly maintained dreadlocks. "The Council of Wizards told us everything. They should have contained the rogue long before he reached you, but once he did—"

"Wait." Ari silenced her with a raised finger, his mouth tightening with creeping confusion. "Who are you talking about, exactly?"

The minuscule unraveling of his nerves redid itself, the knot tighter than ever. Ari refused to acknowledge the gut instinct too soon, though. There was a chance he was wrong, and this situation wasn't quite as filthy as he was starting to suspect.

"Tayvon Osondu," the old man spat. The venom in his voice squashed Ari's hopes and lit the dread in his gut on fire in one fell swoop.

"We know he was here," the thin woman snipped as she pushed her way through the tables to the old man's side. She didn't look at Ari with as much dislike, but she was no less heated. "He was here twice, and in the same week you activated some serious warding."

"Not so coincidentally," the old man huffed.

Ari studied the group for a long moment. He didn't recognize the woman with the locs, though the man seemed elusively familiar. He thought two faces among the silent onlookers might be regular patrons, but couldn't place the others. The youngest of them was a man in his mid-twenties dressed in a death metal shirt and torn jeans, and Ari doubted he ever trailed Six into the shop as an apprentice.

"I'm going to go out on a sturdy limb here and say you've been misinformed," Ari said at last. "The only wizard to threaten me and become subsequently banished was

Councillor Gaines. Far as I know, Osondu's done nothing wrong."

Six jerked her head up, finally looking at him directly with an unreadable look on her slack-jawed face.

Her peers were much easier to read. The ugly warping that crossed their features struck a chord in Ari's memory. He didn't like it.

"Fine." He laughed to himself, uncrossing his arms and bracing his palms on the counter's edge where he leaned. "Let's get this over with."

It wasn't an invitation, but the witches treated it like one. The old man made a single, sweeping gesture toward the largest of the tables, and the witches collected around it like a choreographed troupe. As the apparent ringleader, the elder pulled out two chairs for Six and Dreadlocks before claiming his own seat between them.

With a pinched smile, Six focused on Ari. "Perhaps you'd like to prepare a pot of coffee, and we can discuss things more companionably?"

Ari snorted, eyes narrowing on the contingent of unhappy witches.

"Magic is on our side here, boy," the elder intoned, gesturing to the last available chair.

Beyond irritated, Ari asked, "Sure about that?" and snapped his fingers to activated his wards once again.

Nothing happened.

"Well, that's disappointing," Ari admitted even as his heart sank and his stomach swooped with an influx of adrenaline.

Either Magic disagreed with his risk assessment, or it was setting him up. Either way, it wanted this confrontation. After everything else Magic did that week, Ari honestly hadn't expected the abandonment.

Swallowing the sudden lump in his throat, Ari went to the table on stiff legs. At least his gait was smooth; probably no one else noticed his unease.

"Well?" he prompted, scooting his chair in and folding his hands on the table like this was prearranged. "Out with it, then."

The kid in the death metal shirt sneered at him. "Who died and made you boss?"

"My place, my rules," Ari countered with a mean smile, twirling a finger to indicate the shop.

The lights of the chandelier flickered and a spike of energy zinged through the air. It jolted the witches to attention in the split second before it vanished, like it was never there to begin with. All eyes zeroed in on Ari with renewed interest, each as wide as the tea saucers belonging to Ari's favorite full service tea set.

As if summoned, a warm, solid weight settled on his lap beneath the table.

Ari grinned.

"I should be prepping muffins and coffee for early bird commuters right now," he mused to no one in particular, "but you lot have your panties in a bunch because a wizard started interfering with my livelihood, so now you expect to do the same without consequence." He turned his head to study the grumpy old guy, and was delighted to see that wizened face turn a splotchy red. "Did I get that right?"

The man opened his mouth, no doubt to voice a blustering retort, but Ari struck him speechless in the next moment.

Maintaining eye contact, Ari reached under the table to grab the tray from his thighs. He set the antique tray and matching Neo-Gothic tea set on the table, and more than one person reeled back in shock. Ari reserved this particular spread for private meetings with serious collectors ready to drop significant sums under his guidance.

When Ari first bought it at auction, it included the tray, ornate pot, and four matching place settings; now, however, Ari had to mask his surprise as he revealed eight smaller saucers, each hosting its own miniature cup just large enough for a couple mouthfuls.

The steady trail of steam from the pot's spout was too sweet and rich to identify. Ari didn't know what it was, but he knew how to spot an advantage when it was handed to him on a literal silver platter.

The tray settled on the table with a satisfying chime of heavy porcelain.

"You wanted to talk," Ari said, "so talk."

Ari couldn't have orchestrated it better if he tried. As he served himself a cup of mystery liquid, the witches stared. If they weren't staring, they traded quick, furtive glances. They were silent a wonderfully long while, long enough for Ari's artificial ease to start feeling real.

Magic wanted this conversation to happen. There was no escaping or procrastinating. He understood that now.

That didn't mean Magic had abandoned him. Maybe it was Ari's inner vindictive streak overruling his professionalism at last, but Ari was excited to see what would happen next.

Glad no one else could detect his racing heart, Ari took a leisurely sip of tea.

"How are you doing this?" the old man demanded as he looked Ari up and down, "I see no conduit item or designated communion channel. I heard no incantation."

Six reached out to grip Ari's wrist tighter than he expected from her. Sounding scandalized, she asked "Are you studying to become a wizard, Ari?"

The room froze, the accusation stealing all traces of warmth from the atmosphere.

Behind his teacup, Ari pursed his lips. He should be protesting his innocence right now, but Ari couldn't muster the inclination to do so. It was like someone hit pause on his emotions and dampened his senses to physical touch.

This must be how Osondu felt when his mentor reacted to his spontaneous change in wizardry. Belatedly, Ari wondered why he wasn't scared out of his wits. Death Metal Shirt and Dreadlocks sure looked ready to give him his own black eye as they jumped to their feet.

Was he in shock?

Ari was spared having to answer Six's accusation. While he sat cradling his mini tea cup, noise enveloped the table as the witches voiced their incredulity. Each made their disgust and betrayal obvious, like his hypothetical study into wizardry was a personal insult. No one lunged at him, but a witch in flip flops and deteriorating shorts tried to shove past her neighbor on her way toward the door. Six stood with a hand on the old man's shoulder like he would fly into a murderous rage without her stabilizing touch.

Ari stared into his cup as chaos reigned around him. In his periphery, Dreadlocks tumbled into Flip Flops half way to the exit, and all Ari could think about was the perfectly even ripples working their way across the surface of his drink.

Maybe he wasn't in shock. Maybe Magic drugged him.

"Quiet!" the old man bellowed.

The vein throbbing in his neck jogged Ari's memory. This was Hag Number Three, in the flesh. Ari hadn't seen him since the shop's grand opening weekend all those years ago.

Three turned on Ari with a grumpy pout that begged to be giggled at. Ari didn't make a peep, but it took a conscious effort.

Okay, he was probably in shock.

"I know what's going on here," Three accused. "You're with him. Don't deny it. We know he's been here. We know what he's done, experimenting with forbidden magics! The Council warned us when they called an emergency meeting with the local Morrigans!"

"Oh," Ari whispered, lowering his cup to the table.

Of course this was about Osondu, except for how it wasn't. Not entirely. This was just as much if not more so about Ari. Understanding came to him in a flash, without fanfare or conflicting emotion, but through a calculated numbness. It was shock, he told himself, because life as he knew was over now that this coven thought he was in cahoots with a rogue wizard already marked for death.

The startling clarity didn't feel like shock, though. Pure shock was something he knew. Personal catastrophe was something he knew even better.

This wasn't that. This was a change, a massive one, and it came not long after Ari gave into Magic's insistence and welcomed Osondu into his life.

"Okay," Ari said as he reclined. "You got me. I'm working with him. Osondu. Taye, as his friends call him."

Horrified gasps met this announcement. The poor witches were well and truly stunned.

Six stared at him like he was mutating into a grotesque monster before her very eyes. Ari wished it was the first time someone looked at him like that, but it wasn't.

"You've always walked a thin line between your own kind and the wizards," Six whispered tearfully. "I accepted it because it was always a distinct line. I never expected you to cross it."

Ari heaved a resigned sigh and stood.

That's when the shock began to wane. The numbness

dripped off his brain like a fresh rainfall from the ends of his hair, leaving him in a slow, gradual glide. He thought he felt Magic working along his synapses to restore his emotional awareness without overwhelming him.

For the first time in his life, Ari considered he might be blessed.

"Osondu's only a wizard, a rogue with no right to meddle with Magic he wasn't born to," Three said in a tone that made Ari think he'd find a nemiza decorating his ribs before the sun finished rising. "Neither do you, Jamison."

"I think we're done talking," Ari decided.

Three marched over to spit in Ari's face. Six didn't stop him.

"If this is the thanks we get for leaving you unchecked for so many years, then you can expect a reckoning, boy. The Council and the Morrigans already agreed the rogue's days are numbered. What do you think they'll do to your untrained, loner ass when they learn you're following his footsteps?"

Rage and fear rocketing up his spine, Ari took an involuntary step backward.

The witches around him began muttering, using words like "traitor" and "despicable" and "shameful." The sudden outpouring of vitriol pushed him back several paces, and his guts churned. Bile choked him when he realized they were gathering closer, a united front of blindly furious faces as they stared him down.

It reminded him of being fourteen and having no choice but to take the abuse as his mother's family berated him for being gay. Back then, the incident ended with Ari on the streets, nursing cracked ribs and a bloody lip.

The violence now was the same as the violence then. The differing motivations were meaningless.

Ari whispered a coarse, "Enough," and everything stopped.

The stillness was deafening. No one dropped into a coma or iced over, but all animation ceased. Six was in the back of the crowd with her hands clamped over her mouth in heartbroken dismay. Everyone else was caught with their fists raised, or their faces carved into vicious masks. Dreadlocks had a metal pendant hanging from her fingers on a steel chain, and Ari didn't need to look closer to know it was a weapon she intended to use on him.

"Huh," Ari gaped at the useless mob.

It was beyond disorienting. He could see the awareness in their eyes; he witnessed their collective resolution give way to crippling alarm even as their faces continued displaying the previous emotion. He saw Flip Flop's eyes begin to water, and he struggled to reconcile her newfound fear with the stale hate still etched across her face.

Ari took his time catching his breath. They had no choice but to let him.

"I do not tolerate violence or disrespect in my space," Ari told them with startling firmness. "Not toward me or anyone else I give a shit about."

Magic didn't take him over again. No, this time, it did nothing more than tap open the lock keeping his temper in check and give the slightest nudge of encouragement.

"I'm unsure which esteemed Morrigan you all belong to, but that'll be fixed within the hour," he decided, and the air vibrated with power as Magic rooted him on. "Congratulations, yours is officially the first coven to be banned from Grimoires and Goodies. If I see any of you within spitting distance of my door again, I promise you will walk away with a new definition for the word 'regret.'"

With that, Ari strode to the door and unlocked it was a

single tap of a finger. He grasped the handle and turned at the waist to level them with an unforgiving stare.

"Mindless mobs weren't a good look during the Salem witch trials, and they haven't aged well. Do better."

He yanked the door open and released the freeze with nothing but his will and no distinct thought. They stumbled and quaked back to functional life while Ari stoppered the exit with his foot. He stared them down with his arms crossed.

They got the message. All seven witches scampered past him like souls of the damned given a free pass out of hell with an imminent expiration and zero notice.

As the first rays of daybreak warmed his skin, Ari had to be honest with himself; the sight filled him with satisfaction. What a shame it didn't last.

CHAPTER 8

*H*e should have known it wouldn't be that easy. When Ari found himself opening the store without the banned Morrigan's name, he knew the morning's conflict would come back to bite him in the ass. He just didn't know the exact shape the consequences would take.

For better or worse, he didn't have to wait long.

Taye Osondu wasn't the first customer to walk into Grimoires and Goodies that day, but he was the first one Ari bothered to speak with.

"We need to talk," Ari said even as Taye's mouth opened and one brown hand raised *A Divergence of Magic* into the air between them. "This can wait."

Without breaking stride, Ari snatched the book from Taye's grasp and tucked it behind the register. He could feel those damnably pretty eyes burning a hole in his back as he stormed off to the employees only door. He made a conscious effort to lighten his steps when he realized the troublemaker wasn't following him. Pausing in the doorway to the back room, Ari turned to aim an expectant glare across the store where Taye still stood, blinking toward the register and his confiscated book like a listless idiot.

Jaw tight, Ari growled, "Now."

With one last unreadable look toward the register, Taye shoved his hands in his jacket pockets and slouched after Ari like petulance incarnate.

"Damn, you have an actual kitchen back here," Taye observed as the door swung closed behind him. "I really thought all the bakery stuff was store bought."

Ari's jaw dropped. "How dare you."

Taye shrugged, still studying the crammed backroom remodeled into a commercial grade kitchen. "How do you have time to do all this by yourself?"

Leaning on the fridge with one hip cocked, Ari rolled his eyes. "There's this thing called Magic. Heard of it?"

"You're an ass," Taye countered, but with notable amusement. "What do we need to talk about?"

In response, Ari retrieve his phone from his apron pocket and pulled up the screenshots he took from the security app mere hours ago. He offered it to Taye without fuss.

The brush of their fingers as Taye accepted the phone made Ari's stomach flutter, but the witch chose to ignore that ridiculousness.

"Who are they?"

"Witches," Ari said with a snappishness that earned him a curious glance.

With an apologetic sigh, Ari slumped against the fridge and recounted the whole messy encounter. Taye didn't interrupt save for a few clarifying questions, and Ari was glad to get the story out in one fell swoop. By the time he finished speaking, they were somehow perched side by side on the stainless steel counter in their own little bubble of grave contemplation.

They didn't know each other well enough for the moment to feel so effortless. The fact wasn't lost on Ari.

"So, you can work spontaneous magic the same way I can?" Taye asked after a long moment of silence.

"No," Ari insisted. "Yes. Maybe. I don't know yet."

"Well, then . . ."

The thoughtful quiet returned, but only for a moment.

"We're in this together," Taye stated in a tone that suggested he had mixed feelings about that idea.

"Looks like it."

Taye's next words sounded almost hopeful. "Does this mean I can use your library without paying for it?"

Ari responded with a dull glare. "It's not a library."

"Right. Don't you have a business you should be running?"

Ari wiped the smug grin off that handsome face by shoving its owner off the counter. "Were you raised in barn?" he asked as he slipped off the counter to strut toward the shop proper. "I prep food there, for god's sake."

Taye's low chuckle sent shivers up and down Ari's spine as it chased him out the door.

Said shivers shriveled up and died the moment Ari exited the backroom and walked straight into a solid wall of power, of both the physical and paranormal kind.

"No," Ari groaned as he recoiled. "Not you."

"Not who?" Taye asked as he popped up behind Ari. "Oh."

That last syllable out of Taye's mouth marked a chilly change in tone, and Ari didn't blame him. Taye might not have Ari's sixth sense for the magical nuances surrounding a person, but anyone with working instincts could tell this man was something special. Even if Taye were magically tone deaf, the sparkling citrine and black gold amulet hanging around the man's neck gave him away.

Ordinary people didn't wear artifacts like that on the regular.

"Eren Puckman," the Morrigan introduced himself in that heady southern drawl that once made Ari's knees go weak. "You must be Tayvon."

Puckman didn't offer his hand as he stared over Ari's head. At his back, Ari could feel the growing tension radiating from Taye as he no doubt held the Morrigan's eye. Ari jabbed his elbow back into Taye's gut, successfully interrupting the exchange and earning a grunt directly in his ear.

"He was just leaving," Ari explained. "Do me a favor, Taye, and lock the door behind you."

A sharp inhale from behind warned Ari that Taye was about to object.

"The shop's closed for a private meeting," Ari added in a cold tone that made a slight smile appear on Puckman's face.

Another sharp inhale, then Taye caught on and muttered, "Where is everybody?"

"Something must've come up," Puckman said casually.

Ari could feel the scowl on Taye's face as the wizard said, "All dozen or so tourists and window shoppers suddenly had pressing priorities?"

"I didn't think to ask."

Keeping his eyes on the Morrigan's unrepentant grin, Ari latched on to Taye's arm and shoved him toward the exit. Taye went reluctantly, with a displeased frown barely masking his confusion.

Through the window of the closed door, Taye spared a withering look for Puckman. When the Morrigan gave him a short wave farewell, Taye responded with a deepening scowl and a raised middle finger.

The shop's lock engaged with a metallic shriek of a spray of sparks. The door shook from the force of the thrown lock, and for one terrifying moment, the commotion seemed to catch the attention of a few passersby.

Ari and Puckman held their breath until the mundane shoppers shrugged and continued on their way.

"Impossible," Puckman whispered, gaping at Taye.

"Maybe for you," Ari quipped as he made a covert shooing motion behind the Morrigan's back.

Satisfied with their reactions, Taye shot Ari a wink. Then he took off without a backward glance.

For the first time in over a decade, Ari was alone with Morrigan Eren Puckman.

There were streaks of silver in his dark hair and laugh lines around his mouth and eyes that Ari didn't recognize, but Puckman was otherwise unchanged. He was still tall and sturdy, and unafraid to showcase his muscular form in dark jeans and an evergreen T-shirt that were far cleaner and better tailored than most witches bothered with. His shoes were clean and well cared for, and Ari cringed when he realized they were the same pair Ari bought for him so many years ago.

Puckman noticed his reaction, and after following Ari's gaze toward the floor, he chuckled.

"Something funny?"

"You." One ancient shoe darted forward to tap against Ari's ankle. "I'm glad you noticed your gifts keep on giving. I wasn't sure you would."

"Why are you here, Eren?"

"I don't make a habit of believing rumors, especially when they're about you. Or rogue wizards." The self-satisfied smile dropped from Puckman's face. "I had to see for myself."

"Good job. You saw. Now leave."

"You don't want me to do that, Ari."

"And here I thought we were done with you telling me what I want."

Ari crossed his arms over his chest and arched a challenging brow, but the Morrigan was unfazed.

"The continent's Council of Wizards and prominent Morrigans made a pact two nights ago," Puckman explained with all his usual calm arrogance, "The only reason I'm not delivering Osondu to the Council right now is because you're considered an acceptable distraction."

Ari dropped his arms and stepped back, scanning the Morrigan with fresh wariness.

"Easy, now." Puckman raised his hands in conciliation as he chuckled. "I'm not looking to wind up in the Sahara, after all."

"Then maybe you should go," Ari suggested before thinking, then added, "And leave Taye alone. He's no threat."

"Maybe," Puckman said with a considering nod. "Personally, I'd be less concerned if he weren't also the latest wizard of significant skill to be added to your collection."

Eyes narrowing, Ari stopped himself from squirming. "Meaning . . . what?"

"Meaning Valkyrie," Puckman said on a blunt sigh. "Then Davenport. And now Osondu. Apparently."

Hands going to his hips, Ari raised his chin with a huff that was more defensive than he cared for. "What are you implying here, Eren?"

"Witches and wizards do not mix. You know this." At last, irritation broke through Puckman's cool affect, creating deep lines in his forehead. He shook his head like he couldn't believe he was having the current conversation. "I warned you when you first described your hopes for this place—"

"Yeah?" Ari said with a harsh laugh.

"It's a doomed prospect, Ari," Puckman insisted with clearly failing patience. "It's a culture clash at best. Any attempted bridge between the two will always fail—"

"Oh?" Ari said, flourishing a hand to indicate the shop at large. "This looks like failure to you, does it?"

A faint redness rose on Puckman's cheeks as his mouth tightened into a thin line. "It looks like uncommon good luck that won't last."

Ari huffed a mirthless little laugh and reconsidered Taye's parting gesture. Despite his better reasoning, Ari spat, "Fuck you and fuck off."

He didn't mean for it to happen, or at least he didn't expect Magic's immediate compliance with his errant thoughts, but the door unlocked and sprang open with one emphatic slash of his hand through the air. The door slammed against the wall with a piercing crackle.

As one, the two witches turned their heads to see a deep crack race into existence across the glass door. The damaged glass left the handle embedded in the plaster wall perfectly visible.

It took effort to stand tall and unconcerned under the Morrigan's wide eyed stare, but Ari managed.

"This is exactly the kind of trouble I tried to help you avoid," Puckman said in a devastated whisper. It would have been more touching without the enraged clench of his jaw.

Ignoring the noxious twisting in his gut, Ari shrugged. "No trouble for me. It's everyone else who has a problem."

He could actually hear Puckman's teeth grinding before the witch's hands balled into fists at his sides. "Listen to me,

Ari. This isn't a fight you can win, not even if you had a coven backing you up."

"According to you." Ari sneered. "Come to think of it, you said something similar when I first opened the store, didn't you?"

That was the inevitable point when Puckman's cool evaporated under the heat of Ari's stubbornness. The Morrigan's face blew straight past fiery red and into the purple bluster of an overwhelming temper tantrum.

"How you manage to still be so naive and delusional is mind boggling!" he shouted. "Valkyrie and Davenport have made up for your shortcomings with cash and wizardry so far, but they can't give you the power you'll need to defy the known magical world as a whole!"

"Wow. Rude, much?"

Ari wasn't prepared for the other witch to grab his arms and back him up against the wall. As Ari's skull did a harmless but distinct bounce off the brick, Puckman seethed into his personal space. With his chest heaving for breath and nose nearly touching Ari's, the Morrigan looked as likely to kiss him as he was to throttle him.

"Why are you doing this?" Puckman demanded. "To spite me?"

Ari threw back his head and laughed. "What makes you think—"

"Is this really about Osondu?" Puckman sneered, like the name tasted revolting. "You know you can't help him. Even if Lady Valkyrie took Osondu under her protection, it won't be enough to save him from the Council's judgment."

"She's not protecting him. I am."

The way Puckman gaped at him then was downright insulting.

A strange warmth creeping up the back of his neck, Ari

relaxed under the Morrigan's grip and smiled. "Val and Dazzle are all the support I needed in the past, and that hasn't changed. If adding Taye to the mix has the benefit of finally convincing you to give up on me, than all the better."

The hands on his biceps vanished as Puckman recoiled. "You're seriously going to talk to me like they're your coven?"

Ari shimmied against the wall to get comfortable and shrugged. "They're more a coven to me than you ever were."

"You can't have a witch coven comprised of wizards!" Puckman shrieked, throwing up his hands in absolute exasperation, "That's not a coven!"

"Exactly."

"It's not even a council! That's a . . . a . . . a conundrum!"

Ari longed to laugh in the older witch's fuming face, but he refrained. He couldn't keep the taunting smirk off his lips to save his life.

"Great!" Ari chirped as he strutted over to the door. He gave Puckman a wide berth as he went and donned a rather malicious version of his brightest customer service smile. "How about you run along back to your coven and leave me with my conundrum, then?"

Wonder of all wonders, but Morrigan Puckman seemed to finally accept an answer he didn't like. He didn't leave quietly, and Ari wasted a good ten minutes convincing the neighboring boutique owner not to call the authorities, but he did leave.

Afterward, Ari returned to an empty shop and reluctantly made a sign that read "Temporarily Closed for Repairs" in his finest penmanship. After prying the handle free of the wall and adequately boarding up the shop, Ari returned to retail counter to count the day's cash.

He discovered a fresh mug of coffee waiting by the register. Beside it, a gourmet muffin sat atop a pristine paper napkin with the name of the bakery down the street printed along the side.

"A coven of wizards, huh?" Ari wondered aloud as he picked up the miraculous confection.

It was still warm and soft, as if straight from the oven. Ari considered the treat for as long as it took for his heart rate to chill out, then he took a bite. Maybe it was wishful thinking, but Ari thought it tasted like victory. He only wished it didn't include the aftertaste of a deal signed in blood.

CHAPTER 9

*A*ri wasn't sure what surprised him more: that it took three whole days before he saw Taye again, or that he found him not at the shop, but after work on his couch, cuddling a sequined pillow.

"What the hell is this?"

Instead of an immediate answer, Ari was met with two pairs of rolling eyes. Taye sighed as he set the pillow on the couch beside him, and Val shook her head as it lowered like she was praying for patience. The cat sat upright on the coffee table across from Taye, and from the look of them, Ari had interrupted quite the deep discussion.

"Explain," Ari insisted as he planted his feet and wagged a finger from one sour face to the other. "What's happening here?"

It seemed the pillow was not the only item cluttering Taye's lap, because he raised *A Divergence of Magic* for a split second before dropping it back onto his thighs.

Val's grin was full of fang as she sassed, "We're starting a book club."

Taye glared at her. "You can't take anything seriously, can you?"

"He learns so fast!" she whispered to Ari in a mockery of tearful pride.

"You should probably read this," Taye murmured as he handed over the book.

Despite his words and quickness to offer up the book, Taye didn't look happy to see Ari flipping through the pages. The more pages Ari perused, the more he itched to know why.

Ari handed the book back to Taye with the suggestion, "Perhaps you could use your big boy words to explain, instead of giving me reading homework?"

Val peered up at him. "What shoved a stick up your ass this time?" With a pointed side-eye to Taye, she added. "Besides the obvious sexual tension, I mean."

Taye's tanned face darkened as he snagged the sequined pillow and swung. Unlike Ari's fitful reactions to Val's nonsense, Taye didn't miss.

"Ow!" Val cried with more irritation than hurt.

Taye's next swing failed to hit it's mark only because Val put an effort into evading it. She tumbled to the floor with an involuntary squeak as a result, and Taye seemed satisfied to let the matter go.

"You barely glanced at the page I was trying to show you," Taye acknowledged as he set the pillow aside. His color was back to normal when he narrowed his eyes on Ari. "Why not read it for yourself?"

Ari's folded arms tightened over his chest despite the attempted nonchalance of his tone. "I can't."

Taye's brows rose in disbelief. "You can't read?"

"No." Ari rolled his eyes before jutting his chin toward the book. "I can't read that. The pages are blank to my eyes."

Taye and Val stared at him as if they weren't sure how to react.

After another beat of awkwardness, Taye refocused on *A Divergence of Magic* and pried it open to a random page. He stared, and stared, and stared at the book, chewing his tongue and schooling his expression the whole while.

Val hopped onto the armrest of the couch and bumped her cheek into Ari's hip as she frowned at the mystery book. "You really don't see any of that?"

"Nope."

Val winced at the harsh pop of his final consonant and rocked back to sit on her haunches. "Want me to describe it to—?"

"Yes."

"Okay—"

"But you shouldn't," Ari interrupted her with a resigned sigh. Under her and Taye's curious stares, Ari rolled his shoulders back and released his clenched arms to his sides. "If Magic doesn't want me to see those pages, there's probably a reason."

Val scoffed, "Like what?"

Ari shrugged and caught himself about to cross his arms again, so he redirected his hands into a more casual position, tucked into the pockets of his slacks. He had to swallow a nasty lump in his throat before he could speak, and it tasted a lot like hurt and rejection on the way down.

"Most likely, I'm not ready to know whatever knowledge it contains."

Taye and Val exchanged a look that was far too familiar for Ari's comfort.

"But we are?" Taye asked, doubt as evident in his voice as it was on his face as he refocused on Ari.

Executing yet another useless shrug, Ari came to the

abrupt conclusion that any further discussion would require more caffeine. Without a word, he turned on his heel and made for the kitchen side of the flat. He could feel the combined attention of the wizards like a burning itch between his shoulder blades all the way to the coffee maker.

In the near distance, Ari heard Taye clear his throat. "Do all witches do that?"

Ari wanted to ask "Do what?" but Val was quicker to reply. Her voice was every bit as hushed as Taye's.

"You mean the way he talks about Magic?"

"Yeah. Like it's a person."

There was a pause as Ari tried meditating over coffee grounds, then Val said, "I never asked another witch. The few I've met either weren't friendly enough for prolonged conversation, or they gave the impression it would be inappropriate to ask."

Taye gave a disappointed, "Oh," and they fell quiet.

Ari thought he heard the soft rustling of pages before the pinging of the fresh brew into the pot drowned out any further background noise. Soon, the slow drip rallied into a smooth stream, and Ari scowled as he realized they were still carrying on the stilted conversation.

"It's different for them," Val was muttering under her breath. "More intimate, less clinical. Does that make sense?"

Taye released a long, shaky breath that sounded on the verge of either laughter or tears. "In light of recent events? Yeah. It's starting to."

"Witchcraft might not have wizardry's reliability, but I've never seen Ari make an unsuccessful attempt," Val's voice took on a tone Ari didn't recognize, something speculative and caught between pride and wariness. "He doesn't practice often, but after the years we've been together, I suspect he's not like other witches."

Taye's snort was loud and irreverent, making Ari jump as it shattered the mood of their conversation.

"Dude's unaffiliated with an established foothold in the covens and a working relationship with the Council, and all his friends are renowned wizards. No shit, he's not like other witches."

"Aw!" Val cooed at a return to full volume. "You think I'm renowned?"

Ari's patience snapped like a twig. Slamming his chosen mug down on the counter, he whirled on the cat.

"Seriously, Val? Just how many Lady Valkyries are there roaming the Northern Hemisphere? And while we're at it," Ari mocked, "how many contemporary wizards across the whole-ass globe have been cursed—"

"Blessed!"

"Cursed!" Ari repeated, palm smacking the counter top as he leaned hard across the kitchen island. "You were cursed into living out your life as a literal animal!"

Val didn't try to correct him again. She simply flopped onto her belly on the couch's armrest and licked her claws clean, like the little diva she was.

"Fine. Yes, 'tis I, the infamous Lady Valkyrie."

"Taye? Please smother her for me."

As Ari resumed prepping his coffee, Taye choked on laughter. His cough did nothing to stop Val from divulging her full life's story. Ari managed to drain one cup, go to the bathroom, and fix up a second serving, and Val was still crowing about her adventures as an elite spell caster with Taye as her captivated audience.

When Ari deigned to rejoin them at the coffee table with his third cup of the evening, Taye was holding back his laughter with a fist over his mouth. Val was just reaching the part of her embellished tale where she earned her glorious damnation.

"So, you're saying it was all a misunderstanding?" Taye said with a derisive huff of laughter. "Really?"

"How was I supposed to know he thought we were exclusive?" Val wailed with self-righteous affront. "There was never a conversation! I'm sorry, but in my experience, a few expensive meals and a half decent lay does not a relationship make."

"And you never led him on?" Ari teased rather than condemned. "Not at any time between the thousand dollar steak dinner and the Michelin star crab legs? What about the cheesecake?"

"Oh, no, I put out for the cheesecake," Val admitted, "but I'd still rather you check your toxic masculinity at the door like a good boy."

"Yes ma'am," Ari said with a fond roll of his eyes.

"Damn right." She puffed out her chest and curled her tail around her seated body like a royal donning a cloak. "The point is, in the end, he was left single and heartbroken with a shiny new reputation as a vindictive bastard. I, on the other hand, have been enjoying the most stress free, comfortable life I never had as a woman."

"All thanks to him cursing you," Taye said with an approving nod.

"Essentially."

If Val were still human, Ari would have given her a fist bump in solidarity. As it was, they settled for sharing a knowing look and stifled giggle.

Taye's gaze darted back and forth between them, and his humor melted away to something more contemplative.

Ari's arms prickled with goosebumps, and he squirmed in his favorite chair, adjacent to the couch. "Stop staring like that. You're making it weird."

Taye gnawed on his lip for a moment before sitting forward with a searching expression. "Ever considered that maybe you're the one making things weird?"

Ari squinted at him. "Your tone says that's a genuine question, but your words say you're being a jerk."

Taye's answered smile was angelic. "If you say so."

"I don't think I like you."

"That's a bald faced lie," Val muttered from the sidelines.

Taye leaned back into the couch with a pleased chuckle as heat rushed to Ari's face. Not for the first time, Ari bemoaned the fact he couldn't afford the Olde Town apartment on his own.

He got over it in the next second, when he spied Val tucking *A Divergence of Magic* under the couch cushion. As much as she annoyed him, Ari knew he'd never seriously consider living without her.

Damn it, but he hoped she took it well once the speculation of their coven of wizards became widespread gossip.

ARI WAS THREE STEPS OUT THE DOOR OF HIS APARTMENT building the next morning when Taye hopped into his direct line of sight again.

"Heading to the shop?"

Shoulders slumping in resignation, Ari nodded. "If you want full access to my books, you better be ready to make my coffee and clean up after my customers like my own personal assistant."

"That's fair—"

"Tell me I'm seeing things," snapped a familiar voice from behind him. "Ari, tell me I've lost it, and you're not actually chatting with the community's Most Wanted on a public sidewalk."

Dazzle's arm looped around his stiffening shoulders before Ari could get a word out. Said arm tightened till Ari was squashed into Dazzle's side like a rowdy child on their mother's last nerve. Granted, Dazzle probably didn't look all that maternal in his tie-dyed crop top and bedazzled jeans, but Ari still felt scolded.

"Keep walking, hot stuff," Dazzle advised Taye with a sharp smile. "He's not interested in whatever you're selling."

Ari sighed and didn't intervene as Taye's expression darkened.

"I'm not selling shit," Taye snipped, matching Dazzle's aggression without pause. "And Ari is absolutely interested in everything I'm selling."

A stunned moment followed, then Taye realized what just came out of his mouth, and he recoiled.

"I didn't mean it like that," he protested.

"Oh, no," Dazzle moaned as his arm fell from Ari's shoulders. "He's already adopted you, hasn't he?"

Taye flushed and cast a furtive look at Ari before refocusing on Dazzle. "Adopted . . . how?"

"Ari doesn't make friends." Dazzle gave a long suffering sigh as he gave Ari's head a fond pat. "The universe just shoves people at him till he decides to tolerate and enjoy us."

"Wait," Ari frowned. "What?"

"Poor, confused baby," Val mewled as she popped her head out from his bag.

With a start, Ari redirected his frown toward her. "Have you been in there this whole time?"

"I took a nap on your chair," she admitted. "Then I woke up here to Dazzle's caterwauling with your ChapStick poking me in the eye."

"I do not caterwaul!" Dazzle defended himself.

"Dazzle?" Taye looked the pink-haired wizard up and down with a baffled expression. "You're Dahlia Dazzle?"

It was like a spell had been cast. Dazzle's entire demeanor changed, the snide antagonism evaporating to make room for a beaming smile and the effeminate body language he was known for on stage.

"You've seen my show?" Dazzle asked in full flattered vocal fry.

"Only once," Taye admitted with a charming smile. "I wouldn't mind seeing the next one, though. You were great."

"Oh, thank you!" Dazzle hip-checked Ari, only to grab his arm and tug him close to stage whisper into Ari's ear. "Clearly, he's got good taste. Are we sure he's bad news?"

Ari sighed and pinched Dazzle's side to get him to back off.

Dazzle did, but only so he could offer a dainty hand toward Taye. "Daren Davenport, but you may call me Dazzle."

"Holy shit," Taye said in dawning comprehension as they shook hands. "You're Davenport too? The potions master?"

Dazzle rolled his eyes, but his smile was proud. "Yes, 'tis I."

From Ari's bag came an excited squeak. "I said the same thing yesterday!"

"You guys spend way too much time together," Ari seethed as he shot Taye an apologetic grimace. At the same time, he clamped an open hand on Val's head and pushed her down out of sight.

"I prefer the phrase 'great minds think alike,'" Dazzle said as he pretended to inspect his immaculate manicure.

Taye stepped close enough to grip Ari's wrist and

implore, "Can we go now, or do we have to wait for them to get this BS out of their systems?"

Ari smiled and pried his wrist up till he was holding Taye's hand right back. "You are going to fit in with this group perfectly."

With one last squeeze, Ari threw Taye's hand aside and motioned for both him and Dazzle to follow. He patted Val's side through his bag for good measure and resumed his usual path toward Grimoires and Goodies.

"Come along, my little conundrum. We got shit to discuss."

As he led them to the shop, Ari couldn't shake the mental image of a commander leading troops into war. If he had any good luck at all, it was just his anxiety talking. Then again, it wouldn't be the first time Magic implanted a warning straight into his brain.

CHAPTER 10

Things could have gone far worse than they did, Ari told himself later that day. He was late opening the shop on account of all the explaining he had to do, but in the end, Val and Dazzle were as caught up on the unfolding drama as they could be. With heavy hearts and troubled minds, they parted ways so Val could head home to get in a few hours as remote IT support, and Dazzle left for the office. They agreed to meet up at Ari and Val's apartment in the evening, after everyone had some time to process.

So it was that Ari was left to attend the shop with a new and mostly unwelcomed shadow.

"How do you take your coffee?"

Ari stared at Taye, bemused. "With cream and sugar."

Taye nodded and bounded off to the back room.

That was how the day progressed. Ari conducted business as usual while Taye kept his mug full whenever he wasn't scouring the shelves for his own purposes. Taye floated in Ari's periphery, occasionally flashing that annoyingly charming smile at customers, but mostly putting Ari's arsenal of magical texts to use. Ari noticed fewer customers pestered him to talk, and he wondered how Taye managed to get any studying done while curtailing Ari's most taxing customer interactions.

And all the while, Ari's mug never went dry.

It rankled Ari to admit how seamlessly Taye fitted himself into the shop, like he was meant to be there. If Ari hadn't been so unaccustomed to the constant company, he might have called it enjoyable.

"Are you working magic?" Ari asked him outright during the midday lapse in foot traffic.

Taye looked up from the book he was reading at the corner-most table, his expression drawn and distracted. "Huh?"

"Magic," Ari insisted as he sat down across from him. "Are you using it on the customers? Yourself, maybe?"

Taye frowned. "No. Trust me, if I did anything, it'd be pretty fucking obvious."

Perching his chin on his fist, Ari made a gesture for Taye to go on. "Show me something then."

Taye glanced at the wall of windows leading to the street. There weren't many people passing by, but enough to cause alarm if they saw something they shouldn't.

"They're not paying any attention," Ari assured him. "Come on. You asked for my help, right? Show me what I'm working with."

Sighing, Taye set aside his chosen book and stared around the room for inspiration. His gaze landed on a decorative plastic cauldron acting as a bookend.

"I'll try to make it real," he said with obvious reluctance as he retrieved the prop and set it on the table between them. "Just be ready for any unexpected side effects."

Ari watched carefully as Taye wrapped his hands around

the plastic siding. The wizards brow furrowed as he concentrated on the toy, and his fingers seemed to stiffen.

The change was subtle. Ari couldn't have said when it began. As the minutes dragged on, he noticed the smoothness of the cauldron giving way to pebbled stone. The plastic sheen faded as the cheap base thickened.

"Impressive," Ari admitted, sniffling.

Taye's frown deepened. "Do you smell that? Smells like . . ."

"Smoke," Ari finished, sniffling again.

The fire alarm blared. It was only then Ari realized Taye had brought the cauldron in the window display to life as well, it's fake flames and artificial contents along with it.

THEY AGREED NOT TO MENTION ANY MISHAPS INVOLVING FIRE extinguishers and immature spell casting to Val and Dazzle. Fortunately, they didn't need to hedge around the subject.

Dazzle and Val were waiting for them in the apartment, perched together on the coffee table and looking like someone had died.

"You really think you can work witchcraft?" Val asked before anyone had a chance to voice a more typical greeting.

Ari and Taye exchanged a look, the afternoon's fire still fresh in their minds.

"I wouldn't call it witchcraft," Ari said.

"Show us?" Dazzle asked.

Ari winced, but Taye stepped forward with a resigned expression.

He reached between Dazzle's leg and where Val's tail swayed over the table's edge. There was a small decorative drawer there, but when Taye gripped the handle and tugged, it pulled free as a fully functional pocket of wood.

"No fucking way," Dazzle muttered as Taye reached into the miraculous drawer with intention.

Taye stood up straight holding a vibrant plant Ari had never seen before. It wasn't particularly beautiful, with its bright-green stem and yellowing offshoots, but Dazzle reached for it with an eagerness that suggested a value that far superseded the plant's visual appeal.

"This is something you've been looking for, right?" Taye asked, a bit snappish as he handed it over.

"How did you know—" Dazzle cut himself off when he looked up at Taye's grave expression. Composing himself, Dazzle stood and indicated the yellow-green sprouts. "Radix Astragali is among the rarest herbs in the world. What's left of it in Mongolia is heavily protected, and it costs a small fortune to get your hands on."

Dazzle lowered the plant as he appeared to study Taye with newfound respect.

Ari nudged Taye and asked, "You didn't know any of that, did you?"

Taye nodded toward the coffee table's fake drawer where it was left open. "I knew I could open it and find something that would impress you. That's it. I don't know shit about plants or potions."

"Magic gifted it to you," Ari murmured. He didn't meet anyone's gaze as he said, "It does things like that sometimes. It's not because of anything we do or want, it just . . . does things for us."

Dazzle stared at Ari like he was struggling to recognize his friend. "This Magic, it's yours too?"

Ari nodded, unable to meet Dazzle's eye.

Dazzle cradled the gift in his palms and turned toward Val with conflicted emotions scrawled across his face.

Val sighed and bowed to press her face into her paws.

Ari stepped up to Taye's side and gave Dazzle a hopeful look. "You two talked?"

Val lifted her head with a deadpan grunt of, "Obviously."

"This . . ." Dazzle's words caught in his throat as he lifted the herb and shook it gently under Ari's nose. "This is dangerous magic, Ari. I know neither of you have ill intent, but the Council won't consider that a factor. The existence of such power in a random wizard's hands is all the excuse they need to criminalize it."

Dazzle faltered, like he had more to say, but was too emotionally wrought to continue. His expression when he looked at Ari was miserably apologetic.

"Things will get worse once Fuckman starts talking about his encounter with you," Val added with uncharacteristic stoicism. "By, now you both have a target painted on your backs."

"Yeah, well . . ." Ari sighed and ran a hand through his hair. "From the way Puckman was talking, we're not the only ones."

Dazzle grimaced like he tasted something foul. Hands on his hips as he strode away from the group, he began shaking his pink head.

Val was a stone-cold statue in comparison as she said, "Guilty by association."

Ari knew better than to let his friends stew in their dismay for long. Clearing his throat, Ari tried to imbue his voice with a confidence he didn't quite feel. "I already tried washing my hands of Taye and his whole . . . situation."

He glanced at Taye to see the wizard frowning at him expectantly, arms crossed and brows raised like he was daring

Ari to say something insulting. Ari bit back an involuntary smile, and finished strong despite the distraction.

"It didn't work," he said with a resigned toss of his hands. "Fate wants me involved, so I'm involved."

"Wow," Taye snarked. "You're really selling it with that enthusiasm, bro."

Ari glared at him as Dazzle barked a startled laugh. "I am not, and never will be, your bro," he spat.

Taye's close-lipped smile wasn't exactly pleasant. "Sure thing, boss."

Ari considered it, then declared, "Acceptable."

Taye's expression soured, and Ari gave himself a mental pat on the back.

"As entertaining as it is to watch Ari's attempt at flirting," Dazzle said, "we still have a shitstorm to un-fuck here."

Ari's whole head burned, but Dazzle didn't bat an eye. The potion master's words did a good job at ensuring no one else did either.

"It's one thing to put yourself between a stray wizard or two and the Council, but this isn't cute anymore, Ari. You don't have a coven! It's just you versus the whole fucking North American Council."

"And at least one curse-happy coven," Val added with a pointed look toward Taye. "Ari told us about the nemiza."

Taye straightened under the attention. One hand went to his side on reflex, and Ari realized with a start that the wizard was self-conscious. Somehow, Ari's mental portrait of the guy had become something entirely opposite of that.

"The point is," Dazzle huffed as he stomped over to grab Ari by the shoulders, "I love you, and I know you're capable of great things, but you don't have the means to help him. No offense, Taye."

"No, no, I get it," Taye said in a blasé tone. "If an

innocent person was magically dropped on my doorstep with an angry mob on his heels, I'd probably hurry him on his way too."

Dazzle flushed even as he rolled his eyes. "That's not what I meant."

"It doesn't matter," Ari said, putting himself between them. "Like it or not, I'm involved. And yeah, I'm realistic about the odds being stacked against us here."

Dazzle's eyes narrowed. "But?"

Nodding, Ari said, "But I'm not alone. I have you. And Val."

"How presumptuous of you," Val grumbled.

As one, Ari and Dazzle turned to show her how unimpressed they were. They didn't need to utter a word.

Val's fur bristled as she turned her head away. "Fine. You have me, but only because I've been bored lately."

"Sure," Ari agreed, heavy on the sarcasm. Reigning it back in, Ari refocused on Dazzle with a beseeching smile. "I can count on you too, right?"

Dazzle threw back his pink head with a loud huff. "I'm going to regret this."

Ari spun on his heel to beam at Taye. "That wasn't a no."

Taye stared at them, his furrowed brow casting a severe shadow over his eyes as they hopped from face-to-face-to-face. "For real this time, are none you capable of taking anything seriously? This is life and death we're talking about."

Ari scowled. "I'm always serious."

"It's true," Dazzle chimed as he petted Ari's hair fondly. "Inopportune humor is just his coping mechanism."

Ari swatted Dazzle's hand away. "Really? That's my coping mechanism? Not, I don't know, my trademark pending version of sass?"

"Val already called dibs on sass."

"Right." Ari rounded on the cat with a pout that made her grin. "Remind me, did you claim that as part of your charm, or part of your trauma?"

Val preened. "Yes."

"This can't be happening," Taye said as his gaze flitted between the three of them on another loop. "I run myself ragged looking for help, and this is the best I can find."

In seamless unison, Ari, Val, and Dazzle pinned him with wide smiles that toed the line between expectant and creepy.

"Technically, you only found me," Ari corrected.

Taye flopped into Ari's armchair like a puppet with snapped strings. He stared at nothing and addressed no one as he voiced his thoughts. "We're all going to die."

"Probably," Dazzle sighed as Ari knelt by the chair to ease Taye's hand from his marked side.

"On a related note," Val offered with a slight uptick in her tone, "I'm sure we'll give them hell on the way out."

THAT WAS ALL THE GRAVITY THEY COULD TAKE FOR ONE night. The moment Dazzle hit his limit, he marched out of the apartment with all the gusto of a zombie, Val at his side to ensure he made it home in one piece. Ari suspected the cat had other motives too; after so many years together, he knew when she needed some space from him.

Taye was the last to leave. He lingered in the doorway well after the other wizards vanished down the hall.

"I noticed you didn't tell them about the whole wizard coven idea."

Ari glared at him. "Why am I not surprised you know about that already?"

Taye wiggled his fingers theatrically and said, "Magic. Ta da!"

"You're an ass."

He would have left the conversation at that, but Taye made no move to leave the apartment. "So, why didn't you tell them?"

"I did," Ari said, then he sagged under the weight of Taye's pointed side-eye. "Maybe not directly."

"Not at all, actually."

Ari scowled and crossed his arms over his chest. "I can see how the concept of finesse might be lost on you, but trust me, I laid out the groundwork."

Taye's gaze wandered heavenward as he gave an aggravated chuckle. "And here I thought you were being sentimental. Of course you're not just a snob, you're a master manipulator."

Ari shoved him out onto the apartment's welcome mat. "If I were in your position, I'd probably have nicer things to say about the witch sticking his neck out for me."

With that, Ari slammed the door shut on Taye's annoyingly handsome face.

He turned to survey his empty apartment and stalled out. It was so quiet, too still. It was, in a word, uncomfortable.

"It's fine," he said, nodding to himself like a jostled bobblehead doll. "Val will be back by morning."

A quiet knock sounded on the door directly behind him.

Ari wasn't an idiot; he knew who it was, but with the flat devoid of all life besides himself, Ari couldn't help but lunge for the knob.

No, that was not a euphemism, Ari assured himself.

He expected to find Taye waiting on the other side of the door, but he didn't expect to walk right into a bouquet of white roses in full bloom.

"Jesus!" Ari shrieked, pulling his face from the fragrant assault and blinking rapidly to clear the petals from his eyes.

"That was not my fault!" Taye cried as he threw the bouquet like a lit stick of dynamite.

They watched the flowers bounce down the hallway, spraying leaves and twigs upon each contact with the floor.

"What the fuck, Taye?"

"It wasn't my idea!"

They stopped shouting over each other in the same moment. Ari saw the understanding light up those hazel eyes just as clarity smacked Ari upside the head for good measure.

Magic was at work again.

Stepping into the hall, Ari joined Taye in scowling down at the stray flowers.

"You knocked, though, right?"

"Yeah. I was even planning to apologize, believe it or not."

"Hmm."

"Uh huh."

As they watched, the bundle of white petals and greenery began rolling back toward them. It wasn't fast, but neither witch nor wizard made a move to hurry things along by retrieving the suspicious item. They waited together as one frowning front, like disappointed parents welcoming a problem child home after curfew.

The bouquet came to a gentle, cheeky rest as its tissue wrappings touched Ari's toe.

After a moment, Taye nudged him. "Pick it up."

"You pick it up!"

"I already made contact, it's your turn."

They glared at each other, then at the bouquet. The roses were now a deep, passionate red.

"No way." Taye laughed in disbelief.

Ari echoed the sentiment with a sharp, "Nope," and the two of them ran for the presumed safety of the apartment. It was only after they put a locked and blockaded door between them and the monstrous roses that either of them took a full breath.

"Okay," Ari said as he calmed his panicked lungs. "So, that happened."

"I noticed." Taye pulled at the collar of his sweatshirt like it was strangling him and looked about the apartment. "How am I supposed to leave again?"

Ari froze. He stood there, like a complete idiot, and stared at the door that was supposedly protecting his virtue from Magic's unsubtle insinuations.

"Ari? You do have a fire escape, right?"

Instead of a verbal answer, Ari made to move the decorative half shelf now barring the door back to its original position.

"That has to be a safety violation," Taye groaned.

"It's Olde Town," Ari snapped. "The whole block predates building ordinances. What did you expect?"

He flipped the lock with every intention of letting Taye out and trodding on the damn flowers if need be, but Ari never got to enact the plan. One large, bronzed hand landed below the peephole, clamping the exit shut. Ari's knuckles were white around the handle as Taye's shoulder hit the door with his full weight dumped against it.

"I'm sorry for what I said," Taye said with obvious displeasure, "but I'm more sorry about the magical wingman."

The grumpiness and begrudging acceptance in that statement made Ari burst out laughing. Taye waited for him to smother the fitful noise before continuing with his supernaturally coerced apology.

"Truth is, you remind me of . . . people."

"Oh?" Ari mocked through persistent snickers.

Taye's scowl deepened to new and thrilling depths. He shoved his hands into his jean pockets and loomed over Ari like a very tangible and imminent threat.

"You're an arrogant prick who makes control freaks look chill," Taye stated. "You're only helping me because you have no choice in the matter, and you're incapable of showing anyone a lick of respect."

Ari stopped laughing.

"So yeah," Taye said, "you remind me of a lot of people I'd rather forget."

Stiff and sober, Ari opened his mouth to respond with something suitably scathing. Alarmingly, he couldn't produce a single word.

Whatever expression was scrawled across his face seemed to satisfy Taye, because the wizard pulled back and restored the breathing room between them. A certain tightness remained in his jaw, but Taye's shoulders relaxed as he studied Ari further.

"Coerced or not, none of those people would have done what you did for a complete stranger," Taye added, almost like it was an afterthought. "None of them have ever fostered long-term friendships like you have, either."

Ari frowned and took a wary step back. "Thanks?"

Taye sighed and pinched the bridge of his nose. "I'm not good at this."

"Clearly."

"Look, just . . ." Taye bit his lip as his face crunched with a reluctant conclusion. He sighed again. "I don't know you, but I'm trying to see through my first impressions here, okay?"

"Not really, but go ahead." Ari waved him on before

cocking a hip and folding his arms in expectation. "I'm dying to know if the next words out of your mouth are going to be complimentary or problematic."

"That," Taye fumed, pointing one long finger in Ari's face. "That is exactly the problem. You don't know when to shut up. You always have to have the last word, and it's infuriating!"

With the back of his hand, Ari guided Taye's finger away from his face. "That's your problem, not mine. If you don't like it, feel free to leave."

"And go where?"

An icy frost enveloped them then. It was less about Taye's words than the desperate inflection behind them.

Ari softened as he remembered his first impression of Taye as a homeless person. The way Taye's eyes widened like he hadn't planned to say so much only made Ari's heartstrings that much weaker.

"When was the last time you went home, Taye?"

He knew Taye was going to run for it when he started eyeing the door he still leaned against. Ari stopped him from attempting it with a feather light touch of his pale palm on a dark cheek.

"I'm listening now," Ari said. "If you want to do all the talking, the floor is yours."

Ari swept his hand from the wizard's face into a wide arch that indicated the designated living room. With minimal hesitation, Taye took up the invitation, and that was that.

It wasn't the wild night Magic might have intended for them, but it was a long one. They stayed up late talking and listening, venting more than not. When Ari's eyelids started itching for want of rest and Taye's pauses between thoughts grew too long, there was no need to say goodnight. The bubbling animosity between them was down to a low simmer, though Ari wasn't quite ready to call them friends.

Ari thought he might be well on his way to liking Taye as a person, though.

The evening was enlightening. Ari said little, for once in his life, but he learned much. He learned Taye wasn't just a handsome face with hopes of being a supernatural rock star; while he already knew music was Taye's focus, he hadn't seen any indication that the wizard did anything particularly meaningful with it. Now, however, Ari had at least an hour's worth of stories about all the music therapy Taye did with troubled kids and disabled people. Ari never expected that kind of altruism from the guy, but there it was, in the wet sheen to Taye's eyes and the genuine smile on his face as he spoke.

Taye wasn't willing to discuss his nights on the streets and dipping into nonprofit shelters, but he told Ari plenty about the lead up. His descriptions of abandoning his beloved instruments and studio apartment for a life on the run from every magic user he knew made Ari's chest go tight. Once, when Taye recounted the night his spontaneous magic compromised the health of a client, Ari's eyes even began to water.

No, they weren't friends. Ari didn't speak enough for Taye to learn a fraction as much about him in return. Even so, Ari went to bed relieved to know he was getting into trouble for someone who was worth it. Probably.

CHAPTER 11

The previous night's heart-to-heart notwithstanding, Ari was not prepared to be left alone in his apartment with a strange yet attractive man overnight. This became painfully obvious from the moment the morning sun shone through his bedroom blinds.

"Did you know you drool in your sleep?"

"Ah!" Ari yanked the blankets up to his nose and practically teleported to the far side of the bed.

While he woke up in a dizzying rush, Taye grinned from the foot of Ari's queen-sized bed. He was kneeling on the floor with his chin propped on his folded arms, his posture and bright eyes making it clear that he'd been watching Ari sleep for some time.

Oh, but Ari wished his instincts led him to kick the jerk in the face instead of shrieking like a small child and chasing himself into an actual corner.

"What the fuck are you doing in my room?!" Ari cried as he executed several fast blinks in the attempt to reassure himself that yes, Taye's bare arms and shoulders really were that defined.

"You don't get many guests, do you?" Taye countered before plopping a folded sheet onto the bed between them. Ari recognized it as one of the linens he handed over the night before so Taye could make the couch his resting place for the night.

Turns out, it was a fitted sheet, not the top sheet Ari meant to serve as a blanket.

Flushing with embarrassment, Ari sat up and snatched the fitted sheet to refold it to his liking and smooth out any wrinkles. "I've had guests before," Ari assured him as he worked. "I must have been overtired is all."

Taye arched a dubious brow, and the teasing smirk on his face would have nearly made Ari's heart skip.

Ignoring the growing heat in his cheeks, Ari explained, "Normally, when people sleep over, they share my bed."

Taye second eyebrow rose to join the first.

"Dazzle," Ari spat, face burning as he realized how his words could be misconstrued. "Dazzle's the only person who ever stays over, and it would be disastrous if he and I fought over the bed, so . . . yeah. Besides, we're good friends. Platonic friends."

Taye's brows lowered as understanding dawned, but then the asshole made it a point to ask with a straight face, "Platonic friends who sleep together?"

Ari scoffed in defense without thinking, "With our clothes on, yes!"

Taye didn't laugh at him, at least not out loud. Ari was about to throw the immaculately folded sheet at him anyway, but the wizard chose that moment to stand up and retreat out the door.

Ari's mouth dropped open. Taye was dressed in nothing but an off-white tank and comic book boxers, leaving miles and miles of muscle and mocha skin on display. Ari swallowed on reflex.

"You sleep like the dead, too," Taye said without a backward glance as he exited the bedroom. "I woke up hours ago and made breakfast. Hope you don't mind."

From the chipper emphasis on those words, Ari suspected Taye actually hoped he minded quite a bit. Scowling at the universe at large, Ari deigned to crawl out of bed.

He knew Taye had taken gross advantage of Ari's incapacitation the second he entered the main living space. The mess was obvious even from a distance. Pots and pans were caked in cooling food debris, and Ari's eye twitched when he noticed egg splatter on a cabinet. Every last cupboard door Ari rented was left wide open, and his perfect alignment of cookware and dining supplies were knocked out of place.

Noticing the spice rack was now out of alphabetical order, Ari whimpered and rushed over to correct the mess.

Taye looked gleeful as he watched Ari get to work with a plate in his hands stacked with steaming scrambled eggs, buttered pancakes, and bacon. Ari couldn't remember buying pancake mix or bacon anytime in the recent past, but that was a worry for another time.

"No lie," Taye commented, "I didn't take you for the type to wear flannel to bed. Isn't plaid a little plebeian for your tastes?"

Ari paused with cinnamon in one hand and dried parsley in the other to look down at himself. The pink-and-gray bottoms and loose white tee were his favorite sleepwear, and they looked as comfortable and stylish fresh out of bed as they did when he lounged around the apartment on weekends.

"I have no idea what you're talking about," Ari admitted.

For some reason, Ari's genuine confusion made Taye chuckle as he retrieved a fork from the drawer left ajar.

With a grumpy pout, Ari set his fists on his hips, fingers curled around spice bottles, and demanded, "What's so funny?"

Taye shrugged, still grinning as he jabbed the fork into the heaping eggs. "I just assumed you slept in silk or some shit like that."

Ari's mouth opened in affront, but he stopped himself as his brain finished processing what he just heard. Returning to the spice rack with a smug grin, he said, "Been imagining what I wear to bed, have you?"

The fork tines hit the plate heavily as a poor pancake got stabbed. Taye glared at Ari with his cheek as full as a scavenging chipmunk's. Damn it all, but the sight was adorable.

Before Ari could start fluttering his eyelashes or something equally foolish, he was saved by the switch of a lock and ensuing swing of a door. Dazzle flounced into the apartment with Val in his arms like Ari's personal superhero, complete with armor of the studded leather jacket he reserved for the weekends. The heavy eyeliner and black tips to his fuchsia locks were decently intimidating too.

"Good God," Dazzle groaned in dismay as he took in the kitchen and Taye's state of undress.

"No!" Ari warned. "Get your mind out of the gutter before you get yourself thrown out of my flat!"

Dazzle deflated like all joy had been stolen from his life, but Val perked up and climbed her front paws high onto his shoulder.

"Ah-ha! You're threats are useless on me!" she taunted. "I pay part of the rent!"

Voice low and intent, Ari reminded her, "I can make your life hell, cat."

"Do your worst, you little witch!"

"It is way too early for this," Taye told no one in particular around a mouthful. He swallowed, then held the plate under his chin to begin shoveling food straight into his open maw.

Ari grimaced. "You eat like a Neanderthal."

Taye paused, lowering his plate a scant inch as he grinned around a bunch of omelet. A piece of bell pepper caught between his teeth, and Ari felt it was somehow intentional.

"Ugh," Ari gagged.

At the same time, Dazzle told Val, "Yeah. I like him."

Taye's stuffed grin became more genuine when he turned it on Dazzle.

"I hate you all," Ari announced as he turned his back on them.

The morning was already off to an awkward start, so Ari wasn't about to compound it with the mistake of skipping his usual morning routine. He left the main flat to the wizards for better or worse and locked himself in the bathroom.

Toilet, face wash, and hair, then he would brave the situation waiting for him in the kitchen for the sake of getting his hands on some necessary coffee. He already knew he would need more than one pot before noon.

Everything was going according to that plan until he caught himself primping in the mirror. Without any conscious effort on his end, his skin care routine got carried away. He usually limited himself to washing and moisturizing unless an obvious spot needed addressing, and he liked to leave his hair loose to fall naturally around his face. Instead, he ended up throwing products on his face and styling his hair like he was preparing for a night of dancing at a club. He went so far as to gloss his lips.

"What the fuck am I doing?" Ari asked in a disgusted hush.

He whipped the shiny stuff off his mouth with a twitchy hand, and the running water seemed unreasonably loud as he washed away the evidence.

Emerging from the bathroom, Ari was perturbed to find Taye nowhere to be seen.

Dazzle sat on the couch with *A Divergence of Magic* open over his lap, but Val lounged on the armchair with a perfect view of Ari's wary expression.

"Mr. Tall, Dark, and Handsome is getting dressed," she said with an unrepentant grin. "Since you were taking up the bathroom, I told him to use your bedroom."

Ari seethed under his breath on his way to the coffee maker, "You could've suggested he wait."

"I was being hospitable!"

Ari rolled his eyes, but the display was lost on Val as he faced the kitchen and launched himself at the coffee maker. As he waited on the pot to finish filling, Ari shot a curious glance back toward the couch.

Dazzle's eyes were skimming back and forth across that damn book with intention.

Ari huffed. "You can read it too?"

The temperature didn't actually drop, but it felt like it to Ari as his friends traded wary looks. Slow and not so casual, Dazzle closed the book and set it on the table.

"Ari, darling," Dazzle said with a patient smile, "we have a few things to discuss."

"I assumed as much." Ari trained his attention on the coffee like the lifeline he needed it to be. "You're rarely awake this early on a Sunday. The situation must be dire, indeed."

"I love how you talk like you just stepped out of a Jane Austen novel," Val murmured with a languid stretch.

"Hush, kitten. Don't distract us," Dazzle reprimanded gently. The gentleness persisted as he scooted to the edge of the couch to refocus on Ari. "Firstly, are we absolutely certain there's no way to wash our hands of this situation with the Council and covens?"

Ari gave a soft, sardonic laugh as he poured his first cup of the morning. "We're a good week or more past that point."

"Right." Dazzle sighed, then he launched into a thoroughly thought out game plan. "Then as your friend and accomplice, I suggest we write a formal apology and deliver it to the Council with a gift from my potions lab to smooth things over. I doubt the same thing will work with the Morrigans, but I'll sleep a lot sounder knowing the Council's pacified. Val, it'll help if you can think of something to add to the gift bag."

"On it," Val agreed with a speed that told Ari she was already familiar with the proposed plan. "I know just the artifact, and Ari already has it in stock!"

"You're not giving my commercial goods away," Ari warned.

He hated to shit all over their well-intended hopes, but like Dazzle, he would sleep better once something got done. Unlike Dazzle, Ari had all the information necessary to make a more appropriate decision.

Magic thrummed along his skin with undeniable reassurance. It bolstered his nerve and helped him carry his coffee over to the lounge area and toss Val out of his chair so he could address them from a place of maximized comfort.

Cradling his hot mug and reclining in his chosen throne,

Ari casually explained, "I'll remind you that governing bodies don't negotiate with terrorists as a rule. That's pretty much what we are from their perspective."

Val gaped at him as Dazzle sighed and closed his eyes like he was coming to terms with some aggressively insistent fears.

Rubbing his hands around the mug in search of warmth, Ari continued, "Gaines already admitted they consider Taye's existence an untenable threat, and when I told a Morrigan I was protecting him, it seems I used the same unacceptable Magic to drive the point home. On top of that . . ."

Ari hesitated, but then figured what the hell, he was already in the thick of the mess anyway.

"I'm pretty sure the community thinks I'm forming some sort of bastardized coven full of wizards, which is as blasphemous as it gets among witches. So . . . yeah."

No one said anything for a moment as his best friends seemed to mull the idea over. There were no sneaky looks or attempts at silent communication. Dazzle's forehead folded with a frown as he clutched his hands together in front of pursed lips, and the corner of Val's mouth curled to reveal a fang as her disquieted contemplation led her down conflicting emotional avenues.

Resigning himself to wait, Ari enjoyed his coffee in less than peaceful quiet.

They must have made quite the odd sight, because when Taye reappeared in the bedroom doorway in yesterday's jeans and hoodie, he almost immediately zeroed in on Ari.

"What did you do?"

Ari frown up at him over the rim of his mug. "What makes you think I did something?"

"I think he smacked us over the head with a misguided epiphany," Val said.

"I'm not saying I agree," Dazzle said in slow, measured words as he stared into the void in front of him, "but it's possible we might be magical terrorists. I'm still trying to figure out how seriously I'm supposed to respond to the idea."

"Oh," Taye said as the tension leached from his posture. He sounded both amused and disturbed as he muttered under his breath, "Is that all?"

Silence reigned once again. Ari was the only one who moved as he raised his mug to his lips. The others just sat there, looking forlorn and defeated. In Taye's case, he stood, but he looked no better off than the others.

It was tempting to sink into despair with them. Ari drank more coffee to ward off the feeling. He drained the mug in record timing.

Smacking his lips and wishing he had more to drink, Ari said, "We might as well do it."

The wizards shook themselves from their shared stupor and stared at him.

"Do what?" asked Val.

"Form a coven."

Their staring intensified.

Ari sighed and got up to get more coffee. It was going to be a long, awkward day if they needed him to pitch the idea of a coven of wizards.

CHAPTER 12

There was a first for everything, according to history. Ari kept telling himself that throughout the week, but he couldn't completely shake his nerves. He tried his best to explain what a coven was and how it benefited the magic users within its bond, but even after leaving Val and Dazzle with choice literature on the subject, he doubted they truly understood. In his more optimistic moments, Ari thought perhaps Taye got it, and even then only because he seemed to commune with Magic on the same level Ari did himself.

Despite his doubts, Ari was relieved when Val took it upon herself to set a date for the attempt. They were doing it. They were forming a coven of wizards and one witch. At the very least, they were going to give it a good hard try.

It was an agonizing wait till Friday came.

During the week, Taye was a constant reminder of the impending experiment. He became a prominent fixture in Ari's life with no apparent conflict, either flitting about the shop in pursuit of elusive knowledge, or camping out on his couch and making Ari breakfast like a self-appointed personal chef.

Ari hated admitting it, but the wizard's presence was far more helpful than the hindering annoyance Ari anticipated. Not only did Taye make a decent breakfast each morning, he'd taken to cleaning the main living space in full each night, from kitchen to the boundary of Ari's bedroom. Taye didn't need to be told to keep out of Ari's way during the work day, but he was prompt and cooperative on the few occasions Ari did ask him to run an errand for the sake of the business.

When the fateful Friday evening finally came, his reluctance to close down and leave the shop was almost crippling, but Taye was ready.

"This should be everything we need," the wizard announced as he joined Ari at the shop entrance. He patted the worn backpack hanging from his shoulder and threatening to burst.

Ari eyed the bag doubtfully as he fiddled with the fluffy dice on his keys. "You have the quartz and amethyst from the apartment?"

"Figured I'd save us a trip by bringing them with me this morning."

Ari normally found such obvious competence attractive, but the knowing smirk on Taye's thick lips made him grumble with irritation.

"What was that?" Taye asked, leaning close.

"I didn't say anything!" Ari snapped before ushering them out the door.

Arvada blended into the outskirt of Denver in a way Ari appreciated, because unlike most witches, he preferred city living to rolling around in dirt and frolicking through forests. He rarely ventured further away from the city, but when he did, Dazzle never begrudged him a ride. That was the only reason Ari never complained about Dazzle's Tesla.

Taye had no such compunctions, though.

"I've never been in a car with less personality," he muttered as he ran his hands over the sleek panel where an interior handle and window controls should have been.

In the front passenger seat, Ari stared at the ultra-smooth and too clean dashboard. He might have uttered a short hum of agreement.

"If you can't say something nice, don't say anything at all," Dazzle quoted haughtily as he checked his lip gloss in the rear view mirror. "Leave my Blue Kazoo alone, or I'll make you walk."

They made it to San Isabel National Forest slightly over an hour later, with night skies and empty streets to greet them. They could've chosen a location closer to home, but between all the unknown factors and ceremonial mandate for the strongest natural setting they could find, Ari made the executive decision to drag his band of wizards further out.

Besides, it was after dark, and so long as they steered clear of the designated camp grounds, the long drive was sure to be worth it. The combination of privacy and wilderness couldn't be easily beat.

They kept the flashlights on low as they carved a path from the car through the underbrush. They left Dazzle's car on the side of a dirt road under a quick illusion charm. Thanks to Val's masterful spell casting, the Tesla blended into the darkness seamlessly. It would be undetectable to mundane senses until Val lifted the enchantment, and most supernatural beings wouldn't notice it unless they knew what they were looking for.

Ari and his friends were disconcertingly quiet. Some unnameable instinct kept their usual chatter in check.

Surrounded by the ebony striations of tree silhouettes, shadowy plants, and the eerie backdrop of wildlife's symphony, not one of them dared to utter a word as they trekked further into the forest.

The three wizards followed Ari on silent, but heavy feet. He couldn't hear their footfalls beyond the brief snapping of twigs and undergrowth, but he could feel the stiffness in their movements. Their discomfort was palpable to him, like a cold front creeping up from behind.

It was a stark juxtaposition to his own easy steps. Ari breathed free and deep as the forest seemed to morph around his feet with the practiced grace of a long-term dance partner.

Disturbingly, Ari couldn't remember the last time he paid Mother Nature such a proper visit. The light pollution from the city was completely replaced by stars shining through the leafy canopy. The bustle of vehicles and appliances was replaced by cicadas and the cooing of nocturnal animals. It was a peaceful setting Ari hadn't realized how much he missed.

"This is far enough," Ari whispered upon stepping into a greater patch of starlight.

The space wasn't quite large enough to be called a glade. Roughly the size of his bedroom, the clearing was an awkward shape lined in trees and shrubs. Moss and weeds, grass and dirt made an uneven blanket across the forest floor without rhythm or reason. It was no flourishing garden by any stretch, but when they switched off the flashlights to allow the moon to paint the space in its purity . . . well, then it's beauty became obvious.

At his shoulder, Dazzle's breath caught with a distinct note of wonder.

"Yeah," Ari spoke soft and low, but pleased. "This is the spot."

At his direction, they got to work preparing the clearing for the ritual.

In a way, it was like stepping into an impressionist painting. The sky provided enough light to see by, to detect splashes of greens and yellows, but with little distinction to individual forms. The split second flash of animal eyes peaking from the treeline seemed like sparkling lights more than signs of potential predators. It was an everyday sort of magical, but magical all the same.

Dazzle carved a circle by dragging his feet, Val reinforcing the path by trotting behind him. Taye pulled a book from the tote bag and began checking the sky against a particular page till he found his orientation, then he started setting the uniform candles along the perimeter of the circle.

It was a pitiful circle compared to most witch rituals. The only coven Ari saw gather for a group casting was dozens strong, but they were maxing out at four. Ari hoped the number would be enough.

"Dazzle?" Taye prompted, then when he had Dazzle's attention he said, "Catch."

A ball of carved and polished quartz went sailing through the air. Dazzle's eyes went wide with alarm as he stumbled back, but he caught the precious stone safely against his chest. Hugging it, Dazzle glared at Taye.

"If you ever come that close to breaking my nose again, you'll be paying for the resulting cosmetic procedure!"

"No negativity near the circle!" Ari scolded. "For fuck's sake, we're trying to convince the universe that we're a harmonious power worth sanctifying. Think about it."

Neither Taye nor Dazzle looked at him, but the two traded apologetic smiles. Those smiles were either bashful over their shared immaturity or, as Ari was inclined to believe, they were laughing at him for the shortness of his reprimand. So long as they were on the same page and not bickering, Ari chose not to care about the particulars.

They finished setting up without incident. Val curled up in her designated position on the circle line between two candles, one hefty amethyst placed in front of her. She waited for them to finish measuring and placing the rest of the candles and gems with a curious eye, and she kept any comments to herself.

At least, she held her tongue till the three men joined her at equal intervals on the circle.

"Good job, boys," the cat smiled. "I do love being the de facto supervisor. Remind me to organize a pizza party for you."

Taye sighed heavenward as he struggled to get comfortable in a cross-legged position.

"No negativity near the circle!" Ari rushed to remind him.

Taye glared back at him, but held his tongue.

"Oh! Oh! Oh!" Val bounced in place, her eyes lit up. "Next time, you should bring a water bottle to squirt them when they misbehave!"

"No!" Ari and Taye barked in unison.

Then Dazzle naturally pulled a tiny spritz bottle from his jean pocket and sprayed it in Val's direction, saying, "Bad kitty."

Glittery body oil showered over Val, making the cat flinch and almost tumble backward out of the circle.

"Ari!" Val whined. "You're just going to let him treat me that way? And tonight, of all ceremonious nights!"

"That's enough dramatics, thank you." Ari snapped his fingers without thinking, but his irritation was repaid when the spritz bottle flew into his hand.

Dazzle's arm jerked as the plastic container yanked free of his grasp. He gaped at Ari. "Et tu, Brutus?"

"No negativity near the circle!" Ari seethed.

"Can we please get on with it," Taye begged, "before Ari has a conniption?"

A seeming eternity later, they were all calm and appropriately seated at equal intervals along the circle. Ari, Taye, and Dazzle sat cross-legged between their appointed candles, while Val settled back on her haunches. In accordance with all the reading he'd done that week, Ari gave them a few minutes to relax into position.

The quiet stillness in the fresh air was nice and conducive to meditation. Ari couldn't help wondering why he didn't do this more often on his own. The thought was disconcerting, but Ari couldn't detect any hint of Magic's meddling. Bemused, he decided to reconsider the idea later.

Right now, he had more pressing matters to attend to.

Once everyone seemed settled into their bodies and more or less comfy, Ari cleared his throat.

"Ready?"

Nods all around, and Ari sucked in a deep, bracing breath.

"Okay. Let's start by linking hands and closing our eyes. Proximity is necessary for cooperative witchcraft, so physical contact can only strengthen our chances of pulling this off."

They were far from synchronized, but Ari caught Dazzle's hand in his left and Taye's in his right with surprising smoothness. Peeking through his lashes, Ari spotted Val across the way pouting as the twin grips on her forepaws pulled her into an upward stretch most unbecoming and utterly adorable for a grown cat.

Shutting his eyes again and fending off a smirk at his friend's expense, Ari refocused on drawing ever deeper breaths.

"Expand your senses," Ari instructed, and if anyone else thought he sounded like a ridiculous hipster yoga coach, at least they didn't say it out loud. "Let your awareness sink into the earth and form a connection. There's power there, Magic waiting to be tapped into. You just have to find it."

It took conscious effort not to hold his breath in anticipation. A part of him expected nothing to happen, because why would it? Wizards didn't commune with Magic like this, and they certainly didn't form supernatural bonds. In Dazzle's and Val's cases, they didn't have much hope of sensing raw Magic, yet alone working in tandem with it. They needed their dedicated medium to summon Magic to do their bidding. So did Taye, up till recently.

A week's worth a research hadn't suggested anything else was possible. In all of Grimoires and Goodies, there wasn't a single suggestion on how to make a group of wizards into a coven.

Nevertheless, Ari needed this to work. If Puckman's insinuations were to be believed, they all needed it to work.

Unlike their wizard counterparts, coven witches grew in magical might as their connection to nature and each other deepened. They were among the few magic users who regularly shared their strength and resources, physically, magically, emotionally, or otherwise. They cooperated where most others guarded their power.

Right now, Ari needed that kind of security. He needed it bad enough to set aside a lifetime of pretending he never wanted it.

They sat in stiff silence for too long. Maybe Ari's anxiety was catching, and the others were simply mirroring his tension as the minutes dragged on and on. Ari doubted it, though.

Please, he thought when the ache of keeping his arms stretched to either side evolved into an unsustainable pain. *Please answer us.*

Magic heard his plea, and the relief that flooded him along with the electrifying sense of limitless power almost brought him to tears.

The wizards felt it too. They must have. Ari kept his eyes closed in reverence, and a bit of fear that doing otherwise might jeopardize the ritual, but he could still hear them react. Val hissed a soft little noise of profound understanding, the one syllable conveying an entire shift in her world view. Dazzle released a breathless and tearful laugh that almost drowned out Taye's awed moan.

Ari sent his thanks out into the ether as a wordless mesh of feeling and intention. At the same time, he rolled his shoulders back and heaved a loud and deliberate breath designed to draw everyone's attention without startling them.

"Ari?" Val whispered, shaken.

He opened his mouth to respond, and somehow, some way, he wasn't surprised to hear Magic's words coming out of his mouth.

"All is well," he heard himself say. "It is time we remember who we are."

The sentient power didn't take over his body so much as it guided him with a gentle, but insistent pressure. It was warm and tingly, and Ari couldn't imagine wanting to do anything other than what it asked of him.

It was Magic at its rawest, most potent form. To Ari, it felt like peace.

He let go of Taye's and Dazzle's hands and opened his eyes to see them following his lead, folding their wands in their laps. Taye was pretending not to look at him, while Dazzle kept shoot Ari obvious sideways glances. Across the way, Val crouched on all fours with her wary gaze locked on Ari like she was trying to decide whether she should tackle him or not.

She would have to launch herself over quite a substantial rock if she wanted to follow through on that idea. The amethyst lay in the grass before her, while matching quartz orbs held similar positions before the other wizards. Ari was the only one with multiple stones before him; the book he'd chosen for his instruction manual lay open to the desired pages, with coin-sized stones of every magically charged mineral he had in stock pinning the pages along their edges.

At Magic's direction, Ari waved has hands over the lines of precious stones with symmetry so perfect it had to be supernatural. As one, the stone lifted into the air and began a slow clockwise rotation.

In the safety of his own mind, Ari sobbed with relief. This was happening. The ritual had begun, and it was shockingly easy with Magic helping him along. It was the first time in over a decade that Ari worked witchcraft in front of an audience of more than one snarky cat, but the connection flowed through his body with the familiar ease of a long-lost lover.

The book lay abandoned in the weeds, all but forgotten.

"Find the earth with your skin," Magic instructed with Ari's voice.

Leading by example, Ari lowered his hands to the ground on either side of him and sank his fingers into the soil. His eyes remained on the circling stones, but he felt the movement as the others complied.

"It is not enough to feel it. You must visualize the connection. Welcome it into your body, heart, and mind. Let it meld with your soul like the long-lost piece it is."

Someone uttered a heartwarming whimper. In the same instance, Ari felt the soil grow warm to the touch, and that delicious hint of heat was quick to dance and play its way up his arms and to his chest, inevitably ending with a potent rush to his head.

It sank into him, into each of them, and for one wild moment that lasted eons, Ari knew these three wizards as well as he knew himself.

They knew what was supposed to happen next. Val spent days coaching Ari on his Greek pronunciation for this exact moment, since neither of them expected pig Latin to get such an important job done. Dazzle and Taye were similarly well read on the progression of the ritual, despite having no need to recite the ancient chant themselves.

None of them expected Ari to start speaking in what could only be described as tongues.

The language wasn't just unfamiliar, it was unknowable. It sounded like nothing and everything ever spoken in the world, all at once. If Ari was completely honest, it didn't seem like the sort of thing a human voice box should capable of producing.

Judging from the disturbed expressions on their faces as they gaped at him, his wizards agreed with his take on the matter. Ari wasn't about to interrupt the ritual to reassure them, though.

He held still and composed, utterly compliant as Magic used his voice to make the necessary changes to a ritual meant to form a witch's coven. The various stones he used in place of the typical Morrigan's amulet were still trailing after one another in a perfect airborne circle. The candles flared to life with spontaneous fire; according to the text, the flames were meant to ignite only after the would-be Morrigan finished chanting, but the bizarre words continued pouring from Ari's mouth a full minute after the wick's lit up on their own.

When Ari eventually fell silent, the candles dimmed to a

pleasant glow. The gems ceased their rotation to hang still and expectant as they floated a foot above the open book.

After a long moment, Taye glanced at the others and whispered, "Now what?"

Dazzle shrugged, but said nothing as he eyed Ari's collection of suspended stones. Val gave a low hum of bewilderment as her tail curled around her like a hug.

Ignoring the touch of unease prickling the back of his neck, Ari leaned forward to look over the ritual instructions. The floating stones forced him to shift around in a rather undignified manner for a presumptive Morrigan, but he managed to lock eyes on all the pertinent words anyway.

"I think," he said slowly, "we're done?"

"You're confidence is very convincing," Val sassed.

"I especially like the part where his voice shook," Dazzle added.

"Is it too much to ask for one night of appropriate gravitas from you people?" Taye bemoaned with his face lifted skyward.

"Probably," Ari admitted as he tilted his head various ways in order to study the hanging stones from all possible angles. "If things went entirely by the book, I'd say we should clean up and head home."

"But they didn't," Dazzle said with an impatient sigh.

Ari did another round of considering the scene. The candles should have gone out with the conclusion of the ceremony, but they remained lit. They couldn't leave a dozen precious stones frozen in midair for random hikers to chance upon, either. More than that, as Ari took stock of his emotional and mental well-being, he couldn't detect any new awareness of his supposed coven members; the intimate knowledge he had of them during the ritual seemed to have faded along with the magically charged atmosphere.

They were missing something. The ritual was still going.

It was the only possible excuse. There were no more instructions to follow, and Magic no longer influenced Ari's impulses. It was like the universe was waiting for something special from them.

But of course it was.

"Don't make me regret saying this," Ari warned with a dour look toward Dazzle, before he addressed the group at large. "If your lover did you a life-altering favor, how might you show them your appreciation?"

Dazzle's evil grin made him wince, but whatever wicked taunt Dazzle thought of was held firmly behind his displayed teeth. Val snickered and Dazzle's grin widened to devilish proportions.

"Hypothetically!" Ari snapped.

Val stopped snickering enough to sit up tall and adopt a condescending expression.

"So help me," Ari gripped before she could open her mouth, "if you say anything that involves nudity or bodily fluids, I will flush your entire catnip stash down the toilet the moment we get home."

Val wilted faster than a flower doused in vinegar.

With an awkward clearing of his throat, Taye suggested, "Actually . . . there might be some validity to—"

"No." Ari pointed at Taye like his finger was a weapon. "Not you too. Don't even start."

He raised his hands in supposed placation even as he disregarded the warning. "I'm just saying, there seems to be a certain physicality to most major witchcraft."

"I am not having sex with any of you," Ari announced in a deadpan.

Val and Dazzle snorted, their eyes pointed toward Taye.

Ari just knew they were going to say something he wouldn't like.

"Especially not on a forest floor!" he added in a raised voice.

All three wizards chortled at him, but at least they tried to keep it brief.

"Well, if physical intimacy is off the table," Taye said after getting himself under control, "Physical sacrifice is a regularity throughout most of your library."

"It's not a library," Ari insisted, "and I'm not killing any bunnies tonight, thanks."

Taye rolled his eyes, his smirk waning a tad. "No lover wants a dead rodent."

"Are rabbits rodents?" Dazzle asked Val.

"Not important right now," Ari said. Without second-guessing the wisdom of the action, Ari snatched the confiscated bottle from the ground beside him and squirted Dazzle in body glitter. "Focus!"

As Dazzle preened and rubbed the oil into his cheeks, Ari caught the flash of candlelight on a gleaming blade form the corner of his eye. Taye unfurled an ordinary pocketknife and offered it over, handle first.

"Sacrificing an animal probably isn't what it wants," he suggested, wagging the blade between two long fingers, "It did something for you, so it goes to reason it wants something from you."

"Oh, I know this one!" Val pipped up. "It wants blood!"

"That does sound very witchy," Dazzle agreed.

Meanwhile, Ari's gaze flitted between the knife and Taye.

"As your Morrigan, I think we need to have a talk about what kind of lovers you've had," Ari commented as he accepted the knife.

Taye laughed, and the sound was booming and delightful

in the late-night calm. "I'm not the one having an affair with an omnipotent force of nature."

"Point to Taye!" Dazzle said as he shot the wizard in question a wink.

"Just shut your faces and pray to whoever's listening that this works," Ari commanded.

Without giving himself time to get squeamish, Ari swiped the knife tip across the pad of his left pinky. He barely noticed the sting, but it left behind a thin red line that produced a perfect bubble of blood. Lacking any better ideas, he raised his barely bleeding digit toward the circle of floating stones.

It worked.

Ari wasn't the only one who gasped as the blood blob went from totally inert to zooming off his finger tip. The blood went straight to the center of the circle before flattening out, and it was downright impressive how vast such a little spot of liquid could spread. The red became almost translucent as it stretched to each of the crystals, till they were connected by a sheet of Ari's essence.

Things got weird then. Well, they got weirder, at any rate.

The stones began to glow. The effect wasn't limited to Ari's floating collection either. The giant amethyst and polished quartz in front of his wizards did the same, though their internal light didn't come close to the fierceness of the smaller pieces preternaturally soiled by blood.

"Cool," Dazzle murmured, his eyes locked on the quartz before him.

A glance at Val proved she wasn't quite as transfixed on her amethyst. Her gaze bounced from the rock to random little points in the air around her. She squinted like she might be seeing something the rest of them couldn't, only to relax her eyes again when they returned to the amethyst.

Ari spared a look toward Taye and stiffened.

Taye was staring, but not at the glowing orb nearest him, or any other lit gems for that matter. He was staring at Ari.

"What?" Ari demanded with a defensive pout.

Taye gave a short shake of his head. "Nothing."

"Bullshit," Ari hissed back under his breath. He couldn't read the delicate expression on Taye's face, with his full lips pressed into a thin line that quirked so slightly upward at the corner.

The entire exchanged was hushed to the point neither Val nor Dazzle seemed to notice. Taye kept staring, and Ari kept frowning back at him for a long moment or two while the others entertained themselves with the glowing spectacle. The staring contest might have lasted forever, except Ari got distracted.

As a witch, Ari always felt Magic's presence. It was in the air around him, in the deepest corners of his mind and the ground beneath his feet.

This was different.

Power rushed through him in a visceral blow unlike anything he experienced before. It plowed into him, suffusing every cell in his body. It was like he could feel his very synapses lighting up with it, till his body no longer ran on organic electricity but Magic itself.

It might have lasted an hour, or it could have been mere seconds, but when Ari next became aware of the physical world around him, he was bent over on his hands and knees, the grass pricking at his palms. The air was cool and refreshing as he sucked it back in large gulps. Val's paws were on his shoulder as she shoved at him, and he could feel Dazzle and Taye clustered around him too.

No, that wasn't quite right.

"It worked," he gasped in astonishment, his vision filled with grass and dirt and earth, earth, earth. "We did it."

He could feel so much more than their body heat and spacial proximity. He could sense their Magic like never before, with a startling clarity that gave him full access to the nuances in their magical abilities. It was almost painfully intimate.

"Ari?" Dazzle asked, "What happened?"

It was like he could see the way Dazzle's racing brain worked to formulate the trickiest of potions. He thought he could make out the exact emotional pathways Val used to strength her enchantments. With practice, he was certain he'd be able to read how Taye connected each musical note to a corresponding magical frequency. It was all there, everything and anything he would ever need to know about their wizardry. If knowledge was truly power, then this power was an intoxicating quagmire, indeed.

"You good, man?" Taye said, voice thick with wariness

Ari didn't answer. He was too preoccupied to respond.

Holy shit balls, but did Val know she was capable of massive spell work without uttering a single word? He only ever knew her to use audible invocations as her chosen medium, but it was obvious she didn't need it. If anything, he thought the verbal reliance might be holding her back.

His awareness of her wasn't limited to magical properties, either. The more he focused on the shiny new spot in his mind labeled "Valkyrie," the more he understood her wants and needs. Some conflicted with each other in the purest wizample of human nature, but within the tangled mess was a host of profound possibilities.

"Sweetie, you need to breathe," Val insisted, kneading his shoulder.

With all he could see and understand now, Ari was certain

he could guide her into becoming so much more than she was.

"Ari?"

He could do it for all of them, like he was the key to unlocking their most fulfilling futures. Their potential was dizzying as it painted pictures of groundbreaking magics and incredible lives. It made Ari itch to do something, anything, with the knowledge he now possessed.

For the first time, Ari realized why Morrigans were so revered. No one would ever know his coven members and their true capabilities half as well as he did.

"Ari, you need to calm down."

"I'm fine," he murmured, sitting back on his heels to catch his breath.

That was when he noticed the stones. His collection of magically charged gems lay in the grass beside the book, still open to its useless pages. With a shaky hand, Ari reached for the nearest one.

"I can hear your heart racing," Val pouted nearby.

Ari plucked the little onyx from the grass and the others rose with it. They were connected. At first, Ari marveled at the dark chain that materialized between the stones when he wasn't looking. Then Dazzle turned on his cell phone's flashlight and Ari noticed the deep, dark redness of the spontaneous necklace. Out of direct lighting, the links between stones looked black, but its true color was the exact redness of dried blood.

He had a freaking Morrigan amulet made from his own blood. He was a Morrigan.

As soon as the words took form in his mind, Ari noped straight out of there and passed the fuck out.

When he next awoke, Ari found himself tucked into bed and drowning in high-end sheets and feather down duvet like nothing special happened.

He bolted upright.

Not to be out shown by his dramatic ass, Val leaped into the air with a surprised wail. The sound was so human, it only added to the hilarity of Val's arched back and bristling fur as she landed back on the foot of his bed.

Ari couldn't stop the laugh that burst out of his mouth. Then he kept going till the hysteria made his abdominals ache and Val's ears and fur lay flat with mounting alarm.

The door flew open as Dazzle and Taye tumbled over each other to be the first into the room. Ari couldn't tell if it was luck or sabotage that sent Taye tripping onto the carpet, but Dazzle capitalized on it either way. Ari went from gut-wrenching laughter to having his face squished between Dazzle's manicured hands less than a full second after the door opened.

"What's wrong?" Dazzle implored in his best impression

of a mother hen. "Are you feeling delirious? Feverish? Queasy?"

"I'm fine!" Ari squirmed backward as he pried Dazzle's hands from his face. Glaring at the offending wizard, he rubbed his forehead where he could feel the dent left behind by the edge of a painted talon.

"I've watched you sleep in a non-creepy way for years, and I've never seen you sleep so long or so motionless. You are not fine," Val sassed, practically spitting out the last word.

"You were doing that glow bug thing again," Taye pipped up from the floor like a man begrudgingly accepting his fate.

Ari said, "Huh?" and Dazzle attempted to clear things up with a gentle smack upside his head. Glaring, Ari grunted out a baffled, "Ow?"

"Why didn't you tell us you were possessed by Magic itself!" Dazzle demanded.

"Kind of a big deal, Ari," Val scowled in agreement.

Face and mind going blank under their displeased attentions, Ari said, "Oh. Oops?"

Out of the corner of his eye, Ari saw Taye's head pop up over the side of the bed wearing a dour expression.

"I gave them all the details you left out from the night I showed you the nemiza," he explained. Then with an obvious note of accusation, he added, "You know, since you were incapacitated for three days and unable to answer their questions your damn self."

Ari balked. "I was out for three days?"

"That's what I said," Taye grumbled as he folded his arms atop the mattress's edge. "It's Tuesday."

Ari gasped.

"Ari!" Dazzle shrieked as he shoved Ari's shoulder. "Focus on the bigger issue here!"

Val backed him up by hopping onto Dazzle's knee and

staring deep into Ari's eyes like she was hunting for hidden clues. "How long has this hostile takeover thing been happening?"

Ari shied away from the cat whiskers tickling his nose. "It's really not as big a deal as you're making—"

"Magic doesn't go around taking over people all willy nilly!" Dazzle cried. "Demonic possession is way more likely!"

"Not that we're saying you were possessed by a demon," Val interjected with a quick scowl at Dazzle.

"But we can't rule it out."

"Yes, we can," Taye sighed and bonked his forehead down on his folded arms. Clearly, this wasn't a new argument between the two wizards.

Dazzle rolled his eyes in a way that suggested he would rather be beating sense into Taye instead. They didn't know Taye well enough to judge how he'd react to Dazzle's flippant physicality, but it didn't take a genius to guess Taye could wipe the floor with Dazzle's scrawny butt if he wanted to. Ari thought the eye rolling was a good alternative.

Undeterred, Taye raised his head to look Ari in the eye. "Every magic user knows demons are deceptive, but they have their limits. They can't channel the kind of power you generated the other night without a clear contract with a consenting mortal."

"I'm aware, thanks," Ari snarked before turning his glare to Dazzle and Val. "And that's precisely why I never felt the need to worry you about it sooner."

Dazzle was too caught up in the anxious novelty of the matter to remember the basics. Demonology 101 was an absolute must if a person was going to integrate their life with the magical community, and neither potion brewers nor Drag Queen made an exception.

Ari's disappointed stare intensified as he waited for Dazzle to explain himself.

Dazzle flushed and avoided direct eye contact. In his favorite pride tee and gray sweats, he looked uncharacteristically soft and vulnerable. The near bashful hunch to his body language was one step too far in the wrong direction for Ari to handle.

He didn't need the newfound insight of a Morrigan to know what Dazzle needed most from him, but it was nice to have his instincts magically corroborated.

With a cleansing sigh, Ari opened his arms.

Dazzle dove into Ari's chest. Val wasn't far behind him, shoving her head up under Ari's raised arm to get in on the snuggles.

They were an affectionate bunch, Ari and his two best friends. They hugged and cuddled more than was common, and Ari would never claim not to enjoy the easy contact after an adolescence spent without it. Even so, Ari could count on his fingers the number of times he was the one to initiate said contact.

Naturally, Ari felt Val's fur tickle his armpit, and he finally realized he wasn't wearing pajamas or the outfit he wore out into the forest. In fact, he wore nothing but a pair of his usual briefs and one bloody necklace full of precious stones.

The later was a concern for another day, but the former . . .

"Which one of you fuckers undressed me?"

The room cleared out so fast, he would have suspected Magic if he hadn't known better.

ARI'S FIRST WEEK AS MORRIGAN TO A COVEN OF WIZARDS was both underwhelming and an exercise in patience. It was a relief to get back to the shop and immerse himself in work, but it didn't go as smoothly as he hoped.

He was late opening the shop on Wednesday due to the unprecedented coma, and more than a little pissed to discover he'd slept through two whole work days as well as his only day off. According to Val and Dazzle, they tried opening the shop on Saturday while Taye played nursemaid, and the mere idea horrified Ari beyond his ability to handle further details.

Writing the extended weekend off as a loss, Ari marched over to Grimoires and Goodies with a determined clip to his steps. He threw himself into the shop, going in early and staying late in an effort to catch up on things. His guilt over the unexpected closure had him overcompensating in his customer interactions, and he went a bit overboard in stocking the pastry cabinet each day.

It was a flurry of activity, and Ari reveled in it. His wizards, however, did not.

Ari didn't notice it immediately. His little band of misfit wizards followed him to and from the shop like besotted ducklings, and Ari made a concerted effort not to overthink it. Neither Val nor Dazzle showed any interest in attending their day jobs, and Taye clearly had nothing better to do, so Ari chalked it up to their collective anxiety over his recent incapacitation.

Their worry was sweet, in a way, though unnecessary.

It got old fast.

By late afternoon on Friday, Ari was fed up with them. He couldn't leave the register or go take a piss in his own apartment without tripping over someone. When he exited the shop's kitchen to find all three of them vying to reach the employees only door first, Ari knew something had to be done.

Without a word, Ari strode toward the nearest empty table. His wizards followed without missing a beat.

"Sit," Ari ordered Taye and Dazzle as he pulled out a chair.

He bent down to sweep Val off her feet. She squawked at him with affront that was just humanoid enough to make a few mundane shoppers glance over in disturbed bewilderment.

"Stay," Ari added as he plopped Val onto the table. He took care to make eye contact with each troublesome wizard before storming off to the register.

With three sharp taps to the service bell, Ari had the full attention of the shoppers.

"My apologies, everyone, but I have a private buyer coming in for an impromptu meeting."

Ari beamed about the shop as he reached behind the consumables display to retrieve a tray full of fresh baked cookies. They materialized at his fingertips beneath the counter's coverage, as if Ari did anything more than wish he had something to compensate his customers.

"Please bring your chosen items to the register and grab a cookie on the house. Thank you for your understanding."

Beside a few unhappy sighs and low grumbles, the shop emptied at a nice and easy clip. Several people abandoned their merchandise on random shelves in favor of slouching straight out the door with cookies in hand, but several more took the time to set their desired items on the counter with a smile and promise to return later. Ari rang up no more or less than four purchases, then he walked the final couple to the door with all the superficial pleasantries they might expect. He locked the door behind them with a cheerful wave.

Then he rounded on the two men and one cat sitting in the shop like naughty children resigned to an undeserved time out.

"What's this about?" Ari demanded with his hands on his hips. "I've been back on my feet and back to work for days now. I think we can ease up on the babysitting, right?"

As he spoke, Dazzle began scowling with his legs crossed and one hand of neon blue nails tapping at the table in aggravation. When Ari's speech wrapped up, Val and Taye started exchanging looks full of an understanding Ari wasn't privy to.

"What exactly do you think we're worried about?" Dazzle asked with a sharp edge.

Ari's shoulders slumped. His mouth dried out in a hurry as he began to suspect he'd misinterpreted the situation.

Taye pushed his chair from the table as he stretched his legs and slouched with his arms folded. Frowning down at nothing, he said, "I'm going to go out on a limb and say Ari's somehow missed a few critical points in all the research we did leading up to the ritual."

"Obviously," said Dazzle.

"Ari, don't you know what a Morrigan does?" Val implored.

Ari laughed and tossed up his hands. "Seriously?"

"I'm not asking what you think their role is or whatever Fuckman taught you. I mean the actual job description."

He paused to give the idea due consideration. No one was more surprised than Ari as he realized he hadn't bothered to read up on Morrigans beyond the fact that one needed to be designated for the coven to form. His dismay must have shown on his face, because suddenly he was witness to the disconcerting spectacle that was synchronized eye rolling.

When the fuck did Taye get so cozy with Val and Dazzle

that he could mimic their mannerisms to perfection? On that note, why in Mother Earth's good graces had Val and Dazzle decided to adopt Taye's inclination for severe frowns and no nonsense?

It must have happened while he was unconscious, Ari decided. It was the only explanation.

It was also the wrong explanation.

"In case you missed this too, we're magically bonded now," Dazzle said with a huff. Slow and deliberate, he lifted a blue tipped finger and used it to draw a circle that encompassed the four of them. "All of us, sweetness. This isn't just about you."

Ari made the smart decision to join them at the table then. "Alright. I'm listening."

"Wait," Taye said, halting Dazzle's next words in their tracks. Hazel eyes locked on Ari, Taye reached into the backpack he'd been carrying all week and pulled out the least welcome book of Ari's existence. "Can you read it now?"

With stiff motions, Ari opened *A Divergence of Magic* to a random page. It remained blank to his eyes.

"No can do," Ari admitted with forced levity. "Why?"

With a disappointed frown, Taye returned the book to the bag. "Guess you're still not ready for what it has to say."

Ari refused to admit how much that hurt. Chin lifted, he diverted attention to Val. "You asked me about Morrigans."

She nodded with an uncertain bite of her lip that displayed a prominent fang.

Sighing, Ari explained the impression he cultivated over the years with as little censure as possible.

"The Morrigan is the leader of the coven," he said. "They tend to be the most magically gifted witch around, and the most likely to use"—he bit his tongue to stop the words 'and abuse' from passing his lips—"the supplemental power of the other coven members. They typically hold authority over the others, in whatever capacity they can—"

He stopped himself again. It was easier since this time since Val coughed to give him a fucking clue.

"In my experience," he tried again, shooting her a tight smile, "Morrigans are the ultimate power in their coven's eyes, and their own. They have a more distinct connection to Magic, which is often confused with an increased ability to interpret universal movements, fate, the future, or whatever other term you want to use. But no matter how they portray themselves, they're no more inherently omniscient then the rest of us."

The frown in Taye's resting bitch face grew deeper and deeper with every word out of Ari's mouth. "So, the covens treat them like prophets?"

Ari shrugged. "If that's what you want to call it."

"I don't," Taye declared, as if disgusted.

"Well, I can't speak for Fuckman, or his kind," Val said, "but that's not quite the picture I got from researching the ritual."

"And it's certainly not what we need from you," Dazzle added with a relieved little laugh.

Val chuckled too, but Ari failed to see the joke.

Taye's toe tapped his under the table. With a blatant smirk on his face, Taye said in a stage whisper, "You'd make a terrible spiritual leader."

Feeling like his head was caught in spontaneous combustion, Ari reared back. The table erupted into hearty laughter, and though it wasn't an effect Ari intended, he was happy to take credit for it. The sound filled him with a simmering warmth and the longer it lasted, the lighter he felt. It was like a weighted blanket slipping off his shoulders, one hefty inch at a time.

It didn't feel inherently magical. Perhaps that was why it took him so long to realize it was.

Ari's breath hitched as understanding rammed into him at full speed. "I've been neglecting my coven, haven't I?"

Their good humor faded with pronounced reluctance. Taye winced and avoided looking at him, but Val and Dazzle sent him those annoying smiles that said it was nice to see him pulling his head out of his ass for a change.

It was Ari's turn to laugh, and the sound carried more self-deprecation than he was familiar with. "Less than a week in, and I'm already failing at this."

"It's one setback," Val assured as she scooted over to brush her cheek against his shoulder. She bobbed her head in invitation, and Ari reached out to rub behind her ears. She purred, and he knew he was forgiven.

"You never planned for this," Dazzle sighed. "I think you can afford to give yourself some slack. Moving forward, we just need to find a better balance between the coven and the shop."

That was the crux of the problem, Ari thought. It was the very reason he never held any vested interest in covens or any romantic relationships, for that matter.

Ari's life revolved around Grimoires and Goodies. For as long as he could remember, the shop was either his deepest dream, or his dearest reality, but always his passion. Hell, the only reason he didn't work every single day was because Sunday's cost more than they earned and burnout was a real thing.

Looking around at all the cautiously hopeful faces seated at the table with him, Ari knew there was no going back to the way things were. Val and Dazzle would no longer be content with visiting him for an hour at the store while Ari worked, and supplementing missed quality time with the rare drunken night at Gladys's. Taye seemed the sort to never tolerate that kind of low prioritization in the first place.

Ari ran a shaky hand through his hair and muttered a sour, "I'm sorry, guys."

Val hopped from the table to his lap with such force that Ari's chair rocked onto its rear legs. For one heart-stopping moment, Ari flailed in anticipation of a painful crash to the floor, but it never came.

Taye's hand came down on the edge of Ari's seat and pinned the chair back on all fours. As Val released a boisterous laugh of relief, Ari's focus darted from Taye's discerning stare to the hand emanating warmth beside his outer thigh.

"You're welcome," Taye whispered before retrieving his hand.

This was going to be the biggest change of his life, Ari realized as he watched a self-satisfied smirk cross Taye's lips. On the sidelines, Val was still cackling in wake of the close call, but Dazzle gave him an obscene wag of his brows while pointing his chin at Taye. Such covert messaging wasn't usually within Dazzle's wheelhouse.

So many changes, Ari thought in dismay. So much chaos. Unpredictability. There was no way he would manage to navigate it all gracefully after so many years of micro managing and compartmentalizing his life.

For the sake of his coven, if not his own, Ari hoped he was wrong.

CHAPTER 14

*A*ri's mood plummeted within seconds of unlocking the store the next morning. New signage adorned the door, dictating new weekend hours. Ari had no memory of approving nor creating such a sign. It seemed Magic agreed with his wizards and had taken it upon itself to announce that starting next weekend, Grimoires and Goodies would be closed on Mondays.

On the one hand, Ari supposed he could use an extra day off each week. On the other, however, he was pissed to see business decisions being made without him. The only reason he didn't fly into a rage was because the culprit had no corporeal form and just so happened to be a presumably insurmountable power.

Still, Ari needed some kind of outlet for his impotent ire. Now that Ari had promised to make himself more available after working hours, Dazzle and Val finally deigned to return to their day jobs. This left Taye as the only available target for Ari's temper, and he seemed set on testing it.

"No, you may not touch my register," Ari snapped the second time Taye suggested he take over manning the counter so Ari could catch up on his Morrigan reading. "If you're so concerned about it, then make yourself useful by bookmarking the relevant pages for me to read. I'll deal with it on my break."

Taye started to slouch off in defeat, then paused to shoot Ari a deviously hopeful smile. "And while you're on break?"

"No!"

Ari soon learned the best way to keep Taye from pestering him was to assign specific tasks with an open ended time frame to make good on. The wizard was relentless once he set his mind to a given problem. He stayed out of Ari's hair the entire morning, but the price was a mountain of books and scrolls waiting for him in the back room. Taye was nothing if not thorough.

"Still think you can fit it all into your fifteen minute break?" Taye asked with an obnoxious smirk that sang "Na-ni-na-ni-na-na" straight at Ari's face.

Ari glared back. "Just for that, you can make my lunch while I tackle this mess."

He did not finish before it was time to reopen the shop for the afternoon. In fact, he barely managed to skim through two of the texts. Taye was deplorably smug about it.

Ari wished he could hate him, but he had a weakness for a strong jaw paired with ample sarcasm.

Worse yet, it proved impossible to hate anyone when Ari was so overwhelmed with absorbing info and rewriting misconceptions.

The more he read, the more he realized how warped Morgana the Fey's intentions became in the centuries since her death. The books didn't describe Morrigans as the vaguely religious cult leaders they always seemed to portray in real life. Instead, Ari's lunchtime perusal revealed an image of a humble adviser, not a superior authority. Of the two books he had time for that day, the first described the ideal Morrigan as the witch most in tune with the energies of the world and, as a consequence, someone with more frequent and significant insights than their peers. The second volume had less to say on the topic, but the author held clear respect for the Morrigan construct as "the best and ultimate line of defense" for any coven at risk.

The four volumes Ari brought home with him that night had more of the same to say on the subject. It was a long night of being told he was wrong over, and over, and over.

Ari went to bed with his lip gnawed raw and an emerging headache behind his temples.

His dreams were a tug of war between unhelpful memories and the emerging idea of a benevolent Morrigan. By all written accounts, a Morrigan should be a good person with the health and happiness of their coven as their first priority; Ari struggled to make this image fit with the power-hungry Morrigans he knew, the ones like Eren Puckman who weren't afraid to manipulate and bribe Ari into giving them his power.

Worse still, Ari struggled to see himself in such a role. It sounded like a lot of work for others' sakes.

Needless to say, Ari slept like shit.

The following day was much the same, with Ari's lunch including a side of history and precedent printed in black and white. That night, as Ari closed up shop, Taye selected another armful of research materials from the shop's inventory. The wizard no longer seemed so smug as he helped Ari carry them home.

~

"WHAT DID OR DIDN'T YOU DO, HONEY BOO?" DAZZLE ASKED a few days later.

Blinking sleep from his eyes, Ari unearthed his head from the pillows and frowned at his friends. He found Dazzle lounging on the foot of his bed with Val perched on his pinstriped knee.

"Shouldn't you be at work?" Ari asked, gaze darting from the clock to the sequined rainbow tie of Dazzle's professional attire.

"The office will be there whenever I show up," Dazzle said without concern. "I like to keep them guessing with my schedule. Unlike you, who I could set my watch to. And that's precisely why we're so concerned that you've suddenly taken to sleeping in late."

"Taye thinks you're mad at him," Val piped up in a hurry that suggested she'd been biting back the outburst for a while. "After a whole day of watching you mope with your nose in one book or another, I started thinking you were depressed. When you slept through your alarm for the first time in forever, I called Dazzle to help with an interrogation."

"Wow," Ari drawled, rolling over to dive back into the pillows. "Interrogation. I feel so loved."

"You should." Val pounced, landing on his butt with all four pointy paws, and he yelped. Snickering, the cat raised her voice over his shrieks. "Confess, witch!"

"Get off me!"

Unfortunately for him, this command had the opposite effect. It spurred Dazzle into joining the ridiculousness, and the next thing Ari knew, he was being attacked by hands and paws alike. They tickled him to within an inch of passing out from asphyxiation.

"You're supposed to be talking to me, not killing me!" Ari complained through wheezing laughter.

"No one told me that," Dazzle said as he rolled off the bed with an air of innocence. "Val's the one running this show. I'm just here for emotional support."

"And on that note"—Val planted a paw in the center of Ari's chest—"what's the deal? Shouldn't you be glad to know you're not obligated to become an egomaniac and semi-false idol?"

"Though if that's the route you want to go down, I'm totally here for it," Dazzle said with a meaningful nod over Val's head. "I kinda always wanted to join a cult."

Val craned her neck to stare at him.

"What?" Dazzle scoffed, "I'm not saying I'd drink the Kool-Aid, but it could be fun to hold a cup for a bit and do some mingling."

"Sounds fun," Taye commented.

Ari jumped and gaped at the wizard leaning against the door frame. "Where did you come from?"

"Your couch," he deadpanned.

"That was a stupid question," Val said with a sympathetic pat to Ari's cheek. "He's been hogging my favorite napping spot for over a week. Come on, now."

Dazzle perked up. "Ooh! Maybe you could witchcraft an extra bedroom into the place! Wouldn't that be a neat way to test the limits of rent control and our collective prowess at the same time?"

Val pranced in place with excitement. "Yes! And how practical too!"

"Or," Taye interjected with a long suffering sigh, "we could stop running our mouths off topic for a few minutes so we can get to the bottom of Ari's issues."

"Killjoy," Dazzle muttered as he gave Taye his most adorably conniving pout.

Unmoved, Taye pushed off the door frame and

approached them. He hesitated with a scant inch of space between his knees and the mattress, and Ari was struck with appreciation for the awkwardness. Taye was part of their coven, but he wasn't part of their friend group, not really. He didn't share their history or their impulsive humor. He wasn't one of them, but as he debated between crouching beside the bed or joining them on it, it was clear he wanted to be.

Ari patted the empty stretch of duvet next to him because it was the right thing to do, as a person and as a Morrigan.

Taye didn't react besides the briefest glance up at Ari's face, then he slid into place like he belonged there; and really, that was because he did.

"I didn't mean to worry you," Ari told them with a soft smile full of resignation. "I'm not depressed, just . . . processing."

It hurt to admit, but he didn't see any way out of telling them the cold, hard truth he so recently discovered about himself.

"Not sure if you guys have noticed, but I'm not exactly a people-person."

Taye snorted as Val and Dazzle exchanged unsurprised smiles. No one interrupted him.

"The more I learn about it, the more I realize how involved it is to be a Morrigan," Ari said with his eyes trained on where his hands toyed with the sheet on his lap. "It's not about power, or at least not just about power. It's intimate."

That would have been a perfect time to raise his head and make good and meaningful eye contact with each of them. Ari couldn't bring himself to do it, though. If he did, he had the feeling his eyes might start watering, and that degree of vulnerability was light years beyond his comfort zone.

"I almost wish I was stuck being an egocentric cult leader," he admitted with a dry laugh. "It'd be easier in a lot of ways. I'd probably hate myself for being like that, sure, but at least I wouldn't have to shoulder the responsibility of actually caring for the individuals in my coven—"

Taye interrupted with another irreverent snort. "Like you don't already?"

"Oh, honey," Dazzle said, "I always knew you weren't the most introspective guy, but delusional?"

Ari sighed and rolled his eyes heavenward in a bid for patience. With no other recourse available, he surged ahead.

"A Morrigan should do more than care," he added pointedly. "He should be doing something with all that caring. I'm more than your friend now. I'm supposed to be your adviser and protector. I'm supposed to actively make your lives better, and that's a lot of pressure."

The teasing undertone evaporated from the atmosphere. After a beat of silence, Val uttered a soft, "Oh."

Ari explained, "The basic commitment of joining a coven was a major turn off on its own, but now it's like I've been shoehorned into the heart of one. It's like being put up for a job you're entirely unqualified for, with a gun held to your head. You either make it work despite yourself, or you're dead. Literally, in our case."

He looked around the room, glancing past their ears and focusing on the wall or whatever happened to be directly behind each wizard at the time he passed over them. He was tactful about it, but he still avoided eye contact.

"I'm too selfish to do it right," he admitted. "I wish I had the capacity to put everyone else's needs first, or at least on an equal footing with mine, but I don't, and when I inevitably fuck this up, the few people I do care about will be the ones to suffer most."

He refocused on his lap before he had the chance to get

weepy. When he felt more or less composed, he kept his gaze where it was and began nodding to himself.

"This was a mistake," he thought aloud.

For a long, tense moment, he believed no one disagreed. His pride stung, but it was possible that was simply the only reactive emotion he was ready to name.

"What a load of crap," Taye spat.

Ari was braced for disappointment and shared misery from his coven, but the anger in Taye's voice brought him up short.

"Do you really think any of us would be here, voluntarily bonded to someone who couldn't step up to task?" Taye demanded, "Do any of us seem that stupid to you?"

"Damn," Val whispered, stunned. "He's got a point. And now I'm sad and pissed."

Ari sighed and rubbed at his temples where a weak ache was started to throb. "You're twisting my words."

"No," Taye said with a mirthless laugh, "I'm really not."

He didn't give Ari a chance to argue. Without a backward glance, Taye removed himself from the bed and stormed out of the room.

One down, two to go, Ari thought.

CHAPTER 15

The pity party didn't last long. Ari got a fruitful day's work done at the shop and imbibed half his weight in caffeinated beverages, and his good opinion of himself and his capabilities was well and truly restored in time for dinner that same night.

"I owe you an apology," Ari announced as the apartment door shut behind him.

Taye scowled at him from the couch. There was a smartphone in his hand and his long legs were stretched out, his ankles crossed with his feet propped on the coffee table like an absolute heathen. Unimpressed by Ari's general person, he returned his attention to the phone without a word.

Ouch.

At least Val paid attention to him. She was curled up in a fluffy loaf on the window ledge, sunbathing as she sent a pout his way.

Ari responded with a smile then cleared his throat as he approached the coffee table with loud steps. "I'm sorry for being a shitty, self-absorbed excuse of a Morrigan."

Val sighed and a slight smile tugged at her maw.

Meanwhile, Taye didn't look up. He uttered a lackluster "harrumph" with his lips pursed.

"I'm ready to do better," Ari said, "in case you were wondering."

"Hmm," said Taye, without so much as a twitch of an eyelash.

Ari rolled his eyes before grabbing Taye's ankles and redirecting them to the floor where they belonged. Taye did nothing to stop or assist the endeavor, and Ari despised how the limp weight forced him into an awkward shuffle.

"This is the oddest take on silent treatment I've ever witnessed," Val surmised as she watched from the window sill.

"You accept my apology, right, Val?" Ari said. At the same time, he dropped Taye's feet from about waist height so they landed on the floor with a resounding thud.

Taye grunted, but didn't otherwise react. Dammit, but Ari was tempted to smack him.

"I suppose," Val murmured as she returned her gaze out the window. "But only because I'm relieved to see you're back to your usual healthy ego. The shop reminded you who you were, I take it?"

Ari let her have her air of disinterest because he knew how fake it was. As always, she was meeting him in his comfort zone, safe and sound behind a wall of questionable humor and as far from sentimentality as they could get.

"I was contacted by a lovely witch from a coven in Ecuador today," Ari informed them with a proud lift to his chin and a smug grin. He was practically bouncing on the balls of his feet. "Guess who officially has a foot in the international market? This guy!"

Val's tail whipped up in excitement. "Look at you, fancy pants!"

Ari twisted at the waist to arch an expectant brow at Taye. His grin faltered when he was met with the blatant hostility in those hazel eyes.

"Good for you," Taye said with a thinly veiled sneer as he lurched to his feet and headed for the kitchen. "Really. It's great to know some foreign coven can give you all the props you apparently don't get from your own."

Ari gaped after him. "Run that by me again?"

"You heard me."

"Oh my god, just kiss already," Val begged.

"No," Ari said at the same moment Taye said, "Hell no."

After an awkwardly hurt moment, Ari decided not to take that one too personally. Maybe he should have.

"So, what's the grand plan to do better, as you say?" Taye demanded as he began riffling through the fridge. "I'm assuming it doesn't involve emigration, but only because it'd be ludicrous to suggest you go so far from your precious store."

Ari glared at Taye's turned back, bracing his fists on his hips like he was preparing for a confrontation. And really . . . yes, that was exactly what he was doing.

"If you'd pull that flaming glow stick of jealousy out of your ass, that'd be great. Thanks."

"Glow stick of jealousy," Val murmured. "Is that an actual relic, or are you just being an ass? I can't tell anymore."

Ignoring her, Ari marched over to the island counter that divided the living room from the kitchen and loomed over it till Taye gave in to the pressure and turned around to face him.

"I'm only human, and I'm allowed to have my moments of weakness, thank you very much."

"Sure." Taye shrugged, but his jaw was tight as he mirrored Ari's posture. "So, what's the plan then?"

"I vote for relieving some of the sexual tension before someone combusts!" Val chimed.

"First," Ari jabbed a thumb over his shoulder as he said, "we take her to the Humane Society to get fixed."

"Responsible pet ownership," Taye agreed with a stoic nod. "But then what? How do you expect to do all that caring you were worried about yesterday?"

Ari stood up straight and tall, rolling his shoulders back in sudden nervousness. It was a whole lot easier to feel confident when he wasn't staring back at the temper flaring in Taye's eyes. Ari was past the point of pretending he didn't know where it came from.

He was a Morrigan now. He could feel Taye's hurt, clear as day, and he knew the angry mask wasn't half as firmly set as the wizard would have him believe. Maybe Ari would have bought it if they were still strangers with no magical connection to speak of, but they weren't.

"You didn't come to me for a couch to sleep on," Ari said. "You came to me for help. Correct me if I'm wrong, but you weren't simply looking for someone to protect you from the mean witches and scary Council, were you?"

He hit the nail on the head with that sentence. Taye stepped back from the island with an almost imperceptible sigh and the tension fled from his body like it'd been doused in one of Dazzle's calming potions.

"I haven't forgotten you or your magic," Ari assured with a sheepish smile. "I just been a bit distracted."

Taye gave a slow nod and crossed his arms over his chest in a loose embrace. He backed up till the small of his back leaned against the sink's edge, studying Ari with a mild and unreadable expression.

"This is the part where you kiss and make up!" Val shouted from across the apartment.

"You got a cat carrier to transport her in?" Taye asked without a hint of a smirk.

THE REST OF THE WEEK PROVED SURPRISINGLY PRODUCTIVE after that. Now that Ari was done moping, he was energized by the prospect of a new and challenging project. Taye accompanied him to the shop for the next few days, and when business was slow, the two of them sat behind the service counter for lessons in theoretical witchcraft. While Ari managed the shop, Taye read through the very same texts Ari used years earlier for his own studies into the subject. Between customer interactions and preparing drinks, Ari would answer Taye's questions or regale him with stories of examples. In exchange, Taye let Ari work in peace without making eyes at the register, and he took it upon himself to make them lunch.

It wasn't till one evening when the foot traffic trickled down to nothing for long stretches of time that Taye started asking the difficult questions.

"So, does this make me your apprentice?"

Alarm slithering up his spine, Ari answered with a peevish, "If you like."

Then there was the time Taye asked, "Why don't you ever talk about your mentor?" When Ari made the mistake of admitting he never had one, it led to a whole slew of inquiries Ari wasn't prepared to deal with.

"Why not? Who would have been your mentor if you weren't so damn stubborn? How old were you when you realized Magic was real, and what did that even look like? Are there any other witches in your family? Is it, like . . . inheritable?"

There eventually came a point when Taye realized Ari was getting irritated in a definitively unfunny way, and the intense personal questions were set aside at last.

That wasn't to say all questions ceased.

"You're really self-taught?" Taye asked out of the blue as Ari locked up the shop one night. "Everything you know, it's all from books?"

Ari shot him a scowling side-eye. "Yes. That's been well established."

Taye scratched at the slight scruff sprouting from his chin. He'd taken to shaving his face and neck smooth lately, and Ari was miffed to find the five o'clock shadow more attractive than either the beard or the clean cut look. Taye didn't notice Ari glaring at the prickly growth on account of his own deep thoughts; he seemed to be debating on what he wanted to say.

"Have you ever tried a holistic communion ritual?"

Ari froze. Slowly, his eyes narrowed on Taye's innocent face.

"No," Ari lied. "Why?"

Taye smiled a soft, small smile filled with promise. "Would you try it with me?"

Ari blanched.

Taye's smile widened. "I've been thinking—"

"A dangerous practice for you," Ari sighed and relented, "but go on."

"It'd be nice if we were on an equal footing for my first real attempt at witchcraft," he said with a flippant shrug Ari didn't believe for a second. "A first for both of us, you know?"

Ari shook his head with a stilted laugh. "Now that really is a dangerous practice."

"Why?"

Ari shook his head and refocused on the cash in his hands.

"Ari?"

The disapproving insistence in Taye's voice rankled, and Ari found himself snapping over his shoulder. "Communing with Magic isn't something you do for your first foray into witchcraft. That's like letting a toddler jump head first into the deep end of a swimming pool."

"But—"

"No!" Ari seethed, shoving his hands into his pockets. "Start small, Taye. What you're asking for isn't as simple as a spiritual high, no matter what the books tell you. It requires control. Without it, you run the risk of losing your sense of self."

Taye's footsteps stalled. "I thought you said you never tried it."

"I've heard enough horror stories," Ari countered without looking back at the wizard. "Start small, Taye. Figure out how to direct your magic with intention instead of letting it rule you, then maybe we can talk about a communion."

TAYE TOOK HIM AT HIS WORD AND DEDICATED HIMSELF TO practicing his newfound magic. He no longer followed Ari to the shop every day, preferring the privacy of the apartment so he could work whatever Magic he felt the nerve to attempt.

As it turned out, Taye had a lot of nerve.

Ari came home one day to find the couch on fire and the apartment smelling of incense. Taye's little experiment with tarot cards had been disastrous, but at least the flames were contained in a magical bubble thanks to Val's mutterings in ancient Greek.

"It wasn't my fault," Taye insisted once the fire was out. "I was lighting a candle to help with the reading, and somehow Val knocked it over."

"I'll knock you over if you ever light my tail on fire again," Val said with a glower. "I was clear on the other end of the couch!"

Then another night, Taye discovered his comedic side and Ari's pad Thai became inedible half way through dinner. Taye claimed his incantation was only meant to increase the spice, but at least he had the decency to grovel his apology after Ari made him try a bite. He doubled down on the groveling when he proved unable to correct his miscast spell and Ari threatened to make him pay for the replacement dish. Olde Town wasn't known for its cheap cuisine, and the only Thai place within walking distance was well worth the sticker shock provided couch surfing bums didn't fuck around with the recipes.

Setbacks aside, Taye's control over his witch-like Magic did improve. Within a week of practical application and applying all the tricks Ari learned over the years, Taye's Magic no longer seemed exaggerated. Gone were the magical outbursts that risked exposure to the mundane world.

Taye's relief was palpable. The creases in his forehead seemed shallower, the circles around his eyes all but vanished. He seemed to move more freely, even when not practicing witchcraft. To Ari's Morrigan senses, he seemed lighter than air.

Then, before Ari knew what was happening, Taye moved beyond the need for the usual trappings of witchcraft. As if by instinct, he began tapping into the coven's collective power. Before long, he was effortlessly working Magic of the kind Ari himself could only manage in the heat of the moment.

The toilet paper roll was empty? No problem, Taye would replace it with a literal snap of his fingers. Val's coffee went cold? Taye simply gave the mug a tap, and it began steaming anew. A customer was prattling on too long and keeping Ari from attending other business? Well, it wouldn't be the first time Ari caught Taye narrowing his eyes at said customer with a focus that inspired the individual's bowels to rumble with urgency.

While the little displays of power were impressive and sometimes amusing, they were merely an example of Taye's growth. He learned to identify when Magic was trying to get his attention, and much like Ari, he figured out how to adapt to its unexpected outbursts. Magic had yet to teleport him into a whole different building, but Ari knew if it did, Taye wouldn't let it phase him. Perhaps that was why control came so easily to Taye.

Or maybe Magic was on Taye's side about the whole communion thing. Maybe it was helping him just to stick it to Ari and force him to face his issues head on.

Unfortunately for Taye, Ari had ample experience at curtailing Magic's schemes. He found other matters to attend to.

"Who joins a coven and refuses to acknowledge the Magic it gives them?" Ari huffed.

"Me," said Dazzle.

"Me," said Val. "It's not like I need more magic to be a house cat."

"Work-from-home cat," Dazzle corrected. "Give yourself some credit."

"True," Val purred. "I do pay half our rent."

"A third, actually," Ari commented. "But I digress. When are the two of you going to follow Taye's lead and start experimenting with your magic?"

They blinked at him like deer caught in headlights. Then they blinked at each other.

"Never?"

"I like the sound of never," Dazzle agreed.

"Never, then," Val told Ari with a definitive bob of her head.

Ari should have left it at that. The problem was, he could feel their joint boredom simmering in the back of his mind. It was a constant reminder that his coven was not meeting their potential, and worse yet, that they weren't entirely satisfied in other areas of their life. With Taye exuding determination and rolling satisfaction with every successful spell, Ari couldn't help feeling like the rest of the coven would benefit from doing likewise.

Also, whipping Dazzle and Val into productivity had far greater appeal than doing a holistic communion ritual with Taye.

"I can't just leave them disconnected from the coven's magic," Ari argued the next time Taye suggested he leave the others to their own devices. "Imagine if another coven tried to attack them with a nemiza. They'd be defenseless!"

Ari didn't actually think it was likely, but it sounded appropriately alarming. Hag Number Three and his coven had been quiet for some time, and no one else was speaking out against them like Ari and his friends were demons incarnate. Even the bruised markings on Taye's torso were beginning to fade, the black and blues turning to grays and greens. The Council of Wizards also had yet to address Ari since the encounter with Gaines. All was calm where the greater supernatural community was concerned, and Ari saw no reason for that to change.

Taye didn't think along those lines, though. He accepted

Ari's excuses with a minimal amount of grumbling, and Ari was free to focus his attentions on Val and Dazzle.

At least, that was the idea.

"I have a prior engagement," Dazzle said whenever Ari tried to corner him for a training session. "Rehearsals, you see. Dahlia Dazzle mustn't disappoint her fans!"

Meanwhile, Val wasn't half as convincing with her excuses.

"Management is insisting I be active on my computer for all billable hours," she claimed, "Tech support is such a competitive field, you know. I can't help that they're setting strict work hours that just happen to coincide with your evenings off."

It was a load of nonsense, and they both knew it. So long as Ari didn't bring up magic, his friends were more than happy to while away their evenings with a movie and pizza. A part of Ari even appreciated the quality time for what it was, but it didn't stop his awareness of their Magic from itching at the back of his mind.

As a result, Ari was wholly unrepentant when he kidnapped Val for the day one bright and unsuspecting morning.

"Why!" she whined as Ari deposited his tote bag beside the shop's cash register. The sides sagged to reveal Val, curled up in a protective little ball and glaring around the store like it personally offended her.

"Shush," Ari told her with a patronizing pat to her head as he donned his apron. "We're going to practice magic today."

"Good god, why?"

"Must you channel your inner teenager?" Ari asked as he stuck a hand in the pocket of his slacks. "Come on now, put your big girl pants on and maybe you can have this."

Ari held up a bundle of catnip roughly the size of a golf ball.

Val sat up straight. "I'm listening."

Grinning, Ari stashed the catnip in his apron and explained precisely how she could win it from him.

The goal was to get Val to explore the new limits to her magical abilities. She spent the past week watching Taye do precisely that with witchcraft's added flare, but Ari doubted she'd considered how the coven might affect her own wizardry. When Ari finished explaining that she had to get the catnip out of his pocket with magic but without using speech, there was a new twinkle in her eye. Finally, she entertained the idea of the coven as more than a precaution for Ari's and Taye's sake.

They spent the rest of the morning tackling the challenge. Val lingered close to the service counter as she struggled to find unintelligible noises that might take place of a spoken incantation. Her focus never strayed from Ari's pocket for long. Her odd behavior certainly garnered attention from the shoppers; more than one customer asked after her well-being, and one young lady even offered to ferry Val to and from a vet. Still, they saw no progress by lunch.

"Don't get hung up on the missing words," Ari whispered to her in between customers. "Focus on the intent, and assign your own vocalization to it. Make the sound with the same intention you would normally speak a preexisting spell."

Val didn't know it yet, but Ari planned to eventually get rid of the vocalizations all together. It was an exciting prospect, and seeing her chase it made him grin with pride.

It was the highlight of his day when Val loosed a loud, plaintive mewl and the ball of catnip wiggled in his pocket.

Ari turned his back on a teenager weighing her options between a pair of YA vampire romances and scooped Val up into his arms. Snuggling his face into her fur like any pet owner would their cat, he whispered, "Great job! You're nearly there."

But Val didn't share his excitement. Her claws dug into his shoulder as she issued another sharp meow into his ear.

Ari lifted his head to see the teenager drop the two novels on the counter before racing toward the exit. She wasn't the only one.

The shop wasn't bustling, but there were a fair few people milling about. All at once, each and every one was overcome with a need to be elsewhere. Books and talismans and all sorts of trinkets were left far from their proper homes, abandoned around the shop on whatever convenient surface seemed available.

In a matter of seconds, the shop was empty save for Ari and Val. They were alone.

CHAPTER 16

"Magic," Val hissed. "Amateur wizardry, if I had to guess. It smells like overkill."

Ari's heart lurched. For one wild moment, he wondered if his convenient fear-mongering over their presumptive enemies wasn't so far off. What if the wizards were trying to harm them now? What if the conglomerate of covens who tried to kill Taye were refocusing their energies on Ari's shop?

As if summoned by Ari's spiking anxiety, the employees only door burst open. Taye skidded through it, and for the briefest moment, Ari's living room was visible before the door slammed shut behind him.

"What happened?" Taye demanded, his hands in fists and partially raised.

Ari floundered, his mouth opening and shutting on repeat as he tried to explain. Before Ari's confusion could segue into a full-blown anxiety attack, Val launched out of his arms.

Her paws bounced off the counter, and she landed on the floor beyond, shouting, "Dazzle?"

Sure enough, Dazzle appeared from around the corner in

another one of his business outfits. While the purple tone of the slacks and jacket suited Dazzle to a T, Ari was nonplussed to see his friend in full Darren Davenport getup for the third time in as many weeks.

Dazzle burst through the doorway to Grimoires and Goodies in a flurry of long limbs. His motions were comically spastic, but Dazzle's apparent desperation to lock the door behind him was decidedly not.

"What's wrong?" Ari demanded.

"No idea," Dazzle panted as he tugged the lapels of his jacket straight. "Maybe nothing. Maybe something."

"So help me, Dazzle, I will throttle you if you don't spit out an explanation," Taye griped as he rolled his shoulders back and shook out his hands.

"Nothing happened," Dazzle insisted with paper thin conviction. "At least, nothing I can prove, but I think I was being followed."

Taye and Ari traded worried looks, but Val emitted a low growl as she hopped onto the table closest to the door.

She sat down with a heavy smack of her tail, glaring at the door as an eerie stillness overtook her. Her eyes scanned the street like she was searching for threats, and her sudden rigidity made her seem like a noble statue designed to ward off enemies. Not for the first time, Ari wondered why the supernatural community called her Lady Valkyrie; he asked her once, but after getting a non-answer that devolved into sex jokes, Ari never mustered up the nerve to ask again.

"Okay." Ari heaved a deep breath and beckoned them closer to Val. "Twenty seconds ago, I had a decent crowd of shoppers in here. Now I don't, and Dazzle's being followed. I'm neither optimistic nor stupid enough to call that a coincidence."

Dazzle's face turned red as his eyes widened. "Oh, shit."

Taye popped his knuckles against Dazzle's shoulder. "Explain."

Wincing away from Taye, Dazzle pulled a small object from his pocket, revealing a lopsided carving of a humanoid figure. "I think it's my fault. I activated this when I started feeling like I was being watched, about half a block from here."

Ari snagged the wooden token from his hand. It was rough and unfinished, but he could see the attempt at facial features and the folds of a robe. Whatever idol it was supposed to be, the piece was far from recognizable. The carving was either unfinished, or the carver was simply not very good.

Ari tilted the thing so Val could see. "Amateur work?"

She snorted. "Obviously."

"I got it from a friend who's still earning her certification," Dazzle defended as he snatched it back. "Good thing I commissioned her days before you brought this one home." Dazzle nudged Taye's arm with a pointy elbow as he gave Ari a heavy look. "She won't even talk to me now."

"Don't hold it against her," Val said coldly, her eyes still on the street. "We're not exactly the Council's favorite people right now. They might stonewall her certification if she did talk to you."

Dazzle heaved a lamented sigh, but he didn't seem to disagree.

"What's it do?" Ari asked, gesturing toward the figurine.

Dazzle looked around the shop with an awkward grin. "I asked for an obfuscation charm. It's supposed to help me hide from the notice of untrustworthy folks, but it looks like she overdid it."

Taye glanced between the other two wizards. "Couldn't Val have done that?"

"Nope," said Dazzle.

"Not my forte," said Val.

"Val's an enchanter," said Ari. "But she doesn't infuse materials with staying power."

"My medium is words," Val explained while maintaining her vigil. "I need spoken or written language to cast a spell—"

"So far," Ari interjected.

Rolling her eyes, Val continued, "And I'd have to be present to enact a one-off enchantment."

"Right," Taye said as he plucked the wooden doll from Ari's hand. "This is something Dazzle can reuse on his own. The woodcarving itself is your friend's medium?"

Dazzle nodded. "She started off trying to enchant those flattened pennies from tourist machines, but the magic takes better the more involved she is in the object's creation."

"Ah." Taye nodded with a more appreciative once-over of the doll. "I get that. My music works the same way. I can make a cover song work to keep a house full of drunk college kids under control, but I need my own compositions to do anything more impressive."

Under the impression Taye and Dazzle could talk shop all day if he let them, Ari cleared his throat to regain their attention. "So, who do we think was following you?"

Dazzle's head wobbled in uncertainty as he thought. "If I had to guess . . . a witch? Whoever it was, they kept out of sight, and they didn't immediately go away when I activated the charm. The feeling of being watched disappeared only once I had eyes on the shop."

"That's after the shop cleared out," Val commented. "Makes sense. Between the charm and witch Magic in general, I can see why a bunch of mundanes might feel pressured to leave."

"Not to mention my new wards and the intensity of our coven connection," Ari added, his anxiety finally settling down. The more they talked, the more he could believe the entire thing was a misunderstanding, just the coven reflecting Dazzle's panic and causing all sorts of alarms that needn't be blaring.

"Yeah, sorry," Dazzle said, his grin flushed as he scratched the back on his neck. "I guess I got carried away about nothing. You'd think I'd be used to being stared at by randos by now . . ."

"Sure," said Taye. "But hear me out now, maybe the mass exodus had nothing to do with your little trinket here."

Ari sighed. "You have a better idea?"

"How about the creepy Councillor staring at us from the doorstep?"

Dazzle spun around and promptly muttered, "Well, shit."

Ari had to maneuver around Val and the table to get a good look. Sure enough, when he pulled up between Taye and Dazzle, he found none other than Councillor Robert Gaines baring his teeth in an enraged grimace on the other side of the glass door.

"What happens now?" Taye whispered, as if Gaines were a boogeyman who already had his sights locked on his prey.

"We could run out the back?" suggested Dazzle.

"Fuck that," Val hissed as she flexed her claws. "I can take him."

"Don't be silly." Ari forced her arching back flat with a firm pet down her spine as he headed straight for the door. "We'll face him like the grown-ass adults we are."

"No offense," Dazzle murmured in the background as Ari reached for the lock, "but he doesn't look like he's here to talk things out."

Ari wasn't about to tell him, but Dazzle had a fair point.

Gaines looked livid, his teeth on full display as he seethed, rage in his bloodshot eyes. More alarming still was the peeling skin of his partially healed sunburn. He looked like a mummy who needed one last sacrifice to restore his body. From the way he watched Ari approach, he'd already selected the perfect victim.

His steps faltered, but Ari told himself not to be ridiculous. Gaines was one man, a trained wizard on the Council of Wizards, sure, but he'd already proven himself no match for Ari's wards.

Besides, unlike their last encounter, Ari wasn't alone.

He could feel his coven holding their breath behind him. It wasn't just the anxious tension suffusing the room, it was the kernel of truth Magic fed him on the peripheries of his awareness. In that moment, he knew them as well as he knew himself. Val was ready to fight, her paws itching to run and let her claws fly. Dazzle was a barely contained ball of determination and nerves, and Ari's own palms stung in sympathy for the way Dazzle dug his nails into his palms. Conversely, Taye was almost calm; he was resigned to whatever followed, but more than that, he was willing to back up whatever course Ari set for them.

With a steadiness he made a conscious effort to trust, Ari flipped the lock and opened the door.

"Good evening, Councillor. What brings you by this fine afternoon?"

Gaines sneered and jabbed a finger into Ari's chest hard enough to bruise. "Do you have any idea how long it took me to get out of that damn desert?!"

Ari blinked. Then he made the mistake of laughing out loud. It was a laugh of amazement that the Sahara rumors were factual. It wasn't a personal slight, but a bubble of tension bursting in the face of pure absurdity. Ari laughed because he needed to react to the confirmation that he had done something as incredible as banishing someone to the other side of the globe. He certainly did not laugh at Gaines.

The Councillor didn't seem to care about such nuances. Shrill and explosive, he yelled, "And now I come home to find you making a mockery of wizard kind with your so-called coven!"

Ari's head wobbled in a confused head shake as he weighed his options. "Honestly, I don't know what to tell you, Councillor. What's done is done, and it's probably for the best if we both leave it at that."

Ari had all of a second to prepare before the man issued a furious screech and lunged. A fist warped the collar of his shirt as Ari felt himself stumble backward. His shoulders hit a bookshelf, and Ari had the errant thought that he should really stop getting backed into corners like this by men so much bigger than himself.

This wasn't like the last time, though.

Between one heartbeat and the next, Gaines disappeared. It didn't happen in the literal sense, but Taye was quick and strong, and Dazzle fought dirty; the two of them yanked Gaines off him before Ari could think of being afraid.

The altercation didn't last long. Taye got an ankle behind the Councillor's leg and swept it out from under the man at the same time Val flung herself forward to dig claws into his thigh. As Gaines howled in pained surprise, the cat climbed his body till she could clamp her fangs on the prominent end of his chin. Gaines flailed too much in his attempt to dislodge her, so Ari didn't see exactly what happened, but Val disengaged right as Dazzle planted his knee in a deserving groin.

The Councillor went down hard, clutching himself and leaking blood every time he rolled his head from side to side.

Still situated against a random bookcase, Ari hooked his thumbs through his belt loops and hummed.

"I don't know how, but I am both underwhelmed and so incredibly proud."

Taye frowned at him. "Make that make sense."

"Eh. I don't think I will."

Ari didn't sense Magic working its will on him, but he didn't have a better explanation for why he moseyed on over to the wizard groaning and bleeding on his shop floor. He was running on instinct, or perhaps some kind of shock and belated sense of justice. No matter the reason, Ari heaved a long sigh and crouched down beside Gaines to give the fallen man's shoulder an awkward pat.

Magic didn't guide him, but it was there. Ari could feel it like white noise, floating along the edges of his awareness but easily overlooked if he wished. He didn't want to overlook it, though. Not this time.

"Was it you following my friend around, Rob? Robbie? It's cool if I call you Robbie, right? I think we've reached that point of familiarity by now."

Gaines didn't seem capable of a proper response. Still groaning and holding himself, he managed to raise a hand for the sake of nearly shoving his extended middle finger up Ari's nose. It would have been awfully embarrassing for them both if Ari hadn't leaned back when he did.

"Right," Ari said as he reached and reached for the Magic waiting for him to use it. "I'm guessing this day hasn't gone quite the way you planned. Am I right?"

With tears in his eyes, Gaines shook his head as he made a halfhearted attempt to stem the blood dripping from his face. He used his sleeve, and Ari realized the Councillor was wearing plaid and blue jeans, like any other dude off the street.

With a pang of disappointment, Ari took a moment to fully appreciate just how much he expected better from the Council, in many respects.

"This is going to be the last time we do this, Robbie."

The air vibrated with intent, and Ari heard a chorus of stifled gasps. His coven could feel the Magic and its agreeableness as crystal clear as he could. He didn't know if it was because of him or because of his wizards; regardless, he knew it was there for all of them, woven into the fabric of their little makeshift coven.

His conundrum was special like that.

It wasn't Magic who spoke through Ari's voice then. It was them, the spirit of who and what they were as a cohesive unit. He felt Taye's resolve and Val's righteous indignation as defined as Dazzle's impatience, or his own determination to see this conflict finished. This was long overdue by their collective standards, and it was good and right, and they were going to make it irrefutable.

Through him, the coven said, "We are done being bullied by you, or anyone else. You think yourself superior because you adhere to a code of strict conduct and division, but you're wrong. Your outdated ways don't give you strength. They hold you back."

Following his instincts, Ari set his hand on the Councillor's chest, directly over his heart.

Be it the touch or Ari's tone, Gaines finally caught on that something unusual was afoot. The wizard went still and hyper-focused on Ari like a rabbit who took a wrong turn into a face-off with a hungry wolf.

"You have misused your power for too long without consequence, Robert Bartholomew Gaines," the coven said, "and we've had enough."

Ari knew what he wanted to happen, but he wasn't

convinced it would until it did. The others shared in his doubt and surprise, and it was only right that they shared in his wonder when his desire manifested in a ruthless draw on the core of Gaines's magical affinity.

It wasn't easy, and it was far from comfortable. Ari's every muscle tensed as if he were ripping the supernatural abilities from the Councillor with his own two hands, forced to put his full weight into the act. It was an exhaustive spiritual task that couldn't help but impact his physical body. By the time Ari finished, there wasn't a part of him that didn't ache like he was days into a serious bout with the flu.

Panting, Ari removed his hand from the former wizard's chest. In the back of his mind, Ari felt Val's quiet pity blend with Dazzle's bitter triumph and Taye's somber satisfaction. They knew what he'd just done, and they approved, even if they weren't entirely happy about it.

"Good luck," Ari said as he stood. He struggled with his shaky legs, but managed a smooth transition and cool affect through pure force of will.

Gaines was, in a word, shook. He lay on the floor, shades paler than when he first showed up, and gaped up at Ari. At first, Ari couldn't make sense of the expression on the man's face; much like the plaid, it was so removed from any emotion Ari ever saw Gaines wear before.

Instead of begging for his powers back, Gaines crawled backward into a chair leg. He used the furniture to scramble to his feet without tearing his wide eyes from Ari's.

Belatedly, Ari recognized the look on Gaines's face for what it was: horror.

"What have you done?" Gaines accused, hatred beginning to twist his features.

Ari's gut churned with blooming dread, but he didn't

show any outward reaction. Stoic, he said, "I'm banning you from the shop, Robbie."

"I don't give a shit about your damn shop!"

Gaines took a stumbling stomp toward Ari, but halted in his tracks when Taye darted between them.

"Walk away while you still can," Dazzle sang from the sidelines as Taye crossed his arms and glared, acting for all the world like Ari's appointed bodyguard.

"Don't think I won't bite your ankles," Val added as she trotted up to Taye's side.

Gaines glanced at Val before returning his stare to Ari, eyes narrowed with scorn. He opened his mouth to say something pointless, so Ari lifted his chin in a silent dare. Apparently, that was one threat too far for Gaines.

The Councillor ran for it.

"Huh," Ari said in the unassuming quiet left being in the wake of all the excitement. "Who knew Robbie was a track star in another life?"

Val heaved a long suffering sigh as Dazzle burst into relieved cackles. No one commented further as Taye hurried to bolt the door shut with trembling hands.

Robbie Gaines wasn't the only one disturbed by their apparent victory.

CHAPTER 17

*D*azzle slept over that night. Taye wasn't thrilled to see Dazzle claiming half of Ari's bed, and he made sure to let everyone know with all his glaring and grumbling. Even so, Taye never suggested Dazzle should go home to sleep in his own bed.

There was safety in numbers. After the little showdown at the shop, none of them knew what to expect next, be it from the Council or themselves.

When Ari returned to Grimoires and Goodies on Saturday morning, he did so with a full entourage in tow. At first, Ari felt silly and a tad paranoid for bringing the three wizards to work with him, but before long, he found himself glad to have the company.

The clocked chimed eleven o'clock in the morning, and Ari had a whopping four customers to show for the whole morning.

"Bit slow for a Saturday, isn't it?" Val commented from where she lay curled up in the window display. She didn't bother to keep her voice down; it wasn't like any mundane ears were around to hear the miraculously talking cat.

The four of them were the only souls in the building.

Dazzle sat at the corner table with an open book in his lap, but he lifted his eyes to glance around the shop. "Damn." He leaned out of his chair to eye the grandfather clock and winced. "There hasn't been a single wizard in all morning, has there?"

"Noticed that, did you?" Taye snarked as he slipped behind the service counter to retrieve a croissant from the glass case. "I think that one lady was a witch though."

"She was," Ari admitted as he swatted the arm holding the stolen pastry.

Taye gave a nonplussed stare. "It's not like anyone else is eating it."

Groaning, Ari threw up his hands and spun back to his lonely vigil at the checkout. Pouting, he said, "She bought an enchanted cookbook, but she wouldn't say a word or look at me the entire time I rung her up."

"Who?"

Ari glared at Taye for his inattentiveness. "The witch."

"Oh."

While Taye munched on his misbegotten snack, Dazzle returned to his book and Val resumed people watching via the window. Ari was left to glare uselessly at his otherwise lifeless shop.

"Screw it," Ari huffed before abandoning the counter.

Ari felt Taye staring at his backside the entire way to the backroom. When he returned, Dazzle and Val were seated together at the table nearest the register, their interest perked. When the wizards saw what Ari came back with, all three of them burst out laughing.

Ari raised the pointed witch's hat in one hand and the birch broom in the other, then addressed Val and Dazzle. "Your choice: you can stand on the corner like my fucking mascot and offer free pastry samples to anyone who walks by, or we can lock up early and learn a thing or two about what a coven can do for your magic."

It was a gamble. Even with the Gaines situation lingering around them like the stench of a fresh turd, Ari wasn't sure which way Val or Dazzle would go. An argument could be made that the encounter with Gaines proved they could handle themselves in a conflict more than sufficiently. Ari was ready to rebuttal that point, though, since there was no telling how that might have gone if any one of them had been on their own.

Fortunately, the argument didn't need to be aired.

"Put those silly props away," said Dazzle. "I'll get the door."

ARI WISHED HE COULD SAY THINGS GOT BETTER OVER THE weekend, but they didn't.

For the first time since Grimoires and Goodies opened to the public, Ari was starting to worry about breaking even at the end of the month. There was still decent foot traffic, but it consisted almost entirely of mundane tourists and window shoppers. The few witches and wizards who came through the door were quick to grab what they wanted, and each and every one gave Ari a wide berth; if they could have paid without interacting with him, Ari was certain they would have.

Whatever the supernatural grapevine had to say about the shop's owner and his friends, it was sure to be nothing good.

It was distinctly possible a passing witch or wizard noticed the closed sign and heavy privacy drapes obscuring the shop several afternoons in a row. Ari didn't want to draw any mundane notice as he and Taye taught Val and Dazzle how to draw on the coven's collective power, but that didn't mean the community wasn't aware. With any luck, they assumed Ari's coven was shaping up to be a force no one would want to tangle with.

That assumption was blatantly wrong, but Ari wouldn't be the one to tell them.

"I'm not a witch!" Dazzle bemoaned for the thirtieth time that day. "You can't expect me to visualize magic like one, so just stop!"

Such comments usually devolved into circular arguments where Ari tried to convince Dazzle to try again, and Dazzle would reiterate the point that there was nothing for him to try. Simply put, Ari couldn't understand why Dazzle didn't want to connect with the coven the same way himself, Taye, or Val did; in turn, Dazzle insisted it wasn't a matter of want, but a matter of ability. Neither of them were satisfied with the other's perspective, and it ultimately went nowhere.

At least Val was making progress. Over the course of a few days, her affinity for enchantments went from complete dependency on spoken words to the slightest rumbling growl. It made Ari glad she was on his side in the growing conflict; spontaneous magic was scary on its own, but when the only warning was the low purr of a potentially murderous feline, it became the stuff of nightmares.

It also did nothing to improve their reputation among the supernatural community, but that was a concern Ari was steadfast in avoiding.

Dazzle inevitably called it quits and insisted on returning to his day job. Val followed suit just in time for the Coloradan weather to take a nasty turn.

"This is a giant waste of time," Taye said on the fourth

afternoon in a row of close to no customers. "Why don't we close the shop and go do something worthwhile?"

Ari snorted, but all the downtime was getting to him too. "What did you have in mind?"

It was hailing again, and ice the size of quarters falling from the sky meant no pedestrians. No pedestrians meant no window shoppers likely to wander in to satisfy their curiosity. That week, the handful of witches who braved the rain to stop by were in and out with their minimal spending, and Ari could count on his fingers the number of wizards who frequented the shop. Be they supernatural or mundane, none of the scarce patrons seemed flush with cash, and if they were, they certainly weren't flaunting it at Grimoires and Goodies.

Ari never expected to miss Hag Number Six so much. One visit from her, and he'd probably be able to afford the shop's property taxes for another few weeks.

"I want to try that communion ritual," Taye said.

Ari stiffened.

"You said we'd talk about it after I got my magic under control," Taye added before Ari had a chance to shoot him down.

Without missing a beat, Taye leaned over the service counter to let his wriggling fingers dance over the side of the pastry display case. The rows of muffins and Danishes went stale hours ago, but they fluffed up to freshness at Taye's silent request. Within seconds, Ari saw the condensation collecting on the glass from the reheated pastries.

"As you can see, I have it under control." Taye grinned.

"Nice try, but no. You need to be surrounded by nature and open air for a communion." Ari's scowl deepened as he tilted his head toward the windows. "I'm not going out in that."

Taye turned to watch the rain and hail cracking against the glass. "Okay, fair point, but the forecast says this weekend should be beautiful."

Damn it all, but Ari didn't immediately say no.

"Look around, Ari," Taye said with a soft, sympathetic smile. "You don't have anything better to do."

Stepping back from the register, Ari hugged himself and said, "It's still dangerous."

"The chances of both of us getting lost in the magical slipstream are slim," Taye countered as he rested his forearms on the counter between them. He looked up at Ari through his lashes with the most beguiling smile. "I trust you to bring me back to myself if things go sideways. Can't you trust me to do the same?"

Ari hesitated. Against all his better judgment and past experiences, he hesitated. Maybe it was that stupid half smile on Taye's stupidly perfect face that made him consider it. Ari always did have a problem thinking clearly around obnoxiously handsome men.

Taye Osondu wasn't Eren Puckman, though.

"Okay," Ari breathed out in surprise. "We can try it this weekend."

ONCE UPON A TIME, THERE WAS A BOY WHO QUAKED IN FEAR of himself. He didn't know Magic for the undeniable element it was, only for the risks and inconveniences it caused. He didn't know it was a part of him, didn't want to know it was ingrained in him as surely as his mother's dry humor or his father's blue eyes. He didn't remember much about his parents, and it seemed wrong somehow that this unknowable force of nature was so prominent in his life when they weren't. He didn't know what Magic could mean for him.

He only knew he wanted it to go away.

With this sole goal in mind, the boy sought out his first witch acquaintance. He accepted the first hand that was offered to him. He didn't know any better, especially when said hand arrived attached to the strong male role model he didn't know he needed. All he knew was that this kind, handsome witch was willing to help him. He made promises of relief from an overwhelming force and a network of witches to help young Ari shoulder the load.

That wasn't reality, though. Not back then.

Ari never told Val or Dazzle about the holistic communion he suffered through with Puckman's coven. It went down long before they came into his life, like ancient history best left forgotten.

Perhaps that was the reason his friends seemed so happy to send him on his way out the door for an evening alone with Taye. They didn't know any better. So it was, with Dazzle's car keys in hand and Val's fur decorating his lounge pants, Ari let Taye lead him out of the apartment.

"You can never do this at home," Ari lectured as they walked between the trees. "Low level spells and potions can be done indoors, but the more intense stuff requires proximity to Nature. It's a lot like how a coven can share power more freely the closer they are physically."

"I remember," Taye assured as he brought up the rear with the bag of items Ari packed earlier that week. "That's why we were sitting in the dirt for the coven ritual."

The snarky tinge to that comment made Ari glance back with an arched eyebrow. "Did you want it to fail? Because we could've done it at the shop and kept the backside of your jeans clean, but it would've certainly failed."

Snickering, Taye latched on to the entirely wrong part to counter, "Been thinking about my backside, huh?"

Huffing, Ari marched forward in silence.

They were hiking into the wooded area adjacent to a local park. It was far closer to home than the glade they used for the coven creation, and if Ari strained his ear, he could still detect the noise of the city. The light pollution wasn't ideal either, but it was acceptable for their purposes.

Besides, if they were found by any late-night park goers in the midst of this ritual, they were likely to be mistaken as high as a kite or drunk off their asses. The risks of exposure were slim.

Ari didn't stop walking till he stumbled upon a great big oak tree. Its branches were many and spread a wide net that blocked out the sky. Its roots were just as vast, popping up out of the ground in large mounds. It was perfect.

"Here?" Taye asked.

"Unless you spotted somewhere more comfortable and didn't bother to tell me."

"So sassy," Taye muttered as he dropped his backpack to the ground. He took a knee to open the bag so they could set up for the ritual.

They worked in tandem, moving around each other in harmonious silence. Taye proved himself an adept student who needed no direction beyond what he'd gleaned over recent weeks. Using the natural landscape, they set out twelve white candles to represent peace and clarity, and nine jasper stones to encourage connection and amplify Magic's influence on the earthly plane. Once everything was laid out and firmly balanced either on a smooth stone, leveled tree root, or nestled in the grass, then and only then did Ari choose a place to sit.

Already a step ahead, Taye sat cross-legged at the base of

the oak tree. The intersection of two roots with the trunk made an ideal resting spot, and Ari's chest constricted with a single jealous pang for how cozy Taye looked.

Staring around with his hands on his hips, Ari sought another welcoming seat. As he did so, the ground began to shiver. It was such a slight, localized tremor that he almost didn't notice it through the soles of his shoes.

"Woah," Taye whispered as the shiver spiked to a rumble.

Ari missed the start, but when he turned back toward the grand oak, he found Mother Earth rearranging herself. The soil rolled like ocean waves and the tree roots writhed with the flexibility and liveliness of snakes. It wasn't a flurry of action, but a steady dance that rearranged the ground.

Taye laughed as the forest floor ebbed and flowed beneath him. A sudden bump knocked him off balance till he fell back into the groove where a mighty root curled up to loop around him like a lover's arm. As Ari stared in amazement, there was a powerful groan, and the root on Taye's other side rolled sideways to create extra space.

Stunned and a little breathless, Ari shook his head and joined Taye at the foot of the oak tree. He'd never felt ground so comfortable before.

"Did you do that?" Taye asked, staring at him with near childlike wonder, as if he fully expected Ari to be responsible for the display.

A large part of Ari wanted to take the credit, too. The idea wasn't quite so appealing when Ari realized how close he and Taye were situated. For fuck's sake, but the curving tree roots almost formed a heart shape.

"Not me," Ari hurried to admit. "But I think Magic likes the idea of this communion almost as much as it likes playing matchmaker."

He should have known better than to make eye contact

then. Taye didn't seem to find the idea nearly as humorous as Ari thought he should, judging by the intensity of his expression.

"You're a mess."

Ari balked. "Thanks?"

Taye threw his head back and laughed. "You're like a walking contradiction. Half the time, I think you're super into me, only for you to keep shooting me down at the slightest overture."

Ari flushed and looked away. "That's not—"

"Between your curated wardrobe and anal retentive approach to business, you make a better wizard than anyone else I know," Taye pressed on, waving a hand at their surroundings. "But then I get you out here, and you relax like you're coming home for the first time in ages. You know that healthy glow pregnant women get? That's you right now."

Brow raising, Ari crossed his arms and leaned back. "Interesting," he deadpanned, "seeing as I will never be pregnant nor a woman."

Taye kept on laughing as he stretched out on the ground, ankles crossed and interlaced fingers tucked behind his head. "You really are the perfect Morrigan for a coven of wizards."

Ari sighed and unfolded his arms. "This isn't a coven. It's a conundrum," he said. Then with less sass and more pride, he added, "A conundrum of wizards."

"That's a thing?" Taye doubted, still chuckling at him.

"I'm making it a thing," Ari assured him before sitting up straight and digging the fingers of his right hand into the dirt before him. He offered his left hand to Taye. "Ready?"

Taye's humor waned to a quiet simmer as he took Ari's outstretched hand. "Let's do it."

And they did.

The holistic communion wasn't especially ceremonial, as

far as witchcraft went. It required no chants or ancient language, no runes or bloodletting. All it needed were a few focal objects, such as candles and jasper, oriented in the rough semblance of a circle, and the intent of the witches involved.

Check, check, and check.

Ari closed his eyes and sent out a prayer to the universe, asking it to join them. Beside him, Taye shifted into a more comfortable position, his grip on Ari's hand tightening and relaxing in turns. Ari squeezed back after the fourth time, silently scolding and encouraging the wizarding witchling into a meditative calm.

There was no instant gratification with holistic communion, not according to countless texts and Ari's lone experience. At first, he thought Taye's antsiness was to blame for the lengthy wait, but the longer they sat there in perfect stillness, the stiffer Ari's bones felt and the faster his thoughts swirled.

Maybe, just maybe, it wasn't Taye holding up the connection.

Without permission or any semblance of guidance, Ari's thoughts and memories converged. They trickled into a specific point in his life, a particular event, with a gentleness that left him little warning before he discovered where his mind was taking him.

He was fifteen all over again. Eren's hand was on his shoulder, guiding him down to sit in the muddy grass beside a witch he'd met once before, but whose name he couldn't recall to save his life. Eren wasn't sitting on the forest floor with the rest of the coven; he perched himself on a cut tree stump that sat in view of at least a third of the convening witches.

Ari recalled missing the warmth of Eren's touch. He

remembered the disappointment when Eren chose to sit so far away, despite his prior claims that he would guide Ari through the communion himself, that he would be with him every step of the way. Ari remembered that precise moment when he realized the experience wouldn't be what he was promised.

It hadn't been the first time Eren ushered Ari into something he wasn't ready for. It was merely the first time Ari realized he was being manipulated into sharing himself with a coven he didn't know.

Ari's throat closed up as a vise-like grip ensnared his chest. It took a conscious effort and unknowable minutes for him to remember how to breathe deep enough to wash the incident back into the river of ever-flowing memory.

The effort became astronomically easier once he could sense the world around him again. Taye's grip remained solid on his hand, but the wizard's thumb was rubbing lazy and deliberate circles into Ari's skin.

The tension released like a snappy rubber band, and Ari sucked in a huge, healing breath.

Taye asked no questions, but his thumb stopped moving with the abruptness of Ari's resumed breaths.

It didn't take long after that. Magic rose from the earth around them, swarmed in the moisture of the hinting rain, and floated by on the tender breeze. It enveloped them in its presence, not like a strong hug, but a clinging blanket that started off cool before reflecting a body's warmth. It was like sinking into a hot spring infused with all sorts of happy herbs and minerals. It was, in a word, lovely.

Opening his heavy eyelids, Ari found the forest alight with ethereal sparkles. It was breathtakingly beautiful.

"You're blushing," Ari giggled the next time he looked at Taye.

Taye stared straight back at him and said nothing as he blew strands of grass out of his face.

How they came to be lying on their sides in the nook of the oak tree, Ari couldn't say. He wasn't particularly bothered by the mystery, though. How could he when Taye's eyes were right there? The golden flecks in his irises were brighter than ever, and Ari could have sworn the green-and-brown striations were morphing, wriggling like pretty, pretty worms.

"My eyes are like worms?" Taye gasped through soft, melodic laughter.

"I didn't plan to say that out loud," Ari admitted, but for the life of him, he couldn't bring himself to be mad about it. He knew, in a distant, bad memory sort of way, that he would normally kick himself for voicing such an inane thought, but in that moment, Ari didn't care.

He was comfy. He was lying on the forest floor with a cute guy, getting grass stains on his favorite jeans, and probably ruining an otherwise perfectly good shirt. None of that matter, though. He was more settled in his skin than he could remember ever being before.

Maybe Taye had a point when he said Ari seemed at home in nature, or maybe Ari was under the influence of a Magical roofie. Either option seemed plausible just then.

Deciding to put such thoughts on the back burner for another day, Ari closed his eyes again. He breathed in the scent of petrichor and wood, and his head swam with the beauty of it. With each consecutive inhale, he drew it in deeper, willing the forest to meld with his mind and body till there was no differentiating himself from the Mother Earth.

"I want to kiss you," Taye said. "Is that crazy or what?"

"Or what," Ari answered without thinking.

He didn't hold on to the idea, not of kissing, or his absent speech. He couldn't if he tried. The world was so much bigger than a few petty hangups, and at least for now, he was part of it. It was all at once the clearest and the most obscure thought to ever occur to him, but it was beautifully freeing all the same.

"I'm sleepy," he thought he said to Taye. "Or I'm wired beyond functioning. I can't tell."

"Same," Taye said, the word falling out of his mouth in a slow drawl. Ari could see it floating through the air, the letters wavering on the breeze in a kaleidoscope of colors.

Ari squirmed lower into the sod at the great oak's base. For a moment he was certain the tree was smiling down at him. No, no, it was him doing the smiling, grinning from ear to ear up at the majestic oak like it was a sentient being doing him a favor by letting him rest against it.

A part of Ari knew the tree truly was sentient. Another part knew he was being silly. The Ari living in the moment didn't give a shit either way.

He was right where he belonged, and it was good in ways he never expected.

"Ari?"

"Hmm?"

It was so good it almost hurt. Ari's brain floated along in Magic's stream like a wayward bobble, aimless and innocent. The lack of direction should have been terrifying, but how could something so easy be bad?

Magic swirled around him, caressing his limbs from the inside out, as much as it tickled his skin. It felt like joy and welcome, like nothing Ari had ever done mattered even as it meant everything. He was dizzy with the exhilaration and calmed with the weight of Magic's favor, and somehow, some odd, mysterious way, he didn't splinter apart into a zillion pieces.

"Ari?"

He could have stayed there forever. A seriously large part of him wanted to.

Full, plush lips brushed his forehead in a feathery kiss. The pressure was so light, Ari was sure he imagined it.

"Ari?"

He wasn't part of the tree or the earth, he realized with the slightest sting of disappointment.

"It's time to come back now."

The disappointment faded as his sense of self returned at a trickling pace. It started with a distant awareness that his toes were cold. Where were his shoes?

Ari's heart gave a jittery start.

"Easy. I got you."

With another lurch and a little lunge, Ari's heartbeat picked up speed before his brain could figure out why.

"There you are."

Warm lips brushed high along his cheek, and Ari's heart lost interest in galloping. With a shuddering breath, Ari felt his soul return fully to his body. Blinking rapidly, Ari raised his face from the earth to see Taye looming over him with the softest smile.

"What did you do?" he whispered cautiously.

Taye shook his head and brushed a tuft of blond out of Ari's eyes. "Nothing."

"Liar."

Taye only chuckled.

Slow and lazy, Ari picked himself up and scooted till his back rested against the oak. He gazed around at the lit candles and scattered jasper and realized everything was just as he last saw it.

The only difference was Taye. The wizard knelt in the grass before Ari, bronzed hands on his thighs as he waited with an unassuming smile turning up the corners of his mouth.

Ari shifted under the attention. "I was lost, wasn't I?"

Taye shrugged. He opened his mouth to say something doubtlessly supportive or minimizing, but Ari was having none of it.

"You brought me back."

Taye closed his mouth and went still. Clearly, he was smart enough to know Ari was in a mood, and he wasn't going to risk fanning those flames without further information.

Ari's eyes narrowed as he hugged his knees to his chest. "What about you?"

"What about me?"

"You were fine?" Ari snapped, gesturing at the errant candles and stones. "This was nothing for you?"

The beginnings of a frown creased Taye's brow. "I wouldn't say that."

Sighing, Ari demanded, "What was it like for you?"

"Why are you so mad?"

"Just answer the question!"

Taye's standard scowl returned in full force as he slumped back on his heels. "It was amazing. Like nothing I've ever experienced."

"Yeah," Ari huffed. "Same."

"You're sure?"

"Yes."

He didn't tell Taye how glorious it was in comparison to the nightmare he experienced last time. He could barely admit to himself that he expected the warm sparkles to pass through him, invading his body and making him ill. Even as his head cleared, Ari waited for the discombobulating dizziness, for Magic to prickle along his edges like a threat, but it never happened.

Ari couldn't hold Taye's gaze as he softened his voice to ask, "It wasn't . . . overwhelming? At all?"

Taye blinked once, twice, and by the third blink, he'd schooled his expression into a stoic mask. "No. It was perfect."

That was more than Ari wanted to hear. With an abruptness that startled Taye onto his ass, Ari got his feet under him and started blowing out candles, collecting them as he went. It was probably obvious to Taye, but it took Ari till they returned to Dazzle's car to realize he was jealous.

CHAPTER 18

"What happened?"

"No idea."

"I don't like it. Are we sure the communion worked as it should?"

"Of course it did. Nothing gets Ari's panties in a twist like Magic having its wicked way with him."

"Fine, but at least tell us he had some fun with it?"

"Sure."

"Then why's he aggressively deep cleaning the entire apartment like it owes him money?"

"Beats me."

"I can hear you," Ari reminded them.

Neither Taye, Val, nor Dazzle had the decency to look ashamed. The three wizards remained seated on the couch like an unsanctioned lineup of judges as they stared after Ari. Dazzle nursed a cup of coffee on top a tissue box full of displaced nick-knacks, while Taye hugged the sequined cushion like it a shield. Val sat upright and fully alert on the small stack of Taye's laundered clothing and borrowed linens.

"Are you ready to stop rage cleaning and talk to us?" Val asked.

Ari flipped her a middle finger and resumed scrubbing the kitchen backsplash till the graying grout shined white. For irony's sake, but also because he was peeved at Magic again, Ari used a good old-fashioned Mr. Clean eraser to get the job done.

Dazzle cleared his throat from the safety of the couch. "You know, my associate helped formulate the potion used in those products, right?"

Ari spun and threw the damp sponge at his friend.

It worked like a charm, but better, because there was no Magic involved as the three wizard scattered out of range. Val shrieked her most kittenish shriek yet as she dove over the armrest, and Taye gave an undignified yelp as he rolled from the couch to the floor, still clutching the pillow to his chest.

Dazzle was the only one to form a verbal retort as he scampered around the coffee table on his tiptoes. "I don't care how pissy you are, there's no excuse for throwing chemicals anywhere near my hair!"

Perking up, Ari darted around the island countered and hopped over Taye to retrieve the Mr. Clean eraser. He brandished it at Dazzle with a serious scowl full of intent. "Out!"

Dazzle followed the direction of his pointing finger to the door and bit his lip in indecision.

Still pointing toward the exit, Ari reared back to make another throw.

Dazzle took one last look at Ari's face, and made the wise decision not to call his bluff. "I'm out! You two can deal with this."

The door slammed behind him on the way out, and a

before Ari could finish maneuvering to find another target, Val shouted, "It's all you, Taye!"

"What?" Taye shrieked as Val crossed to the open window in a white and gray streak.

"Last chance," Ari warned, one hand on his hip and the other holding the sponge aloft. "Leave me in peace while you still can."

Taye shot a dirty look toward the window, then the door, before clenching his jaw and squaring his shoulders. Ari should have known Taye wouldn't back down so easily; unlike Val and Dazzle, he wasn't worn down by years of dealing with Ari's Magic-induced tantrums.

The lone wizard opened his mouth to speak, and Ari launched the sponge straight at his face.

It was a direct hit.

As the cleaning product plopped to the floor, Taye stood tall and unmoved as he stared at Ari. "Was that really necessary?"

Ari thought back to the previous night and how Taye weathered the storm of communion with such grace. "Yes. Definitely."

With a sharp turn on his heel, Ari made for the kitchen under the pretense that Taye would grow bored of being ignored eventually. Again, he should have known better. The guy was nothing if not obnoxiously persistent, and he had Magic's favor to boot.

Heavy footsteps followed him into the kitchen.

"Did I do something wrong? I swear, I was only trying to help—"

Eye twitching, Ari rounded on Taye. "What makes you think this has anything to do with you? News flash, not everything is!"

"What the hell, Ari?"

"Oh, shut up. You're not stupid, and it doesn't take a genius to figure out you're already better at this Magic shit than I am. Go ahead, rub it in some more for good measure!"

Judging from the unhinged jaw and wide open eyes Taye was sported, Ari might have misjudged his intelligence after all. That was no matter, though; now that Ari had gotten started, he couldn't just stop. That would be too simple, and not at all his style.

"You've had Magic at your beck and call for mere weeks," Ari spat, "and no matter how much it's disrupted your life, you just keep rolling with it. Last night, you should have been a novice getting tossed around by Magic's whim, but no! With zero experience, you," he stressed, "were the one keeping me afloat. It should have been the other way around."

Taye recovered from his shock in time to attempt an interjection. "But you said you'd never—"

"Magic's been dogging my steps since I was a kid, of course I've tried a communion before!"

"You should have told me," Taye said with a quiet hint of anger in his voice.

Too caught up in himself to care, Ari waved him off with a flippant gesture. "What makes you so special anyway? Why is this so fucking easy for you?"

His voice broke right as his eyes started burning with frustrated tears. Trying to compose himself and stop the waterworks in their tracks, Ari fell silent. He turned away to hunt for a new cleaning product.

For one ugly moment, he thought Taye was going to let the matter go. He expected to hear the door open and close with Taye's departure. Instead, a few light and measured footsteps brought a substantial warmth up to his back, then solid arms wound around his chest and pulled him against a wall of muscle and cozy cotton.

Ari stiffened, and not in the good way.

Taye's chin landed on his shoulder as his arms gave a squeeze. "I didn't know it was so hard for you."

Sniffling, Ari tried to shrug free. "Well, now you do."

Taye didn't let him go, though. "Why do you do that? You say you trust me, but whenever I try to talk to you about anything personal, you deflect. Why?"

There was no censure in Taye's voice. With him safely out of sight, but an undeniable presence holding him in place, Ari could imagine they were still strangers. They weren't, not anymore, but the pretense allowed Ari to slump a little and trust, at least a little.

When he finally spoke, his eyes were dry again, and his voice was quiet with feigned calm.

"I have a track record of trusting the wrong people," Ari said. "My family, for one. Morrigan Puckman for another."

Taye's arms tightened reflexively at the sound of the Morrigan's name, and he made a short, displeased sort of grunt. He didn't interrupt, though.

"I thought I was broken for a long time because of them," Ari admitted while he still had the nerve to keep speaking. "Then there was Val, and then Dazzle."

"You trust them," Taye asserted.

"With my life," Ari agreed. Then with a soft, short laugh, he said, "Then you showed up and I thought, 'Hey! Here's someone just like me!' But you're not. This . . ." He threw up a hand to indicate Magic, or perhaps the universe in general. "This comes naturally to you. It's a disruption to me every time I'm inconvenienced, but you've lost your home, your job, your— I mean, you're living out of a backpack."

"I get it," Taye grunted, digging his chin into Ari's

shoulder a bit harder than necessary. "It's not that you don't trust me. You don't trust yourself."

Ari laughed, but it was a miserable little sound. "More or less."

A touch of snarky pride entered Taye's voice as he added, "And you're jealous."

"I wouldn't go that far," Ari protested.

He squirmed his way out of Taye's embrace, mostly because Taye let him. Turning to face the wizard, Ari felt lighter than he had in years, with the obvious exception of the previous night. Ari wasn't entirely sure that one counted.

"Do me a favor?" Taye asked, stepping in close.

"Depends on the favor," Ari countered, shoving his mysteriously sweaty hands in his pockets.

"Stop thinking so much."

Turns out, that was a much easier thing to do with Taye's lips pressed against his own.

ARI'S DAYTIME UPSET FOLLOWED HIM INTO DREAMLAND THAT night.

"All that power," Puckman said from the trenches of Ari's memory, "wasted on a kid."

It had hurt so much more the first time, when Ari overheard those words in real time instead of recollection. The years and spatial distance softened the blow now, but it still ached with the context of Puckman's soft kisses and strong embrace. He recalled Puckman's hand, always so firm on his shoulder, and how blind he'd been to mistake possession for affection.

In his nightmare, the greed in Puckman's smile was more

obvious than it'd been in real life. Or not; maybe Ari was simply old enough to recognize it for what it was.

"I got you," Puckman said with a nasty smirk.

Gut sinking, Ari's dream carried him away from the apparition.

"I got you," said a soft voice in his ear.

Ari whirled around, and there was Taye.

"YOU DISGUST ME," VAL WHISPERED DAYS LATER. "Seriously, the infatuated grin on your face is sickening. Stop it."

Ari did not stop grinning, but he did shove the cat off his service counter.

Val hit the floor with all four paws and bounced. Taking the dismissal in stride, she raised her tail high and trotted off to bother someone else. The next time Ari looked up from his inventory paperwork, he found her curled up on the corner table between two emo teens, basking in their adoration as they gave a wizard a full-body massage. She caught his eye and winked before rewarding the teens with a meow.

Shaking his head at her ridiculousness, Ari tried to return his focus to the inventory. It was scheduled to be done yesterday, but Taye convinced him to lock up the shop early with his masculine wiles.

"I can hear you thinking," said the man in question.

Ari paused to shoot a considerate frown across the counter as Taye approached. "Literally?"

"No." Taye laughed as he braced his palms wide on the customer side of the register and leaned in. "You're just easy to read."

Rearing back in offense that was mostly for show, Ari

scoffed, "I am not."

"You are super emotive," Taye snickered, "but it's a good look on you."

The proverbial chip on Ari's shoulder evaporated in record time. Chest puffing up as he pretended to refocus on the open app on his phone, Ari said flippantly, "Well, I suppose you're entitled to your opinion, even if you're wrong."

Taye's low chuckle made the butterflies in Ari's stomach burst into spontaneous flight. Ari was just about to tell the wizard off for distracting him when a more professional distraction demanded his attention.

A grand total of three mundane patrons were in the shop that day. Val's emo admirers spent a whole eighteen dollars on drinks and were otherwise treating the shop like a library, but the third was a middle age woman with a working credit card. She wobbled over to the register with a stack of historical fiction centered on the Salem witch trials. Ari nearly wept in glee as he told her the total.

"I guess things are looking up then?" Taye teased, nodding after the woman.

Ari gave him a friendly scowl. "Don't jinx it."

"I TOLD HIM NOT TO JINX IT," ARI COMPLAINED THE following day.

They were six hours into the business day and not a single soul had yet to step into the shop. While Ari was glad Val was providing him some company, he thought the two of them made a rather sorry sight as they sat at the foremost table and stared at the entrance like trained dogs awaiting a belated meal.

There was nothing else to do. Val was well on her way to nonverbal enchantments, and there was only so much practice she could handle for one day. For his part, Ari's hands were raw and sore from scrubbing the floorboards and polishing every polishable inch of the shop he could find. There was quite literally nothing else to do until a damn customer or two showed their faces.

Naturally, the next person to round the corner and power walk his way to the shop's front door wasn't a customer at all. It was Taye, and he wasn't empty handed.

"Is that a guitar?" Ari asked as Taye set the oblong case on the adjacent table.

"You bet your ass it is," Taye said. He spared a second to plant a kiss on Ari's cheek, then he busied himself with unlatching the many weathered clasps.

Frowning, Ari watched Taye pull out a chair and arrange the pale wood instrument on his knee with practiced ease. "You've been bumming on my couch for weeks, free of charge, and this is what you spend your dwindling savings on?"

Taye paused to shoot him a sheepish grin. "It's secondhand."

Thanks to Taye's quick fingers, the instrument released a burst of sound. It was nothing but a brief strumming of the chords, but from the sound came a gentle tickle against Ari's cheek. It almost felt like a fluttering kiss, but when Ari raised his hand to the spot, he found a literal butterfly landing on his finger.

"You got to be kidding me," Ari laughed as he admired the blue-and-green striations in the creature's wings.

"Aw!" Val cooed. "How sweet. They two of you make my teeth rot."

Taye swiped his hand over the strings to produce a jarring

noise, and Val coughed out a little gray moth. When she glared at him, he responded with a grin and raised his middle finger.

Before Val could try biting him, Ari stepped between them and asked, "So, this is the all-important errand you needed to run?"

"You disapprove."

"I didn't say that."

"Your face said that."

"It did," Val agreed.

"I suspect your attitude will change soon enough," Taye explained as he gave the guitar a fond pat. "Believe it or not, but I've been known to draw a decent-sized crowd with one of these. Don't suppose you've considered adding live music to the atmosphere before?"

An hour later, Ari starting kicking himself for not remembering Taye's wizarding medium before now. He filled the shop with a lilting tune that was both beautiful and slightly macabre, in keeping with the shop's general theme. With the door open to the street and no amplification beyond what the cobblestones provided, Taye's music seemed to snare the attention of every passersby who heard it. People of all sorts gathered inside the shop, from the soccer mom with her band of kids to the elderly couple with the matching hearing aids, and everyone in between.

Ari even spotted Hag Number Two-hundred-and-four loitering just beyond the welcome mat, on his tiptoes and craning his neck to try and see through the crowd. Was it wrong of him to have Val chase him off like a rabid beast? Possibly, but neither Val nor Ari would be losing sleep over it.

At first, Ari fretted that the music would prove too big a distraction, but those fears were soon laid to rest. Not long after they got a look at Taye and his guitar, people began to flitter about the shelves, like their curiosity over the music was a transient thing, ready and willing to hop from one novelty to the next. Ari wanted to cheer when the first few listeners made their way to him at the service counter, merchandise in hand and eyes lingering on the pastry case.

Thanks to Taye, Ari turned a healthy profit that day.

TAYE BECAME A SEMI-PERMANENT FIXTURE IN THE SHOP THAT week, but he couldn't keep playing indefinitely. The calluses on his fingers needed to build back up, and his fingers were stiff and aching at the end of the first few days. As much as he appreciated the music, and its subliminal beckoning, Ari didn't like seeing his lover in pain. There was only so many massages Ari could give his hands in between customers, and before long, Ari had to insist on more frequent breaks.

It was during one such break that Dazzle paid them a visit, bearing gifts. He flounced into the shop in a crop top and oversized jeans, a pastel-pink clutch purse tucked under his arm.

"The least I could do was put that Astragali to good use in your favor," Dazzle insisted as he plucked a jar from his bag and proceeded to smear its faintly green contents into Taye's hand.

"I can do it myself," he offered, reaching for the container on the table between them.

"I got it," Ari insisted, planting himself on Taye's knee and snagging the cream from Dazzle.

Taye's breath was warm on his cheek as he passively suggested, "I really can do it myself."

"Shut up and let me pamper you."

"Ew," Dazzle commented, watching them with a wicked grin. "Who acts like that in public? So indecent of you, Ari!"

"Thank you, Dazzle," Ari said as he pushed a spontaneous espresso out from behind the jar of cream. He offered it to Dazzle with all the mocking sweetness he could muster. "As always, your potions are invaluable. Now kindly fuck off."

The shop was once again devoid of paying customers. It wasn't a surprise at this point, but it still sent Ari's anxiety through the roof.

"Alright," Dazzle announced as he returned the cream to his purse and picked up the espresso. "Now that I've done my part to help exploit your boyfriend's talents—"

As one, Ari and Taye jerked upright. "We're not boyfriends," cried one, while the other insisted, "He's not exploiting me!"

" . . . Right." Dazzle studied them with a pinched expression on his face as he stirred his espresso with a miniature spoon. "I'm not touching that with a ten foot pole. You cuties can sort yourself out on your own time, not mine."

Huffily crossing his arms, Ari asked, "Was there something you wanted?"

Dazzle beamed at him. "Now that you mention it, yes!"

"Can I kick him?" Taye asked Ari.

Ari patted his shoulder, letting the touch linger as he said, "Only if he tries to leave without giving us that cream."

"While I hate to drop a bomb on your little love fest here," Dazzle prattled as he reached into his purse, "I'm not about be labeled the bad guy."

With that, Dazzle hand dug into his clutch and the bag's opening stretched beyond normal limits as he retrieved a hefty tomb. Dazzle dropped the book on the table to reveal none other than *A Divergence of Magic*.

Instantly, Taye's shoulder tensed till it felt like Ari's palm was resting on solid stone.

"Thanks for letting me borrow it, Taye," Dazzle said with a sharpness to his smile that Ari didn't like.

"Is now really the best time for this?" Val interjected.

"No," Taye grumbled.

"Yes," Ari and Dazzle said in unison.

Ari removed himself from Taye's knee and glanced between Taye and Val. Neither wizard met his eye. "What's this about?"

"Nothing," Taye said.

Dazzle scoffed.

Taye's chair clattered across the floor as he stood and snatched the troublesome book from the table. Opening it at random, he spun it around to show Ari.

"Can you read it?"

Ari frowned from the blank pages to Taye's expectant face.

Taye didn't need a verbal response. He snapped the book shut and tossed it back onto the table as he rounded on Dazzle. "Still want to do this now?"

"Do what?" Ari demanded.

"He's not ready," Val interjected.

"Ready for what?" Ari shrieked.

They ignored him as they all watched Dazzle return the book to his suspiciously small purse.

Spine stiffening, Ari demanded, "Is this about me?"

Again, Taye said "No," but Val said, "Oh, yeah."

While Ari threw up his hands in exasperation, Dazzle reached out to give his forearm a gentle squeeze. "It's not just you, Ari. It's about all of us. The coven as a whole. You should know what this book says."

"Sure, why not," Taye snarked. "It apparently doesn't

matter if you can read it or not. Dazzle's decided he knows better than Magic itself."

Dazzle's grip tightened on Ari's arm. "You're our Morrigan, right?"

Ari sent a wary side-eye toward the purse. He tried to weigh the endless possibilities against Taye's vehement reluctance to share with him. "You really think I should know?"

"I don't think it's fair to leave you in the dark," Dazzle said. "Your life as you know is being upended, and you should know why. It's not all because you stood up for a sorry street bum."

"Hey!" Taye griped. No one paid him any attention.

Gut clenching, Ari asked, "What does it say?"

With a resigned sigh, Dazzle retrieved the book once more. This time, he took the time open it to a specific page.

"This isn't the first time a coven of wizards was formed."

Ari's breath hitched in surprise. Was a he relieved or more terrified than ever? He didn't know.

"According to the book, witches and wizards used to be more in sync. We weren't so separated by social norms, but like two halves of the same coin. We made each other stronger, enabled each other to perform magic of mythical proportions."

A lump formed in Ari's throat then, hard and unforgiving as he forced himself to listen. This wasn't a history lesson; this was precedent.

"There were other witches, other Morrigans before you," Dazzle continued with mounting excitement, "They were epic, Ari. The magic they performed was limitless, and the way they interacted with it . . . Ari, if you read this book yourself, you'd see. They were truly blessed. No one could touch them."

Ari hugged himself and nodded. His skin felt too tight, the lump in his throat growing to monstrous proportions. He didn't know what to say, and he thought maybe that was because there was nothing to say.

It was too late to back out now.

"This isn't stuff most people know," Taye interjected as he nudged Ari's side. "That's by design. The Council burned almost every record in existence."

Ari reeled back by several steps. "They wouldn't dare."

"They would," Val grumbled. "Why do you think everyone's so horrified by us, Ari? The Morrigans don't like you being their competition, and the Council already knew what a threat we could become. Look at what we did to Gaines!"

"He started it!"

"Doesn't matter," Taye said. He sat with his arms tightly crossed and deep furrow to his brow as he studied the wood grain of the table. "What we've done—what we are . . . Ari, this shit is legendary."

Ari looked from Taye to Dazzle, silently asking if they were sure this wasn't some sort of joke. Taye wouldn't look at him. He just kept glaring at the table and shaking his head.

Dazzle was less than helpful as he bit his lip and shrugged. "Yeah . . . it's kind of Morgana the Fey levels of legendary."

Ari's legs gave the fuck out. The only reason he didn't wind up on the floor was because Magic intervened by swinging a chair under him on the way down.

"Wizards are already avoiding the shop," Dazzle said, undeterred. "A number of witches too."

"If they're not doing it under the Council's direction, they soon will be," Val added. "They want to scare you away from becoming a power in your own right, one who can magically operate independently of the covens, and with a team of wizards the Council can't hold authority over."

Ari shook his head, a hand going to his throbbing temple. "That's ridiculous. My idea of competition is limited to out earning the local Hot Topic and the palm reader down the street!"

Val sneered. "How is she still in business? She's a blatant charlatan."

"Exactly my point!" Ari said with a flailing gesture, "I don't want to wrestle anyone for authority, least of all the Morrigans and the Council of Wizards! All I want is to keep my family and my shop safe!"

"Aw!" cooed Val, her eyes suspiciously shiny. "You really do love us, don't you!"

"Shut up," Ari and Taye snapped.

Ari sat forward in his chair to peer at Taye. "I said I'd be your Morrigan out of necessity, not so I could go toe-to-toe with the Council, or anyone else. Please tell me none of you knew this was going to paint a bullseye on our backs before we formed the coven?"

A flurry of voiced smacked Ari back in his seat as his wizards hurried to reassure him. They fell silent again when he lifted a hand to smother the noise.

Are swallowed the urge to scream. They couldn't afford for him to panic, not with legendary status and all it entailed looming over them.

"I have to think on this," Ari muttered before removing himself from the table. With nowhere else to go, he beat a path straight to the backroom and the relative solitude of the kitchen.

Behind him, he heard Val lamenting, "I told you he wasn't ready."

CHAPTER 19

*V*al knew him too well.

Nearly overnight, Ari became a strict task master. The pressure was on, and he had no time to waste getting his wizards to appreciate what a coven was. Book learning wasn't enough. It could never be enough.

The Council had already decided they were dangerous, so Ari would just have to make sure they were.

Perhaps Dazzle felt guilty for revealing the truth to him in such a blunt manner, or maybe he was as scared shitless as Ari was. Either way, Dazzle was suddenly on board with exploring his newfound magic.

"Close your eyes and find that thread that links you to me," Ari instructed the next day instead of opening the shop. "Imagine it's a direct pathway to my Magic. All you have to do is travel down it, reach along it, and I'll give you whatever you need."

Dazzle's first successful connection was with Val. Her enchantment expertise allowed him to make a sensitive potion in the bland confines of Ari's kitchen with nothing more than the ingredients in the fridge. He enchanted the broccoli to act like a magic-grown herb, and the rest was history.

Taye gave Val the insight to hum a little song to startling effect, and they nearly burned the apartment down with the resulting fireworks. It was possible that last one wasn't entirely Taye's doing, though. All three wizards seemed to have a serious power boost whenever Ari was in the vicinity.

In the week that followed Dazzle's revelation about *A Divergence of Magic*, Ari saw more of his friends than he usually did in a whole month. Dazzle skipped work on multiple occasions, and Val flat out pretended her laptop didn't exist for several days straight. Taye had nothing better to do than exercise his newfound witch magic, at least whenever he wasn't bugging Ari for intimate favors.

All in all, they were quickly growing into a force to reckon with. Air only wished they got there a little faster.

Val and Dazzle were even more easily distracted than Ari.

"Why don't you ever celebrate Samhain?" Val asked one day when she was supposed to be practicing her nonverbal spell casting.

"Ooh, now that's an idea!" Dazzle said, abandoned the text book he'd been studying. He even went so far as to shove it back onto the shelf, without checking to see if it was the right spot. "I for one am all for getting together in the woods and getting drunk on witch's brew."

"I've never celebrated Samhain before," Taye commented from the spiral staircase. He was in the process of returning a stack of Dazzle's discarded texts, earning himself the not-so-coveted spot as Ari's favorite coven member. "I've done Halloween though. Aren't they the same thing?"

"Oh, no!" Dazzle spun around in his chair to stare at Taye

like he'd gone mad. "We will not be celebrating Halloween. I'm not suggesting we dress up in costumes and go hand out candy to children. I want something more spiritual, like the communion thingy you guys did."

Ari sighed and abandoned all hope of getting them to focus on anything serious for the time being.

"Samhain's supposed to be a time to unwind and reconnect with Mother Earth in a celebration of the changing seasons," Ari explained. "Or so I'm told."

"Specifically the end of the harvest season, right?" Dazzle asked with an intrigued twinkle in his eye.

"Yes," Ari huffed in impatience, "and the passage from summer to winter."

"So . . . Fall?" Taye cheekily interjected from the upper level.

Ari shot him a glare and refocused his attention on Val. "Can we get back to work now?"

"In a minute," Val said, brushing past him to paw at a book on a lower shelf. "Tell me more about Samhain. I've always heard it described as a work retreat where you're stuck doing trust exercises and stale team building shit no one asked for."

"Hard pass," Dazzle said with shudder. "I'll hold out for naked dancing in the moonlight, if you don't mind."

"It's so great to hear wizard perspectives on witch traditions," Ari drawled as he leaned back in his chair. "I didn't know you could be so unimaginative, though. Impressive."

Dazzle pouted back at him. "Oh, gee. Thanks."

"Did you just say 'orgy fairies'?"

As one, Ari and Dazzle looked up to see Taye leaning over the upstairs railing and staring down at them with a mixture of cautious alarm and blatant interest. One look at him was all it took to send the others into a ruckus of laughter.

"Orgy fairies?" Dazzle snorted through his cackling, clutching at his side.

"Shut up," Taye said, shoving back from the railing with clear huffiness.

Val laughed so hard, she stumbled on her way from the window to Ari's knee. Wheezing, she cried, "Orgy faeries! Of all the things to mishear, that's not even a thing."

"It is too!" Taye yelled back with such insistence that made Ari and Dazzle doubled over with renewed laughter. "Check urban dictionary; it's right under Monster Fucking 101!"

"It's not even remotely what I said!" Dazzle countered, but the damage was done.

As Taye slipped deep into a hissy fit that seemed mostly for show, Dazzle and Ari succumbed to the unprecedented amusement of it all. Val managed to recover her decorum after the initial onslaught of chuckles, but she wore a wide grin as her head swiveled back and forth between the two men seated at the table with her.

For his part, Ari had never contemplated the idea of such an orgy before. Faeries were too reclusive and their numbers too few for any sort of large scale debauchery, at least in the modern era.

All in all, it was a beautifully silly moment. It was never meant to last.

Abdominal aching with mirth, Ari dug his phone from his pocket after it chirped with an incoming message. He was still chuckling and wiping tears from his eyes as he opened his professional email. A single missive awaited him.

Val was first to noticed Ari's change in demeanor. "What's wrong?"

Ari didn't give her an immediate answer. He couldn't. His mouth went dry at the first glance at the subject line. With every word his eyes traced over next, his stomach seemed to drop another foot.

Soon enough, Dazzle fell quiet and Taye raced down the spiral stairs to throw an arm along the back of Ari's chair so he could read over the blond's shoulder.

"Email from Councillor Sanchez," Taye said, tone grave.

"She's backing out of the deal for the scroll," Ari explained. His voice sounded hollow. "She . . . well . . . She says the Council has issued a formal order to boycott Grimoires and Goodies."

A stunned stupor fell over the table. It didn't stop there, though. It seemed to encompass the whole shop, suffusing the air with a wretched sort of suspense.

Ari gulped. The lump in his throat went down painfully, like swallowing a handful of jagged glass shards.

"They can't do that," Val insisted. She lurched up with her front paws on Ari's shoulder for a good look at the phone. Her eyes darted back and forth across the screen at a dizzying pace before she plopped back on her hunches with a short puff of exhaled air. "Holy shit."

Dazzle whipped out his own cell phone. His glittering gold nails clanked together in his rush to check his messages. Ari knew the moment his friend found what he was looking for, because Dazzle went still and the color drained from his face.

"Dazzle?" Val whined.

"If this is a bluff, it's a good one," Dazzle said.

Ari nearly knocked Taye over as he jumped out of his seat. He made a beeline for Dazzle. "Let me see."

Dazzle didn't look at him as his device went black, and he tucked it away.

"Dazzle," Ari demanded, "what did it say?"

"Lies you don't need to read."

"Dazzle!"

Ari lunged for the phone sticking out of Dazzle's pocket, but the wizard sprang out of reach with matching speed. A split second later, a large hand caught Ari's bicep.

"Knock it off," Taye said, tugging him away from Dazzle.

Ari laughed and shook himself free. Hands on his waist, he began pacing. "I can't believe this."

"Let's not jump to conclusions," Val said in a daze. "The Councillors aren't tyrants. Just because they make a call to action doesn't mean wizards everywhere will comply."

"After all this time," Ari whined to no one and everyone. "After everything I've done for some of the wizards on that fucking Council . . ."

"Jobs," Taye snapped, this time grabbing hold of Ari by the shoulders. "You did jobs for them, Ari, not favors. If they want to cut professional ties because you did the right thing by me—"

"It's not just you," Dazzle piped up. He winced when Taye's sharp gaze darted onto him. "At this point, you're only one of the reasons the Council hates Ari."

Ari almost made it out of Taye's grasp as he tried to close in on Dazzle again. "What did they say to you? Show me!"

Dazzle shook his head, barely managing to meet Taye's eye as he avoided Ari's.

Taye's hand cinched down on Ari's shoulder. "They know about us then. Our coven."

It wasn't a question, but Dazzle nodded like it was.

"That's fine," Val said in stiff tone that was far from

reassuring. "We knew it was only a matter of time before Gaines or Puckman spread the word."

With a watery bark of hysteria, Ari tossed off Taye's hold. He flopped into the nearest chair with his head in his hands, fingers yanking at his hair.

When he managed to lift his head again, he found Dazzle still nodding. The sorry lilt to the movement gradually shifted toward determination.

"The Council lost their chance to screw me over when they granted my certification," Dazzle thought aloud. His gaze grew distant and shrewd as he tapped a manicured talon on his chin. "It's not the sort of thing they can revoke. So long as I keep my copy safe and sound, legally there's nothing they can do to me."

Ari sat up straight, gaping. "Is that what they said in the email? They threatened you?"

Dazzle waved him off, already turning to Val. "Mind holding my credentials under that security enchantment of yours?"

"I'm insulted you felt the need to ask," Val said. She rallied around the promise of action and hopped onto the table with her furry chest puffed up. "What about you, Taye?"

Taye's bronzed complexion went ashen. "I didn't think to grab it before they chased me out of my hometown."

Another round of stunned incredulity made its way around the room.

Ari's stomach rolled. He was going to be violently ill if anyone added another disastrous realization to this damn conversation.

Taye glanced around the room at their daunted expressions. His own hardened. "You know what? No. It doesn't matter."

Dazzle stared at him. "You don't care that the Council

may very well have destroyed any evidence that you were ever a recognized wizard? You'll probably never work again."

"You'll never be granted access to the wiz database," Val added. "You'll be blacklisted from every magical establishment under the Council's authority."

Taye jerked in the most defiant and defensive shrug Ari had ever witnessed. "Fuck them. I don't need people who won't have my back when I need them."

"That's a lovely sentiment," Dazzle stressed, "but we're not talking about a toxic ex. This is the Council of Wizards."

Taye crossed his arms and lifted his chin. "Look me in the eye and tell me they've done anything helpful for you beyond signing an overvalued paper."

Dazzle opened his mouth, then promptly closed it again. He threw up his hands, and when they fell back to his sides, Dazzle looked deflated, but also thoughtful. He looked like he was settling into the idea and surprised by it find how much it appealed.

"Exactly," said Taye.

"It's not like they can take our magic from us," Val mused aloud. "Far as I know, Ari's the first to ever do that."

"Exactly," Taye repeated.

As one, the band of wizards turned to stare at Ari where he remained miserably slouched in his seat.

"What?" Ari grumbled, slouching further.

"We're having a moment," Dazzle said with a gesture to indicate himself, Val, and Taye. "You getting in on this, or what?"

Ari scowled. "Your livelihood might not depend on Council support, but mine does."

Taye coughed. "Tell that to the covens of Ecuador."

"Touché!" Val cheered.

And really, Ari thought, there wasn't any other option for him. Technically, he joined their semi-rebellion the moment he claimed them to Morrigan Puckman's incredulous face.

"This boycott explains some of the lack of foot traffic," Ari said, "but not all of it."

"It must be the witches who cursed the shop, then," Val concluded. "The Council took a legal approach, leaving the magical hack to the covens."

"That's a huge assumption," Taye cautioned.

"My ex-boyfriend is probably behind some of it," Ari lamented. Then he turned an expectant glare on Dazzle. "You're more than likely going to have to become my Sugar Daddy."

Dazzle scrunched his nose in distaste. "Ew. I love you, but like . . . totally platonical."

"That's not a word," Ari sighed.

Dazzle ignored him in favor of shooting a look at Taye that involved narrowed eyes and pursed lips. "I lost interest in him like that after introducing him to the concept of man-spacing. You're welcome."

Taye regarded him back thoughtfully. "You are either a masterful or terrible wingman."

"He's both," Val asserted. "Dazzle's a complex individual like that."

"Why, thank you!" Dazzle preened, channeling his stage person as he fluttered his lashes at Taye and Val.

While the wizards devolved into snarky laughter and gentle teasing, Ari sank as low as he could go without slipping from chair to floor. His heart felt heavy, his chest too tight. He was physically unable to join in their antics.

"Why the shop?" he murmured.

The chit chat ceased.

Ari studied the ground unseeingly and followed the

thought through to the end. "Why are they targeting the shop when they could attack us outright? What's stopping them from imprisoning us right off the bat?"

It was a damn good question. When Ari raised his gaze to find his wizards staring back at him, he knew none of them had an answer.

CHAPTER 20

*A*ri was the only witch to grace the shop with his presence when he reopened for the following week. He spent the day alone, not a single customer to be seen. Locking up a full two hours early that evening, Ari told himself it was a temporary setback.

While walking back to the apartment, his brain spun circles around topics such as mundane marketing and cutting costs. Not for the first time, Ari was glad he didn't have any employees to worry about. He was already going to have to cut loose a vendor or two if things didn't turn around soon.

He was so caught up in his thoughts, Ari didn't notice who was standing in his path till he was almost on top of him.

"What the fuck, Eren?"

Puckman grinned, holding a hand out to the side as if to say "Not my fault, it's a public sidewalk." What actually came out of his mouth was almost as annoying.

"I'm respecting your boundaries and staying away from the shop, aren't I?"

"I should smite you," Ari thought aloud. "I've never

smote someone before, but I'm pretty sure I could do it if I'm really, really motivated."

Puckman rolled his eyes. They were a nice brown shade, and nothing that could hold a candle to the glints of gold and green in Taye's hazel orbs.

Good god, but Ari almost gagged on his inner poet's intrusive ramblings. Fortunately, the other witch didn't notice.

"You left me no other way to contact you."

"It's been years since I blocked your number." Ari sneered, crossing his arms and backing up.

"True." Puckman sighed, but that cocky little grin didn't quite leave his face. "But how am I supposed to resist when you've become so interesting lately?"

Ari's face warmed, but the days when Eren Puckman could turn him into a flustered mess were long gone. No, now he was just pissed.

"That's the problem with you: always out to score an interesting asset," he mocked, uncrossing his arms so he could gesture between them. "There's no genuine connection here, and there never was. After all this time, you're still too self-absorbed to see the problem with that."

Finally, the effortless confidence seemed to leach from Puckman's shoulders. Ari wished he'd lose the leather jacket too. It didn't seem fair for such an asshole to look so attractive.

Shaking his head at Puckman's nonplussed expression, Ari made to walk past him. He got his arm caught in a bruising grip for doing so.

Ari froze, then tilted his head to stare down at the hand holding him. When he raised his gaze to meet Puckman's, he was cold as stone.

Puckman was a good four or five inches taller, and he

outweighed Ari by a good deal. Even so, he let go without a single word being uttered between them.

Ari continued on his way.

"Osondu's not worth the trouble," Puckman called after him. "All you have to do is renounce him. Disband this whole coven idea, and your life can go back to normal."

Ari kept walking, but his hands curled into fists at his sides.

The connection to a coven was as close to sacred as modern witches got, and for the first time, Ari was able to truly appreciate it. The idea of losing access to the collective power was disturbing enough on its own, but Ari shuddered at the idea of losing the intimacy of the connection itself. Losing that sixth sense, not being able to feel Taye and Val and Dazzle like extensions of himself—even in theory— sounded as painful as losing a part of himself.

"I'm begging you, Ari," Puckman demanded. "Disband the coven, and you can come home."

Ari nearly turned around to plant his fist in Puckman's face.

THE NEXT FEW DAYS WERE MISERABLE. THE SHOP WAS NOT only devoid of any wizards, it seemed the witches were on board with icing Grimoires and Goodies out of the community. Ari nearly hyperventilated the one time he dared to consider what might happen the next time he needed to reach out to his contacts for an elusive magical item; at the rate things were going, he would never have such a lucrative commission again.

"No need to panic," Val insisted the next time Ari

succumbed to a fit of sobs at the sight of his empty shop. "It's only been a few days. This won't last."

The next day was an unassuming Wednesday morning. He turned a poor profit off a bunch of tourists and local alternative life-stylists, and sold a genuinely enchanted cauldron to a witch visiting from the East Coast. That was it.

"It won't last," Val insisted. "You're too vital to the community. This'll blow over soon."

Except Val was wrong. It didn't blow over. By Friday evening, Ari's electricity bill outstripped his earnings for the day.

Saturday was no better.

"This isn't right," Taye said to no one in particular.

"No shit," Ari grossed.

They sat together at the table nearest the door, Ari still as a statue in a chair while Val curled up beside his coffee mug. Taye slumped in the seat beside them, his resting scowl deeper than ever as he played with the straw sticking out of his chai latte.

They were people watching. At first, they sat down for drinks while they scoped out passersby and made bets on which of them were most likely to step into Goodies, but as time passed, and no one approached, they began to sulk.

Not even the mundanes seemed to notice the shop. It was like Grimoires and Goodies had ceased to exist.

"It's one bad week," Val told herself.

Taye uttered a dubious grunt.

"You don't often spend all day in the shop, so you don't appreciate how disturbing this is," Ari explained with a weary whine. "It's lunch time, and no one's even glanced our way. I think we've been cursed."

"What did I tell you about jumping to conclusions?"

"Seriously?" Taye interjected with a wave toward the bay window. "Look at that!"

Val turned her head to follow his emphatic gesture toward a pair of middle-aged goths as they vanished beyond the display window's view. Neither figure gave Goodies a passing glance as they strolled by in their black clothes and caked-on makeup. They weren't regulars, but Ari knew deep in his bones that his store was one they would appreciate.

But no. Their eyes skipped over the store with the same regard they might give a vacant lot.

"Okay," Val admitted, "we might have a problem."

Taye's mirthless note of laughter came out as a snort.

Val smacked him with her tail. "Where's your guitar, anyway?"

"Behind the counter," Taye responded as he slouched further. Sullen stare fixed on the busy street outside, he said, "I already tried playing for an hour. It didn't help."

The irritated swish of Val's tail came to an abrupt halt. She stared at him, aghast. "You're serious?" She gaped at Ari next. "Not one person heard the music?"

"They heard," Ari corrected with a heavy sigh. "They just didn't care."

Dejected as could be, Ari trained his attention on his coffee. Thinking about the sorry state of his business was depressing, but at least he had caffeine to boost his mood. He buried his nose in the mug, closed his eyes and took a deep breath, willing the familiar fragrance to momentarily sooth his worries.

Val let out an excited "Oh!" a moment before the unexpected chiming of the door's bell echoed throughout the space.

Ari bolted out of his chair, coffee splashing onto his hand as he dropped it back onto the tabletop.

An old man was in the store. Ari didn't know his face, and considering his grizzled wrinkles and extreme shortness, one look was enough to assure Ari he'd never seen the man before.

Ari rounded the table and went to greet the newcomer. He didn't get so much as a syllable of sound out before the man breezed past him with a harrumph of acknowledgment. The quick interaction was enough to tell Ari the man was no witch or wizard.

He wasn't mundane, though. Ari was certain of it, though he couldn't say how.

Frowning, Ari followed and planted his feet in the man's scant shadow.

"Welcome to Grimoires and Goodies. Is there anything I can help you find?"

The man gave him a skeptical once-over without turning to face him fully. "Just browsing," he muttered.

Ari shot a confounded look over his shoulder at Val and Taye. The wizards remained where he left them, nursing their drinks and watching Ari's desperate attempt at customer service with a mixture of amusement and concern. Neither wizard seemed inclined to offer aid as they studiously refocused on their drinks.

With nothing better to do, Ari wandered over to the cash register on the off chance the stranger bought something. He tightened his apron and began wiping down the counter while he waited, just to keep his hands busy and his nerves pacified.

He waited in vain. The vertically challenged man wandered the entire shop for the better part of an hour, but he left empty handed. Ari's only consolation was some brief eye contact and a briefer nod of dare he say approval on the man's way out.

"That was weird, right?" Val asked.

"An understatement," Taye agreed.

"He's magic," Ari said.

Their heads wiped around to stare at him.

"Shit," Taye murmured, scratching at the several days' worth of scruff on his jaw. "Do you think the Council sent him to cause trouble?"

"It did seem like he was scoping out the place," Val commented.

Ari's eyes narrowed. "Did either of you recognize him?"

"No," Taye said as he stared out the window in the direction the old man took off in. "I wouldn't put it past the Council to try that sort of thing, though. Not after everything else they've done lately."

"Snipers," Val hissed as she hustled to the bay window to resume her custodial watch over the street.

Ari shook his head hard. It made him a little dizzy, but he preferred that to the anxious tailspin their implications were trying to send him into.

"No," he insisted without feeling. "I bought this property without magical connections, and my realtor won't work with anyone I don't approve of. They can't force me to sell . . ."

He trailed off with a lame squeak to his voice. Bravado was much easier without Taye arching a brow and gesturing around the vacant midday store.

HE WAS FORCED TO CLOSED THE SHOP EARLY. AFTER SO MANY days of steadily decreasing business, he didn't have much more choice about closing the shop for the rest of the week. That wasn't to say he was sitting on his ass feeling sorry for himself. Oh, no. Ari was far too shaken for idleness. Instead, he called on his coven and put them to work.

They spent the rest of the week cooped up in the shop, scouring it for insight.

It didn't take a genius to figure out Grimoires and Goodies was cursed. Either that, or Ari himself was under a hex, and he honestly couldn't decide which would be worse. Curses were generally permanent unless a counter curse was performed, and the cure was often as nasty or complex as the initial curse's side effects. On the other hand, hexes were reserved for personal slights; while they were often shorter lived than curses, they rarely left room for any fixes until the hex ran its course.

The only consolation was the likelihood of the Council of Wizards being behind the shop's troubles. While Ari knew of a few Morrigans likely to condone such maliciousness, the Council had already proven themselves petty and violent. It was a peculiar sort of relief, but at least this curse or hex wasn't powered by a collective of pissed off witches.

"You need a break," Val said that Saturday afternoon. She set a heavy paw on the book Ari was studying, all but swiping it from his hands as she pinned it to the table. "You have bags under your eyes, Ari. Bags!"

Ordinarily, such a remark would have him rushing to the nearest mirror in a panic. It was a mark of how stressed he was that he didn't even flinch at the comment.

"I can worry about my appearance after we save my store," he insisted, yanking the book back.

Val hopped forward and sat on it before the book moved an inch.

"You're not the only one who's been cooped up in here too long," she insisted.

With a resigned sigh, Ari followed her head tilt over to the next table over.

Taye and Dazzle sat together amid a mountain of books

and scrolls, with Val's laptop computer open between them. Dazzle readjusted his position constantly as he switched back and forth between a scroll and its leatherbound counterpart. Ari watched on in horror as Dazzle absently chewed on the edge of one of his fabulous nails.

Taye's condition was no better. His posture was deplorable as he bent low over an aged journal, frown lines deep and eyes squinting as he tried to decipher the author's penmanship. Ari's heart sank as he noticed the gray hairs in his short beard for the first time.

"Okay," Ari said loud enough to break the two wizards from their studious trances. "That's enough for one day."

IF ARI EVER NEEDED PROOF THAT HE WASN'T CUT OUT FOR the Morrigan role, he got it when all three of his wizards cheered over the prospect of being anywhere else that night.

A part of him expected them to go home and rest. That was his plan, at least. He really ought to have known better.

Ari was halfway into his pajamas when Dazzle showed up at the apartment with a cream to vanish the emerging wrinkles around Ari's eyes and mouth. Dazzle wasn't in full drag by any measure, but his makeup was dark and glittery in ways that warned Ari they would be going out whether he liked it or not. By the time he was appropriately dressed, Taye and Val were ready to walk out the door, too.

They ended up at Gladys: The Nosy Neighbor. There were only so many bars a cat could attend unnoticed.

Dressed to impress, and surrounded by the bar's unrepentant glitz and glamour, they were ready for a fun night of stress relief. Unfortunately, that wasn't quite what they got.

"Curses are bullshit," Ari lamented over his fourth martini. "And mean. They're like . . . the meanest."

"That's what you keep telling us," Taye grumbled as he replaced Ari's glass with one full of water.

"He's not wrong," Val slurred as she popped her head up from the seat between them.

Taye had moved her off the table after her second beer in the hopes that no one would notice the cat alternating between sympathetic weeping and righteously indignant cussing. So far, they had escaped any such scrutiny. Dazzle assured Taye as much at the beginning of the night, but Taye hadn't known about Gladys's particular brand of chaotic obscurity. Three or four rounds into the evening, and Ari thought he was finally starting to get the idea.

Not one person gave them a second glance as Dazzle stuck one rainbow talon into Ari's water glass and stirred it into a neon blue cocktail.

Ari and Val oohed and awed as only drunk people could.

"You've been practicing!" Ari cried, looming out of his seat so he could wrap his friend in a hug from clear across the table.

"Well, yeah," Dazzle preened. "I'll admit, I didn't take you seriously at first, but the store really was attacked!"

"That's how I see it too!" Ari gushed, gripping Dazzles hand in both of his.

"That's cool and all," Taye commented as he pulled Ari back into his seat, "but it'd be even cooler if you could change it back."

He slid the neon drink closer to Dazzle with his chin lifted in challenge. Dazzle wasn't quite drunk enough to take the bait though.

Wagging a finger at Taye, Dazzle smirked. "Now why

would I do that? Ari hasn't even had a taste of my little potion here."

Without further prompting, Ari snatched up the glass and downed half of it in one go. It tasted like alcohol and raspberries, and Ari lowered the glass back to the table while smacking his lips.

The grin of superiority on Dazzle's face wilted as Ari shoved the glass at him.

"Go on, then," Ari said, sounding almost sober as the task at hand caught and held his attention. "Change it back. I want to see how you did it."

Taye and Val laughed as a fuming Dazzle muddled through a few excuses. Ari didn't hear most of them on account of how disappointed he was not to see more of Dazzle's magical progress.

Mood souring again, Ari took it upon himself to replace the soiled water glass. He left for the bar with every intention of bringing back a pitcher to help the group sober up, but he got distracted. The barkeeper heard the word "water" and promptly dropped a menu into Ari's hands.

The nachos looked divine.

A glance back toward his friends, and Ari saw Val and Dazzle on either side of Taye, the two of them grinning from ear to ear. Taye looked suitably amused, so Ari decided he would survive a few moments more of the harassment.

In his drunken state, Ari saw no reason not to sit his ass on a rickety stool and have himself an unprecedented dinner of greasy nachos, with another drink for good measure. He deserved it, after all. His shop—his baby, his first love—was in danger, and Ari would be hard-pressed to keep a roof over his head if he didn't find a way to break this monster of a curse soon. No one had better reasons than he did to gorge on bar food and drink themselves silly.

It was a moment of weakness if there ever was one.

Naturally, the universe refused to let him wallow in it alone.

"Fancy seeing you here, Mr. Jamison," said a woman as she slid onto the bar stool to his right.

"My, my, how the mighty have fallen," said a man who followed suit to his left.

Not that he'd admit it, but Ari didn't immediately recognize them. He stalled for time by thoroughly chewing his mouthful and daintily wiping his mouth with a paper napkin. When he finally folded the napkin and tucked it under his basket of soggy chips and cheese, he did so with a full recollection of who he was dealing with: Hags Death Metal Shirt and Flip Flops.

At least they were both dressed appropriately for a night on the town, though his studded jacket and her patchwork shawl looked cheaper than the earth-stained garments they used to wear into Grimoires and Goodies. Maybe the grungy attire and threadbare flip flops were meant to be a dig at Ari's anti-witch footwear policy, but he couldn't find the energy to care just then.

"You do realize just because you're banned from my establishment, doesn't mean I'm banned from this one?" Ari asked with leisurely glances for each witch.

The man scowled, and Ari couldn't help noticing how unfortunate the expression looked on anyone but Taye. Taye had the thick brow and strong jaw line to make it look sexy, and Death Metal Shirt certainly did not.

"You're a snob and an asshole," Flip Flops said. Ari almost complimented her bluntness, but then she followed it up by smugly saying, "I'm glad we ran into you anyway."

Ari's eyes narrowed. "Is that so?"

She nodded, and the smugness increased tenfold as she

pointed her nose high in the air. "I wanted to be the one to tell you: Morrigan Harding filed for a business license last week."

Spine stiffening, Ari nodded. "Good for them."

"She's filling your place in the community."

Ari snorted into his next mouthful of cheese and jalapeño. The derisive noise turned into a startled cough as the male witch patted his back with a tad too much force.

"You had a good run, man," he breathed in Ari's ear unnecessarily. "It's too bad. No witch alive is going to step foot in your place now they have an unproblematic source with connections to the whole wide supernatural world."

With one last, achy thump to Ari's back, the guy took off.

Flip flops lingered just long enough to give him a peck on the cheek. She laughed as Ari wiped her cooties away and said, "She's already taking online orders, by the way. Wouldn't that explain a few things, huh?"

She set a shiny business card on the bar top before taking her leave. Ari told himself not to look at it, but he was weak. Dammit all, but the card was nice, thick and engraved with the words "Harding's Magical Goods and Consignments."

As if that wasn't bad enough, Ari detected the faint shimmer of an obscurification charm along the bottom edge. With little more than a thought, Ari banished the enchantment to reveal more information.

In partnership with the North American Council of Wizards.

Appetite vanishing, Ari crushed the card in his hand.

"Who the fuck is Morrigan Harding?" Dazzle asked as he read the crumpled card the following morning.

"It doesn't matter," Ari said from the comfort of his recliner. "She's competition at best."

"And probably a saboteur," Val chimed in, lifting her muzzle from the plastic bowl holding Dazzle's much appreciated hangover cure.

"Let's hope she's not responsible for the curse on the shop," Ari grumbled between sips of his own potion-and-coffee concoction. "We're strong, but there are only four of us. Even if we find the right counter curse, we probably can't outmatch the strength of a full coven."

"Well, how many witches are we talking about?" Taye asked from his favorite spot on the sofa.

Ari shrugged. "No one, but the Morrigan herself probably knows the exact number, but it likely falls in the range of about . . . Oh, let's say twenty-five to forty."

Val choked on a mouthful of potion as Taye stared in blatant alarm.

Ari paused with his mug an inch from his lips to add, "I've heard of the rare coven with up to sixty members."

"Sweet baby Jesus," Dazzle muttered, also gaping at Ari. "We can't compete with that."

"Nope," Ari agreed before burying his nose in his mug.

By unspoken agreement, they knuckled down and got back to work researching curses, hexes, and everything in between.

THEY TURNED IN FOR THE NIGHT WITH NOTHING BUT headaches and frustration to show for it. Val elected to go home with Dazzle, claiming she couldn't handle anymore of Ari's moping any better than she could handle the kicked puppy dog eyes Taye kept shooting Ari's way. Ari had no idea what she meant by that, but he was too tired to look into it too closely.

Once it was just the two of them in the apartment, Ari peeled himself out of the armchair with the intention of putting himself to bed.

"How about chicken and waffles for dinner?"

Ari stared at Taye in incomprehension. "Huh?"

Taye bit back a smile as he approached Ari with the slow patience of a trapper trying to soothe a cornered animal. "You haven't eaten anything since lunch, and I have a hankering for comfort food."

As if on cue, Ari's stomach issued a loud gurgle. Face hot, Ari said, "Okay. You might be on to something."

Taye's quiet chuckle only made him blush harder.

"You don't have to do all the cooking around here," Ari said as he dug his phone from his pocket. "Considering all the exhaustion going around, I'll just order something."

Taye snatched the phone from him and tossed it onto the vacated chair. "For fuck's sake, Ari, let me take care of you for a change."

The irritation in his voice took Ari by surprise. Blinking up at the taller man, Ari asked, "What's that supposed to mean?"

Taye sighed, glancing away as he scratched the back of his neck. For some reason, his reluctance pissed Ari off.

"I don't need you to take care of me," he snapped.

"Yeah. You've made that perfectly clear."

Fists braced on his hips, Ari huffed, "Is that a problem for you?"

Taye opened his mouth to speak, but nothing came out. Snapping his jaw shut, the wizard started shaking his head and staring at the vicinity of Ari's knees.

Ari couldn't help himself. He ducked down and moved in close, getting right in Taye's face. "I asked you a question."

"Here's a better one," Taye snapped, finally meeting Ari's eye with the golden flecks in his own blazing. "When's the last time we kissed?"

Ari reeled back with an incredulous scoff. "In case you haven't noticed, I've been a bit too busy and stressed for fooling around—"

"I didn't ask about sex," Taye spat, taking one step forward for each of Ari's steps back. "I understand not being in the mood. What I don't get is why every waking moment has to be dedicated to the bullshit going on around us. You can't spare a second for a peck on the cheek!"

Sneering, Ari began to say, "So sorry I'm not into PDA—"

But Taye cut him off with a terse, "You were before the boycott started."

Ari blinked. "No, I wasn't."

Much to his shame, Taye proceeded to count off instances on his fingers. He recalled countless kisses hello and goodbye, and how often Val used to mock them for staring at each other. He talked about missing the casual way Ari would touch his arm as he passed on his way back to the register with a customer's drink order. He mentioned the time Ari would sit on his knee and cuddle in the long lulls between customers, when the few people in the shop seemed acceptably distracted.

Taye finished his diatribe strong by saying, "And don't even get me started on how touchy-feely you've gotten in front of Val and Dazzle."

"I'd rather you didn't," Ari murmured.

Ari sat on the edge of the coffee table with his hands crushed between his knees. Blond hair fell in his face as he kept his head lowered, but Ari couldn't be bothered to care about the dishevelment.

Taye remained standing, the constant shifting of his weight belying the coolness of his voice. If he noticed Ari's upset, it wasn't enough to stop him from saying his piece.

"You're not the only one who needs to feel needed and appreciated," Taye said.

"I'm sorry."

"I'm not just talking about me either. Do you know how much the other night at Gladys's meant to Val and Dazzle?"

Pleading notes infused Taye's voice then. Combined with his earnestness, it was clear he expected some kind of response this time. It only made Ari feel worse, though.

"They talked about it for days, Ari. Days!"

Ari opened his mouth to say something, anything to defend himself. The problem was, he didn't know what to say.

"I'm sorry," was all that came out of him. He was such a broken record.

"I don't need your apologies." Taye sighed and crouched down in front of him, his hands landing on Ari's knees. "I just need you be present. Be here, with me."

Taye's hands left his knees so he could hold Ari's face in his palms. With the gentlest pressure, Ari found his face lifted till he was staring straight into the most vibrantly hazel eyes in existence. The greens in Taye's eyes were more defined than ever as he graced Ari with a small, wistful smile.

"Things with the Council and the shop can't keep interfering with the rest of your life," Taye whispered, his thump swiping over Ari's cheek in a soothing gesture. "You can't keep letting it. Sometimes, we need you more than the business does. Yeah?"

"Yeah," Ari whispered tearfully.

A part of Ari wanted to remind Taye that he'd warned them this was a mistake, that he was too self-absorbed to be a good Morrigan—or a lover for that matter. That same part of him wanted to sob and push Taye away.

The longer he sat there staring into Taye's eyes and feeling the warmth of his hands, the smaller that part of him became. By the time Taye kissed him, it was reduced to a shadow at the fringes of his mind.

Maybe, just maybe, if Taye could continue being so patient with him, maybe Ari could learn to be better.

ARI TRIED TO MAKE THINGS RIGHT WITH VAL AND DAZZLE, but with far less touching and kissing involved. They more or less shrugged him off and thanked Taye for pulling Ari's head out of his ass again. Then, at Val's insistence, they returned to the daunting task of identifying whatever spell was influencing the shop.

Things more or less returned to normal. Ari chose not to worry about it unless everyone else was.

Fortunately or not, that normalcy only lasted a few days more. They had Dazzle to thank for it.

"Found it!" Dazzle shouted as he leaped from the couch. His fists rose in victory, but the motion lost gusto midway as reality caught up to Dazzle. "Shit. I found it, but it's not great."

"What did you find, exactly?" Taye said, frowning up at him from one couch cushion over.

Books and scrolls littered the living room, covering the coffee table and the carpet combined. Ari reclined in his chair with Val's laptop open on his thighs, while the wizards fussed with volumes commandeered from the shop. Val was perched on the island counter with a small stack of brand new spell books specializing in curse identification and breakage.

It was a Tuesday. The shop should have been open for business. Instead, Ari and his coven were pouring over ancient and contemporary texts alike, even turning to the internet in a bid for information. If there was any hope of keeping the shop afloat, they needed to uncover what spell was keeping business away, and fast.

"It's an anti-prosperity hex," Dazzle explained as he reread the page of interest. "It's witchcraft. Looks like our initial suspicions about the Council being behind it were wrong."

"Well shit," Taye huffed, tossing aside the book he'd been studying. "At least we're not dealing with a second nemiza."

By this point in time, the bruises on Taye's ribs were faded to a motley yellow. Taye's continued existence remained as inexplicable as the mark's murky persistence.

"Of course it's witches," Val huffed.

Ari sighed as he closed the laptop with one hand, rubbing his aching temple with the other. "Alright, Dazzle, tell me what you found."

In answer, Dazzle flipped his book around and handed it over to Ari. After hours of staring at either a screen or fine print, the new pages seemed to bleed together in a swirl of meaningless, headache inducing nonsense.

"This thing literally drives prosperity and its sources away from the victim," Dazzle relented as he retrieved the book. "I've seen curses to make the shop invisible to prospective eyes, but that wouldn't affect your digital store front the way it has. This, however, is all-encompassing."

"It's targeting you personally," Taye added after standing to read over Dazzle's shoulder, "It's blocking all channels of income."

"Great," Ari gripped as he shut his eyes and sank further down into his seat. "How do I break it?"

No one answered him.

Ari opened one eye to spy Taye and Dazzle silently urging the other to speak up. He knew then he wouldn't like the answer.

"It's a hex," Val chimed in with a long suffering sigh. "We'll just have to wait it out."

Ari whimpered and slumped so far down into his chair, his ass hit the floor.

THE THING ABOUT HEXES IS THAT THEY WERE NOT ALL created equal. The specific effect and longevity were determined by the spell caster, and whatever intent and adjustments they made to the basic spell. The strength of the witch involved in the casting was a major factor in how long it lasted, and whole covens were known to make them last years instead of weeks.

When Ari hit two weeks without making a dime, they concluded they were dealing with a substantial coven, maybe multiple.

"Let's assume the hex went into effect the first day Taye's music failed us," Val surmised.

"Excuse you," Taye corrected, "My music didn't fail. It just wasn't stronger than whoever hexed Ari."

As the two wizards devolving into arguing semantics, Ari rested his head in his folded arms and tried not to cry. Again.

Ari sat on the floor with his arms and head on the coffee table in much the same position he'd spent the past two days. Those two long, miserable days required him to stay home and have nothing to do with work, and he hated it. It was Val's idea, so for now, he hated her too.

"Hex or no hex, you played your fingers raw and Ari still didn't make a sale. Ergo: failure."

"Fuck you, I didn't know about the hex then!"

"Oh? Then what was your excuse for the other day?"

Ari couldn't decipher whatever it was Taye grumbled in retort. Far as he was concerned, it didn't matter.

Nothing mattered because nothing could stop this damn hex.

Val was the clever one who suggested they test the limits of the hex. Her theory was sound and, at the onset, it gave Ari some hope. While Dazzle conducted a one man hunt for the witch or coven responsible for the hex, Val and Taye would run the shop without Ari's involvement. Technically, the hex was placed on Ari himself, so it went to reason that if he wasn't around, perhaps the hex would overlook the shop.

Ari wasn't thrilled to be sitting on the sidelines, but with a begrudging heart, he handed Taye the shop keys and provided him the codes to the cash register. He didn't clue Taye or Val into the fairy-glamoured safe on the upper level for safety reasons, but they otherwise had full run of the shop. Entrusting them with his pride and joy stung, but Ari did it anyway.

It was supposed to pay off.

It didn't.

Even with Taye playing his guitar with an amplifier positioned at the open door, they didn't garner the attentions of a single customer.

"You're missing the point!" Val shouted over Taye's continued grumbling. "Stop distracting me when I'm trying to make a plan of attack!"

"No one's attacking anyone," Ari grunted into his folded arms.

"Maybe we should," Taye said. "They might stop messing with us if we retaliated. So far, the Council's the only one we've tangled with."

"Gaines had it coming," Val interjected. "He shouldn't count."

Taye barked a short, disdainful laugh. "He's a Councillor! Of course he counts."

Ari lifted his head at that. "He was a Councillor. He can't still be one without magic. Can he?"

Taye and Val exchanged wide eyed looks, as if the thought hadn't occurred to them before.

Ari sighed and struggled to his feet. He'd been sitting for so long that his legs were numb. Pins and needles prickled his limbs and made him limp into the kitchen to make another pot of coffee.

"None of this matters," Ari told them as he scooped coffee grounds. "Whether I'm there or not, I'm still the owner and curator. Hell, my literal blood is set into the baseboards of that shop."

He shut the top of the coffee maker with a touch too much force. In the corner of his eye, he saw Val jump as it snapped closed.

"There is no divorcing me from the shop," he stated. "And my absence isn't going to fool a hex that may very well be powered by half the Morrigans of Colorado."

"Let's not be dramatic," Taye advised.

Val snorted. "Have you met him?"

"Not helpful."

It took so little prompting for Val and Taye to go back to bickering, Ari thought as he watched the fresh brew drip into the pot.

The two wizards continued picking at each other well into the afternoon. Ari let them at it; as long as they were entertaining each other, that time couldn't be spent trying to pester Ari into cheerfulness. Their back and forth commentary and thinly veiled insults began to fade into background noise before long, and Ari was able to enjoy three large cups of liquid sustenance in peace, if not quiet.

He was just finishing his third cup when Dazzle burst into the apartment in a flurry of tie-dye and stage makeup. He wasn't in full drag, however, and his short pink hair stuck up in every direction; it was a very legitimately windswept look and totally out of character for Dazzle.

"I have news!" he declared before his attention zeroed in on Ari like the strongest of magnets. "You should sit down for this."

Air hung his head in dejection, but only for a moment. Shaking himself, he poured what was left of the pot into his mug.

"Let's get this over with," Ari said as he crossed back

over to the recliner. "Go on, Dazzle. Kick me while I'm down."

At Dazzle's wide eyed look, Val told him, "We closed the shop early today because there was no point staying on for nonexistent sales."

Blinking slowly, Dazzle walked further into the room and loomed over Ari like a scientist examining a specimen.

"And yesterday we learned my music is no match for the hex," Taye added.

"Oh my god," Dazzle whispered in horror. "I really am going to have to be Ari's Sugar Daddy."

Ari glared up at him as he savored a minuscule mouthful of coffee.

"Okay, then." Dazzle plopped down on the arm of the recliner and flung his arm around Ari's shoulders. "I don't want to break your pretty little brain, but this is too big and time sensitive to keep to myself."

"Out with it," Ari deadpanned.

"Right." Dazzle gave him a squeeze before sitting upright and clearing his throat. "So, remember your little tete-a-tete with those witches at the bar?"

Ari frowned up at him expectantly.

"Well, I was thinking on it, and it just seems really convenient for a couple randos to approach you at Galdys's of all places, just to give you an insulting business card."

"You think Morrigan Harding has something to do with the hex?" Val asked, leaping up with excitement.

"More than that," Dazzle said, gripping Ari's shoulder tight. "It took a lot of sweet talking and greasing a few palms, but I got in touch with one of her witches."

Ari sat bolt upright, twisting to stare at Dazzle. For their parts, Val and Taye seemed to be holding their breath.

Like the little shit he was, Dazzle took a moment to bask in their suspended attention.

"Dazzle!" Val snapped, darting forward to swipe at him.

"Okay!" Dazzle kicked out a foot to keep her at bay. Once the cat settle down a healthy distance away, Dazzle cleared his throat again. "So, I didn't get any confirmation if she was involved or not."

They all groaned.

"But!" Dazzle stressed, holding up a finger to waylay their dissatisfaction. "The little witchling I talked to promised to set up a meeting between my Morrigan and his."

Ari stared back at Dazzle's encouraging grin with his jaw unhinged. He struggled to name the emotion he was feeling, but he knew it was hot and strong enough to turn his stomach.

"Let me get this straight," Taye said. "You want Ari to meet one-on-one with a witch who might be actively ruining his life?"

Dazzle's grin faltered. "I'll admit, I hadn't thought of it like that."

"Absolutely not."

"Well, that's not your decision to make."

"I'm with Taye on this one," Val interjected.

"Again, not your call." Dazzle shook Ari by the shoulder then. "What do you say, Ari? If Harding is responsible, this could be a chance to talk her down. Right? A hex can be canceled by the caster according to all the reading we've done."

"If she's responsible," Val reiterated.

"And if she's willing to change her mind at all," Taye added. "Those are big ifs."

"Not to mention, it sounds a lot like negotiating with a terrorist," said Val.

"Except we're the terrorists," Dazzle reminded them

before giving Ari another good shake. "What do you say, Morrigan Jamison?"

At last, Ari figured out what he was feeling. It was anger, but worse. It was a vengeful, ugly sort of rage.

It made perfect sense, and he knew without a doubt that Harding was the one who hexed him. It didn't matter that they'd never met in person. Hers was the only coven he ever banned from Grimoires and Goodies. Her witches were among the first to witness Ari's unbridled power, well before it could be supplemented by the creation of his blasphemous coven.

No one else had as much reason to want to see him ruined.

"Yeah," he said without pausing to second-guess the fury bubbling inside his chest. "I want to meet her."

CHAPTER 22

There were plenty of places for covert meetings in the Denver area, but not all of them were suited to a witch's particular comforts. With that and the need for neutral territory in mind, Dazzle and his contact in Harding's coven managed to agree on a spot before the weekend.

Washington Park Loop was closed to the public in the evenings, but that was where the Magic came in. Dazzle drove them to the southwestern parking lot with his obfuscation totem activated the whole drive. The plan was for Ari to hike to a predetermined bench along the southern lake's edge to meet Morrigan Harding under the moonlight, far from prying eyes or interfering coven members.

"I don't like this," Taye said as Dazzle parked the car. "I've been practicing an invisibility spell. I could just follow—"

"No," Ari and Dazzle said as one.

"If you're in trouble, you'll need proximity to the coven to help—"

"No," Ari repeated with a sound snap of his teeth.

Yet when Ari opened his door to get out of the car, he

wasn't the only one. Taye hopped out and frowned down out him, making the most of their estimated two inches of height difference.

"You can't assume she'll keep her word and show up alone," Taye warned.

Ari sighed. This wasn't the first time they hashed this out.

"Even if she's not responsible for the hex, she's actively stealing business from you."

"If this goes sideways, it can't be because of me," Ari said without meeting Taye's eye. Now wasn't the time for Taye to realize a big part of Ari's better judgment agreed with him.

"Don't worry," Dazzle chimed in as the passenger window slid down. "Val and I will make sure Taye stays back."

"We'll be right here," Val said as she popped her head out of the car. "Waiting like useless side characters while you go off on your adventure."

Taye nodded toward the cat with a knowing expression. "What if it's a trap?"

"It's not!" Ari and Dazzle insisted, their voice blending with exasperation.

It took a bit longer to convince Taye and Val to sit put, but when Ari finally began the hike toward the meeting spot, he did it on his own.

Truth be told, it wasn't much of a hike. Washington Park Loop consisted of little more than two miles of scenic nature trail. The paved path was flat and surrounded by trees and grass, while the opposing ends of the oblong trail curved around two man-made lakes. It was a lovely spot where raw nature met modern convenience, and the quiet night lent it a softness that wouldn't be possible during the busy daylight hours.

It took Ari mere minutes to reach the appointed bench. It was situated beneath a tree and overlooked the water in a picturesque setup worthy of fine art photography. The moonlight made the water glisten as crickets provided an organic soundtrack for the evening.

It was rather romantic, which was intensely off-putting, considering the circumstances.

Shrugging off his bizarre thoughts, Ari approached the bench.

He was within arm's reach of the bench when the nearby tree made a move. It wasn't the subtle sway of branches in a breeze, either. The tree itself seemed to waver, its trunk turning fluid as it billowed outward. At first, Ari thought it was Magic playing tricks on him again, but then he recognized the feel of witchcraft.

The bulging belly of the tree peeled away from the rest of the trunk. It moved a pace or two forward in jerky motions till it bumped into the back of the bench. At that point, the peculiar mass of wood-like artifice stretched upward, and Ari began to make out the shape of a woman.

It was a strikingly familiar shape, actually.

"You've got to be shitting me," Ari muttered.

The disguise lifted in a series of slow, mesmerizing seconds. A knob in the bark turned into a nose, and moss smoothed out into a cardigan. The cracks and crevices parted ways to reveal fingers and eyelids, and the errant twigs collected into a mane of dark hair.

Ari recognized her long before her mouth was free to utter a defense. Hag Number Six stood before him with a sheepish smile that did nothing to detract from her motherly affect.

"Good evening, Ari."

"Morrigan Jamison," he corrected coldly.

Her smile waned, but not nearly as much as he thought it ought to. "If you insist on formality, than so will I."

"Of course." Recovering from the surprise, Ari crossed his arms and adopted his most professionally cool smile. "You're Morrigan Harding, nothing more and nothing less than the very witch who's trying to destroy my business."

That slapped the smile clear off her face. Jaw dropped, she lifted a hand to her heart and said, "No! I would never wish harm to you or Grimoires and Goodies."

He almost believed her, but he remembered the crinkled and torn business card in the inner breast pocket of his jacket. Pulling it out, Ari crumpled it all over again and tossed the ball of paper to her.

To his chagrin, she caught it. Her face paled as she unfurled it with painstaking care. "Where did you get this?"

"Your coven," he said, short and not so sweet.

She stared down at the card, still shaking her head, but with a new tightness of displeasure to her jaw.

"So, how exactly is this not causing me or my shop harm?"

She closed her eyes as she smoothed the card out and tucked it into her sleeve. When she opened them again, her eyes were convincingly sympathetic.

"You banned me and mine from the shop," she began in a soft and unassuming tone. "You cut me off from much needed resources. I had to start looking elsewhere, and it seemed . . ." She faltered, a subtle blush coloring her cheeks. "I thought a little friendly competition wouldn't affect you much, assuming you noticed it at all."

"I didn't." Ari huffed a mean little laugh. "Or I didn't until your flunkies started harassing me."

"I had nothing to do with that," she said, clasping her hands tight and holding them over her heart. "I swear, Ari—"

"Morrigan Jamison."

"—I will deal with them, Morrigan Jamison. On Magic, I swear no witch of mine will show you such disrespect again."

He felt the power behind the words as she said them. The intensity of it reassure him that she not only meant what she said, she fully intended to hold herself to it by magical means. A vow like that could not be avoided or worked around. Until she made good on her promise, Harding would be increasingly inconvenienced by Magic itself. It would steer her toward addressing the problem at every waking moment, until the universe and Harding herself felt her word had been adequately honored.

Ari's mouth went dry as his anger abated a bit. He wondered if he shouldn't warn her about his so-called affair with Magic, and how it might decide to hold her to much higher standards for his sake.

"You really have nothing to worry about," she said. "I don't have anywhere near the network you do. Goodness, but this little venture of mine wouldn't have gotten off the ground without the Council of Wizards helping me."

"Help you gladly accepted," Ari sneered. "And after all your talk about me crossing lines between us and them. You're a fucking hypocrite."

She cringed, but it was short-lived. "No. My dealings with the wizards are strictly professional. That makes all the difference."

"Right. My apologies. You're not a hypocrite, just a bigot."

For the first time, Ari witnessed her flush with anger. Her round cheeks turned splotchy with redness and her similarity to an overripe tomato almost made him laugh at the most inopportune moment.

"I think we're done here, if you're resorting to name

calling," she said, fists twisting in the hem of her cardigan. "And to think, when Mr. Davenport first suggesting a meeting, a part of me hoped it was to set aside our differences, so we could be permitted back in the shop."

Ari scoffed.

"Grow up, Morrigan Jamison," she spat before turning to march off.

Ari wasn't about to let her have the last word, though.

"You have a lot of nerve hoping for anything from me after what you did."

She came to a screeching halt. Back to him, she whimpered, "What?"

"You hexed me!" he accused, fists at his sides.

Harding whipped around so fast, her hair smacked her in the face. Spitting it out of her mouth, she matched his glare and said, "I have never condoned hexes and frankly, I'm insulted you would suggest otherwise."

"I don't know you like that," Ari argued. "But I know your witches have a track record of trying to fuck with me."

"I've kicked witches out of my coven over the most minor hexes!" Harding seethed, her clenched fist shaking at her side. "They know it's hard boundary for me. Ask any witch around, they know I won't tolerate that kind of maliciousness being attached to my name."

That gave Ari pause. As a Morrigan, he couldn't imagine being so angry that he'd voluntarily amputate a part of his chosen family.

Sure enough, behind the righteous anger in Harding's expression was something mournful. She wasn't happy about cutting off these unnamed witches, but she'd done it anyway.

As if Ari needed the redundancy, Magic swept over him with a ring of truth.

"This hex is destroying my life," he said with the slightest apology to his tone. "If it wasn't you, who was it?"

Her eyes widened then, as if she'd stumbled into a realization. She stared at him like she had that fateful day in the shop, like she didn't recognize him. "Morrigan Puckman was right."

Ari's teeth ground together at the name. "About what?"

"You," she said, and her shoulders drooped with pity. "You're lost, Morrigan Jamison. You've taken on more than you can handle."

Ari stiffened. "Eren's an opportunistic gossip. You should take what he says with a grain of salt."

"That doesn't mean he's wrong," she countered, her chin jerking into the air. "Do you know what I saw when I read your palm?"

Ari sighed and rolled his eyes.

"Promise," she croaked, as if on the verge of tears. "I thought, any day now, he's going to come into his own, and would be glorious. Instead, here you are, more out of touch with the universe than ever before."

Ari gritted his teeth. "Sorry to disappoint you."

"Not yet, I think," she said, back stepping into the shadows. "You made enemies when you took in that rogue wizard. Perhaps one of them is behind your hex."

Before Ari could think of something to say, she turned tail and scampered off into the darkness.

"Damn," Val said out of nowhere the following morning. "We were so sure it was her."

"Well it wasn't," Ari snapped as he finished making his first cup of coffee for the day.

"And we're lucky it wasn't," Taye added as he flopped onto the couch with his curls clumping to one side from a night of heavy sleep. "Imagine if she'd been the criminal mastermind we were looking for; Ari would've been delivered to her on a silver platter."

Val rolled her eyes, but otherwise didn't respond. Neither she nor Ari were likely to entertain Taye's what-ifs for a second day running. While Harding's innocence was a breath of fresh air to Taye, it only served to worsen Ari's and Val's moods. Now, instead of one solid possibility, they had a list of unknowns to look into.

"Hear me out," Val said after leaping onto the counter, so she could meet Ari's eye. "What if the hex caster is someone we've never met?"

Ari shut her down with a quick shake of his head. "Hexes are usually born from personal investment in seeing the victim hurt, and this one's strong. It has to be fueled at least in part by someone I offended personally."

"My money's still on Harding's coven," Taye interjected on his way toward the bathroom.

"He could be right," Val said. "That old guy nearly got physical with you back at the shop, and the two who accosted you at Gladys's prove Harding doesn't have as tight a hold over her people as she thinks."

Ari took the time to sip more coffee before he set his mug down and looked Val dead in the eye.

"Would you risk me breaking your connection to the coven for any reason?"

Val reared back, teetering on her hind legs as if she'd been slapped.

Ari retrieved his mug with a knowing look spared for Val, then he focused on putting together something quick for breakfast. He had a bagel toasting and the makings of a fruit salad out on the counter before Val spoke up again.

"I know I haven't been diligent about the magic practice," Val said, slow and deliberate. "And we haven't really talked about it, but I do value the magical link between us."

Ari paused, a knife in one hand and a banana in the other. He turned to see Val studying the floor with an uncomfortable set to her muzzle and a groove of deep thought drawn between her eyes.

"It's like having my best friends with me everywhere I go," she said. "Like I'll never feel alone ever again."

Magic did its thing then, or maybe Val was broadcasting more than usual, but Ari was inundated with impressions, with vague ideas and emotions that spelled out the story of a lifetime. He'd always known Val was something of a child prodigy when it came to spell casting, but he never stopped to consider how isolating it must have been before that moment. She carved out a place in world as a fearsome enchantress, only to have it all ripped away when she was cursed. In a split instant, Ari understood the journey Val took to be the happy and relatively carefree cat she was today. There had been mourning there, and abandonment when others assumed her value as a person was diminished.

Then there was Dazzle, who welcomed her with open arms with the same fervor he did most of the world's oddities. From there, she found Ari, who hadn't cared about her shedding fur so long as she could cover part of the rent. Smack in between them, she carved another—albeit smaller —place for herself, and like the truest of magics, she found it suited her much better than her old life.

Forming a coven was the encapsulation of all that she suspected and rarely dared to put into words. They were a part of her now, inextricably linked in all the ways that mattered. They were family.

"Oh, Val."

"Don't start," she scowled. "If you cry, I'll cry. Have you ever seen a cat cry, Ari? It's not fun. It's devastating. Do you want to be devastated today?"

Sniffling back any sign of tears, Ari smiled and reached for her. "Come here, you big sap."

"Ugh. If I must."

She didn't come to him, but she didn't object as he scooped her into his arms and snuggled her close.

That was how Taye found them. He came out of the bathroom with his hair in tight coils and teeth freshly brushed, and froze. His eyes darted from the bathroom to the apartment's exit, like he wasn't sure where he should be other than elsewhere.

Before Taye could backpedal into the bathroom again, Ari released Val from his clutches and said, "You're coming to the shop with me today, right?"

Taye and Val relaxed in perfect synchronicity, each of them glad to be spared more awkward sentimentality.

~

"I SEE THE HEX IS STILL GOING STRONG," TAYE COMMENTED as he set aside his guitar some hours later. "Remind me why we're here when no one else is?"

"Principle," Ari admitted without looking up from the banking app on his phone. "If I can't confront the asshole who hexed me, the least I can do is show them I'm unbothered."

"But you are bothered."

Ari sighed and shot him a dark look. "Yes, but they don't need to know that. Ergo, the shop stays open."

With a long suffering groan, Taye picked up his guitar again. This time, his aimless strumming produced nothing but melody; he was well past trying to pique anyone's curiosity with magic.

"It's also practical," Ari added a touch defensively. "How will we know when the hex is done running its course unless we're here to see its effects stop?"

Taye just snorted and continued playing.

Ari didn't recognize the tune, and Taye switched it up long before a full song would reach its conclusion. After the fourth or fifth switch, Ari concluded that Taye wasn't practicing any particular line up; he was simply keeping his hands busy. A part of Ari was tempted to suggest he fill the idleness by practicing his magic, but a larger part figured Taye deserved the reprieve. Of all the wizards in their coven, no one else had shown as much investment or made as great an improvement.

Besides, Ari appreciated the background noise. It made things less tedious.

When lunch time came along, Taye was still strumming along with one foot up on a neighboring chair as he slouched. Ari showed his appreciation by stopping on his way to the kitchen to give Taye's cheek a kiss.

The guitar strings gave a clashing whine as Taye's fingers slipped in surprise.

"Sorry," Ari murmured as he hurried along. "I'll be back in a minute with lunch."

He could feel Taye's stare like a sunbeam burning into his back as he hightailed it to the back room. Taye didn't call out to him or offer any reassurances, and Ari's heart sank. His thoughts spiraled as he threw together some croissant sandwiches.

He pulled cheese and turkey from the fridge and tried to remember the last time he initiated such casual affection between them. He cut the croissants in half and wondered why Taye didn't reciprocate. Spreading mustard coincided with the acknowledgment that he'd slipped back into old patterns too easily, and now Taye had lost all romantic interest.

Ari finished making lunch and took a moment to compose and recite an apology before he returned to the shop proper.

He never got to say it, though.

Two women stood in the shop. The one was tall and willowy, draped in a chic black dress and shawl. Despite the late afternoon hour, she wore the darkest of sunglasses as she trailed her fingers along a shelf of historical literature. The second woman was no less slender, though a good foot behind her companion in terms of height; she wore a bright pastel dress that suited her smile even if it was at odds with the autumnal season.

They were easily the most gorgeous people Ari had ever laid eyes on. After one dumbstruck moment, he recognized the delicate faerie glamours for what they were.

Standing behind the register, Taye gave Ari a wide eyed look as he nodded toward the women.

Ari didn't need to be nudged into action a second time. He deposited their lunch with Taye and moseyed on over toward the prospective customers.

Holy shit, but his heart was pounding away in his throat. His hands felt the slightest bit clammy.

Clearing his throat as unobtrusively as possible, Ari started his usually greeting, "Welcome to Grimoires and Good—"

"You can make a decent cappuccino, can't you?" the tall one asked without redirecting her sunglasses from the shelves.

Her dismissive attitude rankled, but Ari couldn't pinpoint if it was her Louis Vuitton watch or Gucci necklace carrying her glamour charm. All snubs aside, he needed to make some money, and she had it.

"One cappuccino, coming right up," he assured with a coolly professional smile. His expression warmed as he met the smaller woman's beaming eyes. "And for you?"

She studied him from head to toe before answering, but her smile never faltered. "Why don't you surprise me?"

Feeling off kilter and like he was being tested, Ari retraced his path to the backroom. He got out the milk and espresso on auto pilot before a sudden thought gave him pause.

He hadn't sensed any witchcraft or wizardry coming from the two women themselves, only the elusive touch of Fae artifacts. All the recent warnings about the Council's machinations swam to the surface of his thoughts on an unwelcome, but inevitable tide.

Sighing, Ari set the milk to steam before leaning his lower back on the counter and closing his eyes.

It was easy to find what he needed. His coven existed as three bright spots in the background of his mind, and their warmth put the rest of the landscape to shame. Ari reached for them with a noncorporeal hand and asked for aid without words, only feeling.

Val was first to respond. She sent him a flood of power and reassurance, tinged with stony resolve. Dazzle's answer came flavored by surprise and worry, but it came all the same. Then Taye's Magic came rushing toward him in a metaphysical flood.

They gave so freely, it was humbling. Perhaps he was still a little raw from the morning's heart-to-heart with Val, because Ari found himself a little choked up.

With far more power than he needed, Ari compiled the cappuccino by muscle memory and focused on expanding his senses to the other room. He would have preferred a well-constructed communion casting, complete with incense and a tarot deck, but he had neither the time nor the covert access to the tools. It wasn't the first time he'd broken the rules of witchcraft, but it was the first time he did so with intention.

It was smooth. Easy. It was like wading into a warm bath and letting the water sap the tension from his muscles. Magic welcomed him with open arms, and there was a soft trill of joy somewhere in the quagmire of Ari's awareness.

Ari asked for clarity, that was all. Were the mystery shoppers friendly? He knew they couldn't be malicious, thanks to the wards, but were they here with ulterior motives? Would someone tasked with a job on the Council's behalf even trigger the wards at all?

The answer came on a gentle breeze through a nonexistent window. Magic detected no ill intent or covertness on the property, but simple, if intense curiosity.

Interesting, Ari decided.

When he returned to the storefront with a cappuccino in one hand and a green tea concoction in the other, he was startled to discover Taye leaning on the register, absolutely at ease. Ari's heart skidded to a brief stop when he realized Taye was chatting with the tall woman in a most flirtatious manner.

Only two questions occurred to him then: where the hell did that suave little grin come from, and why wasn't Ari the recipient?

"Thank you for waiting," Ari said as he handed over the

goods and hip-checked Taye away from the register in one smooth motion.

While Ari closed the transaction, he felt Taye lingering nearby. The jerk kept silent, but Ari could feel him vibrating with suppressed laughter. As the woman carried off their purchases, Ari rounded on him.

"Is that what you call customer service?"

Taye's mirth dampened to a thoughtful, yet curiously intense frown. "No. If you want that, you'll have to actually pay me."

Ari recoiled, his jaw hanging open. "That's not what I meant."

"No? What exactly did you mean, then?" Taye interjected, folding his arms with an expectant look.

Ari's face heated at an alarming rate. He opened his mouth to retort, but nothing came out.

Slow and too damn attractive, a knowing smirk brightened Taye's face.

"How delightful!" cried the bubbly woman.

Ari and Taye turned to see the two shoppers on the far side of the shop. While the tall one held her cup aloft as she studied the mummified troll in the corner, her petite companion was not so composed. She bounced on the balls of her feet, seeming to dance in place as she gulped her drink and stared around the shop with wonder.

She noticed their attention and bounded toward the counter. She drained the drink as she went.

"You have a gift, Mr. Jamison," she announced, setting her paper cup on the counter between them. She chirped, "I'll have another!"

With a bemused arch of his brow, Ari tossed the used cup in the trash and went to make her another tea. It wasn't anything special, simply the first thing he could imagine the perky woman drinking.

When he returned, Taye wasn't flirting, but leaning on the bakery display with a patient smile as he listened to the woman chatter. Whatever riveting tale she was spinning came to an abrupt end as Ari approached and her focus zeroed in on the new beverage. She paid without fuss and took a long draw from the full cup before reached out to pat the back of Taye's hand.

"He's a special one. I'd keep him close if I were you," she said with a wink.

Then she was gone, prancing off toward her companion like she hadn't a care in the world.

Hands on his hips, Ari studied Taye's rigid posture and stricken smile. "What was that about?"

"No idea."

The strangest part was, Ari believed him.

BUSINESS PICKED UP AFTER THAT. CUSTOMERS RETURNED TO the shop over the course of the afternoon in a slow trickle. It was nothing like the traffic Ari was used to before Taye entered his life, but it was a breath of fresh air after days of negative profits.

Yet Ari's worry didn't let up. Of all the people who visited the shop that day, none of them were mundane. Worse still, Ari couldn't identify a single one of them as a witch or wizard.

"Seems like the hex is finally done with you," Taye commented as Ari closed out the register that evening.

"Maybe," Ari mused uncertainly.

He bit his tongue, wondering if he should tell Taye about

the suspiciously vague Magic he sensed from the day's customers. While he hemmed and hawed over the subject, he watched Taye clear the remaining pastries from the display case into a trash bag.

Now that Ari thought on it, Taye had been far from idle all day. A good amount of recent sales came about after Taye turned his easy smile and a few kindly words on Ari's prospective customers. Even without retrieving his guitar from behind the counter, Taye seemed to act as Ari's personal good luck charm.

As Taye locked up the shop some minutes later, Ari commented, "If I didn't know any better, I'd say you were auditioning for sales associates today."

Mid-stride toward home, Taye froze. His face went stoic. "You offering?"

Ari faltered, almost tripping to a halt. "I wasn't. At least . . . not consciously."

Then they stood there, staring at each other with nothing coherent to say. All sorts of feelings weighed down the air.

Truth be told, Ari wasn't thinking of offering Taye a job. His intentions began and ended with the desire to tease Taye for his casual flirting and seamless rapport building. Once he got over the sting of jealousy, it was humorous how easily people spoke with Taye.

He must have made one hell of a music therapist.

After a prolonged moment of discomfort, Ari blurted out, "Do you want to work with me?"

"Do you want me to?"

Ari sputtered, "Of course. Maybe. I mean . . . I've never had any employees before, but if it's you . . . I think I could trust you. With the store, I mean."

"Oh."

"Oh?" Ari mocked, his laugh incredulous.

A slow, speculative smile crept across Taye's face as his shoulders eased. "I thought you were backing out on us again. You surprised me earlier with that kiss."

Ari cringed and turned to resumed walking, in complete dismissal as he huffed, "Ridiculous."

Laughing, Taye hurried to catch up. Ari heard his footsteps, felt the brush of his hand along the small of his back. He felt it before Taye caught up to him as clearly as he felt the stupid besotted smile crossing his own lips.

He felt a lot, but not the shift in magical energies as a witch activated their runes.

"Ari?"

A dull, throbbing pain enveloped Ari's whole being. It was the first thing he became aware of.

"Ari? Baby, say something."

It was a curious sensation. It wasn't pain in the traditional sense, but a low-grade ache that suffused every muscle and synapse with such totality that it couldn't be ignored. It felt like the flu, only the upset wasn't limited to his physical body. His mind hurt. His soul hurt too.

"You're blinking! That's good. That's real good. Come on."

"Is he alright?"

"Should someone call an ambulance?"

"No, thanks. We're good. He's good. Right, Ari?"

The noise was the next thing to make sense. Ari noticed the concerned mutterings of strangers around the same time he noticed Taye's fervent whispers, begging him to sit up and say something coherent.

"I think he had a stroke."

"Don't be silly. He just fainted, probably from hunger. Someone should feed that boy a sandwich."

The scent of ozone filled his nose to the exclusion of all else. It smelled pungent, making his eyes and throat itch with the cloying taste of metal. There was a touch of something rancid in it too, like his upper lip was coated in a thin layer of sulfur.

"Stand up, baby. Come on. Let's get you home."

His head spun with a series of incomprehensible light points in a sea of dark cobblestone and sky. The hurt persisted, but as Ari found his feet under him, he began to notice the input from the physical world around him. It gave him something to focus on, a buoy to latch on to instead of losing himself in that dreadful, all-encompassing ache.

Taye was there. His hand griped Ari's forearm while the other held him up around the waist. Ari recognized the firm lines of his body even as he struggled to recognize the pinched expression on the wizard's face. The furrows in his brow were deeper than ever, and Ari longed to smooth them away with a kiss.

The grooves of concern didn't lighten as Taye aimed a smile over Ari's shoulder at a bystander.

"Thanks, but that's not necessary."

What wasn't necessary?

"I got him," said Taye, and Ari slumped in his arms with a relieved whimper.

Ari couldn't have said how long it took them to reach the apartment. Between concerned strangers, the scant distance, and Ari's questionable sense of balance, it certainly took longer than it should have. Regardless, they made it to the building to find Val pacing in the foyer and Dazzle fidgeting with his car keys like they were the neck of a witch he really wanted to strangle.

"My God, what happened?" Dazzle whined, reaching for him.

Dazzle wasn't in full drag that night, but the amount of pink glitter on his eyelids and wig made Ari wince. As he buried his face in Taye's throat, he heard Val issue a pitiful, warbling mewl.

"Not here," Taye insisted as he cupped the back of Ari's head and held him close. "Let's get him inside."

They must have picked him up at that point, because all Ari felt were warm arms and swooshing air before the soft give of a mattress welcomed him. He lay there like a dead weight, and the thought was apt enough to make him smile through the full-body pangs.

Closing his eyes, Ari focused on breathing. This would pass. The pain wasn't so severe that it constituted an emergency. It would pass. It had to.

It was easier to tell himself that without the peanut gallery fretting over his prone body.

"Witches," Taye explained to the others. "It was a trap, and he walked right into it."

"Who the hell sets a magical trap on a public street?" Dazzle seethed.

"If I knew, I'd be beating them to a pulp right now."

"I don't understand," Val whined, and Ari felt the cool tip of her nose brush along his cheek. "What were they trying to do to him?"

"I don't know!"

"Well, what the hell do you know?"

"Nothing! Alright? One second he was fine, the next there was this surge of power. I reacted without thinking and if I hadn't already had one hand inside the spell circle when it was activated, I don't think I could've pulled him out at all. Shit, maybe I shouldn't have and that's why he's all . . ."

As Taye's voice trailed off, the notes of self-blame were untenable. Ari made a short, harsh grunt of protest.

"Oh, Ari!" Val mewled, nuzzling the hair off his forehead.

"Not Taye's fault," Ari murmured without opening his eyes.

"Hush," Dazzle scolded. "You rest. We'll get it sorted out after you feel better."

For no good reason, this made Ari's chest go tight. His eyes stung, and he just knew they'd overflow if he dared to open them.

"Where does it hurt?" Val asked. "How can I help?"

Dammit all, but Ari lost the fight with his tear ducts.

Instantly, Val's furry body curled into the crook of his neck and shoulder. As her head came to rest on his chest, Ari felt Dazzle's telltale manicure scratching along his arm in a soft, soothing glide. The bed sank with Taye's weight as he settled by Ari's hip, and a large hand gripped his knee.

They were all there. His conundrum was there, and they wouldn't let anyone hurt him.

The certainty of it rocked through him with more force than the witch's spell could have hoped for. His breath caught, and his heart skipped a beat. For one euphoric moment, the comfort of their presence outstripped the pain lingering in his soul and bones.

The reprieve was too brief. The discomfort reasserted itself not with a vengeance, but in a steady trickle of returned sensation. It was like healing from a pulled muscle, like the moment of ease inspired movement the body wasn't ready to sustain, and the result was another bout of deep seated hurt.

There was nothing to do but wait for it to pass. Rather like the hex, Ari thought.

Bracing himself, Ari opened his wet eyes and raised a shaky hand to give Val's rump a pat.

"There were runes," he said. "I noticed them too late. Someone needs to go back and make sure they're not still there."

"I'll go," Taye said as he lurched to his feet.

"Not alone," Ari admonished. "Val, go with him. If the runes are still there, take pictures so we can cross-reference them. Stay alert."

"Sure thing, boss," Val teased, but there was a hard edge to her voice Ari didn't recognize. "Whoever did this won't get a second chance. You'll stay with him?"

"Obviously," Dazzle drawled as if offended. "Anyone besides you two walks through that door, I'm dousing them in a pot of poison ivy concentrate before I stab their eyes out with my nails."

They all stared at him, but Dazzle only puffed out his chest and flipped a curl of bubblegum-pink hair over his shoulder.

That, clearly, was the end of the discussion.

ARI SLEPT LIKE THE DEAD. HE REALLY, REALLY SHOULDN'T have.

"Oh, thank fuck," Dazzle said as Ari heaved himself off the mattress and into a sitting position.

It took a little effort. His muscles and bones protested the movement, but the pain was minimal. It was like the day of recovery after pushing too hard at the gym. The ache was there, but it was no longer debilitating. There was a dull weakness lingering in the metaphysical corners of his being too, and while it could be ignored, Ari wasn't foolish enough to chalk it up to a nonissue.

Blinking, Ari started up at Dazzle, with his short pink bob and red rimmed eyes scrubbed clean of any makeup.

"How long did I sleep?" he asked.

"Too long," Dazzle gripped as he plopped down on the edge of Ari's bed. "It's morning. Almost time to open the shop."

"Shit," Ari groaned as he made to out of bed.

Dazzle stopped him with five long nails curling into his nightshirt.

Ari stared from the fist holding him in place to the way Dazzle chewed his lower lip. "What's wrong?"

"Taye and Val," Dazzle whispered with obvious reluctance. "They didn't come back last night. I couldn't wake you any sooner."

Uncomprehending, Ari continued to stare.

"They went to check out the runes that attacked you," Dazzle said with strained patience. "They never came back."

Ari shook his head. "That's not right. It's a five minute walk away . . ."

"Taye's phone is off," Dazzle whined. "Why the fuck would his phone be off?"

"Wait." Ari swallowed the jagged rock in his throat and tried to make Dazzle's words make sense. "What are you saying?"

Dazzle tried to answer. He opened his mouth, drew a breath, met Ari's eye and everything. Then he burst into messy, ugly tears.

ON A GOOD, NORMAL DAY, THE SPOT WHERE ARI WAS attacked was about a five minute walk from the apartment. Ari and Dazzle made it there in two, maybe less.

"There's nothing here," Dazzle panted. With his wide eyes and frantic looking about, he looked closer than ever to panicking.

This wasn't an entirely accurate assessment, however. Scrutinizing the area turned up no sign of Taye or Val, and at first glance there wasn't any proof anything untoward recently happened. Despite what his eyes said, Ari couldn't shake the feeling that something valuable was there, waiting to be noticed.

It was early morning and the few people roaming Olde Town Arvada were preoccupied with commuting to work. They were too busy to notice Ari crouching down on the sidewalk and running his fingers over the cobblestone like a total weirdo. The mundane commuters simply stepped around him as they hustled by.

"What are you doing?" Dazzle hissed under his breath as Ari crab walked into his shadow to continue inspecting.

"I'm looking for the runes," Ari answered distractedly, both hands groping the ground.

Ari knew he had the right spot; he remembered passing in front of the new age tattoo parlor right before the world exploded into confusion and pain. As if his memory weren't sufficient, he could feel Magic egging him on like a personal cheer squad breathing down his neck. This was the spot where it happened, and there was proof to be found. He just had to be meticulous in his search.

"Ari, people are staring."

"Shush."

Ari ignored Dazzle as thoroughly as he did the shop owner who harrumphed as she gave him a wide berth on her way to unlocking a nearby storefront.

His fingers stumbled over a thin blob of something smooth and invisible. Ari let out a stunned chuckle.

"You're not going to believe this," he said as he looked up at Dazzle, "They used glue to write the runes."

Dazzle's nose wrinkled in bemused distaste. "Like . . . Elmer's? Who does that?"

Ari closed his eyes and asked the universe for paper and pencil. He felt the paper form under his sweater-vest in the same moment the requested utensil materialized in his pocket. Broad daylight and as publicly exposed as it was, Ari manifested the tools he needed with no one the wiser.

"What the fuck," Dazzle seethed, pulling at his hair as Ari laid the paper on the ground, "You can't just do that in full view of the mundanes, Ari! This is the exact type of shit that makes the Council so nervous!"

Ari was past caring about that. He scrubbed the pencil over the paper, and sure enough, the graphite caught on the underlying glue to reveal a partial rune. The top sections of the symbol were smooth and bulbous where the glue remained intact, but the lower sections were jagged and unfinished. Someone had attempted to scrap off the glue.

Heart in his throat, Ari wondered if that was why Taye and Val never came home. Perhaps they had chanced upon the culprit cleaning up after themselves.

"We need to get to the shop," Ari said as he climbed to his feet with his knuckles white around the rune rubbing. "This isn't a standard symbol I know on sight, but I think I've seen it before. We need to know what this thing does, and who in the community is capable of weaponizing it."

Realizing that Dazzle was being uncharacteristically quiet, Ari tore his eyes from the paper. Dazzle's face was ghostly white as he stared up at the sky behind Ari.

A shock of numbness stole over Ari as he turned to follow Dazzle's stare.

Dark, billowing clouds filled the air above the shops.

They blossomed and rose in a steady stream that seemed both natural and disconcerting.

"What?" Ari whispered, the paper in his hand crinkling in protest.

Distantly, as if through a haze, Ari thought he heard sirens. The wailing grew closer as the peculiar clouds grew larger.

"Dazzle?" Ari whispered, transfixed.

"Yeah?" Dazzle choked.

"That's not close to my shop, is it?"

Dazzle didn't answer him, but really, Ari didn't need him to.

It was a short trip, but they never made it to the destination.

"This is a bad dream," Ari heard himself say as if through a dense fog. "It's just a nightmare."

He knew it wasn't, though. Logically, he knew even his worst nightmares never went so far as to decimate his shop and everything in it. Such a thing wasn't safe to consider, not even subconsciously.

"Ari?" said Dazzle, "We shouldn't be here right now. Let's leave."

Someone tugged on his arm, brushed the soot from his cheek. Ari barely noticed, yet alone cared.

"You don't need to see this."

He could feel the heat from where he stood, several shops down and across the street behind a flimsy barrier of yellow caution tape. By some miracle, the flames hadn't spread to the neighboring stores; they seemed to rage against the constraint with higher and fiercer temperatures in response.

There would be nothing left when the fire finished decimating everything Ari built over the years.

"I don't want to watch this, Ari. Please, let's go."

Dazzle was crying. Ari felt his friend's arms enveloped him and the face against his shoulder drenching him in tears, but he couldn't make himself respond. He knew he should, but his limbs were inordinately heavy, and he couldn't find the energy to lift them. Dazzle just kept on crying and pleading, and all Ari could do was stand there.

He stood there, watching his life's work go up in literal flames.

"A gas leak," a police officer would theorize later.

"Local teens, fucking around and finding out," a firefighter would eventually tell him.

The official story meant nothing to Ari. It didn't matter what the mundane authorities determined. The end result would be the same.

Grimoires and Goodies no longer existed. Technically, the foundation was still intact, but by the time the firefighters could make any progress, the spirit of the store was already burned out. Nothing but ash and mottled shelves remained.

The shop was dead, and a large part of Ari died right along with it.

ARI STARED AT THE FIRE MARSHAL'S BUSINESS CARD LIKE IT would do him any good. He already knew it wouldn't. A gas leak was the current suspicion. They were opening an investigation.

The hex wasn't broken. That was a fact Ari was certain of. The single day of half decent business was a fluke. It was a fucking fluke he paid dearly for.

"I'll take that," Dazzle murmured as he slipped the officer's card off the coffee table.

Ari didn't know where his friend put it, only that it was no longer in front of him. His vision filled with the wood grain of the table top. He'd had the furniture for years, but somehow this was the first time he'd noticed the gnarled swirls in its pattern.

A steaming mug of coffee appeared in front of him. Ari didn't pick it up, so Dazzle's hands appeared to forcibly wrap Ari's fingers around the drink. Ari watched Dazzle's rainbow nails encircle his wrist and guide the coffee toward his face, but it felt like he was watching a movie, not living the actions himself.

"Drink," Dazzle insisted, helping Ari press the ceramic to his lips.

Muscle memory took over, and Ari drank. He didn't notice the taste, but he noticed the heat. It scalded his tongue and made him think about sky high flames and burning books.

TIME PASSED. ARI SPENT IT ON THE COUCH, STARING AT THE imperfections in his coffee table and imbibing whatever consumables Dazzle brought him.

Eventually, enough time passed for Dazzle's patience to expire.

"We need to talk about Val and Taye," Dazzle insisted as he planted his butt on the coffee table across from Ari.

Ari sighed and slumped further into the cushions. "Maybe they wizened up after the attack and took off."

Dazzle stared at him, nostrils flaring with temper. "You don't believe that."

"No, but I want to."

Ari pried himself out of the cushions and promptly folded forward to plop his head in his hands.

"I don't know what to do," he whispered, so low he thought Dazzle might not hear him. Perhaps a part of him even hoped Dazzle didn't.

As usual, he had no such luck.

"Damn it, Ari. I know you're upset, but we can't afford for you to check out right now. Our coven is being picked apart, and it's like you don't even care."

"Of course I care," he said dully. "Val's one of the most capable wizards I know, and Taye's quick on his feet. They'll be fine."

"They are missing," Dazzle stressed.

Ari's heart gave a painful lurch.

"Shit," Dazzle hissed under his breath. "Don't start crying, Ari. That's not— Wait."

"I can't handle this right now," Ari said, shaking his head till his brain sloshed against his skull with a dizzying ache. "I can't. I just can't."

His breath hitched and what remained of his emotional control snapped as clear and sharp as a broken bone.

"Even if the insurance doesn't pay out, you'll be okay," Dazzle promised at some point.

The sky outside was dusky and gray. That was Ari's only indication that the day was wasting away. He'd been in bed for most of it. Every part of him still hurt, but he could no longer tell if the ache was born from the magical attack or coming from his exhausted emotions.

Dazzle stroked his hair. "Don't you worry, Sugar Baby. Daddy's got your back."

Ari sniffled into his pillow and didn't respond.

The soothing strokes to his head halted. "Seriously? You're just going to let that one slide without comment? Not even an eye roll, huh?"

Lacking the energy to do much else, Ari let it slide.

DAZZLE LEFT THE APARTMENT. ARI THOUGHT HE TOLD HIM not to go out alone, but he couldn't remember what was said, if anything at all. He was only half conscious and splayed out on the couch when Dazzle announced his departure.

Where had Dazzle gone, anyway?

Like an answer to his sluggish thoughts, a timid knock sounded on the door. Ari dragged his weary bones over to the door, fully expecting to find Dazzle on the other side.

Instead, he was met with a silver fox of a man wearing a sympathetic smile and a pair of pristine shoes from ancient history.

Ari didn't have the energy to scowl, so he leaned his weight on the door frame with a deadpan stare. "What are you doing here, Puckman?"

The Morrigan raised his hands in apparent innocence. "I'm only here to talk."

Ari frowned.

Hooking his thumbs through the belt loops of his jeans, Puckman toed at the edge of the welcome mat. He seemed hesitant, which was a first in Ari's reckoning.

"I saw the smoke," Puckman said, glancing at Ari through his eyelashes. "I know what happened to the shop."

Spine stiffening, Ari reeled back.

Puckman took it as an invitation. Ari was too stunned and hurt to stop him from waltzing right on in. The bastard even had the gall to take the door from Ari's grip and close it for him.

"Ari, I am so, so sorry."

Ari was shaking. It was a subtle tremor born from grief and exhaustive anger, and it paralyzed him as Puckman stepped closer and enveloped him in his arms. A large hand cupped the back of his head to urge Ari to rest against a sturdy shoulder, but Ari's neck was too tense to bend.

"I never wanted this for you," Puckman whispered, the gentle pressure of his hand unrelenting. "I tried to warn you, sweetheart. I tried so hard—"

Ari yanked free with a suddenness that stunned Puckman into silence.

"That's right," Ari said, sucking back a deep breath and willing his heartbeat to calm the fuck down. "You did warn me, didn't you?"

Puckman frowned, but his eyes were clear of confusion. The expression he wore was all disapproval and frustration, like he thought Ari was fussing over nothing. How many times had Ari been the recipient of that look before he finally tired of it?

"You're not here to comfort me, Puckman," Ari said with a weary sigh.

Puckman's eyes widened before he schooled his face into a sorrowful mask. "I only came as a friend—"

"We're not friends," Ari cut in. "We never were."

Puckman's pitiable frown lifted into a wry half smile. "I suppose not. We were more than that."

"I used to think so," Ari said as he crossed his arms and put more space between them. "But I was young and naive then."

After everything that had happened in the past day or two, Ari didn't have the energy to scream at the other witch. He wanted to. Magic itself probably didn't know how badly he wanted to, but he couldn't.

It was despicable of Puckman to come here, pretending to be sympathetic, so he could rope Ari back into his sphere of influence all over again. If Ari ever needed the reminder that Puckman was an opportunistic dick, this would be it.

Without a second of hesitation, Ari opened the door and motioned for Puckman to get out.

~

MUCH TO ARI'S CHAGRIN, PUCKMAN'S VISIT WAS NOT THE only unhappy encounter within the same hour.

"Just when I thought this day couldn't get any worse," Ari lamented as he dropped the bowl of Chinese takeout on the coffee table. "My chicken's overcooked. If that's not an apt metaphor for my life right now, I don't know what is."

No one responded to him. No one was around to hear him in the first place.

Everyone was gone. Dazzle was done watching him mope, and Taye and Val were missing. He was alone, and not even Grimoires and Goodies awaited to provide him comfort.

Shit. Now he was crying.

Wiping at his eyes, Ari centered himself on the couch and took deep, calming breaths. The tears slowed but didn't stop. Squeezing his eyes shut, Ari tried to find anything to distract him from his worries.

Nothing presented itself.

No, instead of distancing himself from the situation, closing his eyes only made things worse. His throat constricted as his mind summoned images of Taye. He provided himself a crisp picture of that chiseled face and colorful eyes, of his dry sarcasm and stubborn helpfulness. Ari's heart gave a vicious pang against his ribs.

God, but he wished Taye was here with him, holding his hand and rubbing his back.

Ari startled at the prickle of Magic responding to his longing.

"Taye?" Ari whispered, terrified and hopeful in equal measure.

He opened his eyes, but no one was there.

Shutting his eyes tighter than before, Ari turned his focus inward. In his misery and fright, he'd completely forgotten about the coven connection he shared with his missing wizards. His heart lurched with desperation as he sought out the glimmering corners of his mind and soul where Taye and Val belonged.

He found them. They were there, warm and smoldering in the background of his awareness. They were alive, he realized with a jolt of guilt. At least they were alive.

The waterworks overpowered him then, leaking through his closed lids like they were the world's most ineffective dam. Once they started in earnest, they refused to stop.

"I've spent the past day making calls and pounding on doors," Dazzle said as he paced the length of the living room. "Meanwhile, you've done virtually nothing to try and find Taye and Val. Ari, they need their Morrigan right now."

"I warned you," Ari mumbled into his pillow. "I'm not fit to be a Morrigan."

"Ari," Dazzle whimpered.

"They're alive," Ari murmured without lifting his head. "They wouldn't be if the Council had them, or the witches responsible for the nemiza. It's obvious they cut their losses and ran. You should probably do the same."

On the other side of the coffee table, Dazzle was crying. Ari could feel him there, a solid lump of misery dropping onto the table amid devastatingly quite sobs. A part of Ari lit up with the impulse to go to him, to take the wizard in his arms and let them dissolve into a pathetic mess together.

Ari chose to bury his face in couch cushions instead.

It took a while, but eventually Dazzle's tears ran dry. He tried to talk to Ari, but his words turned into warbled junk by the time Ari's brain finished a halfhearted attempt at processing.

"Please," Dazzle begged. "Please, Ari. Potions are useless here. I'm useless. I need you to do something. Anything!"

Dazzle dragged him from the couch, his grip on Ari's arm bruising.

"There has to be something you can do. As a witch, if not as a Morrigan. Look."

Ari didn't have the slightest idea how they ended up on the floor with a book and a local atlas spread out in front of them. On his knees, Ari sat there in a useless heap as Dazzle fussed over him. He didn't activate a single muscle as Dazzle lifted his hand for him to place a thin chain in his hand.

No, wait, it wasn't a chain. It was a necklace. With a start, Ari noticed the uneven nodes along the chain's length. When he looked down into his palm, he found the blood and gemstone necklace that acted as his Morrigan's amulet.

"You can find them," Dazzle said, his speech fast and hushed. "You can scry for them, right? Scrying's something all witches can do, it's like a staple."

Ari shot him a dour look over the atlas. "This isn't scrying, Dazzle. If anything, you're talking about geomancy—"

"Same difference!" Dazzle hissed, gesticulating wildly. "I've been hoofing it around town and badgering every wizard I know for info, but you can use magic to pinpoint their location! I know you can. You can find them this way. Right?"

Ari didn't waste his bated breath on telling Dazzle he'd never attempted geomancy before. It was as equally a common practice as scrying, but there was a lifetime's worth of common magic Ari never bothered with.

For Taye and Val, though? He could try for them. It was too little too late, and he doubted he had the mental or magical strength to pull it off, but he could try.

Ari let the necklace hang from his fist in a double line of linked stones and raw intention. The book Dazzle provided was open to a chant in ancient Greek, but the words blurred too much when he tried to focus on them. With anxious sweat collecting on his brow, Ari closed his eyes and willed the universe to grant him the information he sought.

Magic answered his call, as it always did. It rushed into his head and down his arm, lighting up his fingers before it funneled into the piece of jewelry. The power coalesced in the stones, making them vibrate. The chain swung in a wide circle, gaining speed with each rotation.

Nearby, Ari could feel Dazzle crouching, waiting. He was holding his breath.

Praying he wouldn't disappoint his only remaining friend, Ari pushed all the metaphysical strength and intention of his entire being into the necklace. When he felt dizzy with the effort, Ari extended his arm to hold the dancing necklace over the map.

"Please, work," he whispered, "Help me bring them home."

The necklace whirled in the physical embodiment of his

frantic need. It sent vibrations up his arm, to the point he felt like the limb had gone insensate. When Ari dared to peak, he discovered a blur of unchecked activity spinning beneath his raised fist.

It wasn't working, Ari realized in dismay. He pushed and pushed as hard as he could, but the most he could make happen was the endless movement of the chain.

Panting, Ari lowered his arm till the gems clinked on the floor. His arm was trembling.

"What happened?" Dazzle demanded. "Why'd you stop?"

Ari hated to disappoint him. He turned to tell Dazzle that it wasn't working, and discovered that the one thing worse than disappointment was heartbreak.

ARI WASTED ANOTHER STRETCH OF COUNTLESS HOURS LAYING on the couch and scrolling aimlessly through the apps on his phone. He was vaguely aware of Dazzle giving him a disgusted look before he stormed out of the apartment again. He told himself he didn't care.

He already knew he was a shit Morrigan. It was well past time the rest of them figured it out too.

The conundrum was a mistake, his phone said.

It took Ari a long, convoluted moment to realize he wasn't projecting his thoughts and misreading the incoming text. He sat upright, gripping the phone in both hands as he pulled up the message from an unfamiliar number.

The conundrum was a mistake, it said. Three blinking dots appeared beneath the message, and Ari's heart squeezed.

Far as Ari knew, Taye's phone was still out of commission, but he couldn't help the way his heart leaped in anticipation. Maybe Taye got his hands on a new one. Maybe he really wasn't at the mercy of the covens or in the Council's grubby paws. Maybe he was making a run for it, and had the decency to let Ari know.

And Val was with him. She had to be. Val didn't know about the shop's fate; she would have judged Taye's need for support greater than Ari's.

The dots vanished and his phone vibrated with an incoming text. One glance at it, and Ari knew his brief hopes were in vain.

The conundrum was a mistake. I'm here to help you recover, whenever you're ready. - Eren.

Face warping with enraged tears, Ari threw his phone across the room.

CHAPTER 25

*A*ri was in the middle of smothering himself with bedding and pillows when Dazzle made his reappearance.

"Rise and shine, Sugar Baby!" he crowed, busting in Ari's bedroom door. "Seriously, Ari. Get up. We have company."

Ari groaned as the blankets were yanked off him.

"Holy shit, what happened to you? Your eyes are red and swollen."

Glaring up at his only remaining friend and coven member, Ari attempted to snag his covers back. He was still achy and weak from the attack, not to mention the days of mourning the shop.

Dazzle had no sympathy for his struggles, though. He held the sheets aloft with a flourish worthy of a matador, then he unceremoniously dropped them on the floor.

"I hate you," Ari glowered.

"Shut up, you love me," Dazzle countered as he reached into the breast pocket of his custom lavender suit jacket. Out came a stainless steel flask, which he was quick to unscrew and hand over.

Ari eyed the flask dubiously. "Does your employer know you bring alcohol to work?"

"They wouldn't care if they knew, but even if they did, this"—Dazzle wagged the contraband with an impish grin—"isn't alcohol. Think of it as concentrated caffeine with a little cosmetic pick-me-up thrown in."

"Is everything alright in there, Mr. Davenport?"

Ari froze.

His eyes darted toward the doorway and the vaguely familiar voice. It was a female, he knew that much, but he couldn't place where he knew it from.

Sitting up in bed, Ari narrowed his sights on Dazzle.

Dazzle gave him a knowing smirk and offered the flask again without a word. Ari snatched it up, and Dazzle sashayed out of the room to attend to their mystery guest.

When Dazzle described the concoction as concentrated caffeine, he might have been underselling. One sip and Ari turned antsy with overwhelming energy. He hopped out of bed, and all but flew into a fresh pair of slacks and the first button down his hand fell on. As he rushed past the mirror over his dresser, he noticed the red puffiness from prolonged sobbing was gone. His skin practically glowed with health without the need for his usual morning routine. In record timing, he was put together and ready to face the world again.

Ari skidded to a surprised halt before exiting the room.

He felt better. Not just physically, either. He remembered what happened to the shop, and to Taye and Val, but the knowledge seemed shrouded in a net of numbness. He was aware of the facts and the correlating emotions, but they were dampened somehow. He could function again.

Whatever the flask contained, it was one hell of a pick-me-up.

Shaking himself, Ari tugged his shirtfront straight and

composed himself like he would for a meeting with a private client.

It was a good thing he did.

Ari didn't have the foggiest idea who he would find waiting for him in the apartment proper. When he exited the bedroom, the last person he expected was Councillor Sanchez.

He almost didn't recognize her. Her dark hair was piled atop of her head in a classic bun, and her shapely frame was clad in a gray pantsuit that made her look severe. It added years to her face, and for the first time Ari noticed the fine lines around her eyes and mouth. She made a distinctly different impression than she had the last time they met.

She smiled, and Ari thought he saw a glimmer of warmth reach her eyes.

"Good afternoon, Morrigan Jamison."

"Councillor," Ari breathed.

He failed to mask his surprise as she stood from the armchair to face him. He had a hard time correlating the personable and eager client he knew with the cool, straight laced woman in front of him.

She didn't offer her hand or any other greeting, instead clasping her hand together in front of her hips. Ari noted her body language with a swooping stomach; she wasn't aggressive or reassuring. She was as neutral as could be.

Stowing his sweaty palms in his pockets, Ari asked, "What brings you here? To my home."

Sanchez looked to Dazzle where he lounged on the sofa. "Mr. Davenport assured me I could find you here."

Ari shot Dazzle a sharp look behind her back.

In his defense, Dazzle said, "She has information my Morrigan should probably have."

Ari sighed and folded his arms as he refocused on the

Councillor. "It didn't go so well the last time a Councillor showed up without an invitation."

She held up her hands as if to ward him off. "I'm not here to make demands, Morrigan. I'm looking to make a deal."

Ari didn't budge beyond the narrowing of his eyes. "I was under the impression the Council wouldn't work with me anymore."

Her smile was slight as she said, "The formal boycott was for Grimoires and Goodies, as I recall."

Ari started scowling before he realized she wasn't making a dig at the shop's misfortune. Her smile had a touch of regret to it.

Ari's heart picked up speed, or maybe it was the little burst of hope filling him with nothing but hot air.

Fortunately, Sanchez didn't seem inclined to waste time.

"You haven't been able to locate your missing wizards, have you?"

Ari tensed.

She nodded as if he'd confirmed her suspicions out loud. "The Council has select locations warded against witchcraft. Unofficially, of course."

Ari snorted.

"These wards are infallible," she assured him. "Even to you."

Ari huffed, "I noticed. I assume you're not sharing this with me out of the goodness of your heart."

She didn't even flinch, though her smile turned the slightest bit apologetic. "I want my scroll. In return, I'll give you the location of the Council's nearest prison. I've already confirmed your people are there."

Ari's insides shriveled. The desperately hopeful look on Dazzle's face only made him feel worse.

"I'm sorry, Councillor," he said, slow and sure, "but there was an incident at the shop."

"I heard about the fire."

Of course she did, Ari thought uncharitably. Reigning in his bitter suspicions as best he could, Ari said, "The scroll was lost along with everything else."

She didn't falter, however. "I remember suggesting a particular fairy enchanter to you some years ago. Did you take my advice?"

Ari frowned. "Yes, to disguise the safe."

"I think you'll find the charm was more than a basic faerie glamour." Her voice lowered with excitement and conspiracy. "My guy takes pride in his work. To him, anything worth hiding so well is worth protecting on all fronts."

Ari matched her tone as possibility seized him like a vice. "Even from magically ignited flames?"

Her smile turned grim as she nodded.

Without further discussion, Ari reached out to shake her hand.

THEY HAD TO WAIT TILL NIGHTFALL FOR MUNDANE authorities to clear the scene of the fire. Ari hated to think of his shop like that, but it was a fact; there was no Grimoires and Goodies, only a heap of crispy support beams and so much ash.

"This is depressing," Dazzle murmured as he ducked under the caution tape to help Ari sift through the remains. "Ew. And it's dirty. The things I do for that cat, I swear."

Ignoring Dazzle's running commentary, Ari picked his way through the debris in the direction of the charred remains of the staircase. It led to nothing, but it made for a good reference point. Once he was close, he oriented himself toward what used to be the shadowy corner of dusty boxes disguising his glass safe.

"Seriously?" Dazzle huffed, disgusted as he lifted a charred slab from the rubble between his pointer finger and thumb. "I can't tell if it was a book. Can you imagine if you'd been here when this happened?"

Ari gave a noncommittal hum as he kicked aside the wreckage, clearing a path toward a promising heap.

"I don't think anyone's ever hated me this much," Dazzle said with a depleted sigh. "I'm so sorry, Ari,"

Ari paused before a heap of ravished shelves and broken beams. He wanted to say that this wasn't his first rodeo. He considered telling Dazzle about the day his family kicked him out of their lives, about the pain and the blood and, above all, the outright loathing exhibited by people who should have loved and cherished him above all others.

He glanced over his shoulder to see Dazzle wiping away tears and decided it was a story for another time.

Sighing, Ari squatted to begin clearing the garbage off what he hoped was his safe. He struggled with a burned plank for all of a moment before it lifted with relative ease. As the plank hit the ground and kicked up a cloud of ash, Ari found Dazzle a foot way, slapping his hands together to rid himself of the soot.

"Thanks," Ari said with a tearful croak.

Dazzle smiled wetly and rubbed Ari's back. "Anytime."

Wiping his eyes on the backside of his sleeve, Ari sniffled and laughed. "You're wiping your hand clean on me, aren't you?"

"Who, me? Never."

For good measure, Dazzle's other hand gripped his

shoulder and stroked down hard. A streak of gray was left behind on Ari's sleeve. They both chuckled over it before the pitiful state of their surroundings reassert itself.

Together, they got to work clearing the fallen shelves and their ruined wares until they revealed a neat row of unbothered boxes caked in a thick coat of ash.

"Look at that," Dazzle said as Ari began dusting so he wouldn't have to stick his hand through the soot. "I half expected the faerie glamour to make it impossible to find."

Thankfully, the opposite was the case. The safe's disguise was the only visibly intact thing on the premises. Ari almost started crying again, this time in relief as he pulled the safe upright. He retrieved the gloves hung from his back pocket and slipped them on in record time.

"You got the bag?" Ari asked.

In response, Dazzle whipped out his favorite pink purse and held it open.

Ari eyed the little clutch dubiously.

Dazzle stared at him like Ari was an idiot. "Val enchanted this bag. It's a real life Bag of Holding, fuck you very much."

Ari made the wise decision not to argue further, and a moment later he was inside the safe. His hand closed on the jewelry chest first, and Ari was pleased to see the opening of Dazzle's bag stretch to accommodate it. He managed to stow the cursed skull and mini library of aged texts in a similar manner. Dazzle made a noise of displeasure and wrinkled his nose as the shadiest *Book of Shadows* dropped into his purse, but Ari ignored him.

Then all that was left was the ancient scroll. The moonlight caught on Sanchez's name, and Ari chose to take it as divine reassurance.

"This is going to get Taye and Val back," Ari said as the scroll disappeared into the little bag.

"What about the rest?" Dazzle asked, hefting the bag's strap onto his shoulder. "Could you sell it and use the funds to rebuild the shop?"

Ari hesitated, considering the unknown or dangerous nature of the other artifacts. He didn't like the idea of the nemiza's instructions falling into any random rich person's hands.

Reluctantly, he admitted, "That might not be the most responsible thing to do."

"A bit late for that, don't you think?"

Ari threw back his head and groaned as Dazzle glared to the side. "What are you doing here, Fuckman?"

Ari stepped on Dazzle's toe, hard.

"What did you just call me?" Eren Puckman asked in genuine confusion.

"I said, 'What are you doing here, Puckman?'" Dazzle reiterated without missing a beat.

"None of your business, wizard," Puckman said with an audible sneer.

With a heavy sigh and heavier wince, Ari turned around to face the other witch.

It wasn't an ideal setup, in Ari's opinion. He was covered in ashes and standing in the rubble of what used to be his pride and joy; the last thing he wanted was a run in with Morrigan Puckman.

Sure enough, said Morrigan was as put together and down to earth as he always was. His dark washed jeans and Henley were an unofficial uniform at this point, but Ari was tempted to smear soot into those old sneakers just to get Puckman to stop wearing them.

"It's good to see you, Ari."

"Can't say the same," Ari countered, crossing his arms.

"Quite the coincidence, running into you here the first time I visit since the fire."

"What do you want?" Dazzle demanded.

Ari held up a hand and said, "I got this, Dazzle." Then he lifted his chin in Puckman's direction and repeated, "What do you want?"

Puckman laughed, but he was the only one, and it was short-lived. "I thought someone should tell you; the Council of Wizards has Osondu in custody."

"I'm aware. Goodnight, then."

Ari looped his arm through Dazzle's and made to walk off.

"We need to talk about this, Ari."

Ari glared at Puckman, his grip tightening on Dazzle. "Why? So you can make another attempt at consoling me? News flash, Puckman: you're no good at it, and I'm not interested. We have nothing more to say to each other."

His scathing tone must have stunned Puckman, because Ari and Dazzle made it out of the wreckage and onto the sidewalk before another word was uttered.

"He's gone, Ari," Puckman said with a touch of meanness to his voice. "You get that, right? You'll never see Osondu again."

Dazzle opened his mouth to say something, but Ari's grip turned bruising on his arm as he begged, "Keep walking."

"Look around!" Puckman trailed after them. "This whole coven of wizards idea was the biggest mistake of your life! Look at what it's cost you!"

Dazzle almost jerked free of Ari as he whirled to give Puckman a piece of his mind, but Ari latched on to him with both hands.

"Ignore him," Ari pleaded, speaking to himself as much as to Dazzle. "He's nothing to us."

Ari's whole body shook as he led Dazzle toward the apartment. His face was warm with suppressed anger. He wanted nothing more than to show Puckman that him had no influence over him anymore, but every step felt like a herculean effort.

A part of him longed to turn around, to scream and cry at Puckman till the man was shamefaced. Ari wanted to make him realize just how badly he hurt Ari all those years ago. He wanted to reduce Puckman to the disposable tool he once made Ari feel like.

But what good would it do?

"Osondu's gone," Puckman carried on, trailing behind them like a venomous spider who's silk was stuck to the bottom of Ari's shoe. "You don't need to be concerned with him any longer, Ari, and your coven's practically disbanded with only two of you left. It's time for you to come home!"

Ari snapped and spun. "I am home!"

He snatched up Dazzle's hand, shaking his friend's entire arm as he raised their joined hands in Puckman's gobsmacked face.

"This is my coven," Ari insisted, "Even before Magic got involved, these wizards were my family. They've been there for me every time I needed a hug or a shoulder to cry on. They've supported me through every little hiccup in my life since they day I met them, and they have never, not once, asked more from me than I was willing to give. Can you say the same? No!"

Puckman's mouth hung open as Ari ranted at him, but Ari barely noticed. He certainly didn't care.

"All of the brightest, most fulfilling moments of my life included them, not you, not your coven. You used to say you loved me, but all you really loved was my Magic. Well, now I have plenty of it, thanks to them."

Ari nodded to Dazzle for emphasis, and Dazzle beamed smugly.

"You want to know the secret to all the impressive power I displayed lately?" Ari asked as he rewound his arm with Dazzle's.

Puckman finally closed his mouth, his jaw tight with displeasure.

"It's the same reason my coven's better than yours," Ari said. "We actually care about each other."

"I care about you," Puckman said through his teeth.

"You have a funny way of showing it," Dazzle scoffed.

"You should focus on your own people instead of obsessing over me and mine," Ari advised before turning his back on Puckman. "Now, if you don't mind, I have a coven to rescue."

ouncillor Sanchez was hopefully a woman of her word, whether she wore a sundress or a pantsuit. Ari privately preferred the sundress, though; she was a bit scary as she emerged from the shadows in full Councillor attire. The grim set of her mouth almost made him wonder if she would renege on their deal at the last moment.

Ari was intensely glad he followed Dazzle's advice and stopped at home to clean up. His pinstripe slacks and matching vest felt far more appropriate for clandestine encounters in the dead of night than a sooty button down and jeans. Suitably armored, Ari held his head high as he met Sanchez's eye, Morrigan and Councillor meeting as equals.

"Where are Taye and Val?" Ari demanded. His knuckles went white around the paper bag hanging at his side.

Good God, but was he really about to trade hundreds of thousands of dollars' worth of papyrus for directions? Yes, he told the nervous butterflies in his stomach. Yes, he most certainly was.

Sanchez's eyes narrowed on the paper bag. She frowned in confusion as she pointed. "Is the scroll in that?"

"No, I just like carrying old Safeway bags around downtown in the middle of the night," Ari said. "Of course it is. Now where are my wizards?"

Sanchez pried her eyes from the bag so she could survey the area. "What about Davenport? Where's he?"

"Why do you care?"

She sighed, and the scary Councillor persona seemed to melt away as she rubbed between her brows. "I promised you information, Ari, but I expect you to use it wisely."

Ari's spine straightened in offense. "What makes you think I won't?"

She sighed again, like he was giving her a headache. "You're asking a lot of questions, Morrigan, and none of them are the right ones. I don't suppose you've figured out what the Council has planned for your coven?"

Ari matched her scowl with his own. "At this point, I'm assuming they want all of us dead."

Sanchez flinched, and Ari knew he was right.

"Lady Valkyrie is still respected by a significant portion of the community," Sanchez said without lifting her gaze. "They're likely to hold on to her till after the coven is dissolved—"

"Over my dead body."

"Most likely, yes."

Ari sucked back a breath. For some unknown reason, he hadn't expected her to respond so candidly.

"There can't be a coven without a Morrigan," she stated with a muted shrug. "You were already on the Council's radar with how brazenly you mixed company at the shop. Taking in Taye the way you did simply hastened the matter."

Ari opened his mouth to defend himself, but Sanchez kept talking.

"Above all else, the Council of Wizards is concerned with

maintaining secrecy," she said. "Taye's spontaneous and unschooled witchcraft threatened that in ways we haven't dealt with in centuries. I assumed your strength and lack of affiliation would keep things from escalating to the point the covens would get involved."

"You were too late, then," Ari said as he clocked her use of Taye's given name. "He came to me with death written all over his torso."

Finally, she raised her eyes to look at him. They were wide and wet. "You helped him anyway?"

Scowling, Ari opened his mouth to argue against her poor impression of him.

"Of course you did," Sanchez said, her face softening as she stole the wind from his blustering sails. "You always did what you thought was right, even if it wasn't easy. I admired that about you."

"That's why you sent him to me?" Ari asked.

She nodded.

Ari sighed and stared down at the grocery bag in his hand. "Guess I disappointed you, huh? This can't be how you saw this ending."

She said nothing for a long, awkward moment. Then, with a disbelieving huff, she said, "You're not really going to storm the place by yourself, are you? Won't your odds be better with at least part of your coven at your side?"

Ari grinned. "How knowledgeable of you, Councillor. You've been reading up witchcraft, haven't you?"

Her face reddened as she scowled. "What you're doing is unorthodox, potentially hazardous from certain perspectives. It was worth looking into, especially after everything Taye's been through."

That only piqued Ari's interest more. "He's important to you, isn't he?"

She was spared having to answer him when a shiny Tesla rolled up alongside them. Ari didn't react, but he had an excellent view as Sanchez eyed the vehicle. The car door opened, and a moment later, the Councillor's eyes widened with alarm.

That wasn't right.

Ari turned to see Dazzle strut around the front of the car in full drag. Her sleeveless turtleneck jumpsuit covered an impressive rack with blue rhinestones. Her platforms allowed her to tower over Ari even before the four inches of blown out periwinkle wig were accounted for.

Staring at her in all her fierce glory, Ari couldn't decide whether to laugh or cry. "Nice," he choked, "but a bit impractical, don't you think?"

"Impractical?" Dazzle struck a pose with a hand on her hip while the other framed her face. "Baby, this is my war paint. I told you we should dress to impress, didn't I? Well, this"—she gestured to herself—"is as impressive as it gets."

And really, Ari didn't have anything to say to that. Dazzle stood tall and proud with a confidence that was daunting to anyone who gazed upon her. Perhaps she had a point.

"I think my part in this should be done now," Sanchez murmured.

Ari spun toward her and clutched the Safeway bag to his chest. "Tell me what I need to know, and it's yours."

She looked from Ari to Dazzle and back, utter disillusionment souring her expression. Still, she relented. "I'll do you one better and bring you right up to the front door." Then, sighing like she was already regretting her life choices, Councillor Sanchez raised her hand to the office building they stood in front of.

❧

THE OFFICE BUILDING WAS VACANT. A FEW UNASSUMING LAW offices and tax groups were named on the foyer's directory, but the place reeked with stale air and an atmosphere of general abandonment. Ari half expected the elevator to be inoperable.

As Sanchez promised, the doors opened after a single press of the button.

"She said the sixth floor, right?" Dazzle asked with dismay as she eyed the console.

Ari sighed and jabbed his finger at the blank space below the button for the fifth floor. Sanchez hadn't mentioned an illusion would hide the necessary button, and another magic user might have been stumped, but Ari could practically see the wizardry obscuring the square inch of panel. To him, it felt like a beacon.

"Show off," Dazzle muttered fondly as the elevator thrummed upward.

As the floors passed by, Dazzle reached into the top of her boot and pulled out a dollar store spritz bottle.

"Now is not the time for body glitter," Ari warned.

Dazzle gave him a wicked grin. "It's always time for body glitter."

The doors chimed and opened with perfect timing. Ari caught sight of two men in standard security guard dress, but before they could react, Dazzle stretched out her arm and fired off two spritzes in the guards' general direction.

The men stopped all activity. The dopiest smiles lit up their faces.

Dazzle spared Ari a wink before sashaying over to the first guard.

"Hi," the man giggled, the simple act of speaking making him sway.

Dazzle caught him by the arm with a cheerful, "Hello. You don't mind if we take a quick look around, do you?"

"Nope," the man said as Dazzle settled him on a nearby bench. "I couldn't care less what you do."

The second guard burst into guffaws and stumbled back into the wall. Hitting the wall made him drop the wand that was in his hand. It was only four inches of unpolished redwood, but that was enough to do damage in the hands of a trained wizard.

"Alright there?" Ari asked, a bemused smile stealing across his lips as he kicked the wand away.

The second guard slid down the wall into a pile of loose limbs. His head lulled as he looked up at Ari. "Wow," he said, "Your hair's as pretty as a girl's."

Ari turned to see Dazzle choking on muffled laughter.

"What did you do, you little menace?"

Dazzle shrugged. "Relax, it's a just a little anti-anxiety potion."

Ari shot the discombobulated guards a pointed look.

Dazzle's grin only widened. "So, maybe I put a bit of coven magic into the potency. It's an early prototype."

Shaking his head in disbelief, Ari made his way down the hall. Dazzle fell into step beside him before he reached the first door.

Behind Door Number One was a whole lot of nothing. Door Number Two was the same.

"Are we sure Sanchez gave us the right place?" Dazzle asked.

"Those guards weren't guarding empty rooms," Ari assured him before moving on to the next door.

Door after door revealed no sign of Val or Taye. None of the rooms were locked, and none were occupied by more than a dusty conference table or a few chairs. Other than the two men at the elevator, there was no indication of life anywhere to be found.

Ari stopped in the middle of the hallway and held out his hands to Dazzle. The Drag Queen didn't hesitate before taking them.

"Close your eyes?"

Dazzle closed his eyes, and Ari had to fight back a watery smile at the easy show of trust.

"Think of Val and Taye," he instructed in a reverent whisper. "Envision them as you last saw them, how they looked and smelled, how you felt about them."

Ari remembered the downy press of Val's fur as she sat on his knee during another slow day at the shop. He recalled the softness of Taye's lips as they kissed over a homebrewed mug that emitted a rich, nutty aroma. He thought back to the moment he awoke in so much pain, only to hear Taye's voice coaxing him from sleep and to feel the pleasant weight of Val curled against his chest. Unbidden, his mind played back the scene of Taye and Val standing over Robert Gaines in Ari's defense.

He imagined them as he knew them best, as the undeniable forces who wouldn't stop rattling Ari's every barrier. Like Dazzle, they had blasted their way through Ari's walls and made a place for themselves in his heart.

Ari cringed at the thought of how often he pushed them aside for the sake of a shop that no longer existed.

I'll do better, Ari vowed, sending the thought out into the ether for the universe itself to stand as his witness. Then and there, in that dusty hallway, Ari promised his coven he would show them a better Morrigan, a better friend and lover. If fate saw fit to give him the chance, he would make them his priority.

It worked. It wasn't fast, but a trickle of knowing

reverberated from the corners of his mind and soul bearing Val's name.

Dazzle gasped. "She's here."

Grip tightening on Dazzle's hands, Ari latched on to the tendril of Magic and shoved as much of himself as he could into it. He gave it his intention and need like fodder to a flame, and the string of awareness thickened into something sturdy enough to walk on. Metaphorically speaking, that was exactly what Ari did.

"This way," he said, voice hushed with excitement.

They went straight to her.

"My kitten!" Dazzle wailed upon opening the door.

"My Queen!" Val wailed back in the same instant.

They had her in a dog crate. Val reared up on her hind legs to hook her forepaws in the grating, every inch the picture of a suffering captive moments away from a dearly longed for reunion.

Ari didn't buy the pitiful act for a second. There was a silk cushion and several hardbound books in the crate. Ari even spotted a plate with the remains of a fish dinner on it.

"I knew you'd come for me!" Val cheered as Ari inspected the lock.

It was a simple padlock, nothing special and with no sign of magical finagling. Ari closed his hand around it and wished for the mechanism to switch over without the key. It clicked open with the slightest zap of power from his skin to the metal.

Ari's satisfaction with the lock was short-lived.

"Would you believe Taye thought you wouldn't come?" Val said as she hoped over the grating to freedom. "I kept telling him, but he said you'd wait till the weekend when work hours were more convenient."

Ari and Dazzle stiffened, sharing a wide eyed look of dismay.

"He totally owes me a beer now," Val said, unperturbed.

Pointedly not looking at Ari, Dazzle cleared her throat. "They didn't tell you about the shop, did they?"

Val's tail lowered to the floor. "What happened?"

Before Dazzle could speak, Ari scooped Val from the floor and hugged her close. "It doesn't matter right now. I'm just glad you're safe. Where's Taye?"

His friends looked at him like he'd grown a second head.

"Where is Taye?" Ari insisted.

Val's ears twitched back, almost flattening against her head in upset. "I don't know. They took him away a few hours ago. Oh, shit, Ari!" Her ears sprang forward, her eyes bulbous as she pressed an earnest paw to his chest. "They were witches! I heard the guard use the Morrigan title as he led them in."

Ari's breath froze in his lungs. The nemiza took form in his mind, front and center amid a landscape of badness.

"Taye seemed to recognize one them too," Val said. "I thought he didn't know many witches?"

"He doesn't," Ari wheezed as confusion and fear sent jolts of energy coursing through his veins.

Beside himself, there was only one witch Ari knew Taye would recognize by sight, and the bastard had no business taking Taye anywhere.

Not too long ago, Ari would have griped and groaned over the need to do such extensive witchcraft. He would have begrudgingly closed the curtains on the shop and holed himself up with his little velvet bag of witch's tools, and he would have kept the Magic work to a minimum. He would have been quick about it, regardless of the stakes.

Needless to say, that was no longer the case.

With members of his coven to either side of him, Ari marched into the woods with his head held high and not a trace of reluctance to be found.

He chose the same park he and Taye used for the holistic communion so many weeks ago. Ari didn't know if Taye's recent presence at the site would make a difference, but he was certain it couldn't hurt. Ari wanted every possible advantage, considering how epically he failed to find Taye the last time he tried via magical means.

He carried Taye's backpack over his shoulder. Every known item that Taye owned was in the bag. With any luck, something of Taye remained in his belongings and could be used to form a connection.

"If the geomancy didn't work, what makes you think this will?" Val asked as she trotted along by his ankle.

Ari hefted Taye's bag higher on his shoulder. It was heavier than ever with the additional items Ari stuffed into it before they left the apartment. "I don't know if anything will work, but we have to try. Puckman doesn't have the Council's anti-witch wardings. This time, something's bound to work."

The last comment left his mouth with more desperation than conviction, but no one commented on it. Nothing more was said till they reach the majestic old oak tree.

Ari paused in surprise. The oak's roots hadn't returned to their natural places; the little alcove remained the perfect size for two people to sit.

"That's convenient," Dazzle commented, none the wiser as he plopped down against the tree. He wasn't quite in the same spot Taye once sat, but near enough to make Ari choke on a sad little laugh.

Choosing to take the tree as a sign he was on the right track, Ari settled down beside Dazzle and opened the backpack. He started with the velvet satchel that matched the one he lost in the fire, and as he spread the cloth placemat out on the grass, he noticed Val curling up in Dazzle's lap.

This was going to work, Ari told himself as he shot them a tight smile.

Spurred on by Dazzle's earlier mix-up, Ari started with the ceramic bowl from his kitchen cupboard. Someday, he would have to invest in a proper scrying bowl, something aged and carved from stone by a true artisan, but for now the soup bowl would have to do. He filled it from a plastic bottle of drinking water; according to his trusted internet sources, the quality of the water made no difference, but a part of Ari wished he had something fresh from a wild spring. That seemed like the kind of dramatic utility Magic would appreciate.

He hoped Magic would be satisfied with his willingness in the meantime.

Ari stared into the bowl, his legs crossed and hands on his knees in a comfortable stance. He watched the breeze create the smallest ripples in the water and allowed his breath to flow with the gentle motion.

Slowly, the ripples ceased. The water darkened.

Focusing his sight on the mirrored surface, Ari thought solely of Taye. He pictured his unrepentant grin and the complex tang of his Magic that blurred the line between wizardry and witchcraft. He recalled the feel of Taye's rough hands on his skin, and the entrancing melodies those same fingers were capable of composing. The longer he sat there in contemplative silence, the more Ari thought he could hear the low timber of Taye's voice; it was easy to imagine his laugh as much as his deadpan sarcasm whenever he lost patience.

Then, amid all the obvious traits and cozy memories, thoughts of Taye's steadfast presence arose in Ari's mind. From the moment Magic brought them together, Taye never hesitated to seek him out. He saw value in Ari from beginning, chasing after him even before Ari cared to give him the time of day. And after? When Ari stopped fighting the chemistry between them, Taye never faltered in his attentions. Not once, not even when Ari slipped back into his workaholic tendencies did Taye ever give up on him.

Taye believed in him, Ari realized with a start. As his Morrigan and his lover, Taye truly believed Ari was worthy.

The realization took Ari by surprise, making his breath hitch and his chest constrict, but he didn't fight it. Much like

Taye himself, the knowledge persisted to make an impression.

Sniffling back the emotional revelation, Ari whispered to the water, "*Elphay emay indfay imhay.*"

Ari peered into the bowl with all the longing his heart could muster. He felt Dazzle and Val do the same from the other side.

Magic swirled around the great oak, and Ari was tempted to close his eyes and let it sweep him away. He didn't, though. For Taye, he held fast, sturdy and focused despite the raw Magic collecting around him.

Ari's back ached from his deplorable posture as he pored over the bowl. The top of his head brushed against Dazzle as the wizard followed his lead. Val's nose reflected in the water's surface when she drew too close. Together, they held their breath and waited for an image to appear.

Then the Magic petered out. It settled into nothingness like a passing storm.

Val gave a dubious hum. "Are you sure you did it right?"

Ari glared at her.

"What? You said it yourself, you've never done this before."

"She's got a point," Dazzle said with an apologetic smile. "I'm betting the pig Latin was the problem."

Ari turned his scowl on the Drag Queen and hissed, "You have lipstick on your teeth."

While Dazzle gasped and began fretting, Ari refocused on the bowl.

He tried again. Rather than repeating the same thing till he was ready to bash his head against the tree, Ari chose a different target. It wouldn't hurt to test Dazzle's doubts about the pig Latin.

Magic gathered anew. It didn't swarm like the last time, but spun in a lazy circle around the bowl.

After shooting Dazzle a pointed look, Ari clearly enunciated, "*Owshay emay orriganmay ardinghay.*"

It worked.

The water darkened into a perfect lens. In its center swam a moving picture of Hag Number Six herself. Ari didn't recognize the porch or the wicker swing the Morrigan sat on as she puffed on a vape pen. He watched her kick out her bare feet to get the swing moving and decided the lazy smile on her face couldn't possibly mean anything nefarious.

"See?" Ari exclaimed as he wagged his fingers in the water to replace the image with waves. "I did it right the first time. Not my fault it didn't work."

His teasing tone soured as he finished talking. His wizards noticed.

"Does this mean there's no way to locate him?" Val asked. "What about geomancy?"

"Tried that," Ari said as he slumped against the tree. "It didn't work any better."

"Fuckman can't be guarding against all forms of witchcraft," Dazzle insisted as he snagged Ari's velvet purse. "There's too many to choose from. One is sure to work."

With that rousing pep-talk, Dazzle shoved a deck of tarot cards into Ari's hands.

It led to no success. Magic answered his call with gusto again, but when he flipped the cards over they were inexplicably blank.

From there, Ari stole a pen and a notebook from Taye's backpack, closed his eyes and cleared his mind in an attempt at Automatic writing. He ended up with a page full of Taye's name and a few capitalized cuss words thrown in.

For the first time in his life, Ari drank a cup of tea that left no tea leaves to be read.

They even tried using a few fallen twigs from the oak as dowsing rods, but every question about Taye's whereabouts resulted in a pair of eerily still sticks.

With each and every attempt, Ari's heart sank lower. Dazzle and Val made fewer and fewer remarks. At one point, Val started crying.

Their only comfort came from the faint trickle of life and warmth Taye kept broadcasting to the coven. He was alive, it told them. He was alive and not drawing on the coven's magic for any reason.

By dawn, that little scrap of knowledge remained all they had.

~

ANOTHER AGONIZINGLY LONG DAY PASSED WITH NO CHANGE. Ari continued to exhaust all his options when it came to witchcraft, and even Dazzle and Val made a valiant effort to bring their wizardry to bare.

Dazzle brewed an experimental potion he hoped would elevate his coven ties to Taye into a sixth sense of his location. The first attempt made him violently ill for several hours. The second made him annoyingly aware of Val's every movement; from the way his eye kept twitching while he waited for the potion to work its way out of his system, it wasn't a pleasant experience. The third potion was so foul smelling that Ari refused to let Dazzle drink it for fear of poisoning.

Meanwhile, Val did her best to enchant a map into showing her Taye's location. This allowed her to narrow their search radius down to the North American continent and no further.

It was clear that Eren Puckman was no fool when it came to protecting his better interest. Ari already knew that, but he still wondered how Puckman was managing to hide so effectively.

Regarding this concern, Ari could think of only one person it was safe to ask. At long last, Ari retrieved the slip of paper from his refrigerator door and made the call.

Morrigan Harding was waiting for him on the porch of her rural cottage home. Instead of a vape pen, she held a tea saucer and matching cup in her lap as her swing swayed.

As Ari climbed the porch's steps, she smiled.

"Not so lost anymore, are you?" she asked with a knowing glint in her eye.

Unsure how to respond, Ari just shrugged and leaned a hip against the porch railing. "Did you know the Council of Wizards have developed anti-witchcraft wards?"

She gaped at him.

That was just as well, Ari decided. He didn't need her interrupting while he caught her up on the situation. By the time he was done, Harding had set her tea on her lap so she could clutch her hands over her heart in consternation.

"Eren always seemed like such a nice man," she murmured, "I can't imagine him abducting people, let alone working with the Council."

Ari stiffed a snort and kept his comments to himself.

"Well, he can't be guarding against every form of witchcraft," she assured as she leaned back in her swing. She picked up her tea setting, and the porcelain chattered with the minute tremor of her hands. "I don't suppose he could be working with a Councillor directly?"

Ari's spine straightened.

Over the rim of her teacup, Harding watched him with a pinched expression that said she wasn't a fan of the idea either. "The wizards can only ward against magic they know about."

Ari's eyes narrowed on her unassuming figure. "You know something that might work to find Taye?"

She buried her nose back in her teacup. Her brow was lowered in deep thought.

Ari didn't want to give her the time to overthink. He took a seat on the front steps and, swallowing his pride, bowed his head. "If you were in my situation, what would you do?"

The other Morrigan went still. Slowly, she returned her cup to its saucer.

"You might be better prepared for this situation if you joined my coven when I first suggested it," she said, though not unkindly. "You might have learned a few things that aren't typically found in written records."

Ari bit back the urge to snap at her to get to the point.

Harding finished her tea with a loud slurp that made Ari cringe, then she unfurled from her swing. She removed the tea set to the floor beside the door, then seated herself beside him.

"A Morrigan is more than the coven's leader," she said, "He or She is their greatest protector and guide. I'm sure you've noticed your heightened awareness of their emotional state, but did you know that can be built upon?"

Ari's arms uncrossed of their own accord as he sat up straighter. "I can find him with nothing more than the coven connection?"

He thought back to the empty office building where they found Val. It had been such a short distance, but the same principle had served them well enough to find the cat.

"It normally takes time and practice," Harding said before

holding out her hand to him, "but I can guide you through it. If you open yourself to me, trust that I mean to do what I say and nothing more, than I can show you how to make a temporary tether. I've done it before when my witches became unreachable. It's a good skill to have in case of emergencies."

Ari hesitated. Just how much could he trust this witch? Up until recently, he didn't even know her name.

As if she could read his thoughts, Harding said, "It's not all about trusting me. Mostly, it's about trusting your instincts."

Ari bit his lip in uncertainty. His skin pebbled with goose bumps, and he had the strange thought that he was about to leap off a cliff into an endless abyss.

It ultimately came down to one simple truth: Taye needed him to do this.

"Okay," he whispered as he placed his hand in hers.

She smiled like a proud mother watching her child take his first steps. Then she whispered back to him, "Accepting who and what you are is the bravest thing you can do. It makes you stronger than you may ever know."

Her grip locked on.

Instantly, they were caught up in a maelstrom of Magic.

The world spun, becoming a meaningless splash of colors and convoluted shapes. The porch, stairs and swing included, ceased to exist as Magic coiled around them in a rush of power and gut-wrenching sensation. It was like being on the fastest thrill ride—so intense that it stole all perceptions of the tangible universe.

It didn't stop, but reached a crescendo that broke through time and space to an all new plane of existence. Distantly, Ari became aware of his body still lounging on the steps, but it was a secondary sensation, like the memory of a dream. In that moment, the universe that existed inside himself was all that mattered. They were among the stars, standing solidly on nothing but darkness and surrounded by endless black and pinpricks of light.

"They're not stars," Harding said from beside him. They were holding hands, her grip gentle but sure in comparison to his white knuckles and shaking limbs.

Ari watched the not-stars dance around each other in no particular pattern, all at varying speeds. He didn't need Harding to tell him what they were.

"They're my thoughts," he said as a new burst of light blossomed into being an arm's length in front of him.

As the newborn thought danced off into the crowd, Ari's heartbeat slowed. The suddenness of Magic's enforced introspection leveled out, and Ari discovered a peaceful quiet in its place. He was all at once separate from his thoughts and entrenched in them.

"This is . . ." Ari trailed off as his amazement threatened to overwhelm him. "Something."

"It gives a whole new meaning to meditation, doesn't it?" Harding said with a bump of her shoulder against his. She never let go of his hand.

Her gentle teasing reminded him of his friends. A whole lot of not-stars burned brighter, moved faster. It was surreal to see such a visual representation of his thoughts at the same moment he thought them. They danced in choreography that mimicked his memories coalescing into the prominent idea of the moment.

He was here for a reason. He needed to find Taye.

The light show switched up, different not-stars glowing fiercely as they changed trajectory.

For as long as the coven had existed, Ari imagined his wizards as vague existences in the corners of his mind. The reality was very different. Ari's mind had no corners, and there was nothing vague about the green ball of light that glided toward him, faster and faster the more fervently he thought of Taye.

There he was, that soft warm glow that promised life and Magic and not much else. It made sense to Ari that Taye's light would be green instead of the bright white of his other thoughts. Taye wasn't a thought, after all.

Taye wasn't a part of Ari. Not without the coven.

"Go on," Harding said in a reverent hush. "Take him in your hand. Hold him close to your heart. It's all metaphysical, but the symbolism matters."

Symbolism always mattered when it came to Magic, Ari thought with surprising fondness.

Leaving his hand in Harding's, Ari used the other to scoop the green ball of light out of the air. It was as soft and intangible as smoke, but as warm and inviting as bathwater. It stayed in the curve of Ari's hand like it belonged there.

Ari held Taye's essence to his chest, bundling the ball of light with utmost care. It seemed so fragile. He almost cried as he cradled it close.

"You see?" Harding said in his ear. "The connection's there, and it's strong. As his Morrigan, you can do more than send power and emotion along it. You can manipulate the connection itself. You can form a tether made of ether between you and him, and when you return to your body, you'll be able to follow it."

"How?" Ari whispered.

She showed him, and in that unbelievable landscape filled with nothing but him and his Magic, Ari found it was breathtakingly easy.

~

IN HIS EXCITEMENT, ARI DIDN'T STOP AT THE APARTMENT TO collect Val and Dazzle. He followed the invisible thread that tugged him away from Harding's cottage and into the suburbs of Denver. His confusion grew with every picturesque lawn and three car garage he passed by. Ari knew for a fact that Puckman rented a humble condo in the Georgetown outskirts, but these houses screamed wealth and privileged that didn't align with those expectations.

Nevertheless, Ari continued to follow the internal pressure that was leading him to Taye. He was getting closer. He could feel it.

His chest filled with warmth and belonging as he rolled down another street of tailored lawns and prideful homes. He could imagine the green bundle of light shining brighter, stronger than ever with proximity.

He was close. Very close.

Ari stopped the car in front of a two story house, complete with arches over the giant windows and a porch light that looked like it wanted to be a chandelier. He knew with absolute certainty that Taye was inside.

As much as he wanted to, Ari didn't get out of the car and storm the house. He nearly did, but the mailbox was well within view.

Gaines, it read.

CHAPTER 28

"This is so fucked up," said Dazzle.

"But how is Gaines managing to hold Taye?" Val asked no one in particular. "Why doesn't Taye just magic himself out of there? It's not like Gaines has the means to stop him anymore."

"Obviously, Fuckman's helping him," Dazzle said with disdain. "Fucking hypocrite. He spends years bitching at Ari for working with wizards, but now it's okay for him to do it? What an asshole."

Dazzle's expression said he found this phrase woefully insufficient to describe Eren Puckman. Ari sympathized entirely.

"As much as I would love to listen to you trash talk the bastard for another hour, I really need to focus," Ari said without lifting his gaze from his phone.

The screen was bright white, with few words written in the composition box of his email.

Val and Dazzle respected his request for all of a moment.

"Ari?" Val said as she curled her tail around his ankle. "Are you sure you want to do this?"

He froze with his thumbs hovering over the touchscreen's keyboard.

"This isn't the same as defending yourself from aggression," Dazzle said, his tone cautious. "If you start making threats now, you're committing to the terrorist role."

Ari frowned down at his phone.

Dear Council of Wizards, the screen read. A member of my coven is being held against his will at the home of your disgraced peer, Robert Gaines. I have confirmed this myself. If Tayvon Osondu is not freed within the next twenty-four hours—

"Holy shit," Ari whispered. "I'm a magical terrorist."

In the corner of his eye, Val and Dazzle traded a few grave looks. The wordless conversation ended with Dazzle throwing up his hands in a huff.

"Maybe we should try something a bit more . . . diplomatic?" Val suggested as she hopped onto the armrest of Ari's chair. "Far as we know, Gaines may have been the one behind all of this, even before Taye sought you out. It's possible the rest of the Council doesn't know he's involved with whatever Puckman's up to."

"Right," Ari said, already deleting the misbegotten email. "Diplomatic. I can do that."

"The North American Council of Wizards does not appreciate your threat," Councillor Sanchez stated the following morning when Ari opened his door.

She blew past him to enter the apartment, her heels clicking loudly as she marched toward the kitchen island to deposit a box. Perhaps it was the scowl on her face, but the sharp lines of her navy skirt and jacket somehow made her look tougher than the pantsuit he last saw her in.

"What's going on?" Val yawned as she stretched along the back of the couch.

"The Council got my email," Ari told her. Shoving his hands into the pockets of his pajama pants, Ari gave the Councillor a curious frown. "So much for diplomacy," he muttered.

Her eyes went round. "Morrigan Jamison, you said you would expose the supernatural world to the mundanes."

Ari pouted and folded his arms. "It was more an errant thought than a committed plan of action."

"I knew I should have proofread that email myself," Val bemoaned as she rolled off the back of the couch.

"You can't suggest a thing like that in an email," Sanchez insisted. "Especially when you're not prepared to follow through when things don't go your way."

Ari stiffened as Val perked up, bristling.

"You're not going to give Taye back?" he asked, stunned. "You're not even going to try to help him?"

"I can't!" she cried out in frustration. "Gaines was effectively ousted from the Council the day we learned he lost his magical ability. Whatever he's doing now is on him, not us."

"So, you're just going to let a private citizen kidnap one of your wizards?" Ari countered.

"Your wizard," she spat back. "Not ours. Taye made that very clear when he chose to join your coven."

She stared him down, hard, until Ari lost his nerve and dropped his gaze. Seemingly satisfied that he understood, she drew a deep breath and braced her hands on her hips.

"Do you know why I'm here instead of someone else?"

Ari shook his head, shrugging.

"I'm the only one who dared to," she said, stepping closer. "None of them want to end up like Gaines. Neither do I, but at least I know you're a decent person who won't harm me unprovoked."

Val snorted. "The Council's done more than their fair share of provoking. Why didn't you announce Gaines was stepping down?"

"And have to explain to the community what was done to him?" she asked with disbelieving laughter in her voice. "We were waiting for the next election to avoid uncomfortable questions. You're smart enough to have figured that one out on your own, Valkyrie."

Val bristled, but before she could respond Ari spoke up, "What about the fire?"

Sanchez recoiled, wincing.

"The Council boycotted my business, and when that didn't work, they burned it," Ari summarized as he stepped between her and Val. "Is that not provocation?"

She was slow to meet his eye. "I didn't know about the fire till after the fact. The same goes for the hex."

She might as well have slapped him. Blinking furiously, Ari's hands balled into fists at his sides.

"Bullshit," he spat. "That hex was witchcraft."

Her shoulders drooped in apparent defeat. "They paid off a coven to do the dirty work for them."

Ari didn't quite recognize his own voice as he growled, "Which coven?"

Sanchez reacted viscerally. Her eyes widened as she took a step back, and Ari noticed a distinct glow reflecting in the golden baubles dangling from her ears. Her hands shook as she raised them in placation.

"Morrigan Jamison," she murmured, "I am not your enemy."

"But the Council you represent is."

His words resonated with a sense of finality, a definitive line being drawn in the ether. Ari felt the truth take hold with a pulse of Magic. Sanchez felt it too, given the way she shuddered and appeared close to tears.

"You should leave," Val said with her eyes narrowed on Sanchez.

Warily, the Councillor surveyed the room, taking in Val with her bared fangs and Ari with his Magic no doubt on full display. With a note of desperation, her gaze landed on the box she set on the counter.

"I brought donuts as a peace offering," she said with a lame gesture toward the items in question. "I don't suppose that makes much difference to you now?"

"No," Ari and Val said as one.

She nodded to herself and made for the door. She didn't drag her feet, didn't try to argue, and Ari got the distinct impression she wanted this confrontation to end almost as bad as he did. That was too bad for both of them.

Her hand closed around the doorknob before he stopped her.

"Sanchez?"

She froze.

"The public still recognizes Gaines as a Council member," Ari reminded her. "Whether they want to wash their hands of this or not, I will hold them responsible if he hurts Taye."

This pronouncement startled her into looking up and meeting his eye. She opened her mouth, probably to try talking sense into him, but his reflection in her jewelry only flared brighter. Her mouth snapped closed.

"If the Council won't play by the rules, neither will I," Ari and Magic said as one. "Understood?"

She nodded, and the otherworldly shine reflected in her earrings faded away. She was trembling as she reached for the door again.

"For what it's worth," she said, a little breathless, "I hope you find Taye and kick Robert's ass."

Despite himself, Ari found himself softening. "You really do care about him, don't you?"

She nodded, gaze and grip locked on the doorknob. "I fought Robert for the right to mentor him. Obviously, I lost."

"Gaines was Taye's mentor?" Val said in a mixture of surprise and disgust.

In hindsight, it seemed obvious a wizard as talented as Taye would warrant the attentions of a Council member. It was more obvious that Robert Gaines was the type of man who would beat the shit out of his protégé instead of helping him with any magical mishaps.

After Sanchez left, Ari turned to Val and said, "Remind me to give Robbie a black eye when we see him."

Val didn't question it, though he doubted she remembered Taye's fading bruises from the first night she glimpsed him at Gladys's. She simply nodded her acknowledgment as she pawed at the box of donuts.

Ari left her to it and turned back toward the bedroom, intent on getting dressed then making a foolproof plan to rescue Taye. How he was going to do that, he wasn't sure, but that was a problem for after clothes and food.

"Hey, Ari?" Val said in a nervous tone that dashed his immediate plans. "You might want a look at these donuts. Like . . . now."

Hanging his head in consternation, Ari took a deep breath before turning around.

There were no sugary confections awaiting him in the box. *A Divergence of Magic* lay there instead, nestled in clean pastry tissues like an absolute gift.

ARI STILL WASN'T DRESSED BY THE TIME DAZZLE SHOWED UP with enough coffee and bagels to feed a small army. Unlike him, Dazzle looked fresh and bright eyed in his baggy jeans and crop top, though his pink hair could use another combing. Ari saw a tendril of purple curls hanging from his bottomless purse before Dazzle tossed it and the takeout bag onto the couch.

"Refreshments and reinforcements have arrived!" Dazzle announced as he pried a coffee cup from the holder and delivered it into Ari's waiting hand. "Now someone get me caught up on the drama before I start pulling out my hair from nerves."

Val perked up and began weaving an embellished story that vaguely resembled the impromptu meeting with Sanchez.

While she did so, Ari refocused on the book in his lap. There was a new chapter in the back, and he was only part way into his second read through.

Vulnerabilities Unique to A Close-Knit Coven, it was titled.

Ari finished rereading and double-checking his comprehension. Only then did he raise his nose from the book to find Val and Dazzle perched on the coffee table, side by side as they stared at him expectantly.

"I think I know why none of our magic's been able to find Taye," Ari said in a daze. "He's been blocking us off. If it's not Puckman's doing or Gaines, it's Taye."

Val and Dazzle stared at him, uncomprehending.

Sighed, Ari turned back to the chapter's beginning and handed the book to Dazzle.

"We don't just share Magic with each other," he summarized, "we share *access* to each other's magic. All it takes is the right dark magic ritual, a coven strong enough to perform it, and . . . one of us."

It's was so obvious, it was painful.

Of course Taye was responsible. He was protecting them, not in the grand way Ari did whenever he confronted someone on the coven's behalf, but in that small, quiet way that was distinctly *Taye*. There was no fuss, no demands for recognition, just the simple, blunt action of a man who knew his limits and how to use them.

It was the same way Taye defending Ari delicate sensibilities from *A Divergence of Magic*. Ari had no doubt Taye knew what was written in that final chapter, and he was using that knowledge now, when the book itself decided it was time for Ari to know the full scope of the risks.

The responsibility was crushing. If Ari had known the risks sooner, he might very well have disbanded the coven. It would have been too much to cope with.

Unaware of his dark thoughts, Dazzle and Val continued pouring over the book.

"That's why Taye's still alive," Val concluded. "They can't kill him if they want to steal our power through him first."

"He's been trying to cut himself off from the coven so the rest of us won't be affected," Dazzle said.

Ari hung his head and tried not to cry. "That self-sacrificing asshole."

"Wait," Val huffed. "I mean, that explains what Puckman's up to, but what about Gaines?"

Without lifting his head, Ari said, "Anyone can kill with

any number of mundane tools. The ritual's intended to steal, though. Death is just a side effect."

"Gaines is the recipient," Val said in dawning horror. "They're trying to steal Taye's Magic and give it to Gaines."

"Why though?" Dazzle pressed, glancing back and forth between them. "Why wouldn't Fuckman want the magic for himself?"

"He doesn't need it," Val said. "His coven's huge, right?"

"I don't think this was his idea," Ari thought aloud as he leaned back in his chair. "Even if he needed it, Puckman's not malicious. Egotistical and greedy, sure, but he's not outright mean. Gaines, though . . ."

As Ari trailed off, Dazzle uttered a sheepish laugh. "Yeah . . . plus, we effectually stole his Magic first."

Val spluttered, "We did not!"

Ari waved her off. "We might not have taken it for ourselves, but I doubt that means anything to him. If he's looking for a way to recover any kind of magical ability, then why wouldn't he go the route that includes revenge?"

"It wouldn't be the first time a Council member has looked into witchcraft," Dazzle suggested with a side-eye toward Sanchez's empty donut box.

"Fine," Val said. "I'm convinced, but what next? How do we use this information to our advantage?"

"Easy, we just have to interrupt the ritual," Dazzle said. "Or get Taye out before Puckman's coven has a chance to do it."

"Gaines has wards around his house," Ari informed them. "I noticed it when I drove by. Basic security wards trace the entire property line. I don't know if Gaines can still feel them, but any magic user on site will know the moment an unwanted guest shows up."

"And if Puckman's involved, there's sure to be at least a

few witches hanging around," Dazzle said, tapping his fist on his chin in thought.

"Maybe a counter curse?" Val suggested. "Or a counter ritual? Is that a thing?"

"We went over this when we were dealing with the hex," Ari said impatiently. "Nothing will work unless we know the specifics of the ritual they intend to use!"

Then, as if in answer to Ari's exceptionally valid point, Dazzle's purse was thrown off the couch. It flew through the air, clear over the coffee table, till it skidded across the carpet and knocked into the door. Dazzle's long purple wig came tumbling out of the clutch, along with a tube of lipstick, a cursed skull in its unraveling shroud, fishnet leggings, and the aptly named *Book of Shadows*.

Ari, Val, and Dazzle stared at the mess.

"I have so many questions," Val murmured. "For example, why do you have a human skull in your purse?"

"Another time, kitten," Dazzle said as he scooted closer to Ari. "Do you suppose Magic wants us to use the skull on Fuckman and Gaines?"

"Tempting," Ari said, still scanning the spillage. "Did you pack an entire drag outfit for today?"

"You said to be prepared for another rescue mission!"

"That book smells funky," Val complained. "Ew. Guys, I think it's bound in human skin."

"Ugh," Ari gagged, "Now I really don't want to touch it."

"Let's just use the skull," said Dazzle.

"Agreed," said Ari.

In response, Magic sent the *Book of Shadows* skidding across the floor. It bumped into the coffee table, and the impact forced the cover open. Most mysteriously, many pages followed till the book lay open on the floor to a wall of text and a graphic image of a woman having her soul torn from her body.

Overlaying the image was a blurry, but distinct nemiza.

CHAPTER 29

All at once, things started to make a scary sort of sense. It was all there, in the *Book of Shadows*. If only Ari had turned a page further on that fateful day he first showed the book to Taye, perhaps this whole thing could have been avoided.

The nemiza didn't always kill its victims outright. It could be used in ritual sacrifice.

The ritual in question did precisely as they expected, at least according to the *Book of Shadows*. It would use Taye to gain access to the coven's Magic, using him as a mortal conduit to rip away their power till there was nothing left. It would destroy him in the process.

It even made sense why Puckman seemed so disinterested in Taye until that moment. The transference ritual could only be executed under autumn's final full moon.

"That's tonight," Val said, horrified eyes on the calendar hanging form the fridge.

Ari glanced out the window to see the sun bright and high in the sky. He closed the book and set it aside without a second's hesitation.

They used up too much time reading. The day was mostly gone, and Taye's time was dwindling. The coven's time was dwindling.

As the three of them raced to the Tesla, Ari's lofty dreams of a detailed plan of attack evaporated. There was no time to devise a strategy; hell, there wasn't even time for Ari to change out of his pajamas.

They would just have to rely on brute supernatural force, Magic willing.

Ari expected Magic's favor would be enough right until they pulled up to Robert Gaines's residence. The place was crawling with witches and idling power.

"I thought we'd be early," Val grumbled from Ari's lap, "not fashionably late."

"I blame Dazzle," Ari said as they parked by the curb.

Knuckles white around the wheel, Dazzle glared at him. "I'm not the one who invited a whole-ass coven over for dinner beforehand."

As ridiculous as the idea sounded, Ari had to admit it sounded like a plausible explanation for the gaggle of witches hanging out on Gaines's front lawn. Ari thought he recognized a face or two from back in the days when he thought Puckman hung the moon, but it was hard to tell for sure. Despite the variations to their coloring and ethnicity, they all looked so alike with their grass stains and ribbed jeans or otherwise careless attire. So many bare feet were busy wiggling their toes in the wizard's manicured lawn, it almost made Ari laugh at the cliché.

There were too many to laugh at, however.

"How many witches are in Fuckman's coven again?" Dazzle asked as they watched another handful of witches spill out of the house.

"Too many," Ari admitted.

The witches from indoors spread out, chatting and gesticulating as they spoke to the witches lounging in front of the house. A sense of excitement seemed to spread from the newcomers to their peers, till the whole group was on their feet, fairly vibrating with eagerness.

There were smiles and laughter galore.

Ari's gut churned viciously. He doubted the whole coven had gone psychotic and murderous, but there was no way Puckman branded Taye with the nemiza on his own. They had to know they were dabbling in seriously dark magic, surely.

"Enough of this," Ari hissed before shoving his way out of the car.

A young woman in a hacked up shirt and unseasonably short daisy dukes spotted him first. Her eyes went wide and her jaw dropped. Ari expected a cry of alarm and was already willing the Magic to come to his defense, but her giddy shriek shocked him to a standstill before he could breach the property line.

"Oh my goddess!" she wailed as a manic grin spread across her face. "It's him! Guys! It's him! It's Ari!"

All heads swiveled in his direction, each and every one of their faces sporting some combination of surprise that gave way to delight much too quickly. Before Ari could make sense of it, he found himself enveloped in the crowd. Someone snatched up his hand to vigorously shake his arm, and another patted him on the back like he'd won a prize. The girl in the shorts was sobbing with joy as she hugged his other arm. Nearby, another girl jumped up and down with a complete inability to contain her excitement.

All around him, their voices said his name amid words of welcome. They spoke with a fervor that didn't make sense, like he was some sort of celebrity gracing them with his presence.

"What the actual fuck?" Dazzle shrieked over the din.

A lull swept over Ari's twittering fans. It didn't completely squash the noise, but it put a distinct damper on things.

Ari pried his arm from the girl and spun to seek out Dazzle and Val with wide, confused eyes, but he couldn't see either wizard through the crowd.

He was separated from them.

Ari's heart dropped in the same moment the witches picked up their frantic cheering all over again.

"Oh my gods! Morrigan Puckman told us you probably wouldn't, but we're so happy you came!" said a young man sporting a bun and the spars whiskers of an unfortunate beard. "But did you really have to bring *them*?"

Ari didn't like the way the man sneered the last word, and he certainly didn't like the nasty looks his peers shot in Dazzle's and Val's direction.

"They're my coven," Ari said with a defensive bite. "Why do you think we're here, exactly?"

They blinked at him in doe-eyed incomprehension.

"Right," the girl said with a stilted smile and sarcastic wink. "They're totally your coven."

Ari stared at her, too bewildered for words.

"Come on," said an older witch with leaves and at least one twig stuck in his unkempt hair and beard. He clapped a hand on Ari's shoulder and shook him like they were longtime friends. "No more silliness. There's drinks in the back. What'll you have?"

"I'm not having anything!"

"Don't say that till you see the spread!" the witch said

with a carefree laugh. His grip tightened just enough to steer Ari through the crowd and into the house.

Ari didn't get a chance to deny them. The younger witches launched into a fresh round of fawning and over-animated talking.

"Did you really strand the entire Council of Wizards in the Sahara Dessert?" gushed one.

"I heard you can handle cursed objects with your bare hands!" squealed another.

He caught snippets of similar commentary as they made their way through a crowd of witches who all seemed eager to get a hand on him, even in passing. Their exuberant chattering consisted of half-truths and grossly exaggerated theories about his abilities, at best. The worst of them were outright lies, such as the claim that Ari had trapped the petrified troll in Grimoires and Goodies himself, with nothing but a glower and none of the money he'd actually paid for the artifact.

Ari was too bewildered to let his newfound reputation go to his head. Before he realized he would have to shout to be heard over them, they were already inside the house.

He didn't see much of Gaines's home. He got the impression of a pretentious foyer with its chandelier and golden runner, then he was whisked down a matching hallway. His feet eventually came to a stop on a lacquered wood deck on the other side of the house.

The backyard was a masterpiece of artificial nature. The deck stretched from the back door around to a spacious Jacuzzi where tropical plants created ample shade during the day. The plant life followed the steps down to a vast lawn lined in faux tiki torches. Passion flowers bloomed along the border where their vines clung to the fence. The place was surrounded in precisely pruned greenery.

The amount of wizardry it took to keep the foreign plants thriving in the Colorado autumn was staggering. Ari didn't merely sense it; he could feel it like an extra layer of skin, itchy and gross on top his own.

It made for a beautiful sight, but it forced Ari to realize how overindulgent and magically wasteful wizardry would be.

Someone pressed a Solo cup into his hand, and Ari made himself look past the Magic to the situation crawling all over the yard.

There were a lot of witches. The five utilizing the hot tub were surrounded by a healthy pack vying for a chance to take their places. A few more were out on the grass tossing a Frisbee, while even more sat or stood around chatting.

All in all, there had to be close to thirty witches present, maybe more.

There were also coolers and stacks of plastic cups, and a twice-damned BBQ hot at work on the deck.

"Holy shit," Ari said as he stared at the party going on around him.

He turned and almost ran over the two men and woman who escorted him to the back. They beamed back at him like everything was right in the world.

"I need to talk to Dazzle and Val," Ari said as he handed off his random cup to the guy with the wannabe beard.

The girl stepped into his path. "Sorry. No wizards invited."

"Then give me Taye, and we'll be on our way."

The sudden silence was deafening. Not a single witch spoke. Even the Frisbee players went still and quiet.

Ari didn't let it divert his attention. He stared down at the girl, at her failing smile and the mockery of hurt in her eyes.

"Holy shit," the man with leaves in his hair said, staring at Ari like he was just seeing him for the first time.

"You weren't joking," said the girl. "About them being your coven."

Ari's hands rolled into fists at his sides. "I don't know what Puckman told you, but the only reason I'm here is to stop you from hurting Taye."

A wave of uneasy movement swept over the yard. Still, no one spoke. The Frisbee lay forgotten on the steps of the deck where it last landed.

Ari glanced around him to see a swarm of dismayed and disappointed expressions.

"Do you know what you're here for?" Ari demanded, raising his voice. "Did you fall for a convenient lie, or are you just comfortable with the idea of murdering a man just because he's different from yourselves?"

That broke the silence. Shouts of denial and accusations filled the air, some directed at Ari, but most never directed at all. Ari noticed many people flinching as if slapped.

The girl in the shorts decided to returned the favor.

Ari's head whipped to the side as her hand connected with his face. The smack was loud enough to gather attention.

"You're a liar!" she shouted. "He's a fucking liar! Morrigan Puckman already told us what the ritual would do, remember?"

"That's right!" someone shouted from the crowd. "Our Morrigan wouldn't hurt anyone!"

Ari laughed. He threw back his head and barked his disbelief to the sky. "Yeah, I bet little Miss Daisy Dukes here wouldn't hurt anyone either."

"She wouldn't!"

"She just slapped me! You all saw it!"

"At least I'm not a traitor who cares more about some dumb wizard than the witches whose Magic he stole!"

"What? Taye didn't steal shit—"

The coven shouted over him in a disjointed mess of sound. Ari thought he detected a few notes of disillusioned alarm, but it was hard to tell amid the insults and denials.

"Enough."

The uproar met an immediate end, and there in the doorway to Gaines's house stood Morrigan Puckman. He was as barefooted as the rest of his coven, and for some reason this made a knot in Ari's chest loosen.

If Puckman was wearing those damn shoes tonight, of all nights, Ari might have puked on them.

"Ari," Puckman sighed, a disappointed smile on his face as he shook his head.

Ari lifted his chin and corrected him, "It's Morrigan Jamison to you."

The surrounding witches bristled. Nearby, Daisy Dukes hissed another, "Traitor," under her breath. She wasn't alone.

Puckman doused their grumblings with a raised hand. Heaving another weary sigh, he beckoned Ari to follow him as he crossed the porch.

"Alright then, Morrigan Jamison." His lip twitched like he found Ari's use of the title amusing. "We should have a talk, witch to witch."

Ari hesitated. He eyed the swarm of upset witches that covered the yard from house to fence and back. It wouldn't take much to make another one of them swing at him, and he was alone.

"I need to talk to Val and Dazzle first," Ari decided.

He took a step back toward the house, but the nearby witches closed ranks to block his way.

"So suspicious," Puckman admonished. "You needn't be, Ari."

"Morrigan Jamison," Ari snapped back.

Puckman inclined his head with the slightest rolling of his eyes. "Your coven is perfectly fine. Mine weren't going to let them inside, but they relented after I suggested they show your friends how perfectly fine Osondu is doing."

Ari stiffened. "Take me to them."

"Calm yourself, Morrigan," Puckman said, raising a placating hand. "Your wizards are alive and well, you have my word."

A complicated hand gesture accompanied that final statement. Ari and the other witches felt a small zap of Magic that spoke of truth and transparency.

"They'll be here when we get back," Puckman assured as he watched Ari take the first few steps down from the deck. "Now, will you please come speak with me? There are elements at work here you don't understand."

Thinking fast, Ari eyed the barricade of witches and the posh house beyond them.

He could still feel Magic lingering in the air as witness to Puckman's promise. His wizards were alive and well. That much he could trust. Almost as importantly, he could trust that Puckman never revealed the true nature of the evening's witchcraft to his coven; Ari could sense the power coming off the surrounding witches, and they didn't have what it took for such a dark ritual. They would need their Morrigan.

They needed Puckman in order to do anything to Taye. The best thing Ari could do was keep him away.

With his guts churning with nervous somersaults, Ari followed after Puckman.

~

THERE WAS A WALKING TRAIL BEHIND THE HOUSE, AND Gaines had a neat little cobblestone path leading directly to it from his backyard. Between the popularity of high-rise fences and the various trees maintained by the city, the trail provided ample privacy. Still, Ari and Puckman walked a good ways away from the house before either of them dared to speak.

Impatience getting the better of him, Ari broke first. "What could have possessed you to try a transference spell? And to a member of my coven no less."

Puckman hung his head, shaking it like he couldn't believe he was having this conversation. "Osondu wasn't yours when this was set in motion. You were never meant to get involved."

Ari brought them to a halt as he planted himself in Puckman's path. "A nemiza, Eren? Really?"

Puckman stood firm under Ari's disdain. "I'm merely trying to right the wrongs done to our people."

"Bullshit. You know damn well Taye didn't steal Magic from witches. That's a lie you've spun among your coven to justify your actions."

"No," Puckman said bluntly. "I told them the facts as I've always known them."

"You're manipulating them."

"For example," Puckman continued as if Ari hadn't spoken, "I know Magic manifests for witches when we're children, when we're young and open minded enough to embrace it instead of fighting it. That was always your problem, Ari; you were born with a narrow world view that left no room for the ways of witches."

Ari gaped. "You seriously think that of the two of us, I'm the prejudiced one? I think you have that backward."

"I don't hate wizards, Ari. I simply respect our differences enough to keep my distance." Puckman's smile went from cocky to pitying as he stared at Ari. "On the other hand, you've been loud and proud about your distaste for witches, even yourself."

Ari laughed. It was short and sharp and made his ears and throat hurt. "Just because I don't like rolling around in the dirt or dropping everything to do Magic's bidding doesn't mean I hate myself. For fuck's sake, I knew you never loved me, Puckman, but I thought at least knew me."

A spasm of some nameless emotion crossed Puckman's face. "I did love you—"

"Not really."

"But that was before you fell into bed with a rogue wizard and turned your back so violently on your fellow witches. Morrigan Harding told me what you did to her coven."

"Did she tell you what her coven did to me to warrant that reaction?"

"I understand banning them from the shop, but to use such a force of Magic against your own kind, then proceeding to share that might with a group of reject wizards—" Puckman shook his head, his lips pressed tight in displeasure like his frustration had moved him beyond capability of speech.

"And here we are, right back to square one," Ari said with a mean smile. "Everything's always about my Magic with you. You groomed me to love you because you wanted my power then, and now you're going after my coven because they have it instead."

"No," Puckman gritted out through tight lips. "Tayvon Osondu is a wizard who could not have come into communion with Magic any other way than through nefarious means—"

"You don't know that."

"What's more believable, Ari? That a grown wizard

spontaneously developed a penchant for witchcraft, or that he used dark wizardry to steal it from someone born with it?"

Ari took a step back and considered the question. He watched Puckman closely and noted the tightening of the skin around his eyes, the firm set of his brow, and the depth of his frown. It had been years since Ari made a habit of memorizing Puckman's expressions, but certain things were hard to unlearn.

Puckman truly believed the drivel he was spewing.

"Alright," Ari said, tamping down his anger. "What wizard spell did he use to do it?"

"I don't know."

"Who was his victim?"

Puckman's jaw tensed. He didn't answer.

"If what you say is true," Ari said, slow and measured, "then there must be a spell and a victim that started all this. So, where are they?"

The vein in Puckman's temple grew more obvious the harder the man held himself in check. Not for the first time, something small and undefined in Puckman's stance reminded Ari of the bigoted grandfather who raised him. Ari once tried to talk logic to that old man too, but it hadn't turned out well then either.

"I'm going back to the house," Ari decided. "I'm getting my coven, and we're leaving."

Instead of arguing as his expression suggested he wanted to, Puckman raised his faced toward the sky and heaved a deep breath.

"You should know I was never trying to hurt you, Ari."

"Fuck you, Puckman. What did you think would happen to me when you siphoned off the Magic of my entire coven?"

Eyes still on the dusky sky, Puckman murmured, "I suppose we're about to find out."

Breath catching, Ari followed Puckman's gaze upward. The sky was not yet dark, but the moon was fully visible in the sky.

"Shit," Ari whispered, already turning back toward the house.

Puckman stopped him with a hand on his wrist. No, wait, cool metal accompanied the warmth of Puckman's palm as it encircled him. Ari heard the click of an invisible clasp even as he yanked back.

Instantly, grief swamped him.

"A gift from Gaines," Puckman said somberly. "Did you know the Council's been developing equipment to negate witchcraft? Quite freakishly inventive, wizards are, but useful."

Ari's legs buckled under the onslaught of emptiness. He didn't need to visualize his mindscape to know the bright lights representing his wizards were dimmed and shoved to the farthest reaches of his magical awareness. They were too far away to feel.

"What did you do?" Ari gasped.

Shaking from the involuntary dampening to his magical awareness, Ari's legs lost their strength, and he fell to the ground, clawing at the bracelet. The thin steel band he now wore was seamless and too close to the skin to slip off.

"As I said, you were never meant to get involved," Puckman said with a dispassionate stare. "I've done what I can to make this easier on you, but it's too late to turn back."

Ari barely heard him. He scratched and pulled, pushed and yanked, doing his utmost to shove the bracelet off. Nothing worked.

He couldn't feel them. Taye. Dazzle and Val. They were all gone. He felt hollowed out, his insides raw and exposed to merciless air. It was a numb sort of hurt that reverberated through his person, on all levels of awareness.

"You won't feel their loss," Puckman said, as if Ari wasn't falling to pieces in front of him. "Gaines developed that himself, long before you castrated him. He'll be pleased to know his artificing still works."

Ari's thoughts swam, making him feel lightheaded even as he fought through the rising panic to try and sense any hint of Val.

"It's designed to isolate a witch from their coven. I'm sure this wasn't the way Gaines intended to use it, but I'm glad I could spare you the pain of severing coven ties."

She was there, Ari thought, heart pounding in time with his frantic breaths. Val was there, still connected to him, but so very terribly far away. He couldn't glean anything from her, no emotion and no sense of her Magic. It felt like being ignored, only worse.

"We could have avoided all of this," Puckman prattled on. "If you'd joined my coven when I first offered, you never would have been put in this position. I would have protected you, instead I'll have to settle for taking your Magic for myself."

Ari's fingers went cold and useless against the metal cuff. "What are you saying?"

"I'm sorry," Puckman said, and the sorrow in his tone was almost believable. "You'll have no magic after tonight, Ari. I'll use it well in your name, though. You have my word."

Then the bastard turned around and walked away.

CHAPTER 30

Grief was a powerful thing. It didn't matter that Ari's logical thinking knew better; his heart and soul were convinced his coven was gone. His friends, his lover, they were beyond his reach. Gone. Gone. Gone.

It took him time to regain control of himself. His eyes dried and strength returned to his legs. He caught his breath and stopped grabbing at his manacled wrist. It took several minutes too long, but Ari gathered himself.

The first thing he did was race back to Gaines's yard. He had to lock eyes on his coven, had to prove to himself that they still existed.

The covens were gathered in the backyard by the time Ari burst through the fence's gate. Forty or so witches stood in a perfect circle, three persons deep. Ari had to shove his way through them to a chorus of shrieks and gasps to gain access to the center. That was where he found his conundrum.

The sight of them gave him pause.

Taye and Dazzle were unbound. They sat back to back, flat on their butts as goofy smiles painted their faces. Taye was playing with a handful of grass like it was the most fascinating stuff in the world, while Dazzle's head lay limp and useless on his shoulder. Dazzle wasn't unconscious, but staring up at the sky with the vacancy of someone well and truly doped.

Disbelief warring with dread, Ari couldn't help recognizing the effects of Dazzle's anti-anxiety potion.

Fortunately, not all was lost. Just beyond Dazzle's outstretched legs was a plastic basket overturned and staked into the grass. Despite the stakes, it jerked and bounced from the force of the spitting cat trapped inside it.

"You fuckers are so dead!" Val screamed as she raged against the sides of her makeshift cage. "I will bite all your ankles! It'll be a horror show of severed tendons before I'm done with you!"

Sitting on the basket with his foot tapping in impatience was Robert Gaines, with Eren Puckman looming over him with a holier-than-thou hand on Gaines's head. The two of them froze in shock as Ari burst through the circle.

"The ritual has already begun," Gaines said with a disappointed shake of his head. "It's too late, Ari." Gaines leaped to his feet with an ugly sneer on his face. "Get him out of here!"

"Ari!" Val shrieked.

He made to go to her, but the ranks of witches he just plowed through had regrouped. Hands latched on to him and yanked him back into the circle.

"You can't interrupt a ritual casting, you idiot!" a random witch hissed in his ear.

They shoved him out the other side of the circle, and Ari banged into the fence hard enough to bruise. As he watched, the witches linked arms to bar him from a repeat performance.

He became aware of the chanting then. The joint whispers

of the coven in full made for a thunderously low rumble in ancient Greek. There was an eerily smooth rhythm to their words, that spoke of practice and conviction; it told Ari he'd grossly underestimate Puckman's influence over these witches.

They were going through with it. Not a single one of these witches cared to second-guess Puckman's explanation. Ari had told them the truth, and not one of them cared enough to think it over. They were complicit.

Fury roared through him, burning hot and noxious unlike ever before.

This was wrong on so many levels, but not one of these people were willing to see it. They didn't care what happened to Taye. They weren't willing to consider the consequences beyond their own greed. Why would they listen to the truth, when Puckman had already sold them lies that absolved them from guilt?

Sheep, Ari thought. They were all fucking sheep, following wherever Puckman led them.

Leaning his weight on the fence, Ari stared at the chanting witches with burning hatred.

It was either the perfect or the worst time for him to remember his own Magic. It was still with him. He had time yet to do something with it.

Show them, he demanded from the universe. *Show them they're wrong.*

He didn't know what would happen or how Magic would respond to him ordering it around like a trained pet. He didn't care. Perhaps that was why Magic didn't rush to his side like the faithful, if annoying pet it'd always been.

It answered in slow, tentative sparks. He had its attention, but not its compliance.

Helpless, Ari could do nothing but stare in horror as the

chanting picked up speed and volume. He couldn't see through the rows of witches, but he heard it when Taye began to scream.

"No," Ari whispered as he collapsed against the fence.

Val's mournful yowl joined the cacophony, and Ari's legs gave out. His ass hit the earth and the vines brushed a tear from his cheek as his chest constricted with the realization that he failed.

For the last and most wretched time, Ari failed his coven.

The chanting grew to a crescendo. It overtook the screaming . . . or the screaming died out on its own.

"No," Ari denied, his fingers tangling in the grass as they curled into fists. "This isn't how it's supposed to end."

He closed his eyes tight, blocking any more tears from falling. Desperate, he reached and reached out into the ether for anything that might await him there. It was a last ditch effort to do something—anything—that might change the course of events.

He checked himself from making demands and instead threw his entire heart and soul behind the contact. His body shook and the tears leaked through his clench eyelids, but he didn't relent.

You had our backs when we told Gaines we would not be bullied, Ari prayed with all his might. *Please. Help me prove it now.*

He held his breath. He waited, the voices of Puckman's coven ringing in his ears.

Magic was slow to respond. It began as a wary trickle of warmth at the farthest edges of his fingertips. Ari didn't rush it along, though. He'd already made that mistake.

No, this time Ari willed himself to melt into the earth. His fingers unclenched from the grass so he could seek out the rich soil beneath it. He pressed his head back into the vines, till the leaves cradled his skull and a flower petal graced the shell of his ear. He gave his body over to nature as surely as he freed his heart and mind up to the ether.

The tightness around his chest eased. His breath evened out. his tears dried.

He was done running from Magic. He was done denying the messy parts of himself, the same parts that made him into a fearsome witch of untold power. In that moment, it was almost easy to accept his imperfections and how they'd brought him to this point, from his arrogance and lack of foresight to his preoccupation with the shop at the expense of the people who mattered.

He didn't need to be perfect. His coven didn't need it. They needed him.

It is time, Magic whispered within him.

"Stop," Ari said as he got to his feet.

A few of the nearest witches glanced back at him. He noted their widening eyes, the notable shaking of their limbs as they stared at him. One man jerked, almost breaking the circle in his shock. Their expressions read fearful, and Ari didn't give two shits why.

"I said stop," Ari repeated, and Magic flocked to him in committed waves of power.

Ari wasn't sure what would happen when he raised his hand. He only knew that he wanted it to be impressive and loud enough to stop the ritual. At this point, the only way his coven would survive was if he interrupted the chant and broke the circle. Ari didn't much care how it happened, only that it did.

His Magic didn't disappoint.

A bolt of lightning shrieked out of the crystal clear sky. Ari didn't see where it landed inside the circle, but he grinned at the way the witches shrieked and scattered.

In that instant, the ritual failed.

"No!" Gaines wailed from within the crowd. "I almost had it! You idiots! You stupid, filthy witches!"

Ari stepped forward, and the witches flailed out of his way like he was a walking contagion. They backed away toward the fences and the deck, a few of them even made a mad dash into the house when they caught sight of him.

Ari found his coven more or less where he'd last seen them. Val remained in the overturned basket, though she was now curled up into a protective ball with her fur on end. Taye was sprawled out on the ground, panting and clutching his heart with a stricken expression etched onto his face. Dazzle was half on top of him, his face planted in Taye's ribs and his arms flung over the other man like a human shield.

And there was Gaines, kicking up grass and shaking his fist at the surrounding witches.

"This is what I get for putting my fate in the hands of your kind! You had one job! One fucking— Shit."

Gaines paled as his raving brought him full circle to lock eyes with Ari. His arm shook as he lowered his fist.

Wobbling, Taye lifted his head. His face was drawn and ill, but he gave Ari a dazed grin. "Hey, babe! Look at you, all shiny and stuff." He swatted at Dazzle's face without taking his eyes off Ari. "Look, guys. Look. Ari's glowing again."

Dazzle turned his head, and his heartbroken expression melted with a giggle. "So pretty!"

"I hate both of you," Val whimpered.

Ari took a step toward her.

Gaines jumped like Ari had jabbed him with a shock stick. He lurched forward to yank the stakes free from the ground, then he reeled backward with the basket clutched to his chest like he thought it could protect him.

"It was his idea!" Gaines insisted, pointing one of the stakes at Puckman.

Puckman glared back at him. "If you think Ari's going to take the word of a wizard over mine—"

"You will not speak for me."

Puckman's mouth snapped shut with a startling quickness. At last, Puckman turned to see Ari, incandescent with Magic's favor, and his eyes went wide. It was the first time Ari could recall seeing fear on the man's face.

Ari raised his manacled wrist as his gaze flitted between Puckman and Gaines. "This is disgusting, but not half as much as the unconscionable curse you just tried to inflict on my wizard. I expected better from both of you."

While he spoke, Val sauntered over to him. She leaned against his leg with a rolling growl as she trained her sights on Gaines's throat.

Gaines noticed her attention, and he paled even as he stuck his nose in the air. "You left me no choice!"

Eyes narrowing, Ari said, "Same."

Gaines took that as some sort of attack, because he backpedaled straight into a huddle of watchful withes. Two of the witches were quick to shove him away, back into the spotlight, as they glanced from Gaines to Ari and back while fervently shaking their heads.

They didn't know what Ari was capable of, Ari realized with a start. Rumors were one thing, but now they had seen him call down lightning from a peaceful sky. They were witnessing his power for themselves.

Then again, it wasn't just his power, was it?

Ari bent down and scooped Val off the ground. Cradling her in one arm and stroking her bristled fur down with the other, Ari took a moment to reassure himself she was there, alive and well, and every bit as seething mad as he was.

Taye and Dazzle were still lazing about in the grass at his feet. They would be okay.

"This will not happen again," Ari decided.

An influx of Magic told him he was on the right track. Puckman felt it too, judging by the way he jumped and began backing away.

"Oh my god!" Dazzle simpered as he stared at Ari as if mesmerized. "Look at all the shiny!"

Taye seemed similarly awed as he asked no one in particular, "Am I dating witch Jesus?"

With a dramatic gasp, Dazzle repeated, "Witch Jesus."

Taye rolled over in maniacal laughter, Dazzle quick to follow.

Two compromised wizards aside, no one else seemed to find the situation funny. Puckman's coven continued staring and shying away, like the guilty bystanders they were. Meanwhile, Puckman seemed to be stumped trying to work out whatever puzzle he thought Ari presented. Gaines was past the point of curiosity, though; he was eyeing the exit and nervously licking his lips.

Staring them down, Ari felt nothing but disgust for the two men who caused so much trouble.

"I have to protect myself from you," Ari concluded.

"Getting rid of this should help," Val said as she pawed at his new bracelet. She set her nose against the metal and issued a dangerously low growl.

The bracelet fell away, and there she was, as present and ready in his mind as she was in his arms. Her power flooded him with an immediacy that promised she'd been trying to give it to him for a while.

Along with Val's Magic came an outpouring of emotion. Relief and love were the predominating impressions, but there was also unchecked anger and a healthy dose of fear and confusion. With Taye and Dazzle so high on potions, it was impossible to tell what came from who, and now wasn't the moment to try figuring it all out.

Ari was just glad to feel them again.

"Much better," Val purred her agreement before turning her head toward Puckman and Gaines. "Now put me down so I can make chew toys out of their intestines."

"Aw! Bloodthirsty kitty," Dazzle cooed. "I kinda love it."

"No," Ari said, returning his focus to Gaines. "We're not solving this with violence."

Gaines shuddered as if Ari had sentenced him to torture, but that wasn't what Ari or Magic had in store for him. Then again, the way Puckman squared his shoulders and seemed ready for a drawn out fight, maybe Ari should rethink Val's suggestion.

Shaking his head at such dark thoughts, Ari plucked at the ties binding him to his coven. He sought along them for magical strength and to bolster his resolve. All three wizards responded with immediacy and gusto, enough to make a lesser witch dizzy.

"Robert Bartholomew Gaines," Ari made eye contact with the man before moving on to his partner in crime, "Eren Isaiah Puckman."

Puckman paled at the use of his full name. The defensive edge to his posture fled as reality caught up with him. "Wait, Ari—"

"Consider yourselves cursed," Ari said, imbuing each word with raw power. "From this day till your last, you will have no memory of me or my coven."

"No!" Puckman wailed, reaching for him.

Ari stepped out of range at the same time Val made a vicious swipe for the witch's outstretched hand.

Ignoring the outburst and the way Gaines was moping, Ari continued.

"You will never hear our names if they are spoken within your earshot. You will not see us even if we stand before you. From now on, me and mine do not exist for you."

It was both terrifying and fascinating to watch as the two men lost their grasp on the one fraction of reality. Gaines was first to relent, his wariness and disdain smoothing way to make room for an ever prideful dismay. Conversely, Puckman fought it. With gritted teeth, he fell to his knees, but the desperation of his face gradually washed away. He appeared almost calm as he blinked around the yard with growing confusion.

Puckman turned toward the nearest members of his coven and asked, "What are we doing here?"

If anyone dared to answer him, no one heard it on account of the former wizard waking from a nightmare to discover a whole coven congregated in his yard.

"What the hell are you witches doing here? This is private property!"

"You invited them, asshole," Val snapped.

Gaines took no notice of her. "My property," he shrieked. "Get out! Go on! Shoo, before I call the Council to have you removed!"

"I'd listen to him if I were you," snickered Taye as he snuggled back down on the lawn, arms looped around Dazzle like the potion master was a teddy bear.

Again, Gaines didn't notice. As he continued ranting and flapping his hands at them, the witches finally began to scamper. Two particularly gusty witches got busy herding a very nonplussed Puckman toward the exit.

Each and every one of the witches gave Ari a wide berth on their way out.

Gaines huffed and puffed over the state of his backyard. Shaking his head and fully ignorant of the foursome still trespassing on his property, he kicked a stray Solo cup out of his way as he headed indoors.

"What a way to shut down a party," Val commented dryly.

Ari turned to find her tucked solidly between Dazzle's and Taye's impromptu snuggle fest. She didn't look happy about it, but resigned to her fate.

"Sh!" Taye said as he rubbed his face in her fur. "Save the sass for later, murder kitty."

Hands on his hips, Ari frowned down at his conundrum. "How did this happen, again?"

"Dazzle botched our rescue attempt with his glitter spray," Val grumbled. "There was a fan in the room. He took himself and Taye out along with the two witches who were guarding him."

"Hush," Taye scolded with a carefree snicker. "Ari already fixed it, like I said he would. No harm, no foul."

Ari had a lecture about personal responsibility on the tip of his tongue, but it sizzled out as Taye smiled up at him. There was so much pride and relief in that smile, Ari couldn't possibly hamper it.

Maybe Taye could see Ari softening in real time, because his smile calmed to something a little more serious as he held out a hand.

"We should really get out of here," Ari said even as he set his hand into Taye's.

He followed Taye's tugging and wound up kneeling in the grass. Taye partially disengaged from the cuddle pile so he could lean close to peck Ari on the cheek.

"Love you," he whispered.

Ari beamed.

Naturally, that was the exact moment Dazzle let out the obnoxiously loud snore. As Taye dissolved into giggles and Val whined at the injustice of it all, Ari flopped back onto the solid earth and let their noise wash over him.

There was dirt staining his knees, and half his coven was high on experimental potion. The sky was getting dark, and they were still on enemy territory. The shop was no longer waiting for his return. By all accounts, life should have sucked at that moment.

Ari smiled despite it all. His coven was alive with their Magic intact. He could feel the connection to them thrumming with confidence, as clear and bright as the Magic combing through his hair on the evening breeze.

Things weren't perfect, but they were more than good enough for now.

CHAPTER 31

It took six months for the supernatural community to get over the scandal of Robert Gaines resigning from the Council of Wizards. Within that time frame, no less than half of the Council followed him out of office for unspecified health reasons.

"I believe they were cursed."

Ari nearly spat out his coffee.

"Cursed with misfortune," said his Fae companion, utterly unfazed as she sipped her cappuccino.

Ari bit his tongue and studied the woman seated across from him. Like the time she visited Grimoires and Goodies with her bubbly friend, she wore all black, complete with various haute couture and the darkest sunglasses known to man. She looked impossibly posh and out of place in the cozy dining nook of Ari's new kitchen.

"The Council of Wizards seem to be suffering," she said when Ari remained mute. "One developed boils in the same week he lost his wife to another man. Another's been driven mad by visions of flames and a haunting cat. And those are the more benign rumors."

Ari set aside his mug and donned a professional smile. "Are you here to gossip, or conduct business, Tatiana?"

Her brows sank behind her glasses as she studied him. "You're not the least bit interested? As I recall it, you were afflicted by something similar the first time we met."

With a tight smile, Ari said, "Yes, it was awful. Now, you're here about the necklace, right?"

The necklace in question was one of the many jewelry items he once kept in a fairy-glamoured safe. After the shop burned down and the insurance pulled through, Ari had enough time on his hands to focus on identifying the magical nuances of each piece. Some were little more than parlor tricks embedded in gold or silver, but others proved much more complex and valuable. The necklace Tatiana wanted was fairy made and guaranteed to make its wearer invulnerable from physical harm.

Ari didn't want to know why she wanted it so badly. He only cared that she was willing to pay half a decade's worth of his mortgage to get it.

Sure enough, Ari placed the necklace on the table, and Tatiana's interests in the Council evaporated. Her hand shook with eagerness as she graced the gems inlaid in gold. Ari let the Fae woman fawn over the jewels for a long moment.

That was how Taye found them. Peering in from the kitchen doorway, he said, "Grilmin is waiting in the living room."

Tatiana's head jerked up as she sneered. "Grilmin, the dwarf? I assume he's here sniffing after my necklace?"

Ari refrained from groaning. "It's not yours until you've paid for it, Tatiana."

The Fae woman bristled as she sat up straight. Alarmingly, her sunglasses seemed to slip down her nose. Even after months of negotiations and sales, Ari had yet to catch a glimpse of her eyes, and he was no closer to figuring out what type of Fae she was.

"If you sell it to Grilmin, I will be taking my business elsewhere," Tatiana warned.

Ari sighed and shot Taye a beseeching look.

Taye shrugged, holding up his hands as if to rid himself of the situation entirely.

"Tell Grilmin I'll be out shortly," Ari directed. "Keep him busy for a bit."

As Taye scampered off and Ari turned to face a seething fairy, Ari wondered at the subtle turn his life had taken. There were days he missed the atmosphere of his shop, but he didn't miss dealing with witches or wizards on a daily basis; instead, it seemed he'd upgraded to an almost exclusively Fae clientele.

Turns out, operating a magical artifacts dealership through his home brought its fair share of challenging customers.

"You might not wish to discuss it," Tatiana said once they closed the deal, "but you ought to know the Council of Wizards is seeking advice from the Fae."

Ari paused with his hand on back door's knob. "Alright," he said, quirking a brow at her expectantly. "Are the Fae moonlighting as curse breakers, now?"

For the first time since he'd known her, Tatiana's lips lifted in the slightest smirk. "I'll tell you precisely what I told them, Mr. Jamison: the only one who could break this curse is the witch who cast it."

Ari bit his tongue to hold back a smile. If Tatiana didn't know the difference between a curse and a hex, he wouldn't be the one to correct her.

All in all, it was a successful meeting.

Ari decided to escort Tatiana and her necklace out the

back door and through the rose garden to avoid a scene between her and Grilmin. It wouldn't be the first time a magical fight broke out on the premises, but Ari wasn't looking to make it a frequent occurrence.

He was still rebuilding his reputation, after all. So far, the Fae, one particular vampire, and a few select witches were the only clients giving him the time of day. He didn't need recurring violence on his doorstep to keep the rest of the community away even longer.

After seeing Tatiana off, Ari turned to survey his new home. He closed on the old Victorian house and its acreage only a few months earlier, but he was already adjusting to life away from the city. The house was large, with its two stories of chipping blue paint and white trim, and it had needed the barest magical encouragement to revive the rose bushes crowding the base of the wrap around porch. It was a beautiful home now, after months of Ari and Taye breathing fresh life into the site.

The flowers and grounds were thriving, the house itself brighter than the day he first saw it. It was far removed from the city, and there wasn't a neighbor within sight through the trees. Ari continued to be surprised by how much he loved it.

The summer air was warm against his skin. Tilting his face up toward the sun, Ari closed his eyes and basked for a moment. He wiggled his toes in the grass and smiled at the ticklish sensation. He hated the idea of going back inside to face Grilmin.

Making a snap decision, Ari whipped his phone from the pocket of his slacks and texted Taye to bring their remaining guest outside. He straightened his button down and tightened his bow tie before marching around the house.

Magic must have approved of his decision to hold this

meeting in the garden. He found his patio table decked out with a full tea spread, cookies and bowl of sugar included.

Rolling his eyes and grinning, Ari helped himself.

Taye stalled out as he opened the back door to find Ari chilling with a tea cup in one hand and a cookie in the other.

Grilmin didn't seem to take any notice, however.

"Mr. Jamison," the dwarf grunted in greeting as he squeezed past Taye. "I take it the banshee's gone?"

Ari paused, exchanging a considering look with Taye, who mouthed "I told you so" before slinking off back into the house.

"She's gone," Ari told Grilmin with a polite nod to the chair opposite. "Like I said when you first reached out: your privacy is guaranteed with me."

The air tingled with Magic's agreement, and Grilmin settled into the chair with noticeable loosening of his shoulders and jaw.

This was Ari's second meeting with the dwarf since opening his home for business. Ari didn't count the lone day when Grilmin silently took stock of Grimoires and Goodies like a hired hit man searching for weakness. Nowadays, they weren't friendly, but at least Ari knew Grilmin's name and trusted that his interests were his own.

"You're one hell of a witch, Mr. Jamison," Grilmin admitted gruffly as he served himself tea. "You're handiwork on the Council is causing quite a stir. At least two former Councillors are living out of their cars now, or so I'm told."

Avoiding the dwarf's eye, Ari just sipped his tea and muttered, "I don't know what you're talking about."

The dwarf snorted, but didn't argue. "In any event, I'm confident that if you can't find me what I'm looking for, you'll be capable of creating it with your witchcraft."

Ari set down his cup and folded his hands in his lap,

giving the dwarf his full attention. "That depends on what you're looking for."

Grilmin hesitated, eyeing the door he just came through. "You trust that wizard?"

"With my life."

By this point, it was an open secret that Tayvon Osondu was granted sanctuary and living with Ari. No one who asked seemed surprised when Ari told them they were lovers, and few bothered asking to begin with. Councillor Sanchez assured him that Taye was no longer a priority for what was left of the Council, provided his Magic remained controlled and covert. Most surprising of all, Morrigan Harding treated the subject like ancient history on the few occasions when Ari met up with her for coffee.

Apparently, the matter was not so clearly put to rest where certain grumpy dwarves were concerned.

"You trust him personally," Grilmin amended, his eyes narrowing on the door where Taye had so recently retreated, "but what about professionally? It seems an unprecedented risk to share so much with a rogue wizard."

Ari's smile wilted. "Taye's my assistant. He pulls his weight and makes this process smoother. If you have a problem with him, I suggest you take your business elsewhere."

LATER THAT EVENING, ARI PULLED A LASAGNA OUT OF THE oven to a chorus of appreciative hums.

"Don't get your hopes up," Ari warned his conundrum as he set the food on the table. "It's a freezer meal."

"Any meal I don't have to cook myself is a gift," Dazzle assured him.

Ari went to grab the garlic bread from the counter when a large hand caught his wrist. Taye pulled him down for a quick kiss and murmured, "Thanks."

Ari almost stumbled away from the table. There was so much warmth and intention behind that single word. As Taye held his gaze, Ari wondered exactly what he was being thanked for.

"Ew, gay," Dazzle teased.

"Very gay," Val said, "but also a little sweet."

"The two are not mutually exclusive," Taye said, letting go of Ari's wrist with a roll of his eyes.

As Ari busied himself with the bread, Dazzle said, "I don't know about you, but I like my gay very not sweet."

"You would."

Val snorted a laugh, and the table burst into taunts and jibes. For three people, they made an awful lot of racket. It was a good thing Ari no longer had neighbors to file noise complaints.

Despite the chaos, or perhaps because of it, Ari had a wonderful night.

Like every Wednesday since he bought the house, Dazzle came for dinner and stayed till the following morning when he headed off to work; inevitably, Dazzle would show back up for some undisclosed portion of the weekend. Meanwhile, Val split her time between the house and Dazzle's place. It was an unexpectedly nice and domestic ritual by this point, and even though there was no Magic involved, Ari suspected it had something to do with the thrumming of their metaphysical connection.

Every time Ari mediated on it, he found Taye, Val, and Dazzle growing large and almost blindingly bright to his mind's eye. He had a near constant awareness of them, and it was as easy as breathing to bring any one of them to the forefront of his focus, to give and receive whatever emotion or power was needed in the moment.

It was a closeness Ari never experienced before. He couldn't imagine trading it for anything.

As usual for nights like this, Ari found himself elbow-deep in the freezer in search of ice cream. It was less usual for him to shut the appliance door to find Taye silently watching him like a creep.

"Yes?" Ari asked, a bemused smile on his lips as he balanced the ice cream tub on his hip. "Can I help you?"

Taye continued leaning on the fridge, fighting back a smirk. "You're beautiful, did you know that?"

Ari flushed.

"I mean it," Taye said with a casualness that matched the easy sincerity of his tone. "Not everyone would have turned Grilmin down the way you did today."

Ari sighed. "He was being an ass. Of course I chose you over his money."

"I know," Taye admitted, taking a step closer. "But still. Not everyone would have."

He took the ice cream from Ari and set it on the counter. Then he faced Ari directly and wrapped his hands around his hips. "Thanks for supporting me, for being you."

Taye leaned in, and Ari blurted out, "I love you."

Taye blinked. "I love you too."

"It's just . . ." Ari floundered as his face heated. "I realized I never said it."

Taye's surprise melted into a smile. He chuckled and redirected his kiss to the tip of Ari's nose. "I know, but you got there eventually."

ABOUT THE AUTHOR

K.R. Bady is an author, pro visual artist and a general nerd. She comes from an eclectic background that criss-crosses the country, but she currently calls Colorado her home. Fantastical escapism was her first love, and she still harbors a deep and abiding passion for all things science fiction/fantasy and the supernatural.

As a queer woman who was raised in a religious American household, she aspires to write the sort of novels she wishes were more readily available to anyone who felt similarly disenfranchised. Since making a difference in the real world seems impossible at times, she happily indulges in her obsession of exercising change in fiction by envisioning worlds where people are free to be who they want to be.